Praise for **The Optimistic Decade**

"*The Optimistic Decade* is a stunning and unusual debut. Heather Abel's subjects are political idealism, American-style lust for land, and the perils and pleasures of young love. Her voice is warm, beautifully funny, and completely original. Although the novel spans decades and tackles big themes, its intimate moments and vivid creation of an unforgettable landscape are what continue to haunt me. Once you enter the world of this book, you—like the characters—will find it hard to leave."

—Stephen McCauley, author of *My Ex-Life*

"What does it mean to measure our goodness against wide-open spaces? In Heather Abel's sharp, beautiful debut, American idealism and the obsession with land meet up on a single plateau in the Rockies, leading to a summer of stunning consequences. Long after *The Optimistic Decade* has ended, readers will linger with these pages, haunted by Abel's ability to bring both the spectacular and the intimate to life."

—Mira Jacob, author of *The Sleepwalker's Guide to Dancing*

"The best, worst, right, and left of America's ideologies mash up in *The Optimistic Decade*." —*New York Magazine*

"Abel . . . is a perceptive writer whose astute observations keep the book funny and light even under the weight of its Big Ideas. [She] draws convincing parallels between the rituals of camp and those of activism."

—*The New York Times Book Review*

"Abel's timely debut is bound to draw comparisons to *The Interestings* by Meg Wolitzer. *The Optimistic Decade* follows five characters in Reagan-era America, and explores the limits of idealism and the complexities of well-intentioned activism." —*Entertainment Weekly*

"I loved every minute I spent reading Heather Abel's *The Optimistic Decade*, a sharply rendered portrait of America in 1990. The novel is rich in the conflicting energies of the time—lingering resentments from the previous decade's stark class divisions, a renewed hope for the decade to come—and these clashes are played out over the course of one summer at a Colorado camp. The result is an exuberant and nonjudgmental examination of the unique conflicts of the era." —Arianna Rebolini, *BuzzFeed*

"Sly and funny . . . An exceptional coming-of-age novel, in which Abel proves herself a witty social observer who understands not only the thrum and throes of adolescence, but also the power and beauty of youthful energy and dreams." —*The Seattle Times*

"Politically and psychologically acute . . . Abel's well-crafted plot brings all the strands of the story together into a suspenseful yet believable conclusion. Without landing heavily on any political side, and without abandoning hope, Abel's novel lightly but firmly raises questions about how class and cultural conflicts play out in the rural West."
  —*Publishers Weekly*, starred review

"A sweeping novel about idealism, love, class, and a piece of land that changes everyone who lives on it . . . Speaks directly to our current political moment in the United States, addressing idealism of youth alongside futility of activism, the audacity of optimism alongside the heartbreak of disillusionment." —Bustle.com

"A coming-of-age story set in the age of Reagan and Bush, Heather Abel's wonderful novel asks a question that's more relevant now than ever: Amid the maddening news of the world, how do you go about living an authentic life? Perceptive, funny, and utterly original, *The Optimistic Decade* is a book for anyone who's navigated the twin crises of idealism and youth."
  —Nathan Hill, author of *The Nix*

"Heather Abel's sharp and shining debut brings to life a quirky, specific landscape that brings into focus essential truths about life—growing up and into it, and just plain living it." —SouthernLiving.com

"A sharply funny novel about a Utopian summer camp presided over by charismatic leader Caleb Silver, who's on a mission to teach others to live simply." —*New York Post*

"This witty and psychologically astute debut novel could not be more timely." —Peter Heller, author of *Celine* and *The Dog Stars*

"Abel explores the moral evolutions of adolescence with a charming coming-of-age story about two lonely teenagers and the summer that brought them together. Writing with both warmth and incisiveness, Ms. Abel has crafted an engaging look at idealism and the difficulties in maintaining it. *The Optimistic Decade* is an exceptionally timely look at what it means to be politically aware and reminds readers of the intoxicating power of idealism, particularly when we find ourselves on the precipice of independence." —*Pittsburgh Post-Gazette*

"Within the brilliant, multilayered canopy of the novel's world, Heather Abel's writing comes across as a sincere and tender channel for a story that must be told . . . This strong, astute debut is a study of love in many forms. To read it is nothing less than a mitzvah."

—*BookPage*

"Heather Abel's witty and immersive debut novel, *The Optimistic Decade*, set against the stark and beautiful backdrop of high desert and mountains in western Colorado in the early 1990s, explores the ways that people try to make a difference . . . An engaging and entertaining story about growing up, passion and disillusionment."

—*Shelf Awareness*

THE OPTIMISTIC DECADE

←—•—→ **THE** ←—•—→
OPTIMISTIC
DECADE

A NOVEL

HEATHER ABEL

ALGONQUIN BOOKS
OF CHAPEL HILL
2019

Published by
Algonquin Books of Chapel Hill
Post Office Box 2225
Chapel Hill, North Carolina 27515-2225

a division of
Workman Publishing
225 Varick Street
New York, New York 10014

This is a work of fiction. While, as in all fiction, the literary perceptions and
insights are based on experience, all names, characters, places, and incidents either
are products of the author's imagination or are used fictitiously.

LIBRARY OF CONGRESS CATALOGING-IN-PUBLICATION DATA
Names: Abel, Heather, author.
Title: The optimistic decade : a novel / Heather Abel.
Description: First edition. | Chapel Hill, North Carolina :
Algonquin Books of Chapel Hill, 2018.
Identifiers: LCCN 2017031135 | ISBN 9781616206307 (hardcover : alk. paper)
Subjects: LCSH: Camps—Colorado—Fiction. | Man-woman relationships—Fiction. |
Self-actualization (Psychology)—Fiction. | Nineteen nineties—Fiction.
Classification: LCC PS3601.B435 O68 2018 | DDC 813/.6—dc23
LC record available at https://lccn.loc.gov/2017031135

ISBN 978-1-61620-934-6 (PB)

10 9 8 7 6 5 4 3 2 1
First Paperback Edition

To Adam, Susannah, and Rose

CONTENTS

ONE Utopia Is Greek for "No Place" 1

TWO Yama Low 11

THREE Jordan's River Is Deep and Wide 23

FOUR The Reprimand 37

THE REAGAN YEARS: AUGUST 1982 53

FIVE Wolf 61

THE REAGAN YEARS: JUNE 1983 75

SIX Ishi, Last of His Tribe 89

THE REAGAN YEARS: SEPTEMBER 1982 106

SEVEN In the Beginning, There Was the Myth 122

THE REAGAN YEARS: APRIL 1983 148

EIGHT Rumspringa 152

THE REAGAN YEARS: EARLY OCTOBER 1982 168

NINE Do You Love Me? 179

TEN Across Disney World 193

THE REAGAN YEARS: EARLY OCTOBER 1982 203

ELEVEN Heat Wave 208

TWELVE Down by the Riverside 230

THIRTEEN First the Briny Silence, Then the Boom 241

THE REAGAN YEARS: JULY 1982 259

FOURTEEN Miss Clavel 264

FIFTEEN Rocky Mountain High 273

SIXTEEN Metamorphoses 285

THE CARTER YEARS: OCTOBER 1977 298

SEVENTEEN The Invitation 303

EIGHTEEN Arise, Ye Wretched of the Earth 319

NINETEEN Winter 328

TWENTY Llamalo 343

ONE

◦——◦

Utopia Is Greek for "No Place"

IT WAS APRIL 1990, not even four months into the new decade, and already Nelson Mandela had been freed and Daniel Ortega defeated and the first McDonald's opened in the USSR, which was about to drift apart, ending the Cold War, and still, although increasingly people chose to ignore this, everything was awful when it came down to inequality and Earth destruction and generally being fucked by capitalism. Rebecca Silver, thinking about all of this, walked through residential Berkeley to meet her father for lunch. Above her, a traffic signal swung threateningly in the woolen sky. She passed houses without front lawns, steep spillages of blackberry brambles and nasturtium, stalks of feathery fennel, ice plants with purple faces closed up against the cold, their crawling leaves like the severed feet of ducks. Cement steps led to porches with crappy furniture, painted signs announcing the names of co-ops. Staring at each house, Rebecca found herself locking eyes with a woman—a college junior or senior—on a porch swing, nearly naked in bra and pajama pants, as if the weather affected her differently. She was beautiful, mature, exhaling cigarette smoke, and yet Rebecca, graceless in hiking boots and ski hat, backpack bouncing upon her back, hoped that her own aura of importance might be visible to the woman above.

She was, after all, headed to her first reportorial meeting. Her father, Ira

Silver, publisher of *Our Side Now*, had called yesterday. "I'll be in Oakland for an interview with the Greyhound drivers. A total mess the way they're being strong-armed. Let me take you to lunch. Wherever you want. We should talk about the summer."

He'd never visited her at college, never even called, leaving all direct parental communications to her mom, while he transmitted only his news-paper, sent weekly from Santa Monica in a manila envelope, *Enjoy! -- Dad* scrawled above the masthead, those two dashes standing in, she hoped, for a love so profound it couldn't be written.

But now that she'd be joining his staff for the summer, he wanted to meet with her. He'd been vague as to his purpose, but she couldn't sup-press the hope that he might already have an assignment for her. Maybe there was an article that only Rebecca, having been raised knowing the way of ledes, nut grafs, and the systemic fault lines, could write. Her first byline. Already, the unlikely possibility had become the one she was counting upon.

Turning onto Telegraph, she passed a bookstore with a pyramidal dis-play of *The Satanic Verses*. On a velvet cloth in the next window lay pipes with ceramic faces twisted in agony, like souls suffering Satan's eternal flames. Beside them, a protesting handwritten sign: FOR DECORATIVE USE ONLY. And then she arrived at the restaurant she'd chosen because it had bad food and you shouldn't spend money on good food when others couldn't. Pausing at her reflection in the mirrored door, she took a moment to feel slightly disappointed in the girl with eyebrows like black moss, her angular features far from the impish femininity she admired in others.

A bell jingled her arrival; an odor of cumin greeted her. Nobody looked up. On her left was a lit refrigerated case, depressingly empty except for a bowl of tabouli salad and platter of marinated mushrooms. On her right, a small card table with bumper stickers and stacks of *Our Side Now* for sale. In the second row of tables sat Ira himself, reading a newspaper, not his own.

At her approach, he peered over the paper's rim. "Sweetheart." He hugged her briefly and fiercely. Rebecca had recently grown as tall as him, but he was broader, enlarged further by a nimbus of black-and-gray curls—rising up and out from his head and his chin, tufting behind the collar of his shirt. "Sit," he said. "I only have an hour."

The first twelve minutes of that hour were lost to his attempts to get the waiter to take their order, a period of time during which he found it impossible to do anything but seethe. Six more minutes were given over to the requisite exclamations about Bush: his bellicose bumblings, the Iran-Contra players in his administration, his kinder, gentler covert ops. *Horrifying! I know! Idiotic! I agree!* Had Rebecca read Ira's latest editorial? "Yes," she lied, enjoying, despite the falsehood, how proudly he looked at her.

The food arrived, as if to help them change the subject. "So talk to me," Ira said, stabbing his fork into the weak heart of his salad. "Tell me everything."

She could feel herself smiling back at his smile, the shared pleasure of parent-child parallelism. Despite his rush, he wanted to know all about her. And she wanted to tell him.

She described the special major she was creating—Third World Revolt and Media Studies—and the faculty she'd found to approve it.

"Jimmy," Ira shouted. "Shit! Tell Jim I say hi. Better yet, tell Jimmy fuck you for choosing the *Nation* over us. He judges the Omni Prize. You know about that?" But then he stopped himself, raising a glass of water to the ceiling. "No, no, sorry. I'm listening. Go on."

She listed, for his outrage, the sad lineup of campus political organizations. There was the Democratic Club, if you wanted to waste time being centrist. There were two environmental clubs that spent their reformative energy hiking Mount Tamalpais. But *where* was Ira's coffee? Was it that hard to get a cup of coffee? Ira flagged down the waitress while Rebecca recited the clubs for people with shared identities: La Raza, Southeast Asians United . . .

"Welcome to the nineties," Ira said loudly, interrupting her list as the coffee arrived. "Radicalism has died! Now we team up with those who look like us. *They've* given up on changing the economic structure that keeps their oppressors in power." He sipped. "The coffee, in case you're wondering, is tepid. But the company—you look terrific, Rebecca—the company is fantastic."

She felt so adult, her backpack full of used books with colons in their titles that would teach her everything Ira already knew. She felt, even with her problematic hair, almost beautiful. She began to describe an essay she was working on—"Black and White and Re(a)d All Over: Representations of American Socialism and the Red Scare in the Gray Lady"—when Ira interrupted again. "Sounds terrific, pumpkin. Really punchy and astute. But listen, we need to talk about summer."

Rebecca reached under the table and into her backpack and retrieved a pen and narrow notebook bound spirally at the top, the type he used, which she'd bought for the occasion. She set the notebook on the napkin, uncapped the pen.

He smiled at her provisions. "I've been thinking about that place. That place, you know . . ." He circled his hand as if he might conjure the word through physical effort. "Where David goes."

"David?" She silently ran through the many Davids. David Goldstein. David Grunbaum. David Gross. David Marks. (Ira's friend, Ira's enemy, her SAT tutor, a classmate in poli-sci last semester.)

"David," Ira repeated, bugging his eyes at the obviousness. "*David* David."

"Oh. David."

A young boy walked into her mind, treading on the cuffs of his cords. The son of her parents' closest friends. Once her own best friend. A pierce of pain. *David.* David was now a sullen teenager with whom she shared nothing. A yawn. A thorn. A general disappointment. David cared little about scholastic achievement or political activism. What did he care about instead? She had no idea. He spent his summers at a back-to-the-land camp run by Rebecca's cousin Caleb—"the visionary," as David once called him, when he still spoke to her. She couldn't remember the camp's name either. Did Ira want her to write an article about it?

"That place. Caleb's place. What's it *called*?" Ira pressed his temples until he extracted the camp's name: "Llamalo!" He pronounced it with relief, as well as an embarrassing Spanish accent. *Yama. Low.* "That's it."

But it wasn't quite. "Actually, I think you say the initial *L*. Llamalo." She pronounced the first two syllables as she would a Tibetan monk, Dalai-like. That's how David did it.

"I told Caleb from the start it was a weird name. So, Mom and I were thinking." He paused for coffee. "Maybe you'd like to go this summer."

"To write about it?" *Llamalo,* she wrote in her notebook.

He cleared his throat. "No, hon. As a counselor. Among others of your ilk. Exploring the wilds of Colorado. Fun, huh?"

This could only be a joke. She'd never expressed interest in summer camp as a child, and even if she had, Ira wouldn't have sent her. "Right. What did you used to say? 'Llamalo: where Caleb teaches privileged kids to live simply, so their parents might simply live without them.'"

"Yeah, sure, we made fun of it. We did." Ira was eating as fast as he was talking, helicoptering a lettuce leaf onto the floor. "But look, if you plan on avoiding everything we ridicule, you'll live a very constrained life. You're eighteen—"

"Almost nineteen."

"Okay, then you've been watching us put out this paper once a week for nearly *nineteen years*. Don't you want to do something new?"

The question was so unthinkable she found herself unable to answer.

"Hello? Hello?" Ira called to the passing waitress, raising his arm and scribbling the air with his hand. Turning back to Rebecca: "Maybe we're pushing you into the newspaper."

She'd been the one to ask, as they both knew. "I really don't feel pushed."

"David'll be there, I imagine. You'll already know one person."

"David? We're not exactly close. The last time I saw him, at the pot-luck, the Christmas one, he didn't even take off his headphones. He just sat on the couch drawing those heads, those oversized heads. I can't think of the last time we talked."

"No, he's not much of a talker, is he?"

She had a memory of the kid David once was, reaching out to her in a thicket of eucalyptus. *Come on, chicken. Jump.* Now that boy was gone. All those years she'd spent missing him, and for what? One had to at all times remain free of the delusion that anybody was who you believed them to be.

A fly landed on a tomato in her salad. As calmly as she could, although she was trembling inside, she said, "Do you not want me to work for you?"

"Oh, honey. It's nothing like that. It's just, you know, we never took you anywhere. Jesus, we never even took two consecutive days off. There's so much we didn't do with you. No travel. No camping. I just thought you'd like it. After nineteen years, you deserve something fun. The desert! Supposed to be beautiful. Sleep under the stars. Sounds like a blast to me. But you certainly don't *have* to go."

"Fun? Who cares about fun? The whole world's going to hell," she said, aping Ira's sentiment and inflections.

A waiter slapped the check onto the table, and Ira pulled down his glasses to study it. Rebecca imagined again the moment when she'd tell her friends about her article. "Oh, nothing really. Just a cover story for the most important paper of its kind." She held up the relevant issue. "Oh, that!" A crowd gathered. "Just a three-thousand-word exposé on the S and L crisis and how it robbed public schools." (What exactly was the S and L crisis? She would find out!) But this usually reliably pleasing fantasy was ruined. The crowd dispersed. What had she done to make her father want to send her away?

Ira placed a twenty on the table and borrowed her pen to write a no-tation on the bill, which he folded into his shirt pocket, finally looking at her. "Caleb couldn't have built that camp without me—did you know that? He owes me. So I called him. Made up a whole song and dance about your deep and abiding love for kids." He shook his head. "I was so sure you'd be thrilled. I really expected you to be excited. That's why I kept it a surprise. The thing is, pumpkin, you're already hired."

"You called Caleb?"

He smiled wistfully. "Dumb of me, wasn't it? I had this idea we could go to the camping store, get you some stuff. Sleeping bag . . . What else do people take into nature? Flashlight!" He stood and knocked twice on the table. "But don't worry about it, pumpkin. I'll call Caleb tonight. Tell him you're not interested."

At that, he excused himself to the bathroom. Alone, she considered the possibility that she'd misread the situation. What if he wasn't trying to punish her at all, but to offer her a gift? He'd never given her a gift of any kind before, material or experiential, although of course she'd always wanted him to. And now he had, but he'd chosen wrong, all wrong. Shouldn't he know that she'd hate everything about nature camp—the nature and the camp?

Still, the astonishing thing was that he'd been thinking of her. Although he hadn't called or visited this year, he'd kept her in mind. He wanted to rectify the deprivations of her childhood, and there'd been many. She imagined him triumphant as he landed on the idea of David's place, even though he couldn't remember its name. She imagined him dialing Caleb, calling in a favor in his imperious way. Thinking she'd be pleased, thrilled even. Drove all the way to Berkeley anticipating her delight.

Ira returned to the table, picked up his briefcase, and waited with an embarrassed expression while she packed her notebook and hoisted her backpack. How could he have known her loneliness this first year away? That all she wanted was to get back home? But now if she did, he'd be hurt, her presence a rejection of the gift he'd so carefully prepared.

As they walked to the door, she felt the urgency of tears, and Ira saw this, even though she turned her head. She could tell he saw, because he waved his arm up and down, wanting to comfort her and not knowing how. This gesture was so dear to her that her tears flowed now, and then he, wanting so much, she could tell, to speak softly and with solace, did the very opposite. "Do they think this will *do* anything?" he blustered, pointing to the stacks of bumper stickers they were now passing (IT WILL BE A GREAT DAY WHEN . . . , VISUALIZE WORLD . . . , WAR IS NOT THE . . . , U.S. OUT OF . . .). "A bumper sticker on a Volvo driving around Berkeley? They really think this will change the fundamental injustices of capitalism?"

She wiped her eyes and smiled and said, "Preaching to the deluded," as they headed outside, because the trick was to care so much and then to ridicule all others who cared so much. She'd never want to hurt him. "You know, Dad, why don't I go?" she said, missing him already. "The desert! I've never seen it."

Rain dripped from the brim of her hat and curled into her ears, which is what the half-nude woman still on her porch saw: a freshman of little import, nothing more than a babysitter in nature. But Rebecca could spin a story out of garbage, out of the plastic bags flying past her in the wind, getting pinned by blackberry brambles, shuddering with rain. Ira had raised her to know how to do this.

"Guess what—I got a job at this totally intense utopian camp. No flush toilets, no phones," she said, lying on the floor that evening. It seemed she spent most of her time lying down or lounging uncomfortably on her elbows, as if the purgatorial condition of college students meant that they were both too young and too old for chairs. The kind of parties she went to didn't feel like parties, just people on the floor making puns with the names of philosophers. *I Kant stand up. You can. I Kant.* The kind of party where someone might say, "Actually, utopia is Greek for 'no place.'"

"Exactly," Rebecca said. This party was four people in Megan's room: Rebecca, Megan, and two guys who wanted to sleep with Megan. "It's in the middle of nowhere. The wilds of Colorado. Hours and hours from a city. True Mongolian isolation."

"Wasn't there something about you working for your dad's paper?" Megan asked. Neither of the boys seemed to be listening.

"Not really. Anyway, this'll be a blast."

◆ ◆ ◆

"How'd it go?" Georgia asked before Ira was even through the door. He dropped his briefcase by the record player, his keys in the bowl, and turned to find his wife on the couch with a mug balanced on the cushion beside her, even though he'd asked her not to do that.

"The drive? Nine hours of utter hell."

"Come on. That's not what I mean."

"Fine. It went fine."

"Rebecca said, 'Sure, I'll go. I'll be a counselor'? Just like that?"

"No, not just like that, George. But she came around."

"Is she okay? Should I call her?"

"She's okay. She'll have a great summer. Fun, nature, all the naturey things. It'll be easier for her ensconced like that. It won't damage her so much. She'll be distracted."

Georgia touched the mug and then released it, sending it teetering. "So what's your plan? You'll call her up once she's settled a safe distance from you and tell her then?"

"Jesus, can you just . . . pick it up?" He took two steps and grabbed the mug, finding inside a desiccated tea bag not a danger to anything. Still, he set it loudly on the coffee table in demonstration of proper cup placement. "We'll send her the final issue, and she'll read my letter like everyone else. That way she can, I don't know, process a little before she has to talk to us. Isn't that what you're always pestering me to do—process?" Now standing above the couch, he put a calibrating hand on her forehead.

"Ira, don't."

She was still mad. He walked into the kitchen with a finality Georgia chose to ignore by following him.

"I hope you didn't say 'we.' I hope you didn't say, 'Mom and I want you to go to Colorado.'"

He peered into the fridge, at all the usual uninspiring bowls covered gently with waxed paper. "Look, you wanted me to figure something out, and I did. She'll have a blast there. Or she won't. But either way, she won't be here."

He closed the fridge, then walked into the bathroom but left the door open, because Georgia, he knew, wasn't done. As he was zipping up, she appeared in the doorway.

"I just feel uneasy. She'll think we're sending her away."

He turned on the water and looked at his wife in the mirror. "The hounds'll be all over me. It'll tear her up. You think *I* could stand seeing her like that? My own daughter? No, I can't. I *can't*. I could barely stand to see her today. Do you know how she looked when she said she'd go? All that false happiness for my sake."

"Then don't do it," Georgia whispered, enunciating harshly, as if a change in tone might change his mind. "Keep the fucking paper. It's my life, too."

He leaned his forehead against the cool mirror. "Goddamn it, George. I don't have a choice. Don't you ever listen to me? I don't have a choice anymore."

TWO

Yama Low

DURING THE SCHOOL YEAR, when Llamalo was a world in his head like the Forgotten Realms or Middle-Earth, David drew it over and over during class. Today, he began with the mountain in the center of the page and a wizard (Caleb) in the upper left-hand corner. Along the bottom of the page, he drew the river, shading it with cottonwoods and tamarisks, adding some towering boulders that looked a little lame, but the gnawed metal end of his pencil had lost its eraser. He found the pencil sharpener from his backpack and twirled until the lead was needle-sharp and able to represent in miniature the exact twists of the path up from the river—here's where it's so steep that you feel like puking; here's where that kid once threw a rock and screamed, "Landslide," hitting a counselor in the shoulder. When he finished the path, he saw that he'd drawn it too far up the mountain, so that the plateau at the base of the mountain on which camp was built had to instead jut out from the side of the mountain like Jupiter's ring. What this lacked in realism, it definitely made up for in magnificence. On this ring, he penciled the barn, the ranch house, the garden, Don Talc's trailer, a cluster of tiny people standing with hands raised in awe on the Great Overlook.

From a tape recorder on Señor Thacker's desk at the side of the room came the interminable saga of José and María, who had been trying for the five years that David had been taking Spanish to get to the beach. "¿Vamos a la playa?" María asked in a voice that seemed to David increasingly desperate, with the breathy, high pitch of false optimism.

"Sí, sí," José said, but there was this hesitation. You could hear it coming. A pause and then: "Pero . . ."

"¿Pero qué?"

Dramatic pause. David looked up as if he might see them: Anxious María, whom he pictured like the girls in this class, in skintight pants, pumps, winged eyeliner, and black bangs lacquered into a never-crashing wave above her face. José would be schlumpier, his clothes ill-fitting, undeserving of her endless attention, the two of them standing where nobody else stood—in front of the class, the direction the chairs faced, beneath the ticking clock.

"Pero . . . necesito un traje de baño."

Who the fuck didn't have a *traje de baño*? José—that's who.

While, at the beach, waves crashed endlessly and the churro vendors sold churros to nobody, María and José were stuck inland, boarding an *autobús* for a *tienda* with bathing suits. David drew the arts-and-crafts shacks. Caleb's yurt. Eight sleeping platforms. He made rays of sun emit from the wizard Caleb's hands and land upon these platforms. Every picture, his mom had explained once, had to have a source of light. And then, since this class would never end, he added, in the voluptuous style of R. Crumb, a blonde maiden above the river: Suze.

"Righteous," Yuji said, looking up from his own drawing just as David penciled the exaggerated ellipses of Suze's breasts emerging from overalls.

On David's other side sat Toast, who before falling asleep on his desk had given David a stoned smile of complicity. But David was sober this late April morning. He'd been sober for twenty-eight days now, sober since the Saturday afternoon he'd called Caleb, so freaked when he'd dialed that he'd messed up a digit and reached the Escadom post office, which itself seemed a minor miracle, the simple fact that the two-block town of Escadom existed while he was in an apartment in the swarm of Los Angeles, more people living on his block than in all of Escadom and the outlying rurality. He'd shaken out his hand, dialed again, and there was Caleb's voice. "Hello? Llamalo."

David had planned out what to say, but he'd mangled it and he had to try twice before Caleb understood just what David was asking for: permission to move to Llamalo when he turned eighteen next September. Move there, like, permanently. Without graduating from high school.

"Whoa . . . Huh." That had been Caleb's initial reaction. David held his breath, tried to hear Llamalo through the phone line, some proof of its existence—crickets in the peppergrass, the shrill of a hawk—but he heard only a song from the TV show *Barney* coming from the apartment above. Finally, Caleb continued. "And your parents? How do they feel about this? Their kid moving to Colorado, ditching high school. They're on board?"

If he weren't so nervous, David might have laughed, imagining his dad, Joe Cohen—Harvard grad; *Columbia Law Review*; beloved, if barely paid, lawyer to the farmworkers; recipient of the presidential award for something or other from Jimmy Carter; cofounder of *Our Side Now*; stern and self-disciplined—being "on board" with his son leaving high school. What could David do but wiggle around the facts? "They get it. They know what it means to me."

"I'm impressed. That's some open-minded parenting."

"And besides"—David had rushed on, lest they dwell on his parents—"I'll be legal. Full of sound mind and I don't know, courage, and, Caleb, seriously, my school's bullshit. I'm learning less than nothing. I'm getting the knowledge actively drained from me. I learn more in a single day at Llamalo than in a year here. I can help you with everything. Fix things, build things, clear the ditch for you. I need to be there."

Another pause, then Caleb said, "You know, David, I have to tell you, I've thought a lot about something like this. Getting people up here year-round. And now you're . . . Wow."

"So, I can?"

There'd been a painful pause. Pause without end. José would crumple; he could never achieve such pause. David had opened the fridge, closed it, opened it again, lined up his mom's Yoplait in color order on the top shelf, stared out the kitchenette window at the courtyard shared by the four six-apartment units. There was a small pool, painted teal but empty of water, full of brown palm fronds and diapers and the cardboard from a Coors twelve-pack. What's the worst? he'd asked himself. What's the worst, the very worst that could happen? Caleb could say no, and you'll survive. No, I won't, no, I won't, he responded to himself. He'd been living on hope for months now, ever since he came up with this plan; he couldn't live without it.

His mouth dry, his right palm clammy as it gripped the receiver, David considered blurting out into the pause all the ways he loved Llamalo, but you didn't want to interrupt Caleb when he was thinking. Finally, Caleb said, "Sorry. I'm on the cordless and I saw fox prints, had to follow them awhile. So I should go check on our friends the chickens. See who survived the night. Well, look, David, it's really great to hear how much you want to be here. That might really work for me. It really might. Of course, there's more to think about and now's really not the time for that. How about this? We'll see how the summer goes. Check back in at the end of it."

After David hung up, he shoved into his Vans, flew down the outside staircase, sprinted around his city block without feeling a muscle. Caleb hadn't said no. He'd said, *We'll see.* They would see! They would see! Like blind men granted vision.

Later, in his room, David had more carefully analyzed the words. *We'll see how the summer goes. Check back. See how.* It was, he'd concluded, a sort of test. Caleb wanted David to prove his dedication to Llamalo this summer, and David could do that. No problem. No problemo at all.

Right away, although Caleb couldn't see him, David had begun. While there were limited opportunities for high mesa chores in an apartment complex in Culver City, he kept to the routine of Llamalo as best he could—showers on Tuesdays, eggs for Thursday dinner, washing the dishes in a bucket—although his mom complained and ran them through the dishwasher as if LA were not its own desert and water not scarce.

More difficult by far were the abstentions. For twenty-eight days now—twenty of them at school—David had stopped doing anything disallowed at Llamalo, which meant he no longer drank beer with Yuji and his brother, didn't buy pot from Toast or even smoke when Toast offered freely. He wanted to be clearheaded like Caleb, but this had, honestly, created problems with his friendships. At first, he tried to hang out without participating, but they didn't get it. *You have pneumonia or something? Why you acting this way?*

Without Yuji and Toast, it turned out he was totally alone in this school of 3,100, in this city of three and a half million. He hadn't anticipated the loneliness. Every day around this time—toward the end of fourth period, lunchtime looming—he considered that he might smoke a little, just this once, just to be able to stand with them in the parking lot during lunch. He'd started carrying an array of pens in the pocket of his sweatshirt, with which he wrote *LL* on his books and the back of his hand as reminders to himself, like the straight-edge kids wrote an *X*. Yesterday, he'd drawn *LLAMALO* with a black Sakura paint pen on his locker in the heavily serifed thick block letters like Chicanos used. It looked good and had satisfyingly filled a lunch period and would likely not draw ire from the administration, who turned over Chicano and black kids caught writing on school property to the LAPD gang specialists but generally had a hands-off policy when it came to white kids and graffiti.

But he couldn't spend lunch doing that again. And so what would he do? David reached in his sweatshirt pocket for his Sharpie while a shopkeeper informed José that the store did not carry bathing suits in his size. *Desafortunadamente*, José was too *grande*.

There was nothing David would miss when he dropped out of school, but he did acknowledge that there was a friendliness to the Spanish-language experience. Other than David and Yuji, the class was entirely Chicano—kids who spoke Spanish at home and to each other with a rapidity and accent that Señor Thacker, an aged white man in a guayabera, could only yearn to achieve—but since they were tracked remedial, this was their class. Señor Thacker dealt with the potential for embarrassment by talking as little as possible. At the start of fourth period, he'd turn on the language tape, dim the lights, and lower the blinds, as a kindness for anyone who wanted to sleep.

Teacher and students alike took a break from 10:17 to 11:09, during which time Señor Thacker would sit by the window, listening to his transistor radio with headphones and trimming his bonsai with toenail clippers, as the breeze gently clicked the venetian blinds against the metal window frames.

David crossed his right ankle over his left knee and bent to write *LL* on the white band of his Vans, over and over, until the bell rang and Señor Thacker shut off the tape, calling out, "Adiós, amigos."

"Adiós, Señor Thacker," the class mumbled back, heading to the door in shared somnolence, squinting into the fluorescent vigor of the hallway of the languages building.

David took off before Toast or Yuji could cast a beckoning glance at him. He traversed solo past the parking lot, through the rear courtyard, around the math and sciences buildings, and up the stairs of the English building.

When he reached the top of the stairs, he saw that Chris, Ryan, and Todd, three blond, tousled surfers, princely boys of average intelligence who'd taunted him since kindergarten, were congregated in front of his locker.

Reluctantly, he walked up to them, expecting them to move aside. They knew his locker was below Ryan's; they saw him here most days. But they didn't move. They stared at him. "Um, so, I just have to get something. Right there's my locker."

"Du-uude," Chris said, shaking his head with a faux-friendly expression of disappointment.

Fuck. David knew this look.

"Du-uude." Chris swiveled so he was directly blocking David's locker. "What's up with you, Chewy? You write this?" Chris kicked the locker hard with his heel, the metal reverberating in the hallway.

It would be preferable to lie. Nah, wasn't me. Someone else must've. But obviously, lying wasn't allowed at Llamalo. Caleb never lied. If he was mad at you, he told you. If he was uncertain about something, he'd let on. "Yeah, so?"

"Yama Low? Come on. What's that about, Chewy?"

Even these boys knew the proper Spanish pronunciation of *llama*. In Thacker's "average" class, they'd been hearing María's plaintive cry "Me llamo María. ¿Como te llamas?"

Ryan took a step toward David. He was a head shorter than David, and he cast his blue eyes up at him. "What is with you, Chewy? We're worried about you."

"Very worried."

"Deeply concerned."

"You think you're a cholo now, 'cause you're friends with them?" Ryan said this. "Have you become sadly mistaken?"

Chris and Todd bent over, covering their mouths and muttering, "Oh man, oh shit," a loss of control caused by the mere thought of David, with those skinny arms, in a gang.

"Have you become sadly mistaken?" Ryan repeated proudly, in the stupid the way boys do when they land on something that makes their friends laugh. "Is that it, Chewy? You thought you were in a gang?"

They'd called him Chewy ever since he'd brought his stuffed Chewbacca to the sixth-grade graduation sleepover in the elementary school gym, only to find that it was too late. Chris, it seemed, had finger-fucked Vanessa Slater the weekend before, and in a great unified purging, all sixth-grade boys—other than David and his best friend at the time, Zacky Reznick—had somehow known to leave behind the soft, plush comforts of childhood.

"Yama Low's his gang name," Chris said, turning to the small crowd of girls who'd gathered to watch. "He's in the Yama Low gang," he said, louder now, because someone was walking by with a boom box, playing *It takes two to make a thing go ri-ight.*

Giving up on access to his locker, David smiled foolishly at the girls, making his way through them. "Excuse me. Excuse me. Show's over, folks." He hurried down the hall, down the stairs, outside. What a coward he was.

When David realized he was walking to the parking lot, where Toast and Yuji would welcome him into an intimacy of hilarity, he made himself U-turn. Heading instead toward the admin building, he passed the colorful frippery of the Japanese party kids and the lonely dyad of black band kids, and the math nerds and the attractive soccer players of all races, like a fucking Benetton ad. And then, on the lawn, there was Zacky Reznick himself, holding up a sandwich to make Amy Diamond jump to take a bite from it.

Zacky had attained, if this could be said about a seventeen-year-old, a certain gravitas, immunity from public ridicule bought by wealth and GPA. David hurried past, looking away so that Zacky wouldn't feel compelled to call to him—"Cohen in the houuuuse"—after which they'd have nothing to say, although they'd been inseparable all through elementary school and David still remembered each of Zacky's Transformers and Micronauts, and the way Zacky's mom would wake them up on Saturday mornings with trays of OJ and cinnamon toast and let David tag along to Zacky's Hebrew school, something his own parents would never send him to, religion being the opiate and, also, expensive.

The breach in their friendship resulted from a single standardized test in spring of sixth grade, one week after David's parents announced their separation. The test sorted students into tracks on which they would travel for their junior high and high school journey. Other than David, all the Jews, along with most Asians and a few of the non-Jew whites, were slotted into the gifted-and-talented program, which was called GATE, a fitting acronym. David often imagined an ornate metal gate opening to let these fine students through and then slamming shut behind them. In junior high, they ate lunch and attended all their classes in two trailers across the basketball courts from the average and remedial students. It was the "and" that got to David. His former friends were not just gifted, not merely talented.

After an acrimonious year and a half of divorce negotiations, his parents had finally noticed his academic standing. But what could they do? Should they tell the administration that their darling white child didn't belong in classes with the children of day laborers, domestic workers, and the very farmworkers Joe helped? They couldn't do this. Nor could they afford private school. The only reason they sent David to Llamalo, after all, was because Caleb annually waived the fee in exchange for nine months of ads in *Our Side Now*. Free childcare. Finally, they decided to scrape the money together to hire David a tutor for a few months, a former *OSN* intern, who was the first to introduce David to pot, saying, "School is the prison from which your mind needs to break free to find its own sources of imagination."

On the bench outside the admin building, David took out his notebook. *Please excuse David Cohen from school today at 12:15 for a doctor's appointment.* He signed Joe's name.

The secretary read this without comment or change in expression, accepting his excuse while clearly disbelieving it, because surely she'd show a flicker of facial sympathy for a kid who actually went to the doctor as often as David claimed to. With her signature on his note, David ran down the Greek Amphitheater, a gloriously euphemistic name for some cement steps on which the student body was required to gather biweekly to admire the bodies of cheerleaders below. At the south exit—farthest from the parking lot—he stepped through the metal detector, showed the note to the security guard, and he was free of this particular prison.

He walked westward on Pico, crossing Fourth Street, skimming a line of homeless vets who were waiting for lunch outside the Santa Monica Civic Center. David had been inside this theater only once, when he was six or seven and Joe had taken him and Rebecca to see Pete Seeger perform. Rebecca had brought with her five records—two Weavers albums, one Almanac Singers, three solo Pete, including, she'd showed David excitedly, the live one where he sang "We Shall Overcome" at Carnegie Hall. After the concert, she'd insisted on waiting at the stage door as everyone else from the audience headed to the parking lot and drove away. It was raining, and Joe was impatient. "He won't come," he kept saying. "This is a ridiculous waste of time." But Rebecca refused to leave. It had made David nervous, how cavalier she'd been with Joe's time. After an hour, the door opened and there was Pete, saying, "What have we here?" and taking the records from her hands. She probably had them now in her dorm in Berkeley, worshipped them like some raggedy scrap of shirt from a saint.

As he further developed this fantasy—Rebecca kneeling before her narrow bed, unwrapping layers of Guatemalan scarves, uncovering the LPs beneath, kissing the autograph on each one—he arrived at the corner of Pico and Ocean. And from here he could see it: a beckoning band of blue.

"¿Vamos a la playa?" David asked himself out loud, stepping into the crosswalk against the light.

"¡Sí, sí, vamos!"

He stayed at the beach all afternoon, sitting by the lifeguard station when it was just him and the old guys with metal detectors, buying a churro on the pier when school ended and students overran his spot, standing at the ocean's edge when the sun sank over it and his shadow grew enormous and cartoonish on the sand behind him, grew skinnier even than his real self, already a fucking Kokopelli of a guy. He finally headed to the bus when he couldn't take another minute without human interaction, even if the only human he could interact with was his mom.

When he unlocked the apartment, the lights were off and he could still hear waves, although the ocean was seven miles away. From the open windows came the white of LA night, strobe lights on clouds.

"David, hon?" Judy said from the couch, a T-shirt draped over her eyes. "I have such an interminable headache."

The apartment was three rooms: David's bedroom, the bathroom, and the living room/kitchenette. David crossed the living room to reach the sink and fill the kettle, dropping a Good Earth tea bag into a mug with the teachers union insignia and the words IF YOU THINK THE SYSTEM IS WORKING, ASK SOMEONE WHO ISN'T. When the water boiled, he brought the mug to his mom's side table. With his free hand, he pushed aside tissues, stacked Marge Piercy above Margaret Atwood above Dick Bolles to make space. What color *is* your parachute, Mom? Still haven't figured that one out? He sat on the floor beside the couch. Clicked off a machine that had the sole purpose of emitting oceanic sounds.

Judy pulled the shirt from her head and turned toward him. "I didn't think you'd be home this early. It's Friday night. You have plans to go out later?"

"Nah. I'll be here. We could make fun of *Baywatch* together."

She reached to squeeze his arm. "You never seem to see anyone anymore. I worry, you know."

"Nah, it's cool. I'm good."

"You're good? I shouldn't worry?"

"Don't worry. How was *your* day? Headache-inducing?"

"Alright, hon, I just need to sleep, that's all." She switched on the machine: waves again.

He retreated to the bedroom, turned on a Mini Maglite, lowered his blinds. Friday was Fire Day, and this was his best approximation, since lighting a match had, the week before, set off the smoke detector. He lay on his bed. The way the flashlight shone from his dresser, he could see only the highest of the photos taped to his walls. The oldest photos. Back when Suze and Caleb were together and they stood with their arms around each other and grinned at him.

After ten minutes or so lying there, he sprang up. Walked to his closet door, where his extra sweatshirt hung, and shoved it. "It's pronounced Llamalo, fuckers," he said. "Say it, Chris. Let me hear you. 'Llamalo.' No, not quite. Say it again, Ryan. 'Llamalo.' Can you step the fuck away from my locker? And du-uude, what's wrong with you? Thinking it's a gang like an idiot? Llamalo's not a gang, *dude*. It's a place. I'm worried about you, man. About all of you. It's only the most incredible place on earth, and looks like you'll never see it."

"David," called his mom. "Do you have the radio on? Can you turn it down, hon?"

THREE

Jordan's River Is Deep and Wide

BEFORE LLAMALO EXISTED, THERE was the Double L ranch, and before the Double L ranch just this: a high plateau where the desert rose up to meet the western slope of the Rocky Mountains.

The Ute Indians came up here to hunt, but they lived in the river valley below. When the white pioneers arrived in the final, optimistic decades of the nineteenth century, they didn't pay much attention to the plateau. They were busy killing off the Utes and making the river valley profitable by introducing economies that always fucked someone over. They called their new town Escadom, after two Franciscan priests, Silvestre Vélez de Escalante and Francisco Atanasio Dominguez, who had led the first white expedition through Ute territory a hundred years earlier, in 1776. Escalante and Dominguez nearly starved to death, but they survived to write, in tones that couldn't help but inspire young capitalists, of a "lush, mountainous land filled with game and timber" and "rivers showing signs of precious metals."

Aemon Talc rode into Escadom a few years too late, after all the riverside acreage with its alluvial soil had been claimed for ranches and orchards. He followed the river north from town for a couple miles until the valley closed in, the cliffs on either side edging nearer. He forced his horse to walk switchbacks up the eastern cliff. When he crested the top, he saw that there was another world at this higher elevation. Everything wide and open. The mountains, which had seemed merely gallant from the river valley, here became holy in their magnificence, the nearest one looming thousands of feet above him. Although Aemon was standing two miles due west of this mountain, it seemed he could throw a rock and hit it; there was nothing in his way.

The view to the south held its own enchantment. Strips of brown and ochre and beige as far as he could see. Hundreds of miles of this desert until earth just became sky. To the north, the land rolled into the foothills of the Rockies, and beyond these hills he could see some high faraway mountains, slivers of white like chipped teeth. As for the western view, Aemon could draw it simply with a horizontal line across a piece of paper. Above, sky. Below, the pitch green of the mesa on the far side of the river, pinyon-juniper forest soon to be ripped up to rescue the coal trapped underground.

It was the most extraordinary feeling to stand on this plateau. There was nothing built by humans. None of the verdant, shielding shrubbery of the East Coast. Nothing to box him in. At dawn, the sun rose over the nearest mountain and lit the sagebrush pink. *My soul soars here*, he wrote to his mother. *My optimism is held aloft by the open space. My hubris is held in check by the mountains.* The plateau was flat enough for cattle, although you couldn't call it flat. It rose up and fell down in little hills and shallow declivities and small buttes. Flat enough, though, to lead cows to the mountain's foothills to graze all summer.

But there was a distinctive and unfortunate lack of water. No water to grow winter crops. No water to keep animals or even a small garden. All that survived were drought plants. Sagebrush. Rabbitbrush. Occasional stumpy juniper. Puny greens. A multitude of brown grasses. It was gorgeous land, but worth shit.

Despite that, Aemon applied for ownership under the Stock Raising Homestead Act, and the government gave it all to him for free. Six hundred and one acres, from the edge of the cliff to the toes of the nearest mountain. He joined up with some equally delusional newcomers, including Eustace Sorger, who became his closest neighbor, to build an irrigation system. The men began in the foothills of the northern mountains, at a high-altitude lake that was fed by streams of snowmelt during spring and summer. With pickaxes and horses, they dug a trench six feet wide, three feet deep, and long enough to carry water to each of their homesteads.

It took them years. And as the trench snaked through this parched plateau, it created a green necklace of fecundity; along its banks were wild roses, leaning willows, oyster plants, marsh marigolds. The irrigation trough split Aemon's land in two. The land between the ditch and the mountain remained fallow. He flooded the land that stretched from the ditch toward the cliff, and he ploughed it flat, grew the sharp green of alfalfa.

Aemon named the irrigation trough "the Jordan River," after the river that flows through the Holy Land, but everyone usually just referred to it as "the ditch."

Aemon named his ranch "the Double L" for his daughters, Laura and Linda, whom he also named. He enjoyed naming. He named his son Conway, and when Conway married, Aemon named his grandchildren, the two boys who died in infancy (Aemon and Aemon), the three girls who, being girls, wouldn't inherit his ranch, and the sixth child, who would. He named this boy Donald Aemon Talc. Aemon named each species of the multitudinous brown grasses. He named the oyster plants and the bindweed. He'd have liked to have named the nearest mountain, but it was already called Escadom Mountain, and the river was already called Utefork, after the dead Indians. He named the endless land to the south of the plateau "the Dobies," because it looked like adobe clay out there. The plateau itself he called "Aemon's Mesa," his hubris not entirely held in check.

He built his little white house to face Escadom Mountain, so that as you came upon it from the wagon path that led from the top of the cliff, you saw its back side. On the front of the house was a porch that faced the irrigation ditch and two miles of high-desert scrub and then, bam, the mountain. In his old age, when his son took over the ranch duties, Aemon would sit on his porch for hours, just looking at the mountain.

Caleb Silver ran down these porch steps, hurried northward on the path along the irrigation ditch. It was his ditch now. He was hunting for bindweed, and when he found it, he squatted, unfolded his pocketknife, and sliced through the vine. He tugged at the tail of the creeper slowly, so as not to break it. He could feel little pop-pop-pops as the plant released its hold on the earth. He looped the vine between his left elbow and palm, like coiling a hose. Then he turned and walked back along the ditch until he was standing by two Russian olives planted by Aemon across from the little white house.

Looking toward the mountain, he could see a few blue tarps from the sleeping platforms, glints of sun reflecting off the corrugated tin of the shacks, a flapping sheet that hung from some wooden posts, the yurt's white canvas like a circus tent, nothing that disturbed the view any more than ships out at sea disturb the view of the ocean.

Over the years, he'd built nineteen structures between the ditch and the mountain. Eight sleeping platforms, like wooden stages with posts at each corner, to which you could tie tarps for rain, and a railing between the posts, upon which campers hung towels for privacy. Six arts-and-crafts shacks with three walls and a bit of tin roof. Four composting toilets, shrouded behind sheets. One yurt, from a mail-order catalogue. Caleb had partially hidden the structures whenever possible behind hills or brush, and he'd situated each at a distance from the next so there was no sense of crowding or orderly civilization; much of a camper's time here was spent walking through the sagebrush from one to the next. Empty, the place had the feeling of a long-abandoned mining or refugee camp, a failed experiment, ruins.

But today, the campers would arrive at last. Caleb was alone at the ranch, except for the kitchen ladies, in the kitchen, and the laundry ladies, smoking in the parking lot, ashing on the tips of the orange cones that separated that patch of dried dirt and sagebrush from all the rest of the dried dirt and sagebrush. The counselors had driven the two hours to meet the campers, who flew in pods from airports around the country to Grand Junction. Caleb stayed behind, because who would the kids want to see when they got off the bus? Caleb, of course.

He rolled up his sleeves, crouched, and then reached into the water to tie one end of the vine around a wheel that diverted water to a smaller drainage. He dropped the rest of the bindweed in the water, where it uncoiled, dancing and flailing in the current like a living thing.

Caleb wiped his hands on his pants and walked around the house to the swath of land between it and the parking lot. He'd named this "the Great Overlook" because it offered a harmonic sweep of the endless Dobies. His steps were wide with anticipation. Grasshoppers sprang out of his way. Pinyon jays shouted, *Will you look at that? Willyou willyou?* He looked down the road, but nothing was coming.

He waited until he saw it. The school bus caterpillering along the dirt road in a haze of dust. "Took you long enough," he said aloud, although nobody was with him as he leaned forward on tiptoes.

The bus pulled up in front of the house and sighed as it stopped, a cloud of diesel. The first to step out were returning campers, clutching small boxes of juice. They looked around with unselfconscious grins. From where they stood, what could they see? The cement platform with nine picnic tables that he'd built off the back of the house, leading into the kitchen. The doors of the Talcs' old barn, unable to close for a decade, swung wide. The teepee that Caleb had outfitted as a nurse's station for sunburns and altitude sickness and cramps. A smidge of garden fence. The mountain above. He watched them scanning back and forth, looking for him, and he lifted both arms.

"Caleb! Caleb!" They ran toward him, these kids from Seattle, Scottsdale,

Scarsdale, Amherst, Bethesda, Cambridge. They could see no other houses, no telephone poles, no Little League fields, no swimming pools. The nearest town was two sad blocks of boarded-up shops. They might as well have landed on the moon—except here was gravity, their feet pushing against the dirt as they ran.

He led them around to the front of the house, where there was a small lawn between the porch steps and the irrigation ditch. "Come on. Here we are. Here we are now." It used to be dirt here, too, just hard earth and spiky plants, like everywhere else. Mustard grass, cheatgrass, peppergrass, those thorned, daggered plants that were completely misnamed—nothing like grass at all. But Caleb and Don Talc, his ranch manager, had irrigated and planted seed, and Caleb named the resultant green Suze's Meadow. It was Suze who had always said that kids need a lawn, although she left before she ever saw it.

But he didn't think about Suze now as he stood on her meadow. Or rather, he did, but only with a little zip of pride as he noted how little he was thinking of her these days.

Campers streamed in from the road, blinked against the glare, climbed over each other to sit beside friends. There were sixty-two of them, the largest group yet. A rush of kids on the mesa, a swarm of them, a flock. The youngest was seven; the oldest, seventeen. "Come sit. Come and sit," he kept calling like a circus barker. He couldn't contain his joy.

When all the kids and counselors were seated, he cupped his hands around his mouth. "Come on, Don, get over here. Come out, ladies. Charlene? Denise? You in there?" This was a cue, theatrical. The four kitchen ladies, with their curled hair and flowered aprons, trotted out of the house and down the porch steps, coming to a stop behind the last row of children; then Denise and the other laundry ladies joined the kitchen ladies. Caleb liked everything about these women from town, but especially their sartorial anachronisms—hair held up loosely by two combs; checked shirts tucked into high-waisted jeans; blue and green eyeshadow from lash to brow, shades of Dolly Parton. Looking at them, you'd never know it was 1990. Caleb could see Don, who'd been unloading luggage, walking in his uneven gait toward the Meadow. Everyone was here, and Caleb loved them all. He felt a fullness, which was also a calmness, a post-adrenaline float of satiety.

"Over here, Don," Caleb called, and Don swerved toward him, perhaps thinking that Caleb needed to give him some instruction. But Caleb, in a sudden impulse of happiness, draped his arm around Don's shoulders. He could feel Don stiffen, the muscles tense and shift under his shirt, which was, despite small variations in shade and thickness of plaid, essentially the same shirt Caleb wore. They wore the same Carhartt pants, the same boots. Had he ever done that before—touched Don? He couldn't remember a time. But it seemed the right way to begin this summer, a nod to the fact that it was just the two of them working up here all year—tall Caleb and slight Don, twenty years his senior, whose thin hair was the yellow of faded paper.

"Well, hello, everybody," Caleb said, still with his arm around Don. "You're not here for summer camp. You get that right? Maybe this morning, when you got dressed, you thought you were going to camp." He paused. "*Sorry.* You're here to take care of Llamalo."

How relieved he was to be saying these words again.

Until they arrived, what was Caleb, really? A guy who'd moved to Colorado and bought a ranch—barn, winter corral, house with its back turned to the road, alfalfa fields gone feral and brown.

Until they arrived, Llamalo was simply a chassis—some wood, some dirt—and Caleb was nothing, just a man. He had nobody to whom he could point out the parabola of bird flight, nobody who needed to learn the word "junco," nobody whose life he could strip bare of casual comforts, nobody whose mind he could blow. But now they were back, and Llamalo could become a tone, a muscle, the neuron path of memory, and Caleb could be what he was meant to be, the animating force.

"Have you ever taken care of anything? Have you?" Nobody answered. "Maybe a dog? A hamster? A younger sister once in a while. Adults assume kids can't take care of anything, that *you* need all the care. But that's not true, is it? Or you wouldn't be here. You'd be at some camp with lacrosse, with sailing or team colors." To draw them in, he exaggerated childhood volition; no matter that many of them were sent here without choice. "But you." He paused again, savoring this, slowing it down. "You chose to come to Llamalo."

Don snuck out from under his arm and went to stand beside Denise and the workers from town. High on the crowd's attention, Caleb only barely registered this. "You know that you're not just here to live on a ranch for a summer. You're here to protect it." He squinted at the faces in turn, drawing out the drama. "You're all it's got."

There were, surely, among those listening, six or seven who were dubious about this injunction. It was a ranch. Big whoop. But that would change over time.

"So let's take a minute to see where we are. Start with this right here . . ." He stomped one foot. "Dry dirt. One flicked match, one lightning strike, and this whole place is gone." He snapped. "Like that. This is called high desert. We're sitting six thousand feet above sea level. And Escadom Mountain over there, *our* mountain"—Caleb pointed at the peak behind him— "rises an additional seven thousand feet above us. That's a thirteen-thousand-foot mountain you're looking at. Now the sky. Go on, look up at it. Have you ever seen a sky like this? The whole history of human experience could fill this sky. Now check this out—that empty land to the south. That's the Dobies. No people or the mess we make for as far as you can see. It's wild as the ocean."

As he pointed, the sea of heads shifted to look past him, brown hair and blonde and black, and a tired Mohawk dyed ruby. Caleb spoke faster now, enjoying this. "Those of you who are new will learn pretty quickly that there's a way we do things at Llamalo that's different from how you do things at home. We compost our shit. We take showers once a week, rinse off in the river the other days. We don't make phone calls or watch movies or listen to the radio. We don't walk around after dark, not until we're used to it. We don't tempt mountain lions by leaving food around. We encounter rattlesnakes. There's a way we track elk up on Escadom Mountain. There's a way we treat the irrigation ditch, this stream that flows right through our camp."

He walked over to the ditch. They swiveled to watch. "You see, it's going to get hot this summer. Really hot. A desert heat you might not be familiar with. And you'll feel tempted to cool off in the ditch here. But a ditch like this is easy to get into and nearly impossible to get out of. And the water—stand up and look at the water. The water looks like it's just lazing along, doesn't it? When in fact, it's running so fast that we wouldn't be able to reach for you if the current carried you away."

He could feel a shift in their attention, the charge of fear. He kept his voice calm. "Hey, look at this. Some bindweed got caught in the sluice wheel. You want to find out how fast the current is? Why don't you race it. Let's see who can run faster than this weed. Come, let's run. Stand up, all of you."

Reaching down, he opened his knife and sliced the bindweed free from the wheel. "Run!"

He loved this part, watching them charge down the mesa, galloping over rabbitbrush or between the arms of sage. It was David who bolted ahead of the others, even the counselors. Caleb's breath caught. Look at him go! He was leading them down the field, giving Caleb a soaring feeling, as if he were running himself.

Released from the wheel, the bindweed streamed away. At full length, it was as large as a teenager, and as it buckled and stretched again, it resembled the reaching limbs of a swimmer.

Some ran and then stopped and shielded their eyes to see. Some walked as if pulled by the wake of the running crowd. Some trotted along the ditch path, watching the bindweed disappear. He turned around to see who was left. The kitchen ladies had returned to the kitchen; the laundry ladies, to their cars. A few teenage girls, resisting the joy of movement, stood on the grass with their counselor, his cousin Rebecca. A bit disappointing, so he turned back to the runners.

Caleb let them go as far as they wanted, as long as their legs needed to push. He didn't call them back. He just waited and they came, the bindweed long gone. David returned first, coming to a stop by Caleb, panting and bending forward, with his hands pressed against his knees.

"Good to be here?" Caleb asked.

David nodded. When he caught his breath, he said, "Incredible. I always think it doesn't exist. I get nervous. Like what if I come back and it's not what I remembered? But this time, you know, because of what we talked about, it feels even more exciting. I'm ready to do whatever you need. Just so you know. Whatever you want me to do. Or if you want me to figure it out on my own, some tasks, that's cool, too. I'm thinking about it all the time."

Caleb smiled, unsure what David was referring to. Something they'd talked about? Tasks? But he didn't ask, because now other kids were arriving, breathing hard, their chests startled by the thinness of oxygen, surely pulsing with headache from the nearness of the sun. But nobody complained. They were here now, the torpor of travel forgotten. They were here.

A few kids were walking back so slowly they looked like they might just be standing, but he made everyone wait, didn't yell hurry up, didn't scream, "Come on already," and when they did return, he smiled at them.

"Take a seat." They sat in all directions around him, so he had to turn as he talked. "See, what I'm saying is there's a way we deal with danger here. We trust you. This is different than how you're treated at home or school. We're not going to fence this ditch. We're not putting up a gate. This isn't a playground. We just have the earth here. You and the earth and our trust."

He paused, and when he resumed he spoke quietly. "So think about it. This means that Llamalo isn't normal life. Llamalo is an invitation to act differently, to be someone new. How often do you get that chance?"

◆ ◆ ◆

FROM THE CROWD, REBECCA listened to Caleb skeptically. Why would she ever want to be anyone else? A few weeks earlier, on one of her last days as a Berkeley freshman, she'd cut her black hair into a bob, to look like a Chinese revolutionary—a failure, she understood, on both aesthetic and imitative grounds. She sat with her charges, the campers she'd just met, all of whom seemed to be named Jennifer. Their ponytails brushed against her arm like strands from spiderwebs. She searched the crowd for David. There he was, a few rows in front of her and slightly to her left, with his arms around his knees. She could see his knobby shoulders, bare in a tank top, and a bit of his face. He'd arrived just now with the campers, while she'd already been here for a week of counselor training. It should have been a relief to see someone familiar, but seeing David actually made her lonelier. He seemed merely to refer to someone familiar, to serve as a reminder that he wasn't familiar anymore. The new aquiline nose that looked borrowed from an older adult. His drift of sandy hair held aloft by a rolled-up bandana. One wrist was strung with black rubber bracelets and what looked like pink rubber bands. She felt embarrassed for him: so old and still a camper at nature camp. She thought of how awkward it had been to see him at Samohi, during the year they'd overlapped. She would need to keep her distance from him here as well, she realized. To make friends here, she ought not draw attention to their former bond, which anyway seemed so insubstantial as to be irrelevant.

◆ ◆ ◆

DAVID FELT THE TUG of someone watching him. Twisting around, he expected to see a friend, but it was a new girl. As he met her gaze, she bit her lip and looked away. The funny thing was, she looked just like Rebecca. Same worried face, but Rebecca had always had long hair and this girl had short.

He turned back to Caleb, who was beaming down at him, concluding his speech with the same evocative sentences as always. "When you leave here, you're not going to be the same person you are now. I promise. It'll happen to each of you."

Caleb dismissed the campers to dinner, which was ceremoniously called First Dinner. As they all rose, David saw Rebecca full-length in her ANC shirt, like an ambassador from his parents' world, and then he understood that hair could be cut. What could she possibly be doing here? This question preoccupied him throughout the moment of silence, when everyone held hands around the picnic tables.

The very point of Llamalo was that nothing should change. The Dobies didn't change. Their geological rundown had happened millennia ago. From summer to summer, sage died but more sage grew. The days were the same, matched to their counterpoint on previous years, which meant that this first Monday evening was the same as last year's first Monday evening, with the same menu and activities, and next year, still just a puff of imagination, would look exactly like this.

He took a reassuring look at Caleb, in his usual seat, but in so doing he saw that Rebecca had been seated at the head of table 9, where Suze was supposed to sit. And although Suze hadn't sat there for five years, Rebecca certainly shouldn't have filled her spot. The world was divided into two immutable categories: Llamalo and not-Llamalo. Rebecca belonged to the latter.

Adding to his confusion was the fact that he'd been given no notice that she was coming from either of his parents, which was strange, because one of the few things they still had in common was a deep love of telling him about Rebecca. *Oh, Rebecca, she's so great, she got into Berkeley, she's inventing the most interesting major, she's working at OSN this summer, isn't that fantastic, are you sure you wouldn't want to do something like that?* Rebecca had never shown any interest in Llamalo before. In fact, she had been glaringly uninterested when he'd tried to tell her about it. That was years ago, before he'd stopped trying.

When the dishes had been passed and cleared by the campers in the appropriate ways and Caleb stood, signaling the end of the meal, David sprang up to approach Rebecca, who was heading into the kitchen. On his way, he was ambushed. Three girls—ten or eleven years old—blocked him.

"David. Hey."

"Hey, David."

The third girl wound a strand of brown hair around her finger but didn't speak.

He gave them what they wanted: His attention, a pat, a smile. He slapped-five with Patrick and Matthew, hugged Nicole tightly—yes, it was so great to see her, too—and finally, reaching Rebecca, who was emerging from the kitchen, he offered a gesture of incredulity. You? Here?

At his approach, she bent her head nonchalantly over her steaming mug. "Oh, hey. Just headed . . ." She pointed at the barn.

He wanted to confront her with grand, medieval language: *State your purpose and king!* But all the eloquence he always felt here had vanished under her gaze. She was looking at him like her parents did—with dismay. *Oh, David, what has happened to you and our grand hopes for the regeneration of the species known as Rageful and Depressive Socialist Jew?* He managed only to say, "Wow. Been a while, huh? Kind of surprising to see you here. Heard you were working for your parents."

She shrugged. "If you think about it, I've basically been working for them for eighteen years. I think they can handle one summer without me." She gnashed on her thumbnail, belying the confidence in her voice. Frankly, she looked guilty.

"Yeah, but not really. Wasn't this your first chance to be a reportroire? That's French for 'reporter.' Official journalíste. Journalística nacionále . . ."

"Okay, I get it. I've spent my whole life in that office. What could I even still learn from them?"

"So why come here?" he asked outright. "It's not exactly your scene."

"Well, see, I was in the library at finals. Staring at my enormous pile of books. So stressed out. And all of a sudden, I started thinking about *this*." She pointed at the house, but he understood her to mean the magnificence around them. "How you always used to tell me about it. And I started thinking that maybe this was the remedy I needed. I asked Ira if he could spare me this summer. Begged Caleb to let me come."

"Seriously?" This was immensely satisfying to hear. She'd been listening, after all.

"It's so outside my realm of experience. And I thought, shouldn't I broaden?"

Well, yes, she should. He'd grant her that. "So, here you are. Beauty astounds, doesn't it? Flabbergasts." He felt moved to explain this place to her. Had she heard of vectors yet? She hadn't. "Okay, so picture lines radiating off of us," he said. He knew this speech of Caleb's by heart. "Picture these lines like vectors, and when they hit something—trees in a forest, commuters on a bus, a row of apartment buildings—we feel a psychic prick. Each zap creates anxiety." She was attentive, nodding along. "It's like constant nervous electrocution. But out here—I'm sure you feel it—there's this *tranquilizing effect* of so much open space . . ."

He was using Caleb's words when Caleb himself came upon them, dropping his hand heavily on David's shoulder.

"What do you think, David? Should we go light the first fire?"

David smelled the cough-drop sweetness of Russian olive in the air. He heard the clank of kids washing dishes. The dry wind was hot inside him. It was, David thought, the most extraordinary feeling to stand here on Aemon's Mesa.

"Indeed we should."

As he headed off the platform with Caleb, he called back to Rebecca, still sipping her coffee. "And now that you're here, you love it, right?" How could she not? Brimming with exuberance, he shouted again, "You love it."

FOUR

The Reprimand

SHE HATED IT.

By the third morning of camp, the only thing Rebecca didn't hate was one room, a preference she recognized as counter to the very mission of Llamalo, which was to be outdoors all the time until your cells were changed by the strumming of the sun. But Rebecca liked her cells how they were, which was why she was hiding in the room.

The room was one of two on the second floor of the little white house; the other was locked. The white house was the only structure at Llamalo that had four walls, a roof, and a door that closed. For this reason, everyone was discouraged from hanging out in the house, even though it was much more temperate and less glary indoors and the toilet flushed.

Outside, Rebecca often felt scared. There was a brutality to the exposure, an ominous wind much of the time, and when the wind stopped, the silence was freaky and the air thin and dusty. Her lips cracked and stung. Her nose bled and scabbed over and bled again. It was terrible to walk around here. The ground looked flat from a distance, but it rose in little mounds and fell into small trenches, which seemed malicious in their intent to trip. How, she often wondered, could this be a camp for children? She'd imagined lawns, a dining hall, cabins with bunk beds in tidy rows, a dock, canoes, electric lights, sports fields. But other than that tiny toupee of lawn outside the house, so grandly called Suze's Meadow, there grew only the most awful grasses, each equipped with burrs, like medieval weaponry in miniature. Burrs slipped into her sneakers, bit her ankles, crept into her sleeping bag, and when she pulled them out, they pierced the skin of her fingers.

The room had daisy wallpaper from a long time ago and a darling sloped roof. The sun, so fierce outside, was diluted through two dormer windows with curtains that matched the wallpaper. Rebecca believed that she and the room had a melancholic understanding. She was sad to be at camp, and the bedroom was sad to no longer be a bedroom. It was sad about the stacks of camp brochures, sad about the sprinkler parts, sad about the electric pencil sharpener and the plastic file shelves. At the center of the room was a large metal desk, and atop this desk was a computer and a white cordless phone, and the room was sad about the desk but not about the phone.

Rebecca held her backpack on her lap as she sat at the desk. It was early, prebreakfast, and she'd walked the ten minutes with her campers from their sleeping platform to join the others on the Meadow. She could hear the exaggerated yelps of friendship and the braying of the small herd of guitars. She had no further duties until the cowbell rang for breakfast, which her campers weren't in charge of preparing today. The work here seemed relentless, as the children were to be led through all the chores of ranch upkeep, an ethos that seemed to merely prolong the work, and yet she often found herself with nothing to do.

She was almost never alone. Even on the toilet, she was always a thin bedsheet away from somebody else. During the seven days of counselor training, everyone had been trust-falling, massaging, talking late into the night. Rebecca had slept on a platform with Kai and Nat, but she went to bed long before they did, because she wasn't someone who could blend in, who could chameleon herself to a new locale just by learning the songs and jokes. She needed props or actions to be understood as the complex person that she was, and that's why she'd begun carrying her school back-pack around, even though nobody could see the particulars within.

She bent to look inside it now, imagining herself someone else, apprehending her belongings through this someone else's eyes. Oh, Rebecca, how interesting you are! A Chinua Achebe paperback. Cherry ChapStick, uncapped. *Freewheelin' Bob Dylan*, unspooled. Hair bands stolen from a roommate. A scrunched stack of flyers printed at the computing center, with their double subhed. (WILL YOU BE READY WHEN THE MILI-TARY DRAFT RETURNS? BECOME A CONSCIENTIOUS OBJECTOR TODAY! IT'S TOO LATE WHEN YOUR NUMBER'S UP.)

When meeting new people, there should be a way, Rebecca thought, to offer up an image of yourself that would provide pertinent additional information. She'd like people to see, concurrent with her actual self, a hologram from the day she stood outside the North Berkeley BART station distributing these flyers.

Pleased with this memory, she let it play out for a while, imagining the counselors and campers seeing her as she really was—combat boots, vintage frock, teaching the feint and philosophy of draft dodging—until she recalled, with flaring embarrassment, how the lessons had actually gone. Nearly every boy she'd approached, saying, "Excuse me, do you want to learn about conscientious objection?" had answered with some variation on "I dunno, you want to suck my dick?"

Rebecca, who had some complicated feelings about dick-sucking, never having had the opportunity to try it, unsure of how exactly one did it (teeth?) had found no clever rejoinder. Who felt the pulse, the fright of an approaching war? Not Berkeley's fine young men, all apparently stoned and happy, proud to come of age in peacetime.

So perhaps not a hologram of that precise moment. Amid the discomfort of recalled humiliation, the white telephone began to look like a very compelling portal. She lifted the receiver, dialed.

Caleb had described the rules for phone use with more detail and admonition than he did for chain saws, fires, or bowie knives, casting it as a unique tool of destruction to be avoided except in emergencies, and even then, only at night. Flouting this—it was just a telephone, after all—she'd started calling home willy-nilly. Evening, morning, broad daylight. Her only emergency was the need to say "Don't tell Dad, but I hate it here" and receive sympathetic maternal clucks from Georgia, which would restore her to her full self: knowable, complete, daughter.

Her parents' phone rang twice, and on the third ring, there was a knock on the office door. "Caleb? You in there?"

The door opened, and Don Talc entered, holding a length of hose. "Oh, pardon me. Just looking for . . ."

"Hello?" Georgia said on the phone. "Hello?"

"Caleb. But if you're . . ."

Rebecca hung up the phone. "No, no, not at all," she said to Don, feeling her face flush.

Caleb always deferred to Don. "Don's the one that should be explaining this," he'd say. "He's really in charge of everything." And although Don clearly held no authority and Caleb never asked Don to explain anything, he was entirely allied with Caleb. A sidekick. A trusted assistant.

She began to apologize. It was a true emergency, she said. Her mother was sick. Terribly sick. She said the word "cancer" and then regretted it, seized by a certainty that her mother's healthy cells would now turn malignant by a devious god that toyed with atheists by taking them literally.

Don said he was very sorry to hear about her mother.

"Actually, she's not sick," she said, unable to bear the danger she'd put Georgia in. She knew she sounded crazy, so she began telling him, in a gushed explanation for her erratic behavior, that she was just very much in love with this room and couldn't stay away from it. "I like to think about the woman who lived here, back when it was a bedroom, because, I mean, look around, it was clearly a bedroom, and clearly a woman's bedroom. I can tell."

"Pammy," Don offered, stepping forward to drop the hose on the desk. He took a pack of cigarettes from his back pocket and placed one in his mouth, a gesture that seemed, coupled with his leathery skin, pale mustache, and taciturn demeanor, to be almost too stereotypical, imitating the Marlboro Man imitating a cowboy.

"Alright," she said, surprised that he would play along. "We can call her Pammy. Pamela. I like it." She imagined telling her friends, "Oh, camp? It was great. I got to know this cowboy. We formed a bond over our mutual admiration of a bedroom."

She spoke for a while about how she pictured Pammy picking out the wallpaper, choosing these cheerful daisies over, say, more sentimental roses or maudlin lilies from the pages of a Sears catalogue.

"You can stop making up your stories," Don said, removing the cigarette with two fingers. His gaze focused on the window. "Pammy was an actual person. My wife, actually. She chose the wallpaper, twenty years ago now." He turned to her with a look of malice that surprised her. "That was a few years before she died in this room. It was cancer, just like your mom has."

She'd seen Don's trailer, as small as a four-square court, up the dirt road from the ranch house. Why would his wife have died in this room or chosen its wallpaper? But she said only that she was sorry, so sorry. So sorry. Sorry. She kept apologizing as she grabbed her backpack and ran halfway down the stairs before calling up, softly, so the gods would hear, but not necessarily Don, "My mom doesn't have cancer, though."

On the Meadow, she felt conspicuously solitary. Everyone was in groups or at least paired up, even the little kids. Rebecca puttered a bit in Caleb's orbit. Before she'd arrived at counselor training, they'd met only once, after his dad died. She was just born and he was thirteen, so it was hardly a meeting. But her whole cognizant life she'd been hearing about his mom and stepdad, PR flacks for congressional liberals whose names in the *New York Times* always set off a howl of contempt from her parents, and she'd assumed that their son would be similarly mealy, pedantic, smarmy; somehow she thought she'd be able to discern on his face the boring mind of a middling Democrat.

In actuality, he was tall, brawny, competent, much more of a man than she'd expected. He strolled around camp with purpose but without hurry, a creature totally at ease, carrying his sprinkler nozzles and slingshots. She found herself waiting to be noticed by him, and in that way, at least, she was like everyone else here.

When it became clear that he wasn't going to notice her this morning, she moved closer to a group of campers engaged in one of those mild teenage orgies of permitted touch, flopping against each other, leaning on someone else's bent legs or sitting back-to-back. David was in the very center, a girl braiding his hair. As if they had no idea the loner he actually was. She hadn't spoken to him since the day he'd arrived, but now she felt compelled to flaunt their shared past in front of everyone. "Hey, David," she called. "I talked to Ira yesterday." She was standing far enough from him that she had to shout out her father's predictions about the likelihood of a war in Kuwait over oil.

David shrugged, unperturbed. "That's why it's so awesome to be here. Worlds away."

"And that's a good thing?" she shouted, remembering why it was that she never tried to have these conversations with him. "Just hanging out, pretending a war's not coming? Ignorance is bliss? As if we're not implicated just by the gas we used to get here. *If nothing else.*"

David's friends began laughing at her, not loudly, but the silent, amused chuckle with which the mellow apprehend the vehement.

She set her gaze on them. "And wow, it's funny, isn't it? It's funny that boys like you will be killing other boys and dying. Have you thought about that? Exactly like you. And if there's a draft, then not just boys *like* you, but you." She pointed at the teenage boys in turn. "You and you and you." At last, she felt like herself, the true Rebecca, holographically appearing on the plateau. War resister, Ira's daughter, bearer of bad news. Let them stare. Let them listen. Let a shadow fall across their wide-open futures.

◆ ◆ ◆

ONCE THE KIDS WERE all ushered into activities after breakfast that third morning, Caleb set off from the Meadow to find Kai. Kai wasn't Suze. But she was a girl as beautiful as anything in nature, a girl like Mesa Verde, like the night sky.

And what was Caleb? Walking across the field, he was a tuning fork. That's how he thought of himself. Listening, taking the hum of the place, and then noting who was off. Rebecca zinged into his mind. Or maybe he was more like a piano tuner. Finding the wrong pitch, tightening the offending string inside the soundboard—was that how it happened? In any case, his cousin was plinking wrongly. Her sullen attitude; the way she stood alone, looking willfully pissed-off; her odd decision to tell some boys that they might get killed, which Jenny P. had told him about at breakfast. And yet she'd practically begged to come here. Hadn't Ira called on her behalf, describing her deep desire to be a counselor, her preternatural talent with kids? Caleb decided that he would talk to her right away. After Kai.

Before he even made it across the ditch, however, he came upon Patrick just sitting in the dirt, sifting it through his fingers, his new fat settling like beautiful hills. Caleb loved him, loved all the kids. It killed him to imagine what might have happened to Patrick over the past year, his thirteenth year, the year the world rises up to laugh at you. He put a hand on the soft pudge of Patrick's upper back. "Come walking with me."

"Do I have to?" Patrick asked. He wore a soccer medal over an enormous Lakers shirt and sat in the area of nothingness between barn, shower house, and infirmary teepee. From here, Caleb could see Mikala, a counselor for all eight years of Llamalo, through the wire garden fence. She was crouched over lettuce shoots, her ass and hips in loose jeans, her green tank top, her frizzy brown braid like a furry animal, all so familiar to him, and all still somewhat—even three years after they'd last fucked—turning him on.

"I need your help," he said to Patrick.

Or was it four summers since Mikala? Last year it had been Anja, and the summer before that? Ever since Suze left, someone had come up to Caleb's yurt in the evening after a campfire, the kids all asleep. Caleb had a small repertoire of gesticulatory invitations, a hand resting on a shoulder, slipping down the back, a suggestion of finishing up a conversation later. There was nowhere to knock on a yurt, so the girl had to push open the curtained door. *Oh, hi, I just thought. No, sure, come in.*

"We need to see what's going on up at the Gathering," he said, still looking at Mikala, thinking the phrase "one ass leading to another," and then, "for all time, ass begot ass."

He'd gone all winter without, all spring and fall. It was an appropriate loneliness then, an appropriate hardship, part of living here; hermitage was the cool underside of isolation. Summer, though—summer was different: a jostling busy world, a world of careful calibrations every hour, an explosively alive world. And sex was appropriate in this world.

Caleb helped Patrick to his feet. He never said to the kids, "Why are you just sitting here?" He never said, "Is something wrong?" He said, "Come along with me," and they came. Some chose to spend every morning like this, waiting to be found by Caleb. They pulled on his arm, and as he walked around Llamalo, he heard himself spoken about: *Caleb told me we're having sloppy joes tomorrow. Caleb says that's the most rare hawk to see here.* Even when he'd said nothing of the sort.

Caleb led Patrick to one of the three footbridges he'd built across the irrigation ditch. The Gathering—he often regretted naming it with a gerund—was a fenced-in circle of dirt that had once been the Talcs' winter corral. It was the highest meeting point in camp, beyond the platforms and just after the craft shacks, a twenty-minute walk from the irrigation ditch. Kai would be there now, in her red shorts and with a smile like she was offering a gift.

But once across the bridge, Caleb and Patrick were further detained by another camper, Nicole, who waved a black trash bag, "Caleb, come see!" During announcements, lithe Jamal with the chest-length dreads had stood up, shirtless, to invite campers to help him clear star thistle from the trails that connected the boys' platforms to their toilets. All the girls from puberty on up were now clasping gloved fingers around thorned stems.

Last year, Nicole had worn the same shirt as everyone, tie-dyed, food-stained, oversized (Frank's Farm and Feed sold only larges), as well as a single lace glove. Every day, she unpeeled it for Caleb, and they inspected her skin for signs of tattooing from the sun. "A grand accomplishment!" he'd said, at the end of the summer when she'd removed the glove and waved her latticed hand in his face.

But this year, she'd arrived with two school friends who'd never been here before, Tanaya and Shauna, and they all wore the same white polo shirts, Ray-Bans, Reeboks. At announcements, they sat on plastic bags, lest their khaki shorts be stained with dew. It was these friends of Nicole's, the popular kids, the kids who belonged at camps with competitive sports and weekly phone calls home, whom he worried about more than the stragglers. Would they relax enough to become part of Llamalo?

"Caleb," Tanaya said, "aren't we doing an amazing job?"

"Caleb," Shauna said, "aren't we *so* nice for doing this for the boys?"

Now, all the girls stopped working and gathered around Caleb and Patrick.

"Caleb, are there tacos for lunch today?"

"It's Thursday, isn't it," another girl answered. "Always tacos on Thursday."

"Caleb, are we doing self stories this year?"

"What are 'self stories'?" Tanaya asked, rolling her eyes. "Sounds like something nasty." Her giggling body collapsed onto Shauna's.

Little jappy girls, Caleb thought, but he didn't chastise them. It would happen this summer like it happened before: nail polish chips away, leg hair grows in, alligators fall off, dust settles on white cotton.

The trick, although he never said this to anyone, was simply to love them. He had to feel the love in his chest. He had to listen to them and say "Excellent" and "How fantastic" and "Tell me more at lunch." These phrases now allowed him and Patrick to leave the boys' area, Patrick's soccer medal metronoming their way as they passed the small open-faced shacks: Nat was demonstrating how to make baskets from pine needles, like the Indians did; Scott, laying out black floss to sew patches on the backpacking packs; Jeremy, shaving juniper branches into bows; Rebecca, holding up a clump of mud and asking, "Can you identify this animal track?"

Could Rebecca even identify it? Caleb doubted it. He stopped to listen but was distracted by a cackle and the moan of the generator coming from behind the black sheet that covered the opening of the photography shack. Inside were troughs of chemicals and a red lightbulb and prints hung on a clothesline, but there was no photography on Thursdays.

Caleb walked over, knocked on a wall. He heard a familiar "Oh boy," and then four young boys appeared from behind the sheet, squinting into the sun, followed by David.

"I developed the rolls left over from last summer," David said. "They're drying now."

"Cool. Cool," Caleb said, nodding his head, pleased that David had taken it upon himself to teach the younger boys that the past could be brought back and hung on a clothesline.

The boys copied David—his slouch, the bob of his head—just as David had spent the past eight years copying Caleb, so they all stood there in a semicircle, slouching the same, nodding cool.

"Wanna see them? There's Saskia doing that face. You remember Saskia's face?"

Instead of answering, Caleb rested his hand on David's shoulder. This was perfect, actually. "Could you show them to Patrick? I need to check on something."

Now he could arrive at the Gathering unaccompanied. Four kids, dipping their Farm and Feed shirts into cauldrons of dye, called hello. Kai was kneeling on a tarp, untangling a length of basting string, broken rubber bands beside her. One of her hands was the color of an angry ocean. She glanced at him, returned to her tangle. Her black hair was loose. A T-shirt cut low showed breasts tan and braless. He came to her side and crouched.

"Oh fuck, are you here to tell me I messed something up? I didn't realize the rubber bands would all just snap." She was jocular but defensive.

He reached out to tap her blued fingers. "What happened here?"

Dropping the string, she held the dyed hand out for examination. "I know! I know! I totally forgot to use gloves. It looks awful."

"Actually"—he reached out again and caught this hand and held it—"I like it."

"Are you shitting me?" she asked. He returned her smile and shrugged, and then the first lunch bell rang. But that was fine; he'd done enough.

"Alright, everyone, clean up," she yelled, and her wards set their tie-dyed shirts on a sheet pinned down by rocks. The sheet lapped up blue and green and yellow from the twisted, tourniqueted shirts, straitjackets for clowns.

"Don't wash it," he called, walking away.

Caleb heard the banging noises of cleaning up in the shacks, and then, as he continued the trail alone, he heard aimless guitar-strumming from Suze's Meadow. There was the second *lunch-time, lunch-time* clang of the cowbell that only Scott was allowed to ring, the running of feet to the picnic tables, the silence of the moment of silence, the drum solo of forks scraping, and then voices joining in. And all these were the right noises, washing away in the huge cauldron of sky that was Llamalo, until they were interrupted by the bristled sound of high-pitched giggling, that timbre calculated both to draw attention and to exclude. He looked over to see Nicole, Shauna, and Tanaya, all at the same table, hunched close and laughing.

"Ha," Tanaya said, like a lightning bolt striking a juniper. "Ha," Shauna answered, like a plate of food dropped. "Ha," Nicole echoed. "You're *so* funny, Tanaya."

Caleb rose slightly from his seat, feeling the hot need to shout at them, to shut them up somehow, before he remembered it was just laughing, just children, before he remembered about love.

He forced himself to sit down again and pass the rice and listen as a girl beside him spoke of the remarkable tricks she'd taught her cat. At the end of lunch, campers and counselors gathered on the Meadow. When Caleb came around the house and stood before them, they quieted. He smiled at them and began one of his talks about how you can allow yourself to change when you're in the wilderness, how it's one of the only times in your life you might be entirely open to change. This was not an overt reprimand for those girls, those little jappy girls, but rather words washed in meaning and exhortation, like a rubber-banded T-shirt dunked in blue dye to make blue spiderwebs.

As Caleb was watching everyone head across the footbridges to wait out the hottest hour of the day supine on their platforms, Don approached, squinting up at him. "Wondering if I could take a minute to go over something with you."

"After rest hour," Caleb said. "I need to take this opportunity to conk out."

Don shoved his hands in his pockets and looked out toward the Dobies, a lack of eye contact that always meant he was riled up about something—the wrong kind of feed purchased, a new fecal disaster with the composting toilets. "If you have a minute now . . . it's a matter I know you'll want to hear about."

Caleb noticed Rebecca climbing the porch steps, opening the front door of the white house, ignoring the imperative of rest hour. He told Don that his message would have to wait for another time, and he dashed across the Meadow to the house. Entering, he could hear twanging songs on the radio and the percussion of pots from the kitchen. He didn't find Rebecca in the living room or in the kitchen; the downstairs bathroom door was open, the room empty. He took the stairs two at a time. Tuning fork, he thought. Piano tuner, he corrected. He loved this part of his job. He loved all of it.

◆ ◆ ◆

UNFORTUNATELY, IRA ANSWERED INSTEAD of Georgia. "Rebecca!" he said energetically. "What's the news from the far desert reaches?"

"It's okay." She couldn't complain to Ira, who'd sent her here with such belief in her enjoyment. "It's great."

"Gorgeous, huh?"

"It's nice. Lots of sage. That kind of thing."

"So then what're you doing calling home? Middle of the day?"

Rebecca neatened a pile of invoices on Caleb's desk. "I just want to know what's going on at the paper. I feel out of touch. What's the cover this week?"

"The paper? It's the same old. Isn't that what people say? Same old, same old. And I mean that literally. The paper, like your poor papa, is in its boring middle age. But you! You're young. You're in nature. Mom says you keep calling. Are you worried about us for some reason?"

She wasn't. She was worried about herself, but out of politeness she said, "I guess so."

"Well, you shouldn't worry. You really shouldn't. We're *fine*. It's a waste of your time. You should be enjoying yourself. Have a blast! You're not there for that long, you know. Carpe diem, as they say, although I've always wondered what, exactly, it means to seize a day. Maybe it means, stop calling us. Alright, pumpkin? Stop calling us and try to enjoy it. We thought it would be fun, so try, alright?"

Frozen with guilt over her unhappiness, Rebecca held on to the handset after she hung up, and was still sitting like this when the office door opened.

"That's not going to help."

She set the phone on the desk.

Caleb, taking up the entire doorframe, emanated casual disapproval. "Let me tell you, if you're lonely here, the phone doesn't help. Actually, makes it a lot worse. We should talk, don't you think? Outside, though."

Inside seemed preferable, but she followed him down the stairs.

"I've been hoping to get a moment with you," Caleb said once they reached the Great Overlook, and then he crouched. She didn't know whether she was supposed to crouch, too. She decided to keep standing, which was probably wrong, because now she was looking down at him as if at a toddler. His brown curls were level with her belly. Alone at adult height, she braced herself for condemnation. She expected yelling or that more unnerving quiet anger. But instead, he talked about what he'd seen of her at camp during these past three days and the week of training, how she was open and curious and clearly intelligent and he admired her. It was very pleasing to listen to this.

Then, he paused. His long brow furrowed. "Are you lonely?"

"I'm . . ." Was this a trick question? Was loneliness even allowed here? Llamalo's private language exhausted her. There was a rule that stated which direction the bread basket should be passed and about who should make the batch of sticky herbal lip balm that smelled like urine, and that stipulated it be made on the first Friday of every session. There was a rule about who could ring the dinner bell. But when Rebecca had stopped three kids from pulling mattresses off their platform to build a fort, Mikala had intercepted, explaining that actually this was a fine way for them to explore the world as long as they returned the mattresses afterward.

Even so, Rebecca wanted to please Caleb, who had just praised her so stirringly. But how to answer? If he thought loneliness despicable, she'd disavow it. If, on the other hand, he was sympathetic to the longings of those more susceptible, she wanted to rise to his sympathy. Equivocating, she shrugged one shoulder. "It's just . . ."

He nodded seriously, as if something had been confirmed. "Being lonely can make us antagonistic. I get that. I really do. When I heard what you said, I thought, 'She must be lonely.'"

"What I said? I didn't say anything."

He smiled sadly. "I heard that you told some kids that there's going to be a war over oil in the Middle East. You told them that they might kill and even die in this war. Do you really think they should be thinking about this right now?" He shook his head. "No, see, they're here to figure out how to live."

How had he known? He'd been across the Meadow from her. He was speaking in the same kind tone with which he'd complimented her, but now this kindness encompassed a vast disappointment.

"They've seen shit," he continued, still looking up at her. "Each of them. There's been pain. Even in their family. Especially in their family. There's been love withheld. They've been demeaned. A kid in any family has seen shit." He rose. "And they need you, these kids. They need you to offer something different. To listen to them."

"I've been trying," she protested.

"What if you try to stop holding yourself at a distance? Try that and I bet you won't feel lonely. Keep away from the phone and you'll settle in here better."

The reprimand over, he headed across the irrigation ditch toward his yurt. What a waste, she thought, walking behind him to her platform. She could hear Georgia say that, and she thought it in Georgia's sighing voice: What a waste. Caleb was so charismatic, so good at galvanizing people, at that sort of rousing talk that makes you feel like part of something greater, and *to what use*? To make sure some rich kids were well hydrated? Where was the public good? The whole world's fucked up, Caleb.

She heard the girls as she climbed the steps to the platform, which was built like an open stage, ready for drama. Or rather, they heard her. Someone said, "Shut up, you guys. She's here." The others began squealing, like a tree full of startled crows.

Except for Jenny P. and Jenny L., who lay reading on their own sleeping bags, all the girls were shipwrecked on Tanaya's. Rebecca came to the foot of this mat like a dutiful nurse. "Do you need anything? Anyone want to talk?" They looked at each other. Eyes darting messages. *Uh, no.*

It had been like this since their arrival. She'd carefully chosen books to bring, but they weren't interested in her reading aloud. She'd imagined intimacies, secrets shared, vulnerabilities laid out in front of her like offerings to the gods. She'd imagined guiding them from the pedestal of her nearly nineteen years, from the flashing lighthouse of college, but instead they sat on Tanaya's bed singing Top 40 songs she didn't know.

Lying on her own cot, two Jennifers and six empty beds away from the clique, she couldn't make out what they were saying. She peeled a strip of skin off her fraying lips. In grade school, she'd been a strange girl with inexplicable clothes. Kids like Tanaya had shunned her. But at Berkeley, Rebecca had used her lefty cachet to become a semicelebrity among the nerdier crowd; her friends all knew about the time Angela Davis brought her to see a seal washed up on the oily Oakland sand; the bee sting she'd endured picking lavender at Tom Hayden and Jane Fonda's Santa Barbara ranch; how she'd played hopscotch with the children of both jailed and wanted members of the Weather Underground.

"David," she heard. The girls had become careless in their whispering. "David," again.

She lay still to quell the synthetic shuffle of her sleeping bag. She wouldn't turn her head, so she didn't know who said, "Well, that's the way he looked at me. I'm sure of it." "You wish." "I heard he already made out with . . ." She missed the last word.

David David? What kind of a backward place was this? What garden of misfits, where Rebecca was reprimanded and David revered?

THE REAGAN YEARS: AUGUST 1982

OUT OF THE WHOLE world of objects, large and small, Rebecca, at age eleven, could draw just two: ballet shoes and detonating nuclear bombs.

It was the latter that she'd rendered on poster board, NO MORE HIRO-SHIMAS beneath it in her signature ghost script. Although the rally wasn't until late this afternoon, she carried the placard as she crossed the lawn at Will Rogers State Park to attend a prerally picnic. She was particularly proud of this bomb. Her mom, walking beside her, was complaining about the shame of a well-watered lawn during drought. Her dad, a few steps ahead of them, had a green canvas bag slung over his shoulder. Rebecca was enjoying the clink of apple juice bottles from this bag, and the cheerfully outraged tone of her mother's voice, and the squish of wet soil beneath her sandals. She was imagining the rally: how transit workers would emerge from the accordion doors of their buses, postal workers in pale blue would drop parcels and link arms with whole families of grape pickers, who would grab the hands of students, and President Reagan, known in her house only as "the Fucker," whose fund-raising dinner they were protesting, would glance outside the window of the Century Plaza Hotel and see them—el pueblo unido—and he'd wonder, who was that girl with the bomb poster?

But then Ira stopped short and turned toward his wife and child. "Look, I'm sorry. I can't do it."

"Ira, don't," Georgia said. "Not today."

"I can do the picnic. The picnic's fine. But I can't go to the rally."

Suddenly, the grass was a canyon, and Ira had slipped and fallen in, leaving Georgia and Rebecca on the lip, looking down at him.

"You know how it'll be," he continued. "We'll stand in the area cordoned off by the cops, making sure not to upset them. We'll wave our little signs around." He grabbed Rebecca's poster and pumped it up and down. "And when they tell us to go home, we'll go home and sleep well, as if we've done something."

"That's a lovely drawing," Georgia said, draping an arm around Rebecca. "I think Rebecca really wants to go. She worked hard on her poster."

"No, I don't." Rebecca pulled away from her mother, that cloying shore.

Ira reached out to give the poster back to Rebecca. "I'm sorry if it's disappointing, pumpkin. But who voted for Reagan? The workers of the world. We're their enemy. That's the entire problem. That's the unsolvable. And how do we fix it? We stand outside Reagan's hotel?"

Rebecca saw a thousand placards, a reef of bobbing coral fans, and she was standing in front of them, clutching her poster. By chance, all the girls from her fifth-grade class would happen to pass by, walking splay-toed, with ballet shoes tied over their shoulders. "Is that Rebecca?" "Who?" "Rebecca. You know, the girl who sits in the second row?" "No way." "Yes way." "No way." "Yes way." "No way—you mean Rebecca who doesn't even have hair long enough to French braid?" "Look how she knows all of them—farmworkers and students and union leaders." "I thought she didn't know anyone." Tate, the smartest ballet girl, would purse her glossed lips. "No, she must know all of them. She must know everyone. Even transit workers."

Rebecca looked at her father. Dive in, his expression said. Dive in with me. She dove. "I get it. The rally won't change anything."

Georgia sighed, and they continued on to the patch of lawn that held their friends and their friends' kids—those who were named after foliage and those who were named Jessica or Matthew but had been adopted from Ethiopia and Vietnam. In her gloom, Rebecca chose a spot on a blanket on the outskirts of the gathering and opened *Island of the Blue Dolphins*. No, she didn't want a sandwich. Ira said, "Fine. Suit yourself," and she said, "Fine. I will." He hovered for a moment before joining his newspaper staff in a circle of overturned buckets, commandeering the conversation jovially.

"So my nephew called completely out of the blue." Ira was starting a story Rebecca had already heard twice. "Last saw him twelve years ago. Now he's just out of college."

"We sent him a subscription to the paper for graduation," Georgia chimed in from a bedspread where she sat with Judy, a former dancer, who still cut the collars from shirts and sat with her legs frogged together.

Ira glanced over at Georgia and then continued as if she hadn't spoken. "He called to tell me that he wants to—he absolutely *has* to—go to Wyoming or someplace and start a utopian commune for kids. 'A utopian commune'—the actual phrase he used. I said, 'You mean a summer camp?' He said, 'Nothing like any other summer camp. The kids will never step inside.' In other words, this camp is special because it's *his*, because *he* will lead the youth through the wilderness."

Rebecca watched as other conversations stalled out. The copy editor ceased talking to three women in wraparound skirts. The production assistant turned her head toward Ira's voice as she scooped pasta salad onto a Styrofoam plate. Joe, bald and slight, like Gandhi, stopped lecturing a squadron of bearded fathers and looked over.

"What'd he want from you? Free ad space?" asked a young man. Rebecca couldn't remember the name of the newest intern, but they were all the same: recently graduated from East Coast colleges; thrilled to do menial tasks for free; in awe of Ira.

"Why'd he call me? Why does anyone call me? He wanted my help. Apparently, he needs money for this wilderness experience. Thoreau's cabin in the woods isn't good enough for him. He wants a donor, a *patron*. Let's see, should we make a list of those who deserve funding more than an overprivileged college grad with a hankering for an epiphanic experience?"

Now, even the academics on the far blanket had stopped talking to listen: the UCLA sociologists, the teachers from Hollywood High who had organized the walkout.

"The ten million unemployed," the intern began. "Welfare moms, disabled . . ."

But Ira waved him away. He hadn't meant a *spoken* list—even Rebecca knew that. They all carried the list in their heads. Ira swiveled to face the copy editor and continued. "You know what infuriates me the most? The sense of entitlement. These young men and their belief they can change the world just by being themselves, totally divorced from the social movements already in place. Go to South Central. Go to South *Africa*. Go to Nicaragua. Maybe you'll learn something"

"El Salvadór," the intern offered, with an overdone accent.

Ira looked at the young fathers. "Stop moving to the fucking woods and claiming you're a good person just because you grow your own goddamn vegetables."

"Right, what about all the shitty food options at the supermarkets where poor people have to shop?"

"That's it." Finally, the intern had said the right thing, and Ira rewarded him with a nod. Rebecca watched the intern straighten his back, a proud duck.

"So what'd you tell him?" Joe called out.

"What do you think, Joe? I told him to fuck off."

"Ira! Come on. Tell them the truth," Georgia chided. And then to the crowd, "Even *he* won't treat his nephew that way."

Ira grinned, pleased with himself, arriving at the punch line. "Okay, listen. You're all going to love this. I saved his life. I gave him Peter Finkel's number."

"Finkel?" the copy editor asked incredulously, pushing her round glasses higher on her nose. She'd taken off her blouse to sunbathe in an orange bikini top, despite the wind, and Joe was massaging her shoulders.

Ira drummed on his bucket. "That's right. Because, god knows, Finkel isn't going to part with a dime for this kind of thing. He'll never go for it. Rejection's the best thing that could happen to my nephew. I saved his *life*—got him out of the woods, literally. Now he can do something of significance. Maybe he'll come intern here."

They all laughed—*Finkel!*—Ira the hardest. Rebecca scowled. Perhaps Ira could crawl out of the canyon, but she was stuck down here in the loamy limestone, hands unable to find purchase. She felt a stab of pity for Caleb and his encounter with Finkel, a stab of pity for herself and the placard she wouldn't hold.

And then she saw David running toward her, treading on cuffed cords, windbreaker flapping, blond curls bobbing, skateboard under one arm, the other waving.

Georgia and Ira, Joe and Judy. The two couples had met on a voter registration drive in Mississippi. Ira had convinced everyone to start the newspaper in LA, where Rebecca and, a year later, David were born. Although they went to different schools and were two grades apart—both with late summer birthdays; Rebecca's parents entered her in kindergarten young while David's parents heeded the advice to start boys late—they'd shared a childhood, buckled side by side in cars; sweaty juice-stained legs stuck together; left to amuse themselves during meetings and rallies.

"Finally, you're here," he said, dropping next to her. "Want to play?" No need to specify which game: Years ago, they had invented the land of Unionionion and had spent their childhoods defending its unionized onion farmers against scabs and management. "We are all onion farmers" was their motto.

"I'm reading." She turned a page to demonstrate. "Organized labor is dead—haven't you noticed? Besides, it's really a stupid game."

He spun a wheel of the board he cradled in his arms. "I kind of like it."

She loved it. *I'm suffering,* she wanted to say. "I'm not going to the rally."

"But I thought we—"

"Is Reagan going to end the arms race because of me, holding a poster on TV?"

"Is that what your dad said?" David was clever.

"It's what I think."

He was flicking the wheel faster. "I don't know. I think it'll be fun. Everyone's psyched about the rally. Friends from my school are coming."

Were they? If girls who looked like Tate were *psyched* about the walk-out, if you could know about nail polish *and* Nicaragua, if everyone understood all that the Silvers understood, then what would be left for Rebecca?

"Well, I'm not going."

"Alright." David shrugged. "So let's explore."

She looked up from her book, and David was a lion, yellow and glorious.

A crush could begin that suddenly; it could bubble up from dry ground. One day, there was nothing of note, just the sandy dirt of the desert West. And then the next, the ground was gooey, viscous, a trap.

"There's nowhere to explore," she said and felt herself blushing.

"Come on, Zoomy. This way."

She followed him through a toddler's pink crepe-papered birthday party, toward Will Rogers's ranch house, where people waited to use his toilet and see his spurs. They climbed over a white rope with a swinging NO TRESPASSING sign and walked around to the far side of the house, hidden from parental view. There was no lawn here, just dirt and a scallop of brown ivy against the wall.

Boulders spilled steeply toward . . . well, toward what? Through a thicket of eucalyptus, she could only see dusk and its warnings.

David rushed ahead, prancing rock to rock, but Rebecca froze on a boulder that was too far from the next. If she tried to leap this distance, surely her sandals would slip and she'd fall, slamming against rocks on her way to the ground. When David noticed her hesitate, he made his way back to her and stood on the rock she was aiming for. "You can jump," he said, extending his hand toward her. "I'm here."

She reached out and held his warm hand. She smelled the gaminess of manure and saw eucalyptus leaves, slippery as waxed paper, blanketing the rock he was on.

"Come on, chicken," he said, tensing his grip. "Jump."

Yet instead of jumping, Rebecca jerked her arm toward herself, still holding him tightly, forcing him to lunge forward, stumble, and fall.

The sigh of leaves and then silence, and then David screamed from the ground below.

It was a moment she would mull over in the nights to come, although nobody would ever ask about it, not even David, who just said to his parents, "I slipped." She'd pulled him to her, pulled him close. Hadn't she cared that he would fall? How greedy that first bloom of desire.

She ran to Ira, who called out to his friends for help, but there wasn't a doctor among them; they'd all explicitly let their parents down. Joe, playing the part, inspected palms, rolled up David's corduroys and checked for swelling. After prescribing aspirin, ice, and comic books, he carried David to the car. Georgia folded blankets. Ira flicked Rebecca's shin, saying, "Pumpkin, if you really want to go to the rally, we can."

They sped east on Sunset, past restaurants they would never try. Billboards, skimming by like shuffled cards, advertised movies they would never see. There was a different Los Angeles outside the sun-streamed studios and frozen yogurt and Brentwood Country Mart and Pappagallo espadrilles and everything Rebecca heard about and didn't understand. There was a true Los Angeles that only Rebecca and David knew, and it sang songs that would never become commercials. It sang, *We shall not, we shall not be moved* and *We shall overcome. Deep in my heart, I do believe.*

This Los Angeles walked toward the disappointingly small crowd at the Century Plaza Hotel, a gathering which would never be documented, because there'd just been another shooting on the 405, and every news camera had been sent to cover that story instead. Rebecca pulled on her sweatshirt, because she knew that it was actually cold in this Los Angeles, that if she stood holding a placard and distributing newspapers on an August afternoon, the fog would roll in, and the sky, sand, and ocean would bleach the color of hard-boiled yolk, and how would she ever get warm?

FIVE

—•—

Wolf

IT WAS THE FOURTH full day of camp. The most fragile day of the summer. Like clockwork, kids complained of altitude headaches. A splinter the size of a tapestry needle threaded through a palm. A spider bit the soft epicanthic fold of a sleeping child, who woke screaming that she couldn't open her eyes.

Caleb spent the morning in the infirmary teepee, helping Nat apply iodine and pink calamine lotion. When Don peeked in—"Just looking for you . . ."—Caleb was holding his handkerchief to a bloody nose. "Not right now," he said. In these early days of camp, they communicated largely through notes on yellow paper, tacked to the porch.

Regardless of injury, all kids visiting the infirmary were given honey-and-lemon Popsicles for hydration. As they sat sucking, Caleb, cross-legged on the pile of rugs in the center of the teepee, brushed away mouse shit and told an apocryphal story about a baby wolf born in the Canadian Rockies. This wolf pup was descended from two wolves who escaped the high desert of western Colorado in the 1950s, when all American wolves were being systematically exterminated. ("What does that mean?" "Killed." "Oh.") Now this pup, Caleb said, had never seen Colorado, but somehow he dreamed of it every night. He dreamed of a wide plateau and a tall mountain with the white shape of an animal on its side. One night, when his mother and siblings were sleeping, curled up against each other, this pup took off. He headed south for five weeks, crossing the border when the immigration guards were eating lunch, and he stole their lunch and kept running. He ran through Montana and Wyoming. He spent all winter running.

Here, Caleb drew out the suspense. The wolf was hungry. He grew skinny. He was stalked by hunters on foot and on ATVs and snowmobiles. The wilderness was interrupted by towns and cities and endless subdivisions, and the wolf had to sneak through them at night. Everyone who saw him attempted to shoot him. Caleb described the entire Missoula police force chasing him down Main Street in their cars, lights flashing. The kids listened dreamily, juice dripping on their hands.

The story reached its denouement on a beautiful spring day as the wolf, no longer a baby, climbed over Escadom Mountain, smelled the sage and the rabbitbrush and knew he was home. That night, he looked for cover and found a cave at the foot of the mountain, not far from Llamalo. "Just over there," Caleb said, pointing. Exactly the den his forewolves had lived in.

"Is he still there?"

"I've never seen him. But I think we could this summer. Maybe if we take a hike and get really, really quiet. You think you might want to do that with me?"

All the injured kids nodded, and then Caleb left to check the answering machine in the office. Invariably, on the fourth day, parents left anxious messages. He called them back and reassured:

She's doing wonderfully. He's settling in very well. She's having a fabulous time. We could find a way for you to talk to him if you absolutely need to, but we really don't recommend it. Phone calls really set us back. I hear you, I do, but there's nothing to worry about. Sure, she's made friends, plenty of friends. I'll make sure he writes today.

By the time Caleb finished, the campers had already eaten lunch and rested and hiked to the river. Heading across the alfalfa field to join them, he heard his name, the birdsong of this place.

"Caleb? Caleb!" *Too-wit, Too-wit!*

Don again, standing up from the lawn chair outside his trailer.

"Right." Caleb walked toward his ranch manager, grinning. "You were wanting something. I'm sweltering. Walk with me to the river and we can talk on the way. I need to jump in today."

Don looked away. "Have a few errands this afternoon. Thought you might want to come along."

Caleb stared at Don. Don knew that Caleb never left camp during the first days of summer, when it was up to him to untangle the thread so that it might unspool smoothly through the warming weeks of July and August.

Don pursed his lips. "Thought we could catch up."

"Catch up?" They'd spent every day together for eight years, left notes like lovers.

Don looked pained to have to explicate. He cleared his throat, spit. "Something we might discuss best over errands."

This was so curious, so unlike him, that Caleb relented. "Okay, okay. We'll go. But I have to be back by six at the latest. I'll drive. Need gas anyway."

As they walked together to the parking lot, he wondered what Don might want to say in such privacy. It could only be money. After all these years, Don must want a raise.

And could Caleb give him one? He had plenty of time to calculate finances, because Don didn't speak as Caleb drove him the twenty-five minutes to Frank's Farm and Feed, where they walked through the peeping chicks and scarlet-runner seedlings in cardboard boxes to find the yellow-and-green bottles of Roundup. Don remained silent for the fifty miles to Montrose, where he bought the de-wormer he couldn't find at Frank's. Before they headed back to camp, they stopped at a taco truck for dinner, and finally Don talked, but only about the counselors (he said they were a nice bunch, all in all) and the campers. And the weather, which was too dry even for July—fire weather. They talked about the sow Straw Bale, and whether the kids should be given the option to watch her butchering. Then they were droning northward through a white desert with the truck windows open, conversation impossible over the engine. Caleb thought about how the white flatness was not actually flat, the earth wearing away like skin cells under a microscope. Nor was it white, really, but the very lightest shade of every color as it bleached to white.

By the time they entered the tiny valley town of Escadom, the last bit of sun was bouncing off windows and horse trailers, and Caleb was feeling tenderly toward Don, who was too proud to ask for a raise even after these hours alone together. To give him more time to speak, Caleb drove slowly along the two commercial blocks. Past the movie theater that had shut down eight years earlier, past the Mexican place that had shut down then as well, and all those restaurants that had closed before they'd even opened. Past the Motherlode, the only remaining dining establishment, where the only remaining residents, the coal miners or ranchers or grocery store owners who didn't lose their jobs eight years ago, ate the steak-and-mash special or the chicken à la king and waited for the house band, Tammi's band, to start up with "Islands in the Stream."

Sometimes, on Friday nights during the fall and winter and spring, Caleb and Don and Denise ate here as well, as a threesome, a family, greeting the rest of town. *Hi. Hi. How's it goin'? You get that truck on blocks yet?* Caleb always went straight to the bar to buy the first round, in gratitude for letting him belong in a place where he should never belong. He'd bring Denise her white wine on ice, Don his Jack and Coke, and another for himself. Don and Denise always chose a table in the back, and with them, instead of Don's son, Donnie, sat Caleb, a Swarthmore-educated atheist Jew from Cambridge and DC, like it was nothing.

Of course he'd give him a raise. As soon as he asked.

Caleb turned down Fourth, the town's highest-numbered street, and both he and Don raised their right hands in greeting as they passed Donnie's friends Craig and Travis, soldiers in the town's endless war against mosquitoes, in a teal Chevrolet Silverado. From the truck bed, a contraption the size of a fire hydrant shot a white malathion fog into the evening like a traveling Milky Way.

Should he bring up the subject himself? Say, after all these years, Don, we should reconsider your pay. Caleb picked up speed as he headed up P Road, which followed the river out of town. Clouds chased each other westward. A dog emerged from the cattails along the water. Two trucks were parked in front of the VFW, its POW flag always at half-mast. They were fifteen minutes from Llamalo when Don began tapping one finger against his right knee. "So, I'll tell you about that visit I had with Donnie."

"Wow. Tell me! How's Donnie?" This is what happened whenever Don mentioned his son—Caleb going overboard to pretend everything was copacetic.

"His girlfriend's nice. Marci. Pretty. I mean, exhausted as all hell when I saw her, the baby not yet three months."

"That's great! Good for him."

"Apartment's fine. Small. But it'll do."

Two horses galloping, a roan stallion and a chestnut something, coming to a stop in unison, starting again. A small cluster of cottonwoods swaying to shade a house that long ago burned down. Could anything be better than right here?

But Don kept tapping his Morse code on his knee. And then Caleb realized Don hadn't wanted to talk about a raise at all. There was something he wanted to say about Donnie, and Caleb was going to have to draw it out of him.

"And Donnie? He's doing good?" Caleb turned onto Sorgers Road, which zigzagged up the side of the cliff.

"Something came in the mail a couple days ago. For you. A letter from him. I'll bring it by this evening. I wanted to give you a heads-up."

"Great! Wow. A letter. What about? I mean, if you know." This was where the hairpin was, and although Caleb knew that, he took the turn too fast, sliding the two of them down the bench seat.

Don winced. "He told me to talk to you. When I saw him. Back in March, he told me."

"Talk about what?"

"You know Donnie. Can't let it go."

He left Caleb to grope. "Let *what* go?"

Don turned toward his window, and his voice became quieter. "Thought it was unfair in the way it happened. Thought you were taking advantage of us."

Caleb downshifted as the truck strained up the last switchback and tipped onto Aemon's Mesa. The temperature dropped five degrees. Escadom Mountain seemed to grow as they approached it. A white gash on its side, which usually took on a mammalian aspect—sheep or elk or buffalo—looked simply blobby tonight. He turned the truck away from their only neighbors, the Sorgers, and it was impossible not to think—and to assume Don was thinking—about how Press Sorger had grown up with Don but hadn't lost his ranch when Don had.

Which wasn't Caleb's fault.

Caleb glanced away from the road to look at Don, the back of his neck pink, with white trails where the skin had folded while burned by the sun.

"But we all agreed. We agreed on it." Caleb couldn't keep his voice from wheedling. He was angry. What they were discussing wasn't opinion; it was fact. He'd offered a price for the land, and they'd accepted. This was an irrelevant conversation, and Caleb missed his imagined discussion about the raise. The chance to say "Sure, Don. Of course I can. More than happy."

"Made me promise that I'd come back and tell you his position. I didn't see the point. I told him, past is past, done is done. But you know Donnie. Can't let things go easy. And now he's sent this letter."

"But you're saying you agree with me, right? I just want to be clear. We all agreed."

Don turned to Caleb, his face expressionless. "There's an article I want you to read about thermoformed plastic lining. I cut it out for you." He began to talk about seepage in the irrigation ditch, water loss, cracks in the clay, his usual concerns. Caleb couldn't follow. Did Don agree with Caleb or not? Was there a schism in their friendship, a crack he hadn't known about?

But by the time they parked and parted—Don heading to his trailer, Caleb to the Gathering—he'd reevaluated. Clearly, it was a good sign that Don had told him about Donnie, an excellent sign even, a sign of their closeness. Don was confiding, seeking commiseration: My son, his sad delusions. Whatever was in that letter, Don didn't believe in it. Past is past. Done is done. Water seeped through cracks in the clay ditch bottom, and that was all that mattered now.

At the Gathering, he unlatched the cattle fence and saw everyone sitting there in the sunset of a campfire. Everything was fine this fourth day, this fragile day. Jeremy and Mikala faced the crowd with their guitars. Caleb scanned the heads for Kai. She hadn't come to his yurt the night before, and he'd wondered what that meant. Had she not understood him? Could she be uninterested?

He squeezed in beside her. Kai turned and smiled with half her mouth. "Yello," she said. Her finger brushed the back of his hand. Apparently, she had understood him the day before. She leaned forward until he could feel her breast press against his right arm. Caleb began to sing in a way that, he'd been told, sounded nothing like singing. He couldn't carry a tune, but who cared? He shouted out the words he loved.

◆ ◆ ◆

"I'd fuck him."

That was Nat, whispering in Rebecca's ear just as the wind shifted and carried the campfire's smoke to them.

"Caleb?" Rebecca had been watching across the fire as Caleb wove through the crowd, his tall body settling down beside Kai, which made sense.

Nat laughed, a harsh little *huh*. "I mean, who wouldn't? But apparently, you're tagged the first day if it's you. I mean, he's nice to me and all. He likes me. I *love* him. At least you don't have to deal with the rejection. Better to have Caleb as a cousin and not have to feel sad that you're just not pretty enough."

Rebecca knew that this was her cue to say "No, you're *so* pretty." She wasn't, but she was buxom and game, with a Ren Faire obsession that fit her looks. One could easily imagine her in a dirndl, waving a stein of beer.

"Thanks, but, I'm no Kai apparently. Look at them."

"Well, then who?"

"Who what?"

"Who would you . . . you know?"

Nat pointed a few rows in front of them. Rebecca hadn't noticed David there, his arm reaching around Tanaya, who leaned against him. His back, which was all she could see of him, wasn't unattractive, objectively. But this was bizarre. "David?"

"I mean, look at the way he . . ." Nat laughed again. "You can tell he's not a virgin. That hand!"

How could Nat tell? What cues was Rebecca missing again? It was like in eighth grade, when she'd gone trick-or-treating as a sheep and the other girls had turned into sexy devils, sexy nurses, sexy animals. Rebecca had worn wool upon wool (this was the joke in her costume, a sheep dressed in Georgia's wool sweaters), scratchy and stifling when the hot Santa Ana winds rushed in that evening, inducing the sexy kittens to peel off their black tights.

Then, as now, Rebecca comforted herself with the thought that sex was for frivolous people who had time for sex.

All around them, children sang of a sad train commuter who, lacking appropriate fare, was never allowed to disembark. Why didn't his wife slip a nickel into the sandwiches she dutifully brought him each day? Rebecca had wondered this as a child, truly distraught at the lack of realism or strategy.

Bothered, she stopped singing. "You should see him at home," she whispered. What detail could she provide that might dissuade? How he'd long ago stopped coming to rallies and potlucks? How he was satisfied to languish at the bottom of the academic heap with the druggies and non–native English speakers? Who at Llamalo would even care? "He's a loner," she said with pity. "Really different than he is here."

Nat hit Rebecca's arm. "Those are the ones who're the most interesting, right? Not some blind follower. I mean, I get that he's odd. That embellished way of talking—I'm sure his high school friends can't appreciate it. He should be done with that bullshit. He's clearly smart enough. God, too bad he's not older. Caleb would kill me if I fucked a camper."

Rebecca watched that unvirginal hand. That copulated hand. Those fingering fingers. When David removed his arm and shifted a few inches away from Tanaya, Rebecca found herself pleased beyond appropriate measure, as if she'd succeeded at something.

◆◆◆

DAVID PRESSED HIS PALMS against the pebbled dirt in order to stop himself from standing up and grabbing Jeremy's guitar to show Caleb what he could do.

In the four days since David had arrived, Caleb had made no mention of their phone conversation, and the one time David had alluded to it, Caleb seemed not to understand. This freaked David out until he realized that Caleb wanted to keep their agreement a secret to avoid jealousy or confusion over David's role here. David could get behind that; he'd tell nobody that Caleb was testing him, that he was assessing David's dedication to Llamalo, and that, in all likelihood, David would move here in the fall. David wasn't entirely sure how to prove his dedication. He already enthusiastically participated. He already knew more about this place than all the other campers and most counselors. Still, every day he tried to do a little extra.

Right now, for example, it would be awesome to show Caleb that he knew the chord progressions for every song at the campfire. Over the last year, he'd borrowed Georgia's guitar and taught himself to play, sitting on his bed for hours each day. Although he couldn't do anything fancy yet, he was definitely proficient enough to stand up there, if only he had a guitar.

David watched as Scott crouched to toss on a log, and sparks leapt upward and the fire made the sound of someone falling and falling. With a shrug, Jeremy asked Caleb, "Is it time?"

Caleb pressed a button on his watch, emitting into the dusk a small green glow, and nodded, "Yes, it's time." David noticed all of this, and he was the first one standing. He reached for Tanaya's hand, pulled her up.

At the first campfire, that first summer at Llamalo, Caleb and Mikala had taught them hippie songs: "Teach Your Children," "For What It's Worth," "Will the Circle Be Unbroken," "Leaving on a Jet Plane." Songs with repetitive choruses so everyone could join in. The last song that night was "Rocky Mountain High." David had been sitting between Suze and Caleb. There'd only been thirteen kids that first summer. "This is ironic, right?" Suze had asked Caleb. And yes, it had started out with irony. They'd sung it the way Ira and Joe sang "The Star-Spangled Banner" when the police had come to arrest them. Too loudly, tongue in cheek. *I've seen it raining fire in the sky.* But in just a few nights, it was sung differently. With the sweet sincerity of believers. They sang it every night at every campfire that summer, and still they sang it, always the last song of the evening, standing and holding hands in an amoebic ring. It was how they said goodbye to the day.

This was one of Llamalo's rules, although "rule," David thought while singing along, wasn't exactly the right word. More like a ritual, although that wasn't right either. David had a memory of sitting on the floor with Zacky Reznick, one of the mornings he'd been allowed to tag along to the classroom of the Wilshire Boulevard Temple. The rabbi, in surf shorts and a crocheted yarmulke had perched on the desk and talked about the difficulty of belief, about actions that help you, that bring you closer to

God. That was the word he was looking for. Mizzo? Metzi? Something like "matzoh," but not that.

"Act well, and belief will follow," the rabbi had said, smiling at the wonder of it all.

David remembered that Zacky had been screwing off, whispering stupid knock-knocks to David. But David had only wanted to listen to the rabbi. Actions to bring you closer to God! How had his parents never mentioned that such a thing was possible? Why weren't they doing these actions all the time? When he'd brought this up with Joe and Judy that evening, they gave each other a look of shared superiority. Smiling at his naïveté, they explained that Judaism was regressive and discriminatory. The rituals David had become so excited about, they said, were either superstitions left over from a time before scientific explanations for disease, or rules put in place to maintain hierarchies. Don't eat shellfish. Wear a little hat. Women pray behind a curtain. That had been the abrupt end of his religious education, and now he couldn't remember this word. Mezma?

"What's it called?" He nodded his head toward Tanaya, who was much shorter than he was. "That thing that Jews do? You know, actions, deeds?"

"What?"

"Like what Jews do to get with God, good deeds." You weren't supposed to talk during this song, but he needed to know.

"Are you talking about mitzvot? And if so, why the fuck now?"

"Mitts-vote? You do a mitts-vote?"

"You do many mitzvot, plural. V-O-T. You do a mitz*vah*, singular. V-A-H. Come on—bar *mitzvah*, bat *mitzvah*? Don't you remember anything from yours?"

He raised the hand that was holding hers. "Look, nothing on my wrist. No Swatch for me. Wasn't bar mitzvahed."

He resumed singing, looked up at the watchful mountain. Everywhere else, the country was going to shit. Cows lived their whole lives in cages the size of bathtubs. Humans slept on cardboard on the sidewalk until the cops beat them for fun. Toast's brother had been convicted of "gang activity" and sent to an adult prison, where he was murdered. Bush followed Reagan. Surprise, surprise. There was no stopping this slide toward increased inhumanity. David's parents hadn't stopped it. Rebecca's parents hadn't stopped it. The only thing to do was to get the hell away. This was what Caleb taught them. Live out here, with kindness and love, without buying shit, without watching shit. Every night singing "Rocky Mountain High." Doing the mitzvah of John Denver, getting a little closer to God.

◆ ◆ ◆

THE DARKNESS WAS ALL darkness, pricks of stars. Caleb, alone at the fire, poured water on it, stirred the burned wood and ash, poured more water, and stirred until the sizzling subsided and gray smoke rose and dissipated, and darkness settled again. During these early days, the campers needed to be on their sleeping platforms before dark to reduce risk of falling. "Until you get your sea legs," he told them.

By the time he reached his yurt, all the flashlights had been turned off in the boys' and girls' areas. He stood on the edge of his wooden platform, pissing into darkness. The patter of liquid on dry earth and then silence. He could hear a cough, sounding as close as if the cougher were just behind him. Noise traveled strangely on the plateau at night, sliding everywhere at once. When Kai came, he'd tell her, "Quiet. We need to be quiet," and then quietly he'd push up her shirt, no bra, his thumb against her nipple. He was nothing but anticipation, his whole body anticipation.

As he slipped between the yurt's curtains, he could hear a crunch, a crackle, the weight of a foot or paw landing on the dried arrows of peppergrass, but there was no way to tell how far away it was. When he heard nothing else, he swept his hand over the surface of an upturned crate until his fingers felt the worn cardboard of a matchbook. A flick of his hands and there was that primordial glow. He lit the lantern by his bed. Within milliseconds, the moths arrived, batting against the glass of the lantern, and other strange insects as well. Ungainly, triple-jointed. His yurt a jungle of wings. He reached into a milk crate, digging beneath books and T-shirts for the bottle of Jack Daniel's. He took a long sip and then another, moths head-butting the bottle; they too wanted that amber glow.

When he lowered the bottle, he saw the moon-white envelope on his bed. Caleb ripped it open, unfolded the unlined paper within. Before he read, he was surprised by Donnie's handwriting, the verticality of it, like insect legs. There was a moment when against all rationality, he felt the springiness of hope. Donnie had written to him! After eight years of silence, perhaps they'd be friends again, checking in on each other by mail, visiting even.

> Caleb,
>
> Do you know about the words Wise-Use?
>
> Do you know what this means Custom and Culture?
>
> Do you know about the movement across the Western States to
>
> TAKE BACK OUR LAND?
>
> Do you know that land transfers sometimes are Illegal?
>
> Consider this -- The DOUBLE L is not yours
>
> You can make this easy or hard
>
> Some things to think about.
>
> Donnie

Caleb heard a bright snap, a foot against a twig.

"Caleb? Knock, knock!"

Kai pushed aside the curtained door, peeked around. "Oh, hi." As if surprised to find him there.

Caleb shoved the letter under his pillow. "No, sure, come in." Nothing in here but his mattress and the crate, but from the hole in the roof they could see stars. He picked up the bottle and held it out. "Want some?"

Afterward, he took her outside to watch the moon rise over the final, most western of the Rocky Mountains. It shone a spotlight on Escadom's snowy summit, slid light down the mountain's royal alpine body, cast its white eye over the oceanic and unaccommodating desert, which began in the folds of the mountain's kingly robes and spread out southward as far as they could see.

He held her hand. Naked and content, he decided that he would forget about Donnie's letter. His yurt was washed in moonlight, and the letter dissolved into the darkness from whence it came, and he howled into the night to make Kai laugh. The campers who woke to the howling thought, "Wolf," and went back to sleep.

THE REAGAN YEARS: JUNE 1983

CALEB WAS ALONE AT the ranch when the camp's very first counselors arrived from the humid east. It was a Saturday, so the Talcs weren't working, and the only sounds were the scratching searches of insects and birds. A van pulled up beside the house, expelling the counselors, who blasted out with their road-trip peppiness, their in-jokes, their Big Gulps.

He knew two of them—Scott and Mikala—from an outdoor adventure trip he'd led during their freshman orientation at college. They were four years younger, enamored with him, had eagerly agreed to work for free and to bring along two friends, Suze and Anders.

The counselors oohed over his land in a way that made him feel they didn't quite appreciate it. He'd planned a game that involved closing their eyes and listening, but instead he led them on a hike to the foothills of the mountain. It was midday, June, hot, and there was no trail. As they wove their way between sagebrush, he recognized that he was punishing them because the moment of their arrival hadn't lived up to his expectations. He'd wanted to feel the flick of the ignition switch for Llamalo, the moan of the motor starting up. When he finally let them stop for water, three of them dropped onto the dirt, chugging, panting. Suze walked past them, climbing a nearby mound. She spun a slow 360, then walked down to him. "Do you ever want to let this place just annihilate your sense of self?

Like just get rid of everything, absolutely everything you own, everything you need, and give yourself over to this? I mean, I just want to fucking *eat* this emptiness."

He looked down—she was short, even for a girl—and everything shifted, as if someone had taken a tangled sheet and, with a flick of the wrists, spread it smooth. "Well, guys," he said, turning away from her. "She's figured it out. The whole point of Llamalo."

They hiked back side by side, and he saw that she was more remarkable than he'd initially allowed. That hers wasn't an obvious first-glance beauty provided him the additional pleasure of recognizing something subtle that others might not be able to. She had sunken eyes and pale lashes and a fierce nose, but somehow she was stunning, with a confidence that defied the Deadhead skirt, the multitude of bracelets. There was a corona of happiness around her, a glee, the ethereal manifestation of her hair, which was a yellow fishnet tangled up and set upon her.

That night and the next, he found her often beside him. She asked questions about every detail of his plan for Llamalo. He liked her wrists. He liked her collarbone. He ridiculed his mother's elitism, and she, her mother's anxiety. They came up with a rating scale of all outdoor places—forest versus desert versus ocean versus little stream with a hammock next to it versus sweeping mown lawn versus lake—and agreed on all stages of the hierarchy. Of course, mountains were supreme, the higher the better, preferably above tree line, just rock. The gods on Mount Olympus were the most dangerous and the most sexy to be near. Sexy. Suze said that word.

In this way, the first days of Llamalo buzzed with an audible erotic charge, the sound of power lines across the Dobies. On Sunday afternoon, when they all stripped to swim in the river, piling their clothes on the white stones, he was aware of his body in a way he hadn't been for some time. Not just aware, but pleased. He was pleased with the way he ran over the somewhat-painful rocks and dove under the frigid water. He was pleased, when he surfaced midriver, so cold in the snowmelt that he was almost burning, to see Suze floating naked. Treading water, he was pleased with the water lapping in circles on her breasts, her nipples like rocks, the meeting of her thighs. He was pleased when her eyes caught his, looking at him looking at her. The promise of pleasure was itself so pleasurable that he almost wanted to prolong this expectancy.

THE NEXT DAY, DONNIE's Trans Am pulled up beside the house while Caleb and his crew were still eating oatmeal on the porch. "Check it out," Scott was saying, letting the needle skid against a record. "This song? *So* cheesy." He'd dragged a record player and its speakers to the porch, along with a stack of LPs that Caleb had bought at one of the auctions in town in the wake of Exxon's oil shale bust. He'd bought their encyclopedia sets and board games and axes, their lamps, their pellet stoves, their storm windows, their mason jars, their twin mattresses. For costumes, he'd bought their clothes. For art projects, their dental tools, coin collections, vacation slide shows, Bible figurines.

Donnie and Don stepped out of the car, squinting up at the porch. Caleb ran down the steps, saying loudly, over the oompah of the music, "Hey, guys! Hey, the counselors are here. Come up and meet them!"

Don gave a militaristic salute and headed toward the ditch. Donnie stood still, blinking. The counselors emerged in a line at the porch railing, peering over, holding their bowls, steam rising over their faces. Suze had jumped in the ditch earlier that morning, and wetness from her hair seeped into her camisole. Mikala wore overalls over a leotard. Scott was in cutoffs and knee-highs, his stringy shoulder-length hair in his face. Anders wore the cap he'd bought at Ute's Market: EXXON — SIGN OF THE DOUBLE CROSS.

Looking up at them, Caleb felt sorry for Donnie. How disorienting it would be to meet people your age but with a style and worldview you couldn't comprehend. He called up to the porch, "Come on down, guys! Come meet the Talcs."

The counselors gathered beside Caleb, and he put an arm casually around Suze. "Everyone, this is Donnie. Best thing about Escadom."

The counselors all began reaching their hands toward Donnie like he was a celebrity on one side of a red velvet rope. He shook each hand dutifully.

Caleb kept his arm around Suze while she and Donnie met. He noticed Donnie's handsomeness; he always did. And he noticed Suze's beauty, it was practically all he could think about during those days. But Caleb also noticed, with a small amount of pride, that these two people shaking hands belonged to different worlds, and only he belonged to both of them.

SUZE WAS PAINTING THE rear wall of the barn the next afternoon, rendering within view of the mountain a facsimile of the mountain. Caleb had chosen a task a few yards away. He was trying to convince a rectangle of ashen dirt between the barn and the ditch that it should resemble garden soil, and from here he witnessed Donnie banging his way into the house and then out again and coming to stand behind Suze.

Caleb saw her turn to him. He saw Donnie pull his hat low. "You get to paint pictures like a kindergartner while I'm out there in the heat?"

Suze paused a moment, looking Donnie over, and then set down her paintbrush on a piece of cardboard before saying, "So what exactly are you doing out there in the heat?"

"Fences. Fixin' em."

She started singing "Don't Fence Me In" but seemed to have forgotten the words. "*Give me some land, landy land, landy landy landy land.*" A voice like the tumble of rocks in a riverbed. "Willie's song. Don't you love him?"

Caleb loved Willie Nelson, and that song, that paean to the western breadth, to solitarily surveying the horizon line, well, that song was anthemic to him. He'd teach her the words.

"Willie's aright." Donnie ladled on a drawl. "Willie's my kind of man. Not sure about the pigtails though. Think they'd look good on me?"

She cocked her head, considering. "Awful. Sometimes he has that one long braid. I could see you in that." She sang again. "*I want your land landy land under landy landy land.* Isn't that how it goes?" Caleb realized she was teasing Donnie, egging him to sing the correct words back to her. Caleb was sure Donnie wouldn't know them, but then he began to sing the first few lines, slowly, in a surprisingly confident tenor, while staring at her.

But did Donnie know that the song wasn't actually Willie's? Caleb did. It was by Cole Porter, although even that wasn't entirely true. Tasked with writing a cowboy song for a soundtrack, Porter had borrowed a poem by a highway engineer in Helena. It was a Hollywood song, inauthentically Western, plagiaristic. Did Donnie know any of this?

When he finished singing, Donnie, as if emboldened by the performance, stepped forward and grabbed a hank of Suze's hair. "You could do the pigtails. We'll call you Wilhelmina."

He pointed at the mural. "What's that supposed to be—an albino space alien?"

"Fuck. Tell me you know it's a sheep."

He released her hair. "You ever see any real live sheep, Wilhelmina?"

"They're the pink ones with snouts, right?" With a finger, she snouted her own nostrils.

"Nice look on you. Stick with me and we'll get your farm animals sorted out." Donnie tipped his hat and headed back to the alfalfa field, passing Caleb without looking at him.

Caleb allowed himself to think, I went to a college so small and important you've never heard of it.

DONNIE PARKED HIS TRANS Am beside the house on Wednesday morning and stuck his head out the window. "Wanna help us with the fences, Wilhelmina? I don't think your artistic endeavors will be missed."

Suze was sitting beside Caleb on the porch stairs, mug of coffee in both hands. "That's cool, right?"

Sharp sun on the irrigation ditch water, the chattering of birds. "Well, it's . . ." Caleb raised his left hand to signify that it was conceptually a fine idea, commensurate with his plans for Llamalo, but practically speaking it was maddening and unnecessary. "If you wanted to finish the painting later, then . . ."

"Hop in," Donnie called. Suze left her coffee cup on the steps.

The Trans Am returned in the heat of the afternoon. The three other counselors were napping inside the living room. Caleb remained in the would-be garden, culling rocks from dirt, a headache behind his eyes from the sun. He'd moved Scott's vehicle and his own from their usual spot at the side of the house, parking them four hundred feet to the south. He watched the Talcs get out of the Trans Am and then Suze appear from the back seat, her arms and legs muralled with dirt, the hem of her skirt tucked into her waistband. Don went straightaway to the Russian olive by the side of the ditch where they kept their lunch boxes, but Donnie detained Suze. As they talked, she touched his arm twice. Finally, with a wave to Caleb, she climbed the stairs and entered the house.

"Beautiful day, isn't it, boss," Donnie called out to Caleb.

"Not bad," Caleb said, walking over to him.

"There something you want to tell me?"

"It's about your car. You can't park here anymore."

Donnie looked at his car. "Isn't this where we park?"

"See, we realized this . . ." Caleb gestured toward the wooden archway that said DOUBLE L and beyond that to where the plateau ended and you could see the far mesa, a horizon line of dark green. "Where you were parking your cars, that's the best place to sit and watch the sunset. Totally on fire. We're calling it the . . ." He hadn't yet named this area, and what came forth from his imagination was "the Great Overlook."

Great Overlord connotations came too late; he was stuck with it.

"The Great Overlook?" Donnie frowned. And who could blame him? This area was only slightly higher than the plateau to the south, the same elevation as the western expanse. It hardly looked over anything.

"There." Caleb pointed at his car and Scott's bus, which, now that he realized it, kind of ruined the view of the Dobies from here. "That's the official parking lot."

Donnie stepped into his car, revved, and drove toward town, leaving his dad beneath the Russian olive, peeling a hard-boiled egg. He came back fifteen minutes later, though, parking behind Caleb's Honda in the official parking lot.

AT DUSK, TWO DAYS before Llamalo's first campers arrived, Caleb was washing dishes in a bucket when Suze ran over with delight on her face, skirt flapping. He stood to meet her. The attention she gave Caleb had lost focus, from spotlight to fog light, but now it seemed like she might run straight into his arms, and he couldn't help but open them, bubbles dripping off his fingers. She stopped short, out of breath.

"So Donnie invited all of us to the Motherlode tonight. You should come. Friday night in exciting Escadom!"

"I don't know, Suze. There's still so much to do." He felt rage like eggshells between his teeth.

"Not *that* much. You don't mind if we go, right?"

The counselors piled into Scott's VW and left Caleb alone again on the mesa. He made notes for the first day, rechecked supplies, and lay atop his sleeping bag—in the alfalfa field, where they all slept—listening for them. It was thick night when he heard a motor approach, shut off. He stumbled into his boots and walked with his flashlight past the barn to welcome everyone back. But when he rounded the house, he understood that it hadn't been Scott's bus he'd heard.

The Trans Am was parked on the Great Overlook. Caleb flicked off his light.

He heard two doors shut. Donnie's voice said, "No, not *that* way. You may be a good singer, Wilhelmina, but you've a shit sense of direction." Suze giggling. Donnie again: "Believe me, I know where to go for privacy

around here. Hold my hand. We don't want you falling in the water."
For a few minutes, during which they must have been crossing the single
board he'd laid over the ditch, he heard only Donnie—"That's it, careful
now"—and then the faint sift of displaced stones.

He feigned sleep when the others returned. He heard them whisper
drunkenly about not waking him, then brushing teeth, pissing, the rustle
of nylon sleeping bags, snoring. His stomach clenched; his jaw ached.
The constellations blinked back at him, the Milky Way drifted across the
sky. He couldn't get the fucking song out of his head. The tune of "Don't
Fence Me In," but with Suze's rewrite, which cut to the chase: *I want your
land, landy land, landy landy landy land.* Over and over, until he felt frantic
that he'd never stop hearing it. He was sure he wouldn't sleep, but then he
opened his eyes to find that the sky was mauve. There was a tumble of yellow hair out of Suze's sleeping bag, and when he ran barefoot toward the
Overlook, he saw that the Trans Am was gone.

A DAY THAT CALEB had been looking forward to had been stripped of
every joy. The plan was to drive most of the way to Denver, camp in Rocky
Mountain National Park, and pick up the thirteen campers at the airport
on Sunday midday. The evening dragged on. Suze displayed an exaggerated joviality, but the others seemed to be waiting for him to speak, to set
an edict—no fucking the locals, perhaps?

At the airport, he met and then dismissed the parent chaperones and
hurried his thirteen campers into Scott's van, which Caleb drove, and Caleb's Honda, which Scott drove. The campers were aged nine to fourteen.
Six were related in some manner to the counselors. The other seven—
spawn of hippies, he assumed—had responded to the ad he'd placed in
his uncle's newspaper. Caleb had spoken reassuringly to each of their
parents.

Small aesthetic variations aside, they all looked alike in the way of
suburban white kids. Girls wore shorts with tucked-in shirts announcing school plays, winter choral jubilees, aquariums. Boys wore the same,

untucked. They had knee socks with a yellow stripe at the top or ankle socks with pink pom-poms. They looked entirely unprepared for eight weeks in the high desert. How could he love them?

Five hours later, when they finally crested the rim of the plateau, carsick and hungry, spilled apple juice dribbled down their shirts, the van decided to slow, then stop. Caleb revved for a while, in an aggressive attempt at onwardness. But soon, he had to admit that although the wheels were moving, the van wasn't.

He hopped out and landed softly.

Sixty years earlier, Eustace Sorger had paid for a road to be carved and paved into the cliff from the river valley to the plateau, so it headed straight to his house, which was upriver from Aemon's. To get to Llamalo from the rim, you turned right onto an unnamed dirt road and headed south along the cliff on a slight downhill slope. There was a spot where the ditch, which was a good distance from the road at Llamalo, sidled up right next to it on its way from the Sorgers'. And it was this spot where the road had melted into mud. Grayish mud with strips of red clay.

Two feet ahead of Caleb, there was a desert anomaly: water streaming across the road and pouring down a cliffside.

He stood staring as the Honda stopped behind the van. A door slammed, and Scott came and stood beside him.

"This is unexpected."

By unexpected, Caleb meant "a horror." By unexpected, he meant everything was ruined. By unexpected, he meant Donnie was a fucking asshole, a vindictive fuck. But he was trying hard not to show the depths of his alarm.

"It doesn't make any sense," Scott whined.

Caleb nodded. It made perfect sense. That was the problem.

"It didn't even rain," Scott continued. "How did this even happen?"

"Over there." Caleb pointed to the irrigation canal. In it, wedged between the sod walls of the divider, loomed something white, plastic, unearthly.

"The fuck is that?"

"Refrigerator door."

"A what?"

"Fridge door."

"In the ditch?"

"In the ditch. Blocks the flow."

"But why? Who would even do that?"

"No idea," said Caleb, although he knew exactly who and precisely why.

"Shit. How do we drive past?"

"We don't."

"Okay, so what? We stay in a hotel 'til they fix it?"

Caleb explained that even if he could spin free of the mud, Rocky's Mountain Motel had shut down last fall during the oil shale bust, as had the Sleep Tite. The nearest motel was in Grand Junction.

"Two hours away?"

Crouching by the gully, Caleb saw that it was flowing so quickly across the road it could easily drag a kid down the cliff. Without a clue as to how to proceed, he tapped on the van. "We're here. Everyone out."

Counselors and campers emerged, standing on the dry islands of the road, appraising the runnel before them. "Welcome to Llamalo." Caleb forced a grin.

"Don't tell me this is it." The girl had a freckled pancake face. The others tittered.

"Yup. This is it."

Another girl—the freckled girl's sister—smacked her forehead dramatically. "Oh *jeez*."

Scott said, "What's wrong with a night in a motel? We'll get the people out here to fix the road."

"What people?" Caleb said.

"*I'd* rather a motel," said a girl.

Caleb told them to empty the van of luggage. He'd be back in a few minutes.

A papery panic crumpling inside his chest, he ran northward for fifteen minutes until he came to one of the planks Press Sorger had laid across the canal. It was warped and splintered, maybe six inches across and nine feet long. He ran back with it under one arm and set it across the ditch, just before the washout. Crossed over and then back again, testing it, feeling the wood bow beneath him. Nearly lost his balance as everyone turned to watch.

Caleb considered that they could carry their luggage through the sagebrush to Llamalo, about three-quarters of a mile away. But the ground was uneven, fissured, with great opportunities for kids to break a leg. The road was direct and relatively smooth, even if this meant everyone crossing the ditch twice.

He told the kids to stay where they were while the counselors, with their adult agility, crossed the plank in a few steps, carrying suitcases and sleeping bags. Caleb followed, picking up the plank behind him and placing it across the ditch just after the washout. The counselors crossed to the road, set down the luggage, and went back for another load.

Once the bags were all safely on the dry road, Caleb set down the plank near the campers, calling to them. "Come on over!" The freckled girl approached sassily, ponytail swinging. She put one foot on the makeshift bridge and took it off again, eyeing the swift water. "No way."

Caleb crouched, held out his arms. "Ever walked on a balance beam? Same thing. Fun, actually."

Her round face had turned stony and determined. "I can't do that."

He cajoled for a while, but the girl shook her head. All the kids were watching from her side, the counselors from theirs. He wanted to scream, to force her across. It was her stubbornness that was ruining everything. Instead, he crossed the plank, placing a hand on her back and gesturing to everyone else. "Come here." Only the curly-haired boy from LA held back.

"You," Caleb said to him. "Stand right here."

He looked around as if Caleb couldn't mean him.

"David, right? Come next to me."

Caleb felt cold energy flowing through him like a rivulet through mud. "All of you just flew a long distance. You drove the entire afternoon. Where are we? We're nowhere. Nowhere like home. You're about to be braver than you've ever needed to be. You're about to cross an irrigation ditch. You're not going to fall. I promise you." He paused at the audacity of this vow that was not his to uphold. "But first, let's say goodbye to all the things that you left, that you think you can't live without. Say goodbye to your television and your telephone. Say goodbye to shopping malls. Say goodbye to clean clothes and dry feet. And sidewalks. This morning, you said goodbye to your mom and dad and pets, and that was sad. Now we have to say goodbye to the rest."

The kids twitched and looked away.

"No, really. Say it." Sweat tickled his back.

In singsong mockery, a girl said, "Good*bye*, television. Good*bye*, telephone."

This was never going to work. Fuck you, Donnie.

"Not like that. Say it like you mean it. Let it be sad."

He was looking at David while he spoke, and it was across David's features that he first noticed the shift in expression. The boy's face let go of its skepticism and then quite suddenly billowed with joy as he shouted, "Goodbye, Pac-Man! Goodbye, Defender!"

"What about junk food?" Caleb asked. "Think how you'll miss that."

"Goodbye, Funyuns," David shouted, and now the others joined: "Goodbye, Oreos! Goodbye, Doritos!" They shoveled all their travel fatigue and dislocation and fear into shouting. "Goodbye, *Barney Miller*. Goodbye, *Battlestar Galactica*." Caleb felt the relief of this cacophony filling so much silence, like a crayon scribbling across blank paper. And he felt the coasting thrill of being listened to, of being obeyed.

"Okay. Let's try again." His hand still on the girl's back, he led her to the plank. She set one tentative foot on the plank, inched the other behind it. She undulated—shoulders this way, hips that way. He willed her not to fall. She shuffled her front foot forward, dragged along the rear foot. Caleb could barely watch; he was asking too much of them. But she crossed.

One by one they came, nervously, arms out for balance. Last was David, practically dancing across. Caleb picked up the plank, brought it past the washout, set it over the ditch, and willed them across once again.

Finally, the kids sat on their bags, looking ragged. Faces were slack and smeared with dirt. They licked their already-chapping lips. It had taken an hour to travel twenty feet. Still, Caleb guided them into a bucket brigade, each person two feet from the next along the road. "See that house?" He pointed at the white house nearly a mile away. "We'll get everything there if you toss gently. Work at a rhythm, which I'll set."

"Just a minute." Anders broke out of line. "The kids are beat. We could just carry everything. The counselors, I mean. What would it take? Half hour max?"

Caleb hadn't considered that. He saw the sweat drip down Anders's red forehead. Suze was standing next to Anders, and Caleb hadn't been able to look at her all day. He said, "Don't you understand Llamalo?"

"Hold up." David unzipped his duffel, pulled out a skateboard. "What about this?"

David held it steady as another camper balanced a suitcase on it, and then he released it. The road had just enough of a downhill slope to offer a slowly accelerating ride. When the board jumped a rock, the suitcase flipped, skidding. "Good try," Caleb called. "Come on, take your places."

But David was already running after the board, and the kids were clamoring—"Try *my* bag." They decided that the law was that all the bags had to roll the entire distance to the house, no matter how many wipeouts occurred.

Caleb took position in the sagebrush, trying to block the board from bulleting off the road. Standing there, he watched the kids and counselors running back and forth, dirt in gray maps on their limbs, fallen luggage lying like casualties all along the road. He loved them all. He looked up at the sky, at the immeasurability of blue, and he could fucking eat the emptiness. He thanked the ditch for overflowing its banks. He thanked the road for washing out. He even thanked Donnie, because he was sure it was Donnie who'd shoved the fridge door in the ditch. It couldn't have been anyone else.

They were fully cut off from the world now. Nobody could get here; nobody could leave.

Suze came running toward him, a girl's hand in hers. She let go of the girl when she noticed him, came over to say "It's *so* awesome how . . ." But he interrupted her. Caleb kissed her in full view of everyone. It was the first time, their first kiss. She kissed him right back, pressing her palm against his chest. And then he went diving for the board.

The NEXT DAY WAS a Monday, and Don showed up to work without Donnie. He told Caleb that when he'd seen the washout, he'd parked at the Sorgers' ranch and asked Press Sorger to come by later with a winch hooked up to his tractor to pull the VW from the mud.

Caleb asked about Donnie. "Is he feeling sick? Is he coming later?"

Looking away from Caleb, Don said that he'd woken up on Sunday morning to find his son gone. His Trans Am, his clothes, everything he owned, gone. He hadn't even left a note. "Shame about your ditch," Don said, still looking away. "Not likely we'll ever know who did it."

SIX

Ishi, Last of His Tribe

ON THE FOURTEENTH DAY of Rebecca's tenure as a counselor, she did something unforgivable. When her girls found out, they placed their hands on their small hips. Their gaping mouths shimmered with lip balm. "No way," Tanaya said, and six other fourteen-year-olds echoed: "No *way*." "Oh god," she said. "Oh *god*," they said.

They were sitting around one of the green-painted picnic tables on the eating platform, a cement outcropping behind the kitchen door. Nobody carved initials into the picnic tables. Nobody drew cocks in black ink. They loved it here too much. All around them, kids were smearing peanut butter and jelly onto brown bread, preparing to spend the morning hiking with their counselors to a beach along the Utefork River or the smaller Marcellena Creek, where they would stay until dinner. This was Llamalo's routine every Sunday. It was a time to be removed from the social intricacies of the camp, and counselors, discouraged from encountering other groups, signed up for the coveted and the undesirable spots. That is, if they knew the difference. Rebecca had chosen at random: the evocatively named Salamander Spit.

"What's wrong with Salamander Spit?" she asked vaguely while scanning the honeycomb of tables for David. There he was, ass on a table, feet on the bench, laughing at something a girl had said. Over the past two weeks, she'd begun to feel like her unhappiness was his fault. It seemed there was a fixed amount of happiness allotted to the two of them. At home, a disproportionate share went to her—in proper payment for how hard she worked to please teachers and parents. But here at Llamalo, the scales of happiness tilted heavily toward him. She watched as he leaned down, cupping his hands around the girl's ear, whispering showily, making the kids nearby lean close. All those years Rebecca had thought him unable to speak, when it seemed he'd just been choosing not to speak to her.

"Don't you *know?*" Nicole asked.

Looking away from David, she noticed her camper's peeved stance. "Don't I know what?"

"What's wrong with Salamander Spit. God, don't you know?"

Well, no, she didn't. "It'll be fine. Why would Salamander Spit even be an option if it wasn't fine?"

Tanaya rolled her eyes, muttered something. "Freaker," Rebecca heard. Those nearest clasped their mouths, astonished smiles behind their hands.

Rebecca felt her eyes brimming, the rising tide of childhood come back to get her. Unlike in her actual childhood, she knew enough not to cry in front of her tormentors. "Wait here—all of you." Walking away, she stopped in front of David, ignoring the girl gazing up at him. "Do you have a second?"

But once she led him to the Overlook, to the precise spot where Caleb had crouchingly reprimanded her, this seemed like a bad idea. She and David had hardly spoken at Llamalo, ignoring each other like at school. "Actually, never mind." She turned.

"Hold up, Rebecca. You look—what is it?"

"It's really nothing."

Nat marched past them singing, followed by a line of seven-year-olds clutching lunches, hearts full of a von Trapp family crush on their leader.

"Okay, fine then," she said, as if he'd pressured her. "Although it's not like you can do anything about it. If you really need to know, it's that they hate me."

"No! Nobody hates you." His tone was faux-incredulous, his smile wide. "That's the thing about Rebecca. Everyone likes Rebecca."

"*They* don't."

"Who's they?"

When she told him—they, those girls, especially darling Tanaya—he laughed, "Oh! Oh!" He took a few steps back, as if shot, but by a revelation instead of a bullet. "I get it. It's your first time! Your cherry popped."

She blushed at the insinuation. "First time at what?"

"First time being hated. Disliked. Disappointing people. I can't imagine it's happened to you before. That's what you're upset about, right? That's why you're looking like that. Do you *know* how many people hate me? Do you know how many people laugh at me?"

"Here they don't."

David raised his hands. "And I'm here what? Seven weeks of the year. Round it up to two months. You look surprised. David can round up? I thought he failed math."

"No, I—"

"No worries. Anyway, that leaves ten months not here. Out of twelve. So five-sixths of my life, people are laughing at me. Ignoring me, at best. My dad sitting me down, saying I'm ruining his life, because he can't figure out what he did wrong with me. The problem is—the problem *is*, Rebecca—you're so good you've never had the wild fortune of experiencing this before. Honestly, what's the worst thing you've ever done?"

No examples rose to the still surface of her do-gooder's brain.

David grinned. "We both know, right? When you took those rubber bands off your teeth. That was your grand transgression. Your life's single misdemeanor."

"David, we're heading off," Scott called. "You ready?"

"Indeed! Just a sec!" Turning to her: "Rebecca. It'll be fine. I promise. The world doesn't end when someone hates you. You can trust me on that." David started walking away backward. He was joyful, flamboyant with his limbs.

Caught off guard by his gentleness and that he'd referenced their shared past—she hadn't known he remembered any of it—she found herself calling, "But wait. What should I do?"

"Take them to the river. Have fun! Fuck 'em. Fuck 'em if they don't like you. Think of your people, Rebecca. All those heroes of yours you put all over your room. Your Emma Goldman. Your Rosa Whatever-Her-Name. What about Ira? Your own dad? Isn't that what you like about all of them? That they don't give a flying fuck?"

As she watched him leave, with his gangly stroll that had once seemed so embarrassing and now seemed simply relaxed, Rebecca became gripped by an appalling thought. What if she'd been doing it all wrong?

LIKE THE PROW OF a boat, Nicole, Tanaya, and Shauna led the way down the steep path toward the river, the other girls and Rebecca in their wake. They were descending a red canyon, passing the gnarled shapes of sagebrush. The air was thin and hot. A single bald-headed mountain towered above them. But did the girls notice any of this? Shauna stepped on a lupine. Jenny P. picked a columbine and then dropped it.

As the trail turned to follow the river, Rebecca could see, all along the shoreline, first one group from camp and then another already spread out under the shade of tamarisk or floating in the green water. But Salamander Spit turned out to be, unsurprisingly, neither shaded nor sandy. Just a length of sun-blasted shore with small cement-colored rocks and the occasional rusted, crushed can. Even the river seemed stale here, brown and shallow. Just downstream, the river narrowed and bucked dangerously, pushing between boulders that balanced atop each other, as if frozen midtumble. Upstream, two strands of barbed wire were hung with a BB-pimpled sign: KEEP OUT. PROPERTY OF THE TUCKER RANCH.

Rebecca caught up to the girls assessing their bad luck and dropped her pack. The back of her shirt was soaked with sweat. "It's going to be fine," she said, holding her shirt from her skin. "I brought cards, you know."

"*Cards?*" Tanaya said.

"I might already have heatstroke," Shauna said.

"How about we just go back to camp?" Tanaya said.

Rebecca removed a gray plastic canteen from her backpack and told the girls to drink. She saw that upstream, beyond the barbed wire, beauty resumed. A single cottonwood cast its leafy umbrella over the beach. Large flat stones, perfect for lying on, jutted from the water like resting seals. There, the river was deep and dark, the rocks causing it to pool into flat eddies.

"Let's go," Rebecca said.

"Thank *god,*" said Shauna.

"I mean, this way." Rebecca walked toward the barbed wire. At the fence, she pushed down the lower wire with her foot and held the upper cord high, forming a diamond for them to crawl through. "Come on."

"No *way.*"

"I'm not going through there."

"We're not *allowed,*" Tanaya said. "That's someone's *property.*"

And so Rebecca told them, standing with her boot on the wire, about a man named Ira Silver who walked wherever he wanted, a man who spit when he said the phrase "private property," who bounded over NO TRESPASSING signs, proclaiming that the land belonged to everyone, this land was your land, this land was mine. She didn't mention her scraped palm, her tincture of pride and shame—proud of him, ashamed of her own fears—as he'd pushed her through the barbed wire on Catalina Island just to have a picnic on some greener pasture beyond.

Soon they were sitting on the roots of a tree on the Tucker Ranch, enjoying its shade, eating flattened sandwiches. The girls asked her to tell them more about Ira. She described the wiretappings, the FBI file, the time he'd taken her to trespass at the Nevada Test Site, passing around her cloth diapers as a nuclear bomb exploded underground and contaminated soil hummed into the eyes and mouths of the protesters.

As the girls reconsidered their counselor, she could feel herself changing—her hair glossening and flattening, her splotchy cheeks paling, her features taking prettier form. There was, she felt, a cheapness to the transformation this time, but how would she live without it?

After they finished eating, they shucked off their halter tops and plaid shorts, exposing small fluorescent bikinis and examining each other. *Oh, I love yours. No, I love yours.* Rebecca realized she wasn't wearing a suit and shoveled through her backpack, knowing already that she hadn't remembered to pack it. Here was the always-lurking embarrassment, of doing it wrong, not knowing, forgetting the essentials. The girls began racing to the water. "Wait!" she shouted.

She didn't know what she would say, but as they turned toward her, their ponytails bobbing, their small faces expectant, she understood that she could, right now at least, make them do anything. "We're not wearing suits here."

They tittered.

"No, really. It's a Llamalo rule. At the Tucker Ranch, suits are completely forbidden."

They looked around as if she might have read a sign they'd missed.

"I'm serious about this."

She bent down to unlace the double knots of her boots. She pulled off her shirt and unfastened her bra. She tugged down her shorts and underwear simultaneously and stepped out of them. All the while they stared, arms folded in front of their bodies, and in their silence, she heard the rapids, the roar of pride, the roar of shame.

Finally, Tanaya shrugged. "What are you all waiting for?" She untied the small nylon strings and there she was, a branch-like little girl, her breasts like small mounds of salt. The other girls looked carefully downward as they, too, undressed, but Rebecca couldn't help but glance at everything they worked so hard to hide.

The water was colder on a naked body, greener and slippery. They hollered as they emerged, gasping for air. They were kids now, splashing each other, diving under, becoming sea creatures. The sun sloughed off a cloud, and its light hit the water, turning algae into glitter. After a while, Rebecca climbed out of the water and onto a rock. There was bird shit on it, along with brittle dried grasses, but she lay down. They climbed up after her and stretched out on rocks near her, panting with the effort, pressing their wet hair against the white-streaked shit and sand. She sat up and saw, against so much skin, little hillocks of fur like hidden animals.

"Tell us more," they said. "Did you really never see TV? Not even *The Facts of Life?*"

"What's that?" She said this just to please them.

They asked her for more stories, but she was, perhaps for the first time, bored of her own history and aware of how at turns strident and coyly naïve she would become in the telling of it. Her limbs were suddenly weighty, as if she'd been swimming against rapids, and she wanted nothing but the press of her chilled skin against the heat of this rock.

"Imagine the Indians who lived here first," Rebecca finally said.

They were quiet, and she realized they might start laughing at her, but Jenny L. asked, "Where'd they go?"

She told them the story of *Ishi: Last of His Tribe*, which was one of the books she'd brought, although, since she hadn't read it for nearly a decade she worried she might be confusing it with *Island of the Blue Dolphins*. Ishi, she explained, had been wholly insulated from the white world until the rest of his tribe died one by one from something. He only knew the

Indian language and the Indian way of cooking with manzanita branches, but he'd heard that there was a world out there, and he understood he couldn't live alone. He walked over mountains and across rivers, eating his manzanita berries.

Here she paused, still expecting their derision, but Jenny P. said, "So? What happened to him?"

Ishi, Rebecca ad libbed, having forgotten this part entirely, made it to Redding, California, where he saw buses and electricity and sandwiches. In the end, though, a professor brought him to a museum, and he spent his days on a Navajo rug, under a sign that said LAST LIVING INDIAN.

Rebecca's girls wanted to hear another story, to stay all night, to sleep on the boulders, to never return to camp or put on clothes again, but she wouldn't defy all the rules. When they had dressed and become teenagers again, sexier with short shorts on than without, she said, testing them, "How about we pretend we're Ishi while we're walking back. We're Ishi, walking to find the people who we think will rescue us but who will imprison us instead."

They bent to crawl through the barbed wire, and as they stood they were each of them Ishi, walking alone and silently, assessing all they were losing. On the trail above the river, they came upon another camp group, but Rebecca's girls wouldn't look at them, wouldn't respond to their calls, couldn't even understand their language.

Rebecca, too, was Ishi, the last of her tribe, walking up the hill to become an exhibit in a museum. She thought she would always like to feel this loneliness, with her lonely girls following her. Now they saw what they hadn't seen on the hike down: A clique of black-eyed Susans. Bees humming over a pool of blue lupine. The trembling lips of columbine. And high and gray above them, the single mountain, as lonely as they were.

OF COURSE, ONCE THEY returned to camp, the spell of the cool river was gone and they were brats again, pushing to be first across the bridge, whispering loudly, "Doesn't Jenny L. walk like a ballet bitch? Hey, Jenny, why are you walking on your toes?"

They ran up to the platform while Rebecca stayed behind to sign in her charges on a clipboard hung from a nail outside the barn. Turning to leave, she saw Caleb and David approaching, arms around each other, one skinnier, one taller, two heads bowed in some intimate Llamaloian discussion. She didn't leave.

Caleb hadn't reprimanded her again. Instead, he'd periodically appear beside her, touching her arm and telling her the name of some nearby plant or thistle or snake, as if a linguistic gap were the source of her suffering. During these moments of focused kindness, which were like feathers falling from the sky, she couldn't help but share in the camp's collective crush on Caleb. He was unattainable, charismatic, at the apex of the social hierarchy. And so, whenever he leaned over her, smelling of onion and sweat, she would wonder—as she was sure they all did—if he might be noting her particular charms, if he might take her aside and . . .

But the fantasy never had time to develop, because as suddenly as he appeared, he would turn away from her and focus on someone else.

The only person Caleb singled out for particular attention was David. And David glowed inside it.

She watched them. The afternoon wind swarmed the mesa, bending the sagebrush, shivering through the willows along the ditch, filling her with the world's longing. She was familiar with the way the world's longing can choose to inhabit you in the late afternoon. She'd lain in her dorm room, listening to the Weavers, nearly overwhelmed by wanting something undefined, and she was sure that's what she felt now. The sweet pain of being a surrogate for desire.

What held her here? Surely not David. Could Rebecca notice his appeal only now that Nat had said she'd fuck him? Or did Caleb, as he walked around camp with his arm around David, transfer not just attention, but attractiveness as well? An exchange of the pheromones and ease that made

Caleb so mesmerizing? Or maybe it was just the muscular beauty of a body wanting to be in exactly the landscape it's in.

"David," she called. He pulled away from Caleb, who waved and walked on toward the infirmary teepee. Close by, David touched her hair. "So you swam. In a goddamn river. In Colo-fucking-rado. Don't tell me it all sucked." She could see the white islands of callus on his palms, the golden hairs on his arms, the down above his lip.

"Come here." She walked inside the barn, surprised by the sudden dimness, the sweet smell of hay. He hesitated in the entrance. From where she stood, it looked like he was in a church, within a rectangle of sunlight.

"What?" He began walking toward her.

"Over here." Along the wall behind her, rakes and hoes and shovels hung over stenciled shadows of rakes and hoes and shovels.

She lost her nerve. "Nothing, never mind. Just wanted to tell you that I didn't give a fuck, and they loved me. So, actually, maybe I did. Give a fuck that is. If not giving a fuck is in the interest of getting them to love me, then it's *not* not giving a fuck, right?"

"No, right, true. Not giving a fuck has no ulterior aim and is a state only attainable by masters of fuck-it-ness. But Rebecca, for your first attempt, we salute you!"

Him and what queen? There was a terrible pause. Surely, he was wondering why she'd led him in the dark to tell him this fascinating report of her day. "Well, okay," she said, heading back to the daylight. On the way through the door, he brushed against her shoulder, causing within her an electric twinge, like a mosquito in the zapper on the porch, like the smell of burned hair.

◆ ◆ ◆

THAT SAME AFTERNOON, AS Rebecca sat on the small patch of grass that was called a meadow, Ira began writing a letter. Not a letter to

Rebecca, or at least, not solely to her. A letter to thirty thousand readers. He finished it on Monday and, sending the entire production staff home early, put the issue to bed by himself. Georgia was spending the day in an actual bed, their bed, although perhaps that pronoun was inaccurate, because Ira had been spending his nights on Rebecca's twin, as Georgia wouldn't have him nearby.

When he arrived home, their (her?) bedroom door was closed. The only sign of his wife was the collection of Dannon containers in the sink: Breakfast. Lunch. Dinner. He ate cheese, drank beer standing at the kitchen counter, and then, by habit, sank down into a preshaped indentation on the far left cushion of the living room couch. He flicked on the lamp, also habit, and then found himself at a loss.

He'd never known a day not to end with newspapers. The *New York Times* and the *LA Times* had to be read cover to cover and clipped. The weeklies—*In These Times* and the *Nation*—couldn't be ignored for longer than their appointed seven days. He did allow himself to delegate the puffery of the glossier mags—the *New Yorker, Mother Jones*, etc.—to Georgia. Each morning, the post office dropped off three waxed boxes filled with dailies from cities across the country—the *Gazette*s and *Republican*s and *Tribune*s and *Post*s—arriving a day late. The interns were responsible for reading through these and bringing him a folder of relevant articles. He read their clippings each evening as well, recycling most, attaching sticky notes to the others with a reporter's name and FYI, an acronym Georgia always claimed he meant to stand for "Fuck Your Ignorance."

He read it all. He knew it all. Every piece of state and national legislation. Every instance of institutional bias, every legal challenge, defeat, and subsequent appeal. All the factions in the Movement, in the various movements; there was no Movement anymore. He could call anyone and make them talk. He could get a quote from a rock. From the most reluctant Republican, the most dishonest Dem. He could find the addresses of people who weren't listed in phone books, show up with coffee and donuts, and come away with a story. He could file a FOIA request in his sleep. What good had it done anyone?

His scissors and blue pen were on the side table. Three stacks of sticky notes. The trifolded *Times*es from both coasts waited on the coffee table by his feet. In a burst of purposefulness, he stood to examine the bookshelf Georgia had filled with novels, the female authors plus Dickens on the upper shelves, Philip Roth relegated to the bottom for crimes of misogyny. But no. He'd never understood why anyone would read about imaginary people. Even now, with nothing else to do, it seemed like an indulgence.

So he sat, reading nothing, until 10 p.m., which was a respectable time for sleep, although he wasn't tired.

Before dawn, he set off for Rancho Cucamonga, arriving just after seven, when the sky was the color of milk.

On a street of warehouses, Ira rang an illuminated bell at the only worker-owned printing plant in California. He waited for the buzzer, pushed in the heavy metal door, and entered a small anteroom, where he could hear, but not see, the grinding of Gutenberg's heirs. The churning of verbiage. The optimistic pressing of prose to paper.

"Ira? The man himself?" Debbie sat in a wooden chair with her legs on a metal desk, holding the Metro section of the *LA Times*. *Morning Edition* on KCRW came from a radio on the windowsill. News, news: everyone wanted it; nobody did anything with it. Ira hadn't seen Debbie in years—his production director now drove the proofs to press—and he noticed that she'd made the jarring decision to age. Her gray hair was cut short and spiky.

"I wanted to deliver it," Ira said, settling the portfolio of page proofs beside her metal desk. "Last one."

"I'm well aware. We're screwed, so thanks. You were our only remaining large client. Apparently, everyone else does it themselves at Kinko's now."

Ignoring this, he said, "Well, the occasion seemed to require certain formalities." He nodded toward the coffeepot on the windowsill. "Mind if I . . . ?"

"Go ahead."

He poured the coffee into a mug ringed with brown residue, tore open two sugars, and emptied them. He took the chair across from Debbie, crossed one leg over the other. He remembered fifteen years ago when she and her girlfriend—Barb? Eileen?—formed a CR group with Judy and Georgia and three women who later moved to Oregon to become potters—or was it weavers? All of them so sexy. Deb would wear this little black vest over her T-shirts, and he wasn't supposed to stare. Every Tuesday, Ira and Rebecca, banished from the house while consciousness was being raised in the living room, would walk hand in hand to eat mu shu pork and egg rolls at Green Leaves, their own consciousness as low as ever but their spirits raised delightfully by the chemical compounds of salt and sugar and MSG.

"Think you'll miss it?" Debbie asked, a coolness to her blue eyes. Still sexy.

"Miss what? Miss futility? Miss preaching? Miss the choir? Miss insisting that, despite all evidence to the contrary, we're helping the arc of history bend toward blah blah blah?"

"So, no then."

Sitting here, he could almost muster nostalgia. There used to be such a charge to it all, an indisputable urgency. A frantic, purposeful six days. And then that lacuna of time after he'd drop the paper off with Debbie and before he discovered the issue's mistakes. Eight hours spent in an addictive stoned-out satiety of a job accomplished.

But then, a few years ago, depression, sludge in his veins. Every new subscription was equalized by a canceled subscription. He spent his time begging for money from foundations, trying to tailor articles to their mercurial enthusiasms—the environment, one year; "positivity in politics," the next. He couldn't exist like this anymore.

102 | HEATHER ABEL

"I didn't tell anyone," Debbie said. "Followed orders like a good soldier. So your secret's in there?" She pointed at the portfolio. "Your reason for jumping ship? What comes next for Ira Silver?"

"Georgia calls it my 'suicide note.' She refused to read it, and I wouldn't let anyone copyedit, so you'll be the first."

Debbie swung her legs off the table, leaned toward him. "And then what? Everyone learns in a few days when they get the paper? What's your plan for when the barrage comes? Sit in the office and field angry calls?"

"My actual fear, Debbie, is that fewer people on the left will muster anger than we might like. A tide of complacency is sweeping our shore. And I'd like to believe the reactionary press will be cheering, but the truth is they've ignored us for years." He drained his coffee, put the mug on her table. "Look, could you talk to Georgia maybe? Reach out?"

"Why?"

"She's in a bad state. She's not taking this well."

"Ira, seriously? She's not *taking* this well? You made the unilateral decision to shut down the newspaper. You're basically firing her. Have you even given this any thought? We warned her. We all did. We said, 'Don't have your husband be your boss.' But she insisted you two were equals, making equal decisions. She always felt this compulsion to help you, since the day she met you. And now she's supposed to take this well?" Debbie stood up. "I have to get your pages back there. Unless you want to deliver them yourself? Some closing formalities?"

"It's all yours."

He walked out empty-handed, the street of warehouses a fitting backdrop for this anticlimax. But what had he expected? Gratitude? A gold watch for his service to the cause?

He took side streets to the 134 to forestall his return home to Georgia and the empty hours (what *did* come next for Ira Silver?), and just before the highway on-ramp, he further delayed the inevitable by turning into the vast and largely empty parking lot of a shopping mall.

Why not spend his free day the way all other Americans spent theirs? Obedient to the purring demands of capitalism. He strolled inside. A mall, it turned out—he'd never been in one before—mimicked a village: narrow streets and women sweeping, turning on lights, and calling to each other. The menfolk were in the fields.

Was that why all the women smiled at him? They walked in twos, sweat-suited, sneakered. He soon found himself in an atrium of potted palms and a penny-pelted fountain, the heart of the mall, where the twin escalators acted as artery and vein.

Ira escalated. Only one store had not yet turned on its pulsing music, so he entered it. The shopkeeper stayed near him as he ran his fingers along the sleeves of hanging shirts, wondering how she'd arranged them equidistantly. She seemed to really want to help him, and Ira, encouraged to please her in turn, said, "I'm trying to buy a gift for my wife."

Did Georgia prefer soft fabrics or structured? Was she a winter or a spring? Was she petite or full-bodied? Here, the shopkeeper mimed breasts, flat and full, in front of her own lovely plum-hued chest.

The store smelled of cinnamon air-fresheners; the woman was deeply tanned (yes, her skin was a cinnamon color, but he scorned others for describing brown-skinned people as spices or teas or chocolate or nuts), with something sparkly around her neck. She wore a soft, tight purplish shirt—not a blouse, not a sweater, something else.

"Are you a winter?" he asked.

"A fall."

"And do you perhaps sell that particular shirt?"

She smiled, touched her actual chest. How did he look to her, with his newly elongated forehead, his hair receding and graying? Like Debbie, he'd made the mistake of aging.

"Could I buy it?"

"Of course. So she's a fall, too, your wife?"

A fall? "Well, I guess! She wears shirts like that." Although he could only picture Georgia in the blue button-down. "Or, I should say, she likes autumnal colors. At the very least, she talks about missing fall. We're originally from back East. Traded in the land of seasons for the land of smog."

"It's not strange to not know what size your wife is," the woman said, guiding him to the rack where the shirt waited. "Most men don't."

"She's not very big," he said, appraising her, the skin of her shirt as plush as deer antlers.

"Then perhaps she's small?"

How would he hand it to Georgia? Would he leave it on their bed? Her bed? Would this gesture be enough to allow him to sleep there again? Or, at the very least, would it enable him to stand by the sink chatting while she cooked chicken? Here, with the quiet encouragement of the saleswoman and the cloying spice smell, it seemed likely.

"Small. I suppose that would be logical."

She plucked a shirt from the rack, wrapped it in rose tissue paper, just a shade lighter than the shirt, and sealed the paper with a silver sticker. Ira had no idea if this was standard shirt-buying procedure, and he considered that he might have been awarded something special. He whistled some lines from the Gilbert and Sullivan tape he'd been listening to in the car as she made an impression of his credit card and he signed his name, returning her smile at the accomplishment of a completed transaction.

On the highway, with Georgia's downy shirt in the passenger seat where hours before the newspaper had sat, he hummed happily. So shopping did indeed have salutary effects. Americans were not dumb after all!

Only when he pulled up to his own driveway did he feel the grim irrevocableness of his actions. Soon, the printing would finish. The distributors would haul away the stacks, slap a mailing address on each copy, trucks and airplanes conveying them to the chill of a West Coast summer and the swelter of New York apartments and to the earnest subscribers in the Midwest, to every college town, to every mediocre library that hadn't lost its funding. A few days later, papers would arrive in the hard-to-reach rural addresses. Three for the environmentalists in Yaak, Montana. Twenty-seven in Hawaii. Eighteen in Puerto Rico. One for a counselor in a small mining town in Colorado. A few days after that, airplanes would cross oceans, carrying papers to England, Spain, Italy, Japan, Portugal, South Africa, New Zealand, Poland. It had taken him years to build up this subscription base. His paper would soon be gone, all gone, and he was left with this: pink tissue and a shirt his wife would never wear.

THE REAGAN YEARS: SEPTEMBER 1982

THE ORTHODONTIST TUGGED YELLOW and green rubber bands between the hard knobs of her teeth to separate bone and allow, in the coming weeks, wire and metal to enter, and Rebecca thought about David. The orthodontist hovered his bearded mouth over hers, his breath as brackish as seaweed on the sand, steaming with flies, and she thought about the beach and David.

She had a crush, she knew now, gazing past the orthodontist's face to the stickers on his ceiling—QUEEN, KISS—something to distract recumbent kids, but nothing she knew. David would explain the difference, sitting on her bedroom floor, her tape player between them. It had been a month since she'd seen him at Will Rogers, but he'd be at her house this evening, and what would happen then? The orthodontist sang along to the radio, "It's the eye of the dah-dah, it's the thrill of the dah."

When he levered her chair upright—"You're all set, sweetheart"—it felt difficult to close a mouth that had been stretched open for so long. He told her to come back in two weeks when he'd remove the spacers and put on braces, and ta-da! Straight teeth. "It'll hurt tonight. Take an asprin or something."

In the lobby, a dark room with an inky fish tank, she stood clutching Ira's credit card, but the receptionist refused to look up from the mausoleum of file cabinets. Outside a small window, rain fell. Rebecca took the opportunity to study the other patient, perched on the edge of a chair, a girl with such a tiny nose. Tiny hands with a unicorn ring. Tiny emerald earrings glittering in tiny ears like mushrooms. A tiny silver bracelet on her wrist spelled what must be a tiny version of her name: PMG.

She looked nothing like Rebecca. And yet, her prettiness offered Rebecca hope. It seemed possible that Rebecca was actually this girl. Now that she had a crush, she was no longer herself; she might instead be tiny, too.

Without responding to any visible or audible signal, the receptionist called, "Patricia Gonzalez. He's ready for you now." The girl passed by Rebecca, who closed her eyes in the hopes that some loveliness would transfer osmotically into her.

AT HOME, SHE FIXED her hair in an approximation of PMG's, something involving a white scrunchie, like a cloud over the hillock of dark hair, and rehearsed a greeting in the bathroom mirror: "Hey, what's up?" She felt proud of the rubber spacers that could be glimpsed between white enamel when she spoke. She changed from sweatshirt to sweater and back to sweatshirt again and was ready for David hours before he would arrive.

A short struggle with the kitchen's sliding door and she was in the backyard, where rain shook the bougainvillea petals and bowed the heads of dandelions. Worms, released from the soil, climbed upward into the grass. She stepped quietly into the garage and could hear Ira, although her view of him was obscured by the intern cubicles.

"I *can't* ignore it, Georgia. Don't tell me to ignore it. They're acting like *idiots*."

So many afternoons spent here, reading on the floor while Ira made phone calls, the cynicism in his voice comforting ("You expect me to believe that?"). He'd hand her books on Tubman, Truth, Chavez, Gandhi, X, Debs, Ethel and Julius, but it was Ira whose story—of SDS and arrests in Mississippi and Chicago—she admired most. To love him was to bask in his surety.

Rebecca walked around the cubicles to stand at her father's desk. Against the far wall, Georgia twisted a paper clip at her desk, listening with pressed lips to her husband. "It would be negligent *not* to write about their idiocy," he shouted. "They're pledging total loyalty to a company, the richest company in the world, that doesn't give a shit about them. So if I'm attacked as antiworker, because I say that the workers are acting like idiots, I'm sorry, but it doesn't take an Ivy League education to figure all this out. The oil companies are speculators. They *will* pull out. This is not a new situation."

"But what I'm saying is that it's Exxon's fault," Georgia said. "That's what you need to focus on."

"Of *course* it's Exxon's fault. That's indisputable. I'm just saying, who's going to hold Exxon accountable if the government won't and the workers won't?" Ira stood as if propelled upward by his outrage and began walking back and forth as he talked. "It's total collusion in Exxon's fantasy of a free market without externalities, a fucking lovefest between the assholes who make the profits and the idiots who sell their labor. Carter pronounces energy self-sufficiency to be the 'moral equivalence of war' and suddenly everyone, even the unions, bends over backward to let Exxon rape American land. They should be prepared. They should be *organized*. It's a voluntary refusal to connect the motherfucking dots."

Who else saw the world the way it really was? What other father connected the motherfucking dots? She wanted to be worthy of him, an impulse that—with nothing else to offer—made her lunge toward him with her mouth open. "Look, Dad."

He stared at her without saying anything. It was too warm in here to wait so long, too musty and moldy. Spores grew on paper, and there was plenty of that: tombstones of newspapers and columns of computer printouts and obelisks of spiral notebooks, and on the walls, yellowing cartoons, curling posters, against this, for that. All the paper was quietly waiting.

Finally, he said, "What are you showing me? Does something hurt?"

She pointed.

He gazed uncertainly. "That's new? All those little colored bits? Jesus Christ, of course. You took my credit card. Everything I've scraped together going into your teeth. Poor people don't have teeth, much less straight ones." He directed his shouting to the back of the room: "Everyone, sell more ads, pull the lead. We're going to kiss Exxon's ass, get some of their money. Rebecca needs new teeth." This was Ira's kind of joke, except that sometimes he was serious.

All the paper in the room whispered, You idiot girl. What have you done?

She offered, "I don't actually need braces."

"Sweetie," Georgia said, "could you just give us a minute?"

How had Rebecca forgotten the day? Monday, when the week's proofs needed to be finished, so that they could be driven to the printer at five the next morning. That is, if she didn't get in the way. "I was just getting this," she said, picking up a reporter's notebook from the floor. "I just needed some paper, that's all. I wasn't going to *bother* you." Georgia offered her a vague smile, and Ira sat down and reached for the phone.

Later that evening, David lay on his stomach on her rug drawing superheroes. Or villains; she couldn't tell. His parents were at an ACLU fundraiser. Rebecca sat on her bed with fractions. Nobody had called her and David for dinner. He mentioned that sometimes, during a crisis, he was picked up from school and driven to Oxnard or Long Beach and given a hamburger at Bob's Big Boy on the way to the farmworkers or the longshoremen. Rebecca had never been inside a fast-food restaurant, but then the life of a public-interest lawyer was more glamorous.

David said, "Your folks seemed really frantic when I got here."

Rebecca couldn't see the purple ink on the ditto. *Poor people don't have teeth* . . . She took too much, asked for too much. Her role in the family was avarice. She was not helpful, could not edit. She scooted to the bed's edge.

"It's okay, Rebecca. It'll be okay." David tapped her arm lightly and spoke the way Judy spoke when he was heaving like Rebecca now was, preparing to cry.

"Take them out." She bared her embellished teeth. "I don't want braces now."

"Why?"

"I don't need them. Why should I get something I don't need?"

He seemed to consider. "Won't they mind?"

"They'll be relieved."

"It'll be hard, I bet." David, who had always been there, leg to leg, understood: if you want to help poor people, you can't be above them, can't want Izods or jellies.

His fingers pushed into her mouth. She rolled her tongue, that dangerous tongue, against her top palate. His were smaller fingers than the orthodontist's—curious, tapping her teeth, skittering like mice. "This one's loosest." His eyes were blue-and-green classroom globes. Her tongue snuck down, brazenly licked his finger. He tasted of potato chips and eraser. She licked again.

He looked up at her, but he didn't say anything. For that moment, she was awake in a way she'd never been before. She was, she thought, electrified. Then, he looked back at her teeth.

As he removed each spacer, the pain it caused on her gum and teeth abated, until her entire mouth was hers again. She hid the rubber bands in the trash, covering them with tissue, and they went into the kitchen and made toast with butter and white sugar. They found the sleeping bag in the broom closet and, shoving aside her math dittos and books and crusts of sandwiches, laid it on the rug. David, wearing his clothes, fell asleep right away. She changed into pajamas under her covers. David was turned away from her. She could see only his hair out of the sleeping bag. She still had electricity coursing through her.

She put her forefinger in her mouth and pressed her tongue to it. Dried it off on her pajama shirt, licked again. She was trying to separate her own cells from herself, so that her tongue was foreign to her body and she could feel precisely what he'd felt. She tried to focus on the wetness, the spongy movement. But it turned out taste was the superior sense. Her tongue, insisting it was her own, tasted her skin, sweet with residue of sugar. She dried her finger on her sheets, licked once more, and the sugar was gone and her finger tasted the way it always did, sour and dirty, not like his at all.

"Why are you doing that thing with your mouth?" Georgia asked the following Saturday as they toured open houses in Laurel Canyon that they could never afford, an activity Georgia loved and therefore only rarely allowed herself to indulge in.

Rebecca quickly stopped sliding her tongue across the smooth expanse of her rubber-band-less molars. "I'm not doing anything."

"You were. You keep doing it. You've been doing it for days."

"No, I haven't." As if this would prove her point, Rebecca began to read aloud from a spec sheet about earthquake retrofitting as she headed up a terracotta staircase. "All modifications have been made to ensure that your new abode is at the topmost level of resistance to seismic activity."

"In other words," Georgia said from behind her, "don't sue us when your house slides away."

"It'll serve them right." Rebecca spoke the party line against the rich, although she was thinking that she'd love to live in this house, even if at any minute it would set sail for canyon and doom.

"The more it costs, the farther it falls," her mom said, pausing to look wistfully out a window on the landing. "Luckily, that means ours will just slouch."

Georgia turned the bronze fish handles of the Jacuzzi in the master bath, bounced on the striped window seat in one of the children's rooms, pointed out the Mexican tilework on the backsplash. They stood for a while in the living room, looking out the two-story picture window to the kidney-shaped pool and, behind that, the tumble of chaparral and palm down the canyon.

"Bourgeois pleasures," Georgia said, leaning against her daughter and stroking her hair.

Back home, as they were preparing lunch in their own, untiled kitchen, Ira came through the sliding glass door, clearly upset. "I just got off the phone with Peter Finkel, of all people."

"Finkel called?" Georgia asked, staring at the open refrigerator. "And you deigned to talk to him?"

"I would've passed him off to you, but you were paying witness to conspicuous consumption. You won't believe what happened." As he talked, he took a red apple from a plastic bag on the counter and stared at it. Rebecca watched them from the kitchen table, where she was slopping lemon yogurt into a bowl. She was assessing. She'd had a good morning with her mother, but it seemed doubtful that she'd have a good afternoon with her mother and father. A good time with both parents was what she most wanted, but it was the slipperiest arrangement.

"Is everyone okay?"

"No, everyone's not okay, and it's my fault." Ira placed the apple, a plate, and a knife on the table. "My nephew's off searching for the perfect place for his camp that's not a camp. As we speak. In other words, I ruined his life."

"Caleb?" Georgia brought over a peanut-butter jar.

"Finkel took the bait."

Georgia affected a drop-jawed awe. "Why? A joke?"

Ira quartered the apple and handed the pieces to Georgia. "Why're you smiling?" he said. "This isn't funny. Caleb's out there with Finkel's money looking for someplace where he can bring kids to re-create those camping trips Robbie took him on—whenever Robbie didn't fuck it up. He wants to glorify an asshole. The thing is, Caleb was so young when Robbie killed himself. Thirteen! He never got to see what a schmuck Robbie really was. He's chasing a dream, some ideal that never existed."

"We should all be so lucky to always think of our parents that way." Georgia spread peanut butter on the apple slices, handed two back to Ira.

"But it's idiotic, and he has nobody telling him." He chewed as he talked. "Whatever Robbie told him on those trips, all of Robbie's life lessons—remember that, how Robbie was always trying to tell us his life lessons, reciting those clichés as if he'd made them up? Not that he actually lived those life lessons. All that money he borrowed from me. All those lies, those blatant, embarrassing lies. His convoluted excuses every time he got fired. That teenage girlfriend! Shit Caleb never knew about. I'm sure Mimi never told him. Should I?"

"You need to calm down," Georgia said. "It wasn't Robbie's love of nature that made him a loser. It wasn't because he hid away in a mountain hut. You're confusing causality, which isn't like you. It's sweet, honestly. Caleb just wants to be near his dad, keep his dad alive. Remember what a darling boy he was? We should help him out."

"That's what I was *trying* to do. Help Caleb reappraise his direction. I was planning to call when Finkel turned him down, offer sympathy, maybe an internship here, where we could get to know him, steer him, guide him toward purpose, utility, *engagement*. But it's too late for that now."

"So listen to me," Georgia said. "No, don't make that face. We need to make sure it works out. That it's not a total disaster. We can give him ad space. We can tell our friends to send their kids. Maybe Rebecca?"

They turned to her for a brief moment of potential, during which she considered the lovely possibility of herself at camp. Such a generic lanyard-making opportunity had never been proposed before. But Ira shook his head. "I'm not sending Rebecca."

"Okay, but we can make this a good thing for him. And as a bonus, we get to piss off Mimi and Aaron."

Rebecca could tell from the mention of Caleb's mom and stepfather that the conversational tone was to leave the tragedy of Robbie and enter the comedic realm of ridicule.

"What about Mimi and Aaron?"

"What's their worst nightmare? That we'll brainwash Caleb, bring him to the dark side." Georgia wiggled her fingers to summon the occult. "The spooky radical left."

"But that's hardly what he's heading out to—"

"That's not the point, Ira. The point is, they can't differentiate between narcissistic homesteading and class struggle. As far as they know, if we're involved, he might as well be joining the Sandinistas. Which means we've won. If only in their imagination."

"No, you're right, you're *right*."

"It's sort of funny, actually."

"I'll concede. It's not unfunny."

They began smiling at each other, and Georgia shrugged shyly, and Ira's face softened into proud, childish delight. Rebecca licked her spoon, happy as she always was when her parents rallied together in their contempt for someone else. It would be a very good afternoon, after all.

But Georgia turned to her, pursing her lips. "You didn't have another orthodontist appointment, did you?"

"Why?"

"But you had rubber bands. He gave you those spacers, those bands. Weren't you supposed to keep them on?"

"Oh, give her a break, Georgia," Ira said, and Rebecca could tell he didn't want the good mood spoiled either.

Georgia turned on him. "You don't even *see* it, Ira. You don't even notice. Where'd they go, Rebecca? Where'd they go?"

Rebecca put her hands around her yogurt bowl for support. "I took them off, but wait, listen. It was so that you don't have to pay for braces. It was because I don't *need* them. And so why should I have them?"

Ira stared at her. "Why on earth would you be so wasteful? We already paid for that appointment. Now we have to pay for him to put them on again? Do you know how much it costs each time you even look at the orthodontist?" He stood up from the table. "Where's this money supposed to come from?"

Rebecca sat very still.

Georgia said, "Rebecca, would it hurt you to think about someone besides yourself?"

Ira dropped his plate in the sink and slid open the door to the backyard. "You just took them out? Without asking?"

"Wait, Ira," Georgia called after him, her anger like a Santa Ana wind. "You're just going to leave? We're not done here. *Wait.*"

In bed that night, Rebecca imagined David wearing a white button-down, just like the one Ira sported in the photo of his and Georgia's city hall wedding. He'd come to take Rebecca to Mississippi. They were needed, he whispered, crouching by her bed. Unionionion had just been practice; this was real: squash the scabs, shame the property owners, organize the powerless masses. They'd asked for her specifically, Ira's daughter. Rebecca's hair was long, her dress mini. Swung on David's back was the guitar that had been handed down from Woody to Arlo to him.

He said, You don't need to worry about the rubber bands.

She asked, How'd you know I was worried?

He winked. Teeth, he said, shrugging. Bourgeois pleasures.

Besides, he added, it was worth it. Meaning his fingers pressing on her lips. Meaning the pile of rubber bands on his thigh. Meaning her slippery tongue on his finger.

On the way to Mississippi (or should it be Soweto? Managua?), he crushed her, that is, he lay upon her, his chest pushing on her chest, his legs pressing against her legs, so she couldn't flitter away, so she belonged.

FOR THE NEXT WEEK, Ira and Georgia remained morose, bickering. Each of their outbursts, while ostensibly about grants not received, subscriptions canceled, egregious fact-checking, the wrong kind of dish soap, seemed to have only one true subtext: What were you thinking, Rebecca? Selfish, stupid Rebecca.

And then, one morning, Ira ran into the kitchen waving the *New York Times*. "Check this out!" Rebecca had a spoonful of buckwheat flakes halfway to her mouth. Milk sploshed. Georgia was eating pink Dannon with one hand, holding a paperback open with the other. They leaned toward what he showed them, front page, above the fold: EXXON ABANDONS COLO. SHALE OIL PROJECT. The prognosticator stood above them, delighted. What he'd said would happen had happened.

The next day, the *Los Angeles Times*, in an editorial about Exxon's abrupt pullout from its $5 billion project, praised *Our Side Now*'s "prescient, insightful coverage of the damaging cycles of boom and bust," adding, "As usual, we could all benefit from heeding that feisty rag." In the days that followed, the Ford Foundation, the Pew Charitable Trusts, and the Tides Foundation all called with intimations of increased funding. Ira gave interviews—to *In These Times*, the *Nation*, and *Mother Jones*—until his quote was stone-sharpened. Rebecca could hear him on the kitchen phone, saying, "Only the wealthy will be shielded from the shock waves of the bust. For the thousands of workers who were hired to build Exxon's grandiose Shangri-La, who were urged to take on debt to join the so-called American dream, the bottom will drop out. In small towns across Colorado, towns like Parachute, Rifle, and Escadom, we'll see hunger, homelessness. But thanks to generous bailouts from the Reagan administration,

Exxon will emerge unscathed, its managers relocated, their padded paychecks protected."

The *OSN* board meeting, held that week in their living room, took on the beer-bottle clanks of a party. Rebecca could hear the shouts bleeding through the door; she stayed alone in the kitchen with a bag of Pepperidge Farm.

Each Milano cookie was like an unformed baby. If it were a fetus, it should have the chance to be aborted. That was every mother's right. But Rebecca wanted hers as born babies, and she laid them in a circle on the blue-flowered plate, heads touching, feet splayed, a circular nursery.

She raised the plate and set it back down. It wasn't enough. She was trying to make it up to them, to get them to understand—despite what she had done, despite the money she would cost them to re-rubber-band her teeth, she hadn't changed, would never change. She remained the Rebecca they had loved.

To adorn the cookies, Rebecca went into the backyard and found honeysuckles wrapped around the rotting plank fence that separated her yard from the neighbors'. But these blooms offered too little: a drop of tepid juice and the same sickly beige as the cookies. For what she wanted, she had to brave the way-back, where banana peels swam in the brown water of the compost bucket and Ira's tomato vines curled up the wire fence to the alley.

An aloe owned half of the way-back, its limbs like a dragon's spine. Crouching beneath it, she could hear the oceanic laughter of smokers far away on the brick patio in front of the house. She reached for the orange, shrimp-shaped nasturtiums, plunking them into a brown lunch bag, but there were only six. Needing more, willing to steal for them, she came around the side of the house, past the smokers—"Hey, Rebecca! How's it going, sugar?"—to the front yard, where the neighbor's nasturtiums spilled over clay planters.

She heard him before she saw him. Over the sidewalk, under the fronds of the palm tree lurking on their front lawn, David scraped his skateboard to and fro.

She hadn't seen him since the evening he'd removed her rubber bands, and he looked shorter than she thought he should, after all those nights imagining him. He stuttered to a stop and said, "Hey, Zoomy."

"D'you want to do something?"

"Not really." But when she didn't move, he relented. "Okay, what?"

She couldn't say.

"What?" he repeated, levering his board with one foot.

She tried a cryptic message. "Let's say there was a huge crisis some-where, like Nicaragua, well, like there already is, duh, and you needed to go help, they asked you to choose someone to bring with you. Who would you pick?"

David itched a mosquito bite on his elbow. "Are you trying to talk about superheroes? Do you even know anything about superheroes? Be-cause it doesn't usually work that way."

She was mortified. She'd actually believed he'd say, "Of course I'd pick you." She'd actually hoped that he, too, had been lying awake, imagining the two of them together. How idiotic she'd been. Rebecca thought about how Ira had told her that there would be a nuclear war in her lifetime. Would her skin fall off? Would her shadow burn into the sidewalk? Fine. Let it happen now.

She ran to the door at the side of the house. He called after her: "Iron Man?"

Back under the kitchen's fluorescents, the nasturtiums appeared limp, their petals closing. She felt a surge of chaos, the sort of throat constriction that used to precede a tantrum. Goddamn it all to hell. How could this convey both her apology and the pride she felt in her parents? She threw the blooms in the garbage, but alone the cookies were albino, anemic, and she fished the flowers out again, laid them stringily between the cookies.

She opened the drawer of aging spices and sprinkled cinnamon, a scattering of paprika. It was inadequate but would have to do. Balancing her offering, she kicked open the door to the living room. Six people sat on the floor, four on the couch, three propped against the fireplace. These were the people Rebecca spent her days with, but she was nervous. Nobody needed flowers the way they needed justice or equal pay, or like Judy, her hand jutting out as if throwing an invisible football again and again—"Can I just say . . ."—needed a chance to talk.

Rebecca wanted to put the plate on the coffee table and flee, but it was cluttered with back issues, a bulk-bin bag of walnuts split down the side and spilling, an empty bottle of scotch, a sweating metal bowl of melting ice cubes. Georgia was doodling curlicues over last week's masthead. Ira, regal in the rocking chair, pushed himself forward and back with his bare toes while talking, ignoring Judy. This way. They'd do it this way.

When he finished, Georgia pointed at Rebecca, still standing with the plate. "What's all over the cookies?"

"Cinnamon, duh," Rebecca said. "A brown powder we use on desserts. Ever heard of it?"

"What for?" Judy asked.

"For congratulations."

Ira beckoned. "Let me have one."

She leaned against the wooden chair as her father examined, chose, and bit, puffing a cloud of cinnamon. Crumbs rested in the nest of his beard.

For once, it was like she'd imagined it would be. The others cooed: "For congratulations." "That's *very* pretty, Rebecca," Georgia said. "Bring me one, sweetie." "Perfect," Ira said, finishing his and looking at her in such a way that Rebecca knew she was forgiven. "That was simply perfect." And it was.

Until Ira broke the mood, saying to all those chewing, "You know, we're only happy because we're right. We have to admit we didn't make it any better for anyone. We didn't warn anyone." His rocking resumed.

"All those without a job are just as screwed as they'd have been if we didn't write a fucking sentence. Okay, take the cookies away, we can stop patting ourselves on the back now." He was right, of course. This was no cause for celebration.

Returning ashamedly to the kitchen, she beheld a miracle out the sliding glass door: smoke rising from the pink bugle of a hibiscus flower. She yanked the door in a hurry to investigate, imagining herself, as she so often did even under less exigent circumstances, dousing a fire that was already consuming the walls of the garage, saving the Silvers' most precious possession. Oh, Rebecca. Thank you, Rebecca. Did you hear what Rebecca . . . ? But once on the porch, she saw that, as with most miracles, there was a prosaic explanation. One of the Silvers' coffee mugs had been left behind in the planter, two lit cigarettes inside.

Pausing in disappointment, she heard a bird call. Like a mourning dove but more guttural. A cat in pain—its foot trapped? She followed the sound and saw, on the parched grass between the plum tree and the line of bamboo, Joe. David's father, lying down. Such a nice man; he'd taught them gin rummy, which had proved a very useful skill, and bought her hot chocolate from a vending machine at the air traffic controllers' picket line. And yet he was squirming atop an intern.

Later that night, when she closed her eyes and imagined David taking her to Mississippi, he pinned her down right on the dirt. She could barely breathe with him falling on her like that.

He came to her like that night after night for the rest of the year. Even when she started junior high, with all of its wartime distractions, he came to her. Even though he stopped tagging along to her house, because he was old enough to stay home alone, he came to her. Even when his mom sat at their kitchen table and cried, he came to her. Even when Rebecca began eighth grade, with its concomitant requirement to repeatedly announce one's object of attraction, he came to her. His name was the name she offered, the name she wrote on her notebook. *David Cohen. Who? Goes to John Muir. Oh, Muir—cool.*

The crush was fed by nothing; it was a desert plant in the rainless West. Because they never played together after the day at Will Rogers, the day she'd pulled him down the boulder. Or, if it could be called playing, after the evening he'd removed her rubber bands, one by one. And the night of the meeting—the victory party that wasn't victorious—was one of the last times they'd even talked. *Iron Man?* he'd said.

Then, one blue-sky Saturday when she was fourteen, she was walking on the wooden planks of the Santa Monica Pier, and she spotted him inside the dim, thrumming arcade. She hadn't seen him in ages, but she was sure it was him in the blue sweatshirt and blue Vans. She dragged her two friends with her, their frozen yogurts dripping. "David. *David,*" she called. When they reached him, in front of the Skee-Ball machines' flashing lights, he didn't seem to recognize her. He squinted, extended one hand slowly to touch the wooden paddle in her yogurt, and ran off without saying anything. Her friends, conscientious girls, giggled nervously. *That's David? Like, who you always talk about? That's seriously your crush?*

He never came to her again. Without its defenders, Unionionion fell, becoming a town like all others, scabs slobbering for jobs.

SEVEN

In the Beginning,
There Was the Myth

STANDING IN THE DOBIES, watching his campers hike past, Caleb wanted to stop time, to make every day of the year this day, this moment, this long twilight in the midpoint of the summer.

Toward the front of the procession, a group of girls were looking for a hard-headed woman.

Farther back, morning had broken, like the first morning.

Then, a patch of little girls not singing. *Because what if you could put one of those moving sidewalks that you have in an airport and you'd never have to hike again. Or a ski-lift type thing.*

Somewhere near the middle of the procession, ten-year-olds of both genders were being followed by a moonshadow.

A long stretch of nobody, and then the voices of the oldest boys, followed by the boys themselves, David and friends in high spirits, screaming rather than singing, "How can I try to explain, when I do he turns away again." They waved at Caleb without breaking stride.

It was 1982 Night, a celebration he'd created in 1985. At the time, three years had seemed a long enough stretch. Llamalo's founding was ripe for commemoration. The way Caleb decided to celebrate then had become, in the way of all rituals, how they'd celebrated since. The first 1982 Night had been on the twenty-third day of camp. And while this date was chosen for no meaningful reason, now they always observed 1982 Night on the twenty-third day of camp. That first 1982 Night, they'd eaten a bagged dinner out in the Dobies, so now they always ate a bagged dinner in the Dobies, where it was so stark and hot and the high desert so unending that some teenager would always try out a newly learned word: "postapocalyptic." That first year, Caleb planned for the entire camp to sleep in the Dobies, but one girl forgot to bring her sleeping bag, and Caleb had decided that they would all return to Llamalo and sleep on the Great Overlook instead. Now, of course, they always slept on the Great Overlook. That first year, Caleb woke at dawn, unable to fall back asleep, and he decided to wake the whole camp. In the dim, he told the story of how he found Llamalo. Or not *the* story exactly, but the story he'd created on the spot.

Tonight was the sixth 1982 Night. Dinner was done. Its refuse was packed in Caleb's backpack. He was standing to the side of the trail that a group of campers had constructed over the previous days, marking its circuitous route with cairns. He would bring up the rear to make sure nobody became lost out here.

Most kids and counselors waved to him and kept going, but when Scott saw Caleb, he stopped close, his own need for personal space non-existent. "I totally forgot. Don was looking for you earlier today. Gave me this for you." From the grungy pocket of Scott's famously unwashed jeans came a folded but pristine white envelope.

Caleb held one edge of the envelope, the paper flopping down like a shot bird. No return address, but the same postmark as the letter he'd received three weeks earlier, the letter he'd thrown away and, until this moment, forgotten: Quartzite, NM. Of all the nights, really, for this to arrive. Even if it had come in the mail today, Don should have had the decency to hold on to it until tomorrow. Caleb tore the paper just as a trio of older girls approached behind him.

"Ca-leb." The half-whine, half-flirt mew of a fourteen-year-old. "We need to *talk* to you."

His finger still in the envelope. "Great. I'd love to. But it's 1982 Night. Everyone's on the way to the Overlook. Why don't you catch up?"

"It'll be so quick." Tanaya nudged Nicole with her hip. "Tell him."

"We have this thing. Okay, it's not a thing." Nicole giggled. "It's a performance thing we do?"

"A lot." Shauna shook her head wearily.

He slipped the envelope into his pocket. He was surprised at how much the three girls annoyed him. He could love all the kids—the farters, the bullies, the whiners, the hitters—but he found it impossible to love girls most similar to those who'd ignored him in his own high school.

"A ton of times. First at the youth group, then at the regional, then at—"

"Temple Beth El Home for the Elderly," Shauna said.

"And that other old people's home? The one with the soft-serve?" Tanaya said.

"I'm getting to that." Nicole was self-assured in a way she hadn't been last year. Like her friends, she parted her long dark hair far to one side, her head perpetually tilted as if from the asymmetrical weight. "Basically, we performed it everywhere in Saint Paul and some other cities, too. So, we want to perform it here?"

Caleb realized this was a question. Everything she said had a teenage interrogative inflection, but this was an actual question. "But what *is* it?"

"Tell him." Tanaya shoved Nicole again. They were all of them so twitchy, thrusting out their chests, jiggling their legs, pushing up on tiptoe.

"Okay, so, it's this man who wants everything to be the old way, and his daughters don't. He has three daughters, see, just like us. Three. And their names are—"

"I'm Tzeitel. Oldest and wisest," said Shauna.

Nicole spread her arms, blocking Shauna. "And then there's the middle daughter, and her name is Hodel, and that's me, and then there's—"

"Chava." Tanaya spun around. "I'm the youngest and most beautiful.

Duh." Already at fourteen, she had the sorrowful, agitated look of women who choose not to eat.

"You want to perform *Fiddler on the Roof*? Here?"

Shauna blinked at him. "Not the whole *show*. It's like a medley. Like, we'll make a set. And get this, we brought our costumes. I mean, you're Jewish, right?"

"That's not even . . ." So tenuous was his relationship to his inherited religion that he couldn't finish the sentence.

Tanaya grabbed his arm. "We'll do it at the talent show. Please, Caleb, please?"

"There's no talent show here," Nicole confessed to the ground.

"God, what camp doesn't have a talent show? I'm beginning to think we walked into a freak camp," said Tanaya, releasing Caleb. Nicole scratched her shin guiltily.

He looked down at their small, sarcastic faces. He knew what to do. He needed to soften toward them, to detect the wanting beneath all that twitching, to love. First he should crouch, because kids act differently if they're not looking up at you. Then he should say, "So, *Fiddler*. It's a good story, a timeless story. Tell me what you like about it."

But instead: "Are you out of your minds? You heard Nicole. We don't have performances here. Not what we do. What we do is this." He pointed. "See them hiking—that's what we do. That's what kind of a camp you ended up at. Come on, you've fallen behind."

They followed along the trail, chastened into silence. He blamed them for making him act like an asshole, even as he knew it wasn't their fault but the fault of the envelope in his pocket, that crinkle of paper beneath denim, the fault of Don, who was too cowardly to bring the letter to Caleb himself, the fault of Donnie and whatever idea had lodged in his head.

By the time they reached the Great Overlook, it was dusk, and then, after they laid out the foam pads and sleeping bags, dark. He couldn't read the letter now. It was his own rule that nobody could use flashlights on 1982 Night. Scott lit the fire as Mikala distributed graham crackers in waxed sleeves and counselors led kids away to pee.

Once the fire was underway, Caleb took a few steps from the campout, and then he stopped. He had to be careful. Anything added to this night could become ritual. Scott's fucking bongos, for example. But what was he thinking? That he'd be stuck, year after year, sneaking off to read yet another letter from Donnie?

He made his way to the house, which was darker than the sky, reaching for the banister to the porch steps. The windows of his office faced the barn, not the Overlook, and so on this night of no lights, he could switch on the overhead without being found out. He tugged the paper from its sheath. This letter was shorter than the last. No salutation, just:

I know what you did 8 years ago. I have proof now.
If you do not give me back my land I will find a way to get it.
This is happening all over The West. Look at Elko. Read from
Take Back Our Land by Lawyer Hobart R Billings Esquire.
The Sagebrush Rebellion Lives On. The West Is not For Tourism
and Enviro-Nazis. The West is for the Working people who under-
stand it and who made it what it is. It's NOT your playground.

Oh, come *on*. What had he done? He'd been lucky, sure, but that's all. He'd done nothing illegal. He drummed his fingers against the metal desk then balled up letter and envelope and tossed both in the trash can underneath the desk, the paper falling with a puff.

A drink wasn't possible tonight with all of them sleeping outside. But he couldn't just sit here and he couldn't go back yet. He yanked open the window so that the pane would stop reflecting the room. Through the screen was nothing, blackness, a plonk, a creak. He reached across the desk for the phone and picked up the receiver with a little shake of his head, as if admonishing someone else: Oh, Caleb, not again. His desperation was humiliating. He wouldn't be doing this if he could fuck Kai tonight.

The female voice was bored and loud, from another world. "Operator. Can I help you?"

"Spokane," he whispered, pressing the receiver against his shoulder.

"What?"

"Spokane."

"Business or residence?"

"Residence. The name is Guenther. *G* as in 'giraffe.' *U* as in 'unicorn.' *E* like 'ear' . . ."

In years past, he'd tried Portland, Lander, Flagstaff, Denver, Taos, Missoula, etc.

"You have a first initial?"

For a while, after she'd left him for Steve in Crested Butte, some counselors still saw her and brought back pieces of information that Caleb ruminated on until they were wrung out and offered up no more fodder for supposition or fantasy: She'd left Steve for Greg. She'd left Greg. She'd left Crested Butte. But since then, everyone had lost touch with her. She'd always said she would grow old in a shack near the tallest mountain imaginable, owning nothing but a toothbrush. But he'd called every Western town and never found her.

"S."

It wasn't even just her anymore, but an entire orbit of associations, any of which triggered an almost enjoyable longing. Or not longing exactly. He felt instead like he was waiting. The amount of time he devoted to thinking of her seemed to mean something, as if he were doing the necessary and generative work of hurrying along her return. Campfire songs were about her. The lawn was for her. Not only was blonde hair Suze, but so was anything yellow. And the letter *S*. It had been five years. How could he tell anyone that? The letter *S*.

"Did you say *F* as in 'Frank'?"

"No. *S*. *S* as in 'Suze.'"

"Nobody here by that name."

Back at the Overlook, no time seemed to have passed. When he returned to the encampment and found a seat by Kai, the kids were still eating graham crackers and singing either the same song they'd been singing when he left or one that sounded the same: too many verses, animals of various sorts acting violently, erratically, bumblebees eating other insects, a wedding gone horribly wrong and everyone dead in the end.

◆ ◆ ◆

IF YOU SAW THE Great Overlook in the middle of the night, David thought, it would resemble a battlefield in the gory after-hours. Seventy-one bodies scattershot, this way and that, curled, stretched, stricken.

He'd woken to find that the fire, which had been burning when they all fell asleep, was now extinguished. Caleb, ever careful, must have soaked and stirred and soaked again. There was no moon. And so, as David lay on the ground, the stars were all around, doming down upon him, pulsing, and even though he was doing the watching, he felt himself beheld by them. Through their eyes, he was shape-shifting. One moment, he felt enormous and important, and the next, infinitesimal and anonymous—back and forth like this.

A light flashed on, a little bling, a mislaid star. It jiggled around, then lowered to the ground, where it illuminated its owner. Rebecca was shimmying out of her sleeping bag. Stepping into boots. Now the light wove between bodies to the road and bobbed slowly away.

All summer, communiqués had arrived: Tanaya *liked* him. But Tanaya was young, another camper. She wasn't interesting. What was interesting was the way Rebecca looked at him, the way she watched him; she was always watching him. That was a surprise. Only Rebecca made him nervous. When he met her gaze, he was on the verge of remembering something.

The only adjective he could think of for her was "Rebecca." The color of her eyes was Rebecca.

The light stopped moving and flicked off. He knew she was crouching, panties pushed down. The splatter of pee on hard earth. It was enough to turn him on. When the light sparked on again and began bobbing back down the road, he climbed out of his own bag, stepped into his Vans. He didn't bring his flashlight.

On the road, he felt light pierce his eyes. "Hello?" she whispered. "Hello?"

He shielded his eyes with one hand. "Jesus, can you—?"

"Hello?"

"Just me. David." The light swooped onto the ground, so he entered and left its spotlight as he walked toward her.

"Fuck. I thought maybe . . . like a mountain lion. Your eyes looked red."

"Yeah, when you shine directly on them. Here can I see that?"

"Why?" But she handed him the plastic flashlight.

With his thumb, he flicked it off. They both disappeared, but the stars came back. "You'll actually see better without it."

He had no saliva. Could he even kiss with no saliva? He wasn't usually this nervous to initiate, at least not here, the only place where he'd ever initiated. Of all the people in the world to kiss, though. Rebecca? He hadn't thought of her in years, except as someone his parents wished him to emulate. But here she was, with all the force she'd had as a girl. He wanted to be next to that again.

She sighed. "That's exactly the kind of counterintuitive thing everyone says here. But you know what's great for seeing? Electricity. Edison's finest. Maybe you've heard of it?"

She was the one who was always watching him. So why didn't she, with all her collegiate wisdom, make the first move? *Here I am, Rebecca.*

"Well?" she said. "What?"

Almost like an invitation.

With his free hand, he reached for her arm. Found a hank of sweatshirt and held on to it. He banged his lips on the top of her head. Then his cheek brushed against her nose. Finally, his mouth on hers. He'd expected her to do something, but all he could feel was the air from her surprised exhalation moving into his mouth.

She pulled away. "I have to go." She turned on her light, sprinted down the road.

So he'd misread the situation. Who cared. Who gave a flying fuck. There was Tanaya; there was every other girl here.

But he felt surprisingly crushed. Only Rebecca, after all, had hair the color Rebecca.

◆◆◆

THERE WERE BONGOS IN her dream of David.

Rebecca woke, but unfortunately the bongos remained. She felt the embarrassment she always felt upon hearing bongos. A beat trying too earnestly to be liked. Sitting up, she pulled her sleeping bag to her shoulders. It was a murky light, not black, not yet dawn. The cold air smelled of smoke and dust. The only movements, human or animal, were Caleb crouching before last night's fire and Scott whacking on a duo of drums, head bowed and bobbing, as seemed required of bongo players. *Boom boom. Look at. Me now. So cool.*

Around her were chrysalises. Red, yellow, pink, and Power Ranger–print cocoons. She watched as the bongos insisted their way into everyone's dreams, and the cocoons began twitching to life beneath the sky, which was now thick and gray, like cat fur. Shadow shapes of sagebrush thrashed about.

And then she remembered. It had taken place in the dark, which made it feel like it had never happened. But she had a tactile memory: his lips dry as paper. Rebecca had gone from being someone who had never kissed, could never kiss, to someone who had. Earth was a malleable, windy place.

For the first time here, she liked everything she saw. A scrim had been lifted from her eyes, except she was still Rebecca, so what she liked wasn't the beauty. Liking the ugliness involved a type of morality that she was very familiar with, and so she noticed happily how weird and stark Llamalo was, an ugly dreamscape. She suddenly wanted it even more isolated, more benighted, but she felt satisfied that it was, as is, quite isolated, quite ugly.

The way the camp awoke was dreamlike, too. All these kids, and nobody fucked up by talking. They were whispering, sure, and reminding each other with animated gestures that they weren't allowed to talk, but they all followed the instruction given the night before, which was to put on their shoes and walk silently to Caleb.

She joined the crowd around the reignited fire, scanning for David, and when she saw the back of him, those whorls of bedhead, she willed him to turn around and look at her. She could nearly feel the jolt that would bring. Scott finished in a rapid crescendo and then sprung his palms from the drumheads. Caleb stood, his face crinkling handsomely into a smile. "I'm going to tell you about the first time I came here. How I discovered Llamalo. How I found the Double L and turned it into Llamalo. In the beginning . . ."

He paused, and everyone laughed.

"In the beginning," he began again, theatrically. More laughter. "In the beginning," he said once more, "there was just me. And my truck. You know my truck, don't you? She's old now, so try to imagine her younger, spry."

And then he stopped. He was looking at something beyond them, and Rebecca turned to see a man approaching.

Don stopped just outside of the group, like Caleb's shadow. The two of them, dressed so alike, were the only ones standing. Don removed his hat as if this were a church, and held it with both hands in front of him, elevating the event's solemnity.

Caleb pulled down the brim of his own hat and began again. "You know my truck." Now unsmiling, he looked nearly put-upon, as if they'd dragged him out of bed before dawn and forced him to speak to them.

"Well, I'd been driving around by myself for a while, just exploring, and I turned down that road." He pointed and seemed to regain some enthusiasm. "I saw the mountain, this mountain, and this stretch of land, and boom!" He clapped his hands, and Rebecca startled. "It was that sudden. I felt a pulse. I knew I couldn't leave. It was like I'd been led here, like I was supposed to find this land. I knew that I could never go back to San Francisco, where I'd been living after college. My life there . . . Well, all at once, it didn't mean anything to me. I parked right here, exactly where we're sitting."

He paused again for a long time, and Rebecca worried that he'd forgotten what happened next in his story.

Mikala called out, "So what I did was, I tracked down the owner . . ."

Caleb glanced down, seeming to notice them again. It was a relief when he resumed talking. "Right. So what I did was, I tracked down the owner, one of the *two* owners. I started talking to him—his name's Donnie. Our friend Don's son. And I found out that he was in trouble, serious trouble. The family was in trouble. See, a developer wanted to buy this place, chopping up everything you see here and paving it over for a condo development. Can you imagine? Well, the Talcs couldn't afford to stay, but naturally they couldn't bear to see this land destroyed. And they were devastated at the prospect of moving away from the land they'd grown up on. I knew right then that I had to help them."

Rebecca looked over at Don. Her familial education had been in discernment. She knew which stories were worthy of emotional attention and which weren't. She knew to be moved by narratives about the poorest, the neglected, victims of systemic prejudice. How many times had she read about Sadako, the girl who died of leukemia after Hiroshima? That book about Manzanar? Chavez's biography? She knew to be skeptical of self-satisfaction, the smug charity of the privileged. There was only one bumper sticker Georgia had ever approved of, all others dismissed as trite, simplistic, dim-witted: IF YOU'RE NOT MAD, YOU'RE NOT PAYING ATTEN-TION. Rebecca and her parents were always paying attention.

Although now she wasn't, actually. Thoughts of her parents had aroused a distracting guilt. They'd considerately sent her the most recent *OSN*, which had arrived like their miniature selves in her mailbox three days ago, and while she had meant to read it each rest hour, she hadn't even un-folded it. Caleb had told her that her mother had called twice, but Rebecca couldn't call back until she'd at least skimmed the cover story and found something to say about it.

When she returned her attention to Caleb, he was saying, "And then Donnie said to me, 'Caleb, all my dad and I want is for our land to be saved. We don't need to ranch here anymore, but we want the land to remain. For nothing to be built on it. No asphalt. No condos. Just as my great-grandpa Aemon found it. I'd be thrilled if you could help us out. I'd be thrilled if you took care of this land next, but it's a lot of work. It's difficult land, dry land.' I told him I could do it, but I knew I needed help. So I invited you. I planned a summer camp, and I sent out the letters. It was that urgent. And amazingly, you responded. Year after year, you've responded. This is why you're here. To help me save this land. To save Llamalo."

Rebecca turned again to look at Don. His expression was as serious as always, but clearly, she thought, he must be pleased: his land saved. She wanted Georgia and Ira to hear this, to ask them, don't you feel moved by this small unsystemic act? In first grade, she'd come home singing "America the Beautiful" and Ira had raged—genocide, whitewashing, separation of church and state—but Georgia had said, "Still, it *is* a beautiful song," and she'd sat with Rebecca at the kitchen table and sang it through, even the tricky second verse. *America! America! God mend thine ev'ry flaw.*

"Why's it called Llamalo?" David shouted this out, and she bit her lip to keep from smiling at the sound of his voice.

"Llama*lo*?" Caleb answered.

"No, really, why?"

"Llama*lo*."

Caleb raised his arms and widened his eyes with exaggerated ingenuousness. Everyone laughed, and Rebecca realized that the whole exchange was performance, ritual, because they all knew that *llamalo* was Hebrew, and it meant "why not."

Caleb pulled a folder full of loose yellow papers from his backpack and called out each camper's name in turn. The papers had a sentence or two of commendation and then an assignment: I KNOW THAT YOU'RE READY TO TAKE CARE OF _____.

Morning slop bucket to the pigs or weeding the sugar snaps— something a kid could do without adult supervision from this day until the end of camp. As the campers stepped forward, the sun pushed its way over Escadom Mountain, and Rebecca's sweatshirt was suddenly too heavy. Birds swooped in, small and black, shouting *Will you? Willyou willyou?* as if surprised anew that the sun, the glorious sun, was returning again. She watched the birds skim over the sleeping bags on their way to the irrigation ditch, because they could, because the ranch remained. No asphalt, no condos.

Once all the letters were distributed, everyone was free to speak and head to the eating platform, where the kitchen ladies, who had arrived two hours earlier and parked on the road near Don's trailer so as not to disturb the ritual, were working in dimmed lights. But the campers didn't talk, not much, just smiled at each other and clutched their letters, and she understood the desire to hold on to the heady feeling.

David walked by without a glance in her direction. She took her time stuffing her sleeping bag, even though all the others were left curled like spent firework casings. She was thinking about a story. Two childhood companions who knew each other best. A separation and then, amazingly, a coming back together. She'd tell her friends, "It was as if fated."

When she arrived at breakfast, though, David stood talking to Tanaya.

She called his name. As if he didn't hear, he turned his back to her and took his assigned seat.

Rebecca sat before a spread of oatmeal steaming in aluminum pots, boxes of Barbara's Corn Flakes, milk in enamel pitchers, yellow jackets plunging into bowls of canned peaches in syrup. Next to her, thirteen-year-old Patrick said, "This morning was totally awesome, wasn't it?"

But the day had lost its dazzle. She shrugged. "Bongos? I hate them. Everywhere I go, I hear them. Every single rally has these dumb drum circles, and then outside my dorm window. It's hard to take anything seriously that has bongos."

Patrick looked down at the yellow paper in his hand. He folded the paper again and again until it was hard and small. "Oh, well, I kind of liked it."

◆ ◆ ◆

"HEY! SO YOU JOINED us this morning. Nice! Total surprise, though," Caleb said. On his way to the house to look for the gold-panning sifters, he'd stopped short when he'd seen Don moving irrigation pipe on the Meadow.

A muscle in Don's cheek twitched. "I'd been hearing about it for so long, thought I'd see."

"It's just a . . ." Caleb grinned and raised his hands in mock surrender. "Oh, you know. It gets them going. Makes them feel committed."

Don nodded. "Is that so? A story like that?"

"The letters, though. Donnie's letters . . ." Caleb trailed off with a shrug of false cheeriness, as if talking about a shared annoyance: heat, drought. His heart was thumping with the mad hope that Don might trivialize his own son's ranting.

"Well, I guess . . ." Don looked around. "I guess you're Caleb. You figure everything out. So you'll figure this one out."

Caleb climbed the porch stairs with an enraged vigor. Sure, he hadn't told the truth this morning, but the myth stood in for the truth, which was all anyone wanted anyway. He knew that Don didn't traffic in myths, but clearly he might see their utility over the muddy truth. How much imagination did that take?

Half of what Caleb did as a director was incantation, recitation. Half of what he did was ritual: Platform Night, River Night, Taco Night, 1982 Night. This is how you make a trail. You walk the same path over and over. They were stacking cairns, walking a path again and again until it seemed like it had always existed.

Caleb burst in on his office, forgetting that he'd asked the girl from town, a Jehovah's Witness with a sneaker-length skirt, to do the billing. She sat at the desk surrounded by soft piles of invoices. Startled, she began neatening the pages.

He found the sifters in a box labeled TUNA SALAD, but he didn't leave. "Can you just give me a minute?" he asked, annoyed at her presence, although he had no real purpose in the office.

"Should I wait downstairs?" She stood, taking a few steps toward the door.

"Great. That's perfect." Heading the other way around the desk, he dropped the sifters with a clatter and picked up the phone in a show of urgency.

She hesitated. "In the living room?"

The dial tone was loud in his ear. "Sure, or the kitchen. Wherever."

He depressed the zero button. Nothing, zip, help.

Still she wouldn't leave. From the doorway, she asked. "Do I take this off my time? You want me to stay later?"

A pearly voice said, "Operator. Can I help you?"

"Denver." He palmed the receiver. "No need to stay late."

"What's the name?"

He waited to speak until the girl had finally left the room, as if she'd discern the foolishness in this attempt. "Guenther. Suze Guenther." He tried Boise, then Bozeman.

As the operator was searching her Montana database, Caleb heard the dolphin noises of kids out his open window and swiveled in his chair to watch. Nicole and Shauna were emerging from the barn, each holding one handle of a wheelbarrow. Behind them came Rebecca. To see better, Caleb pushed the daisy curtain aside. And it wasn't Rebecca out there at all; it was his dad. Robbie. Dark eyes, strong eyebrows, that dissatisfied twist of mouth.

He pressed his forehead against the screen. He'd seen the resemblance before, but never this strongly. Like his dad was here.

"Sorry, no Guenther there. Anything else I can help you with?"

"I don't know. Maybe San Francisco?" He knew Suze would never live in a city, but he was rattled.

He saw David crossing the footbridge, something flashing in his hand. Nicole and Shauna dropped the wheelbarrow, raked fingers through their hair. "Hey, Da-vid, whatcha doing?"

David swerved around them with a smile and a wave, but he stopped right in front of Rebecca.

"First initial *S*?"

"Yeah."

It annoyed him afresh how sullen Rebecca was here. How she always looked blank or skeptical. Couldn't she try to be happy here and show him Robbie like that?

"Please hold for your number."

Caleb swung away from the window.

◆ ◆ ◆

"It's mullein," David said. He set the jar he was carrying on the ground and leaned forward to pick the leaf from Rebecca's fingers. She liked the concavity of his chest, the way his shirt hung.

"Alright."

"You can use it as teepee."

"Teepee?"

"To wipe your ass. It's soft."

"Oh, TP. Well, we're just collecting leaves for sachets." What a ridiculous word to say out loud. She studied Spanish, not French, the language of the oppressed, not just the oppressors. It sounded wrong. Sashay, like the dance move? Shimmy-shimmy? How did one go from talking to kissing anyway? His mouth looked faraway and utilitarian. She couldn't reach it.

To make matters worse, he started to back away, rubbing a rash just above the neckline of his shirt. "Look, I didn't mean anything last night. Shit, Rebecca, I'm really sorry."

"Sorry?" She had to go home. She'd give Caleb any excuse, although the emergency would need to be of a certain magnitude. She'd take the risk—or Georgia would—of cancer, breast, ovarian, lung.

"It seemed like you, you know, weren't that into it? You kind of, well, you ran away."

"It was the middle of the night! Anyone could have seen!" Although these statements contradicted each other, her chest tensed with outrage. She could remember bickering over the rules of Unionionion. The whole point of the game was the people united, but someone *did* have to be in charge.

"You ran away because it was the middle of the night?"

Well, no. She'd run because she needed to be alone in order to contemplate the implications of having kissed. And she'd run because, stricken with an admixture of embarrassment and elation, she hadn't known what else one did next.

"The whole camp was nearby. Anyone could've seen." Her hands were on her hips; she was ready. She would argue until it was clear that only she should lead the leaderless collective.

"So perhaps we're in need of some clarification. Maybe come to some agreement of the basic principles?"

"Principles?" Without a fight, she was at a loss.

"Well, firstly, I was wanting to kiss you. And secondarily, you were also wanting to kiss me. All who agree say aye."

Admiring the arrow of his mouth, that borrowed adult nose, and the flush on his cheeks, she wanted to say aye, but, still pugnacious, she said, "Wait."

"No!" He turned and stage-whispered to a rangy little juniper that waggled amiably at the attention. "But she makes me wait. For what are we waiting?"

There was something she wanted to establish first, besides mutuality of desire. How, she wondered, had the past turned into the present? Where had he been? She hemmed: "It's like I know you. Because I knew you forever. But honestly, I don't know anything about you."

He held his hands wide. "Ask me. What do you need to know?"

What she needed to know was this: Was he the same David who tried to teach her to bounce or catch or hit a ball in his cemented backyard while the parents argued inside because something terrible and irrevocable was happening with Russia? Who slept with a Chewbacca doll? Who showed her a book with photos of the shadows of people blasted onto the sidewalks in Hiroshima after the people themselves had dissolved?

Of all the questions she had—What had happened that time they saw each other at the pier? Had he really not remembered her? And all the times they'd seen each other since, him with his headphones on, barely looking up to wave hello, what had he been thinking of her then?—she blurted, "Where do you want to go to college?"

"College? College, Rebecca? I'm not going to college. Look, I can't exactly tell you what I'm doing instead, but how about I put it this way—I'm going to the glorious of gloriousness. To the heart of the matter. Trust me, it'll all become clear soon enough."

Cryptic and exaggerated. All that was clear was that he didn't care about anything she did. And yet.

"Now can we proceed?"

But no, they couldn't. How did people change, and what remained after? How did the interior change, and what about the exterior? She was still ready for a fight. "Don't you want to know anything about me?"

He smiled like crushed tin. "I know you. You're Rebecca."

Rebecca, daughter of Ira and Georgia. The same, but with boobs. And he was so tall. When had that happened? She looked around for anyone who might witness this. Nobody was anywhere. She grabbed his bare arm to pull him down. Lips collided once, then twice, then she pulled back. "I have to go."

"Of course you do. You're Rebecca. You're on the go."

For a moment, before she walked away, when they were still half-smiling and staring at each other, it felt like they were in his childhood, predivorce house again. Like that stucco cube was perched on this mesa, like they were in the living room with its Ho Chi Minh flag, a yellow star against red, the newspapers piled on top of the record player, the Nicaraguan woodcuts spelling COHEN, and the parents arguing in the other room.

♦ ♦ ♦

DAVID REACHED THE OVERLOOK in a state of distraction. He held his glass jar under the cooler spout but didn't turn it on. He was remembering the time—he must've been seven or eight—when they'd all watched Reagan defeat Carter, on a TV rented for the day from the library. Ira had placed it on a pile of books and plugged it in. David sat next to Rebecca on the floor. Georgia walked back and forth between living room and kitchen, taking spoonfuls of yogurt, saying something like *We're doomed, we're doomed*—he couldn't remember the exact phrase. But he knew precisely what Ira and Joe, the two gods on the couch, shouted as they pointed their wrathful fingers at the TV. *Motherfucker, mother*fucker. David remembered thinking about the words "mother" and "fucker," then combining them into what he'd learned was a compound word like "buttercup" and "firefly," and then unwittingly conjuring the image of it. Judy was on the rug, legs spread, leaning this way and that—her legs spread so that she could remain limber as the world burned. Mother*fucker*.

Most of the time at the Silvers', however, Rebecca and David were alone in the house— dropping imitation vanilla extract into oval mounds of sugar and calling it ice cream, listening to Ira's Tom Lehrer records. Now he remembered the way Rebecca would rush ahead of him to push the crusts of peanut-butter sandwiches under her bed before he entered her room, along with her flowered underwear, but she always left out her 100 percent spelling tests—*Fantastic work, Rebecca*—so that he could see. And sometimes they could hear Georgia shout from the garage, "Goddamn it all to hell, Ira," like she hated him, but it was Joe and Judy, who'd seemed so content, who split, his dad moving to Marina del Rey with sexy Monica, Joe not a motherfucker anymore.

To stem this march of images, David pressed the cooler spout, filling his jar. He considered what might be the mitzvah of water. In a place as dry as Llamalo, surely saving water was holy. The dishwater came from the well, and the drinking water came from the cistern in Caleb's truck, refilled in town and poured into large coolers, which were set around Llamalo. When you needed a drink, you brought the jar assigned to you. No matter how many times you washed it, the jar smelled like salsa or peanut butter. The water was the temperature of your mouth or warmer. Sometimes you'd see something floating. A small shape, less defined than a fly, but with a skeletal outline, the curve of a shrimp. You'd look away and keep drinking. He wished he had his notebook with him to write this down now, while the mitzvah was fresh in his mind.

And what if, he considered, looking around him with an inadvertent smile, as if someone might read his thoughts and corroborate, there was a mitzvah of increased attractiveness at Llamalo? What would Zacky's rabbi say about that? At thirteen, David had kissed Daniela in the darkroom. At fourteen, he'd felt up Mara, lying on top of her until she'd said, "Move. I don't want to get pregnant." As if his sperm, as eager as the rest of David, would swim from the mess in his boxers, inside her shorts, underneath the elastic of her panties, and, glorious, inside her. To amend whatever he'd clearly done wrong, he'd pointed out Pleiades and Cassiopeia, but she'd refused to put her glasses back on. Fifteen was a hand job from Heather L., and sixteen was making out and making out and making out with Aura, and then the day after her period, to be safe, sex that lasted only the length of "Go Tell Aunt Rhody," in a culvert outside the Gathering, coming as seventy voices sang, *The old gray goose is dead.*

Last night, he'd thought that Rebecca wasn't into him, that she could only see David as he was in Santa Monica. But no. That wasn't it at all. The mitzvah of David's increased attractiveness worked on everyone on Aemon's Mesa. It was simply that she didn't know how to kiss. Rebecca, who knew everything, who dropped HUAC (all one word, like "hew-ack") into low-level conversation, didn't know how to do this, and it made him like her even more.

◆ ◆ ◆

CALEB HAD HER NUMBER now, scribbled on an invoice. Like a lock picked, the teeth sliding into place, the bolt sprung. San Francisco? He couldn't imagine her there. She'd always claimed to hate cities, so it seemed more than coincidental that she'd chosen to live where he'd lived before Colorado, as if she'd followed the shadow of him.

All he wanted was to hear her voice on the answering machine. It was noon on a Wednesday. Who would be home?

"Hello?" a woman said. "Hello?"

Her voice had the familiar low rasp, as if she always had a cold. He found himself smiling, the way one's mouth responds automatically to a baby's smile. "Is this Suze, by any chance?"

"Speaking."

"It's Caleb."

She didn't say anything.

"I know, I know. A blast from the past, huh?"

"Caleb. Caleb Silver." She sounded amused.

"Just thought, it's been years, but I thought, why not? Find out what's up with Suze. So how the hell are you?" His jaw ached from smiling.

"This is so strange. I was just thinking of you *yesterday*."

Of course she was. Of course. How could he think of her so often without reciprocation?

"Wait, are you calling from camp? Are you at Llamalo?"

"Where else?"

"Oh, Llamalo—I *miss it*." No mention of how she'd walked out on him, saying she couldn't stand it there anymore. But of course she missed it.

"It's so different. You'd be amazed." In a rush, he told her about the Meadow, how there was actual grass now, and four new platforms, a darkroom, a ton of kids—he rounded up to eighty—and last night was 1982 Night, which he knew she loved, and could she imagine the morning of silence with eighty kids?

The question wasn't rhetorical—*could* she imagine it?—but she just said, "Wow, really great." He could hear water turning on, metal banging against metal. All these years waiting for her and she was just a voice, a voice in San Francisco, of all places, doing dishes.

"Actually, this morning had an interesting twist." He was throwing this out as bait, trying to hook her attention. "Don showed up. Five in the a.m. Just walked across the field."

The water shut off with a whinny. All quiet in San Francisco. "*Don* came to the 1982 story?"

"Stood there with his hat in his hands. Can you believe it?"

The low blast of a train whistle, the most familiar laugh. "No, no, no. God, Caleb. You must've been losing your shit."

He laughed with her; now, he could see the humor in it. "When I saw him walking toward us, I froze. Completely forgot what I was going to say. Thought about changing the story, because of course Don knows how it really happened, but then everyone who'd been hearing it for eight years would find out I'd been lying."

"But you said it, right?"

"Same way I always do. Condos, developer. How Donnie begged me to take care of his land."

"And Don? He didn't say anything, did he?"

"Not a word."

"He gets it. Okay, no, what am I saying? He doesn't *get* it, but he's probably already forgotten about it. He's thinking about the ditch. Is he really ever not thinking about irrigation?"

"But wait. That's not all." Caleb told her about Donnie's letters, to catch hold of the golden strand of her interest, to pull her closer. He told her about Donnie's insinuations that there was something illegal about the land sale. The weird phrases he'd used. Custom and culture.

"Donnie, Donnie, Donnie, Donnie. Such an angry young man." It was immensely gratifying to discern no lingering affection for Donnie in her voice.

"There's this threatening tone." He aped a cinematic Germanic voice: "I vill find a way to get it!"

"Get out."

"Freaked me out, actually."

"He's all bluster. What could he do? Demand his ranch back? Him and what army?"

"An army of Craig. Remember him? He can show up with Craig."

"My god, Craig! With his mullet. Is *he* still around?"

"Still driving the malathion truck. Still spraying every living thing with poison in order to kill the menacing mosquitoes."

"Oh, Escadom—will that town ever join the modern world?"

Her sentence was interrupted by the tonelessness of call-waiting, a periodic abeyance of noise. "I have to go, but wow—great talking to you. Weirdly easy, don't you think?"

"So let's do it again. I'd love to find—" But she'd crossed over to the other call.

He replaced the phone in its cradle—an ingenious invention—and walked outside.

On the ground was grass, and above was sky. A jay flew from one branch of a juniper to another, and the boughs bobbed with weight gained or lost. Outside the barn, Mikala squatted in front of six white waxy boxes from the post office, sorting mail by platform. Mikala. She had three syllables in her name, and Suze only had one.

Noticing his gaze, Mikala turned. "Hey, what about those gold-panning sifters? You find them?"

He laughed, because it was years earlier that he'd gone to look for them. "Right! I'll get them for you."

He enjoyed each step, the smooth scissoring of one leg and then another, heel hitting, then the toe. His body was light as balsa wood. The first lunch bell rang out into the thin air, a perfect note, trembling.

He paused on the Meadow to watch the kids arrive for lunch. They crossed the footbridges unhurriedly, talking in clusters or walking solitarily and dreamily, and all of that delighted him. When he saw Tanaya, Shauna, and Nicole cross the Meadow, he called out to them.

They turned their sullen and disdainful faces toward him, and at last he could see their pain and the way they worked to hide it, how they'd learned at fourteen to conceal so much.

He crouched, one knee on the grass, as if proposing to the trio. "Okay, so tell me. What is it you like about *Fiddler on the Roof*?"

Shauna remained skeptical. "Really want to know?"

"I really do."

"God, *everything*," Tanaya said with exasperation. "Like, I like the songs."

"Sure, the songs are catchy," Caleb said. "But why this particular story?"

"It's about the generation gap, you know?"

"Like how our parents want us to be one way and we want to be another way," Nicole added.

"Okay, this is good." Caleb was excited now. His job was to be patient, to bring them around the slow way, to love the JAPs as well as the farters, and he was good at his job. "It's a timeless story. Even I can relate to it. My mom doesn't approve of me living out here, running this camp, this 'freak camp,' as you called it last night."

Tanaya smiled sheepishly. "I mean, not exactly."

"So, I have a challenge for you." They stepped closer to him. "I'm going to let you perform your thing, your *Fiddler on the Roof* thing, but . . ." The girls began jumping and clutching each other. He continued, imagining Suze listening. "But there's more. The catch is, I want to see it reflect who you are *here*. You're not the same girls as you were when you left Saint Paul. I can see that already. You're more aware of what's around you. You've changed just by being here." He couldn't see this, of course. But his job was to make it happen by saying it.

The second bell rang, and he sent the girls around the house to the eating platform. He entered the house to pick up the sifters from his desk, his office holding an erotic echo, because that's where he'd spoken to Suze, despite the glum mien of the girl who had resumed her position among the invoices at his desk. He tossed the sifters up and caught them again as he headed into the kitchen, through the cloying fog of garlic and steam.

He pushed open the door to the eating platform and held it, waiting a moment in the doorway as if on the cutwater of a ship, studying the ocean for its tidal answers. He noticed Don, who was invited to join all the meals, sitting next to Scott, and surely Suze was right. Don's mind was on irrigation. Caleb noticed Rebecca looking over her shoulder at something, and her eyes were radiant, her mouth barely hiding a smile. So she was happy here, after all. He felt a thrill course through his own body. He remembered how contagious it had been when his dad was on, lit up. Being with Robbie when he was happy was like jumping a train, moving that fast.

When he came to his table, everyone on the eating platform stood and silenced, even Don. They would stand, holding hands, as long as he did. He never took advantage of this, allowing for only a quick moment of contemplation, but now, in his contentment, in his joy, he kept them standing for a long time while he thought of Robbie. Kids started fidgeting, coughing. Flies buzzed on the food. Counselors glanced at him. But he let himself remember everything he could about his last night with Robbie.

They'd been camping in the Poconos when it had started raining and Caleb said, "Let's put up the tent." "What tent?" Robbie said. "We don't need a tent. We don't need sleep." They sat up all night under a tree, Robbie telling him again about the year he'd spent on a kibbutz and how kids were free there, living away from their parents in the children's house, how childhood was a sorrow everywhere else. Whenever Caleb asked him why he did anything—why he moved from Massachusetts to Wyoming and from Wyoming to Utah, why he quit graduate school, why he worked in a tire factory, why he didn't have a phone number where Caleb could call him—Robbie would answer in enthusiastic Hebrew. "Llama*lo*! Llama*lo*!" And no, they hadn't stayed awake all night, or at least Caleb hadn't. At some point, despite rain dripping from the leaves above, he'd fallen asleep against Robbie's shoulder, and when he'd opened his eyes, it was light and all the green grass and leaves shook with green water. Robbie was still awake, his shirt dark with rain, his hand on Caleb's hair, saying, "Look at this beauty, all this beauty."

Caleb sat, and the meal began.

THE REAGAN YEARS: APRIL 1983

CALEB, NEW LANDOWNER, WAS walking beside his irrigation ditch, thinking that this would be the day he'd set fire to it.

The ditch, which had been empty of water since November, was all anyone in Escadom talked to him about once they learned he'd bought the Double L. They told him stories, the same ones Donnie had told him—about a rancher collapsing with a heart attack at the headgate, who hadn't been found until he'd bloated like a beluga; about the boy who fell into the ditch and was resuscitated by his uncle but retained brain damage from lack of oxygen—repeating each other in a transpersonal old-fogeyism, until it seemed the ditch was the collective song of the place.

These days, every time Caleb drove to town, someone would remind him of his responsibility to burn away the brush in the ditch so it wouldn't clog anyone's dividers when the water flowed again. Soon, they said, the snowcaps would begin to melt, pouring into the high-altitude streams, which would spill down the mountain, filling the Upper Escadom Reservoir, which was what Aemon's lake had been turned into in the 1930s. The reservoir would slosh over its retaining wall, and Press Sorger, president of the ditch company, would turn a metal wheel and allow water to flow into the canals once more.

Caleb had already bought for this purpose a propane tank with a rubber hose extending from it and a steel nozzle at the end of this hose. Of course, he couldn't do it alone. The Talcs worked for him now. He'd found them last month in Escadom's trailer park, which sat on the dry spit between the slosh of the sewage treatment plant and the river, and he'd asked them to build the wooden sleeping platforms and train him in irrigation and well maintenance and general ranch management until the counselors arrived in June. He'd hired them as a way to help them stay in town. It was seven months after the oil shale bust, and Escadom was still shedding jobs, shrinking, becoming ghostlier each day. And he'd hired them with the daring hope that, with the land purchase behind them, he and Donnie could resume their friendship.

Which hadn't exactly happened yet.

Still, as he walked northward, he began to imagine that Donnie was beside him in the ditch, holding the propane tank and blasting the brush behind them in order to char it into oblivion. He imagined himself saying, "Hey, can I have a turn?"

And Donnie would look up, wary at first, but then relieved. "Sure. If you want. Come on in."

They'd walk together, devastation behind them.

Caleb glanced at his watch and knew that they'd be arriving soon and that he should turn around, this doubling back always accompanied by a slight sadness, the walk no longer full of possibility, the immeasurability of scale out here suddenly measurable simply by the distance he'd traveled. As he turned around, he imagined saying to Donnie, "We just leave it like this?" This would allow Donnie to resume his proud didacticism of last fall. "Shit, we got a lot to teach you. We gotta make sure the fire's out." And then the two of them would begin stomping on the little licks of flames.

Once he passed the Sorgers' land and could see the ranch house, Caleb pursued a few more plot points of the fantasy, but it was too late; the dream was dissolving. Even so, the aura of resumed friendship remained. He understood this wouldn't happen immediately, but surely over time.

When the Talcs drove up, the car coming to a stop beside the house,

Caleb had already leapt forward months to a time of forgiveness. He pulled a folded yellow sheet from his pocket, pretended to peruse a list. "So, where to start today? I was thinking maybe burn the ditch?"

"Tryna kill us," Donnie said to his dad. "Tryna scorch the mesa."

Don jutted his chin in the direction of the mountain. "Windy as fuck." He took the list from Caleb. "Okay, so for the lumber for the platforms, you thinking pressure-treated?"

"Can you lay out the pros and cons?" With embarrassment, Caleb noticed the wind he'd somehow missed before, dirt swirling in furious little ellipses, grit crunching in his teeth.

Donnie assessed him flatly. "Your decision, not ours."

It was a few days later when, returning from town, Caleb drove onto the plateau and saw a length of the ditch smoldering, a freight train of smoke, steel gray and moving. Donnie had set fire to it without him.

Over the next few weeks, the Double L became Llamalo, wooden platforms and the shower house rising up on the dead field as spring unfurled around them. Because the buildings were deliberately rudimentary and unfinished—Caleb specified that the least amount of material should intrude on the kids' experience of nature—they looked like ruins. They looked, more specifically, like the riverside camps set up during the oil shale boom and abandoned after the bust. Caleb loved it. He hiked the back route on Escadom Mountain to see the newborn green of aspen daggers, snapping stalks of wild asparagus along the ditch and leaving them as offerings on Donnie's Trans Am.

There was no dampening his optimism until one afternoon when he was on the porch and Donnie appeared, cradling his right hand, a seam of blood across his palm. Neither of the Talcs had entered the house since the land sale, but without looking at Caleb, he pushed the door with his left hand. Caleb followed Donnie into the house after a few minutes, and Donnie's presence made Caleb feel like a guest, like he was seeing it for the first time. He noticed the wood paneling again, the plaid curtains, the smell of bacon grease and generations of cigarettes. There was a dot-to-dot of blood along the living room carpet, up the carpeted stairs.

Near the top of the stairs, Caleb could see Donnie in the upstairs hallway. He'd wrapped his palm with gauze and was looking in the open door of his old bedroom. Caleb had been using it as a closet, a dumping ground. There was a river of tangled shirts, jeans, boxers. There were balled-up yellow papers, cassettes, apple cores, a boom box with an open mouth, a tent city of overturned books: *A Sand County Almanac, Desert Solitaire, The Man Who Walked Through Time.*

Donnie's face in profile looked blasted, like an accident victim on the side of the highway as the semis barrel past. Caleb nearly climbed the remaining steps to him, but for what reason? To hold him? He reminded himself that he was helping out. He'd employed them, allowing them to stay in Escadom these months, and he would do more. He'd invite them to work on the ranch all summer, even the fall, the winter, although he wasn't sure yet what they'd do. Caleb noticed now that Donnie's blue snap shirt was the same one he wore. He wore the same Carhartt jacket as Donnie, the cowboy boots, the brown hat, of course. Like a mirror, but not at all like a mirror. There was the jolt of Donnie's beauty, the pronounced ridge of eyebrows over dark eyes.

"Is it okay?" Caleb called, meaning the hand.

Donnie turned and saw Caleb, and his face registered an intensity of hatred that Caleb had never seen. "Clean it up in there," Donnie said.

Just then, Don called from the bottom of the stairs. "Is Donnie there? Donnie? You okay, Donnie? I saw blood on the post."

Donnie started down the stairs to his concerned father, and Caleb leaned against the wall to allow Donnie to pass by. How could he be jealous of someone who'd lost everything?

EIGHT

•

Rumspringa

REBECCA WHISPERED, "HEY, YOU here?"

"Nope," David answered. "Not here."

"Shh. Quieter."

"Nobody can hear us, Zoomy. You can't even see me. Find me."

There was the mitzvah of hiding in the barn after swimming, alone with the creep of black widows in the woodpile, until Rebecca arrived and they ate each other's mouths. The hiding could take ten, twenty minutes, the eating only a few seconds. He would hold her hand or touch her shoulder blades through her shirt, and she would kiss in that insistent pecking way. And then, before he could move his hand, she would rush off.

David was crouched in a rear stall, his back pressed against the wooden divider, plucking strands from the hillscape of straw, releasing the gaminess of manure even though livestock hadn't been in here for a decade or more—long dead, eaten and transformed into people cells, and some of those people had also died.

"But not eaten. Presumably," he said aloud.

"What are you even talking about?" Rebecca said. "Can you just be quiet? I can't find you." He heard footsteps pattering nearer, and that was enough to make him half-hard.

"I'm in cow apartment 2A. Cowpartment. Cowndominium."

Her head appeared around the wooden barrier. "God, there you are. What're you even doing?"

"Cownhouse."

Sigh of annoyance.

She always acted like this at first. What was he even doing? Well, he was waiting for her, as she knew. As he'd done every Sunday, Wednesday, and Thursday for the past three weeks. (On the other days, she'd determined, there was no safe time to meet.) Hiding as she'd asked him to do. Discreet, discreet. Now the rest of her emerged, her hips in a crumpled flowered skirt he'd never seen. From his delightfully low vantage point among the ghosts of bovine shit, he could see a slab of stomach and the up-down of her breasts, the movement of which he'd been studying even on Mondays, Tuesdays, Fridays, and Saturdays.

"Look at you. All ready for your big night out." He was still in his swim trunks, increasingly uncomfortable.

She smoothed her hair, and it fuzzed back up. "Should be fun. It's cool of Caleb to allow it. Like a tension release. Apparently, it gets kinda wild."

"Yeah. I've heard stories. Almost asked Caleb if I could go, but I figure he'll need help around here."

"Need a hair tie." She took off her backpack and, holding it with her chin, started rummaging through.

"He'd've let me, though." David couldn't help but drop hints. Summer was nearly over, and it had gone very well. Caleb always seemed pleased with him, resting his hand on David's shoulder, talking seriously with him. It was so hard not to tell Rebecca that he'd move here in September, that she should plan to visit him on breaks from college, the two of them sharing a tent.

"You think?"

The day after their second kiss, the one by the ditch, she'd said she couldn't do that again, quoting Caleb's admonition during the week of counselor training. "Any counselor suspected of sexual advances"—she'd hesitated but carried on—"defined as widely as possible, will be asked to leave immediately. Will you need to walk to town if you don't have a car? Yes. Yes, you will."

David had explained as vaguely as he could that Caleb didn't think of him as a camper, not at all, that he was exempt from such rules, more a counselor than some of the counselors. Anyway, although Caleb himself never had a girlfriend, never replaced Suze, because only she was worthy of him, David couldn't imagine Caleb getting worked up about this, about a little kissing, and, hopefully soon, some more involved making out.

In a way, David was older than Rebecca. He did the reassuring, the cajoling, made the moves. Each time, she acted like they wouldn't kiss. Like now, pulling from her backpack a copy of her parents' newspaper, which she began flapping around. "Look what I've been carrying around forever! They sent this to me when—two weeks ago? Three? And I haven't even read it. Did you?" She dropped the backpack on the straw, but now his view of her was foiled by the newspaper.

"Did I what? Read that one?" *Any? Ever?* Gee, no, he hadn't had the chance.

As he stood up, she glued her gaze on her beloved newspaper, determined, avoiding. She hadn't even glanced down at him, at the comic tenting, the straining against nylon fabric. Just prattled on about Ira's latest apocalyptic warnings. He couldn't help thinking that more attention should be paid to his hard-on. Did she know about dicks and where they were? Wasn't she just a little curious? He would be.

But no. "See this article—'What Threat Saddam?'—Ira was telling me about it when I was home. He's talked to some people *in the administration* who think involvement can be avoided."

As if they'd simply met up in cloistered secrecy for a leftist study group. She had no moves. She was entirely moveless. Gave him the confidence to say "Come here."

"I mean, doesn't everyone understand that a war would just be about oil?"

Her brow furrowed from the force of the roiling white-capped rivers of concern for global stupidity and avarice that rushed through her day and night, while all his blood simply made its way downward. The way she'd said "in the administration" was precisely how Ira always said it, demonstrating that he had access while simultaneously disparaging those with access. She licked her finger to open the front page, and the newspaper flopped over as if exhausted by its own shrill voice. She was determined to be on the wrong path, the prudish path, the fogey path, and only one person could pull her back to the right one.

"Zoomy. Come here."

◆ ◆ ◆

A SHOAL OF COUNSELORS was waiting for Rebecca. They were packed closely—the analogy to sardines had been made several times—in the tin can of Scott's VW bus, ready to drive into town.

As they waited, they said they would die if they didn't get cheese fries soon. They said fuck the cheese fries; it was so hot they wanted a pitcher of beer all to themselves. They said that after two months up here, didn't it always seem like magic when night came at the Motherlode and electric lights went on? They said that more than anything they just wanted the swamp cooler. They were going to stand under the blast of the swamp cooler until their skin turned blue.

This was their Rumspringa. The last Tuesday of camp. The afternoon when counselors left en masse and emerged into the world as a team, comrades from the land of Caleb. The world they always chose to emerge into was the Motherlode, because the Motherlode, caught as it was in the past, was the best evidence that they weren't in Portland anymore, that they weren't in Ann Arbor or Austin or Providence, or even Phuket or Goa or

Puerto Escondido—there was no Lonely Planet guide to what they were doing out here among the unexotic poor.

They said that if they didn't leave this minute, they might scream from heat exhaustion.

But Rebecca, in the barn, was otherwise occupied. If this was a kiss, this thing that never ended, this Möbius route through dark woodland, then what exactly had she been doing before? She was somewhere she'd never been, led here by David, whose tongue tasted of tomato and probed everywhere, encouraging her to do the same, to keep her own mouth open, until all her little pecks and nervous licks ran together like a river, dense and insistent. With one thumb, he was stroking her cheek.

Then there was the additional etymological question about what exactly was tap-tap-tapping against her hip, bringing to mind Poe's raven. It was a very friendly tapping, she felt. The nosing of a badger or vole against a pine in the woodland.

She wanted to stay here forever, and so, impulsively, she pulled her face away. Still at close range, David was a Cyclops blur, one-eyed, two-nosed. A spider's thread of saliva linked them. "I just want to know something."

"Well, okay." He was laughing at her.

"That time I saw you at the pier?"

Tapping ceased. She didn't look down.

"What time?"

"Don't you remember? Like five years ago? I was with my friends in the Skee-Ball place. The arcade. And you acted like you didn't recognize me?"

He leaned his head back, two-eyed again and frowning. "Nah. Couldn't have been me. 'Cause I don't remember that. I would remember, and I don't."

"That's so weird. All these years, I thought it was you and you were ignoring me. It looked like you. And when I said your name, you came over to me."

"My doppelganger, clearly," he said, moving his hand along her back.

"He's been known to roam the streets of Santa Monica impersonating me. But seriously. I have no memory. Five years ago?"

She frowned, unconvinced but distracted by the slow movement of his hand on her skin. She was feline, petted. Oh, kiss me, kiss me, kiss me, she thought. "You go," she said. "You go out first."

"No, Rebecca."

"It's better that way." He wasn't careful enough. If she left first, he would come out seconds later, and call, with exaggerated, and thus obviously faked, surprise, Why, Rebecca, you're here, too! What a coincidence! She, on the other hand, would wait cautiously, not emerging until five minutes had passed, and then, poker-faced.

"But I can't. Not yet."

"Just go."

"Uh, don't you get it? I physically can't go out there." His face was animated by a pure form of pride, unmiserly, wanting to share his bounty.

She couldn't look down now, but she wished she'd looked before, because she wanted to understand how it worked. Was it horizontal or vertical? At a jaunty angle like a flagpole off a building or, more sinister, a "Heil Hitler" salute? So she'd actually felt one!

Rebecca ran from the evening of the barn into the sunshine, Eve's original knowledge now hers. She climbed into the bus amid cheers, dragging her backpack. All the seats were taken; she crawled past the hillock of Scott's laundry and sat on the floor behind the last row of seats. The bus bucked down the dirt road, bashing her sacrum over and over against the metal floor, but Rebecca was smiling, immensely pleased by what she'd felt.

"You want?" Over the seat, Jeremy was holding out a small wooden pipe.

She refused; she'd done enough new things for one day.

◆ ◆ ◆

As the dirt stirred up by the VW resettled on the road, and the camp was left counselorless, Caleb paged warily through the letters, the bills, the rifle and seed catalogues in his mailbox on the outside wall of the barn. It had been twenty days since 1982 Night, when he'd last received a letter from Donnie. Although neither of the two letters had been addressed to Caleb directly and had gone instead to Don's PO box, the daily task of checking his mail had begun to fill him with trepidation, and lately he found himself forgetting to do so altogether, allowing the mail to sit abandoned for a few days.

At the moment of relief—nothing from Donnie—Caleb saw David sauntering out the barn door in his swim trunks. It was so easy to love this boy who was always happy. Calling to him, Caleb said, "Scott's gone. Would you mind ringing the dinner bell in his place?"

David flushed, even happier. "I mean, that'd be great."

Together they walked to the house to retrieve the cowbell from its usual place on the bookshelf, where they found, anchored by the weight of the instrument, a white envelope addressed to *Caleb, c/o Mr. Donald Talc, Sr., The Double L, Escadom, Colorado 81428.*

"You go ahead," Caleb said, opening the door to allow David to step onto the porch and clang the bell the requisite seven times. Shutting the door behind him, Caleb ripped open the envelope.

Howdy Caleb. My Dad told me about the lies your spreading up at your camp. How you tell everyone we were so happy when you came and saved our land from the developer who wanted to buy it. HA HA. You think we didn't see through your plan but we did. I have proof now.

It's a proven and recorded fact that it was the enviro Nazis who came to Colorado to shut down Exxon and take away our Jobs. And then, when we had nothing, who showed up in Escadom looking for land? You did, Caleb. Coincidence???? Now I know. It was your plan all along. First, you shut down the oil shale plant. Then you come and pretend you don't even know anything about Escadom. Well what made us foreclose?? <u>You</u>. I know from lawyer Hobart R Billings Esquire that is called an Illegal Taking. There are ways to settle this. The West is being taken back by the people who live here and belong here. You can wait until I come there or you can clear out Now.

From,
Donnie

♦♦♦

WALKING INTO THE MOTHERLODE, Nat and Saskia gripped Rebecca's arms as they cooed over the ducks in gingham dresses and Murphy's Law carved into wood, hung on the orange-and-brown wallpaper. Two waitresses with bouffants frozen in both time and space watched as the group took over three tables near the jukebox and pool table.

Rebecca had been told that on this day wonders would occur: censorious Mikala would happily buy the underagers beer; puritan Scott, who shook nutritional yeast on all his meals, would lead the candy run to Ute's Market. And indeed, soon Mikala was pouring Rebecca a beer from the pitcher she'd bought while Scott was spilling out the contents of three plastic bags.

Rebecca found herself seated beside Jeremy, listening to Jeremy, which is what one did with Jeremy. He was overly tall and prematurely balding—he shaved what was left—and he seemed to misread these genetic accidents as proof that he was a divine translator of life's complexities.

He sat with his legs wide and angled toward her, saying in his stentorian manner, "First word that comes to your head when you think of this town? Drowsy, right? Dead. Deceased. Over. Done."

Rebecca had to nod yes, although she wasn't thinking of the boarded-up storefronts or of the broken windows held together with duct tape.

"And yet," Jeremy said, "I have this theory that, hard to believe, this town is headed for major change. Major change-o. Wanna hear it?"

Rebecca was thinking of the penis. What was the right word? Cock? Dick? Phallus? Thanks to one year at college, she could spot phallic representations in paintings, literature, rock formations, and wallpaper, but despite one year at college, she'd never been so close to an actual one.

Jeremy flicked the back of her hand in a plea for attention that seemed more aggressive than was called for, as if he could view the salacious competition of her wandering thoughts.

"No, yeah. Tell me."

"Okay, here's the thing. Escadom's on the cusp. This is big. There aren't many cusp moments for a town. The first one was in 1852. When white people came. You're looking at me like, whoa, how's he have all the dates memorized, but I actually wrote a whole paper on it. My senior thesis last year was on Escadom and Caleb. I gave Caleb a copy at the beginning of the summer. He seemed way pleased."

For a moment, Jeremy looked distracted, and Rebecca thought she'd be spared his theory, but he regained himself, resting giant elbows on giant knees, cantilevering ominously toward her. "So remember? 1852. Three men on a scouting expedition. Looking for a way through the Rockies for the topographical engineers. These are tough men. Men who could maneuver through avalanches, fight off Indians." Jeremy maneuvered through the English language like a cautious explorer, pausing to rest after each phrase. "They saw the river. And boom! They knew it. This was a fertile valley. Fertile. Soon as they're done with the expedition, they come back. Kick out the Indians. Name the town. Escadom. It's theirs."

As he talked, Jeremy was scraping the remains of a Now and Later off an incisor with his thumb's ragged, tormented fingernail, his cheeks reddening from his excitement at being the bearer of both history and prediction. What had David done once Rebecca left the barn? Had he waited, watching it (penis, cock, dick) droop, deflate? Had he jacked off alone? And how would he do that anyway? She pictured him humping the ground, tapping against the straw.

"From then on, Escadom was all about what you could get from the land. To sell. Coal. Shale. Crops. Fruit. Cows. See a pattern? Nothing produced for people's souls. Or minds. Nada. Until now. Until right now."

She'd seen the hand motion for jacking off, of course. Once, in high school, she'd made the mistake of miming carrying a sign at a rally, up and down, and set off hoots. That was the same, apparently. Subsequently, she'd thought a lot about the phrase. Jacking off. To jack off. Something sly about it. When what she did was simply, clinically, called masturbation.

"Enter Caleb, stage left. His arrival is as monumental as those dudes on horseback a hundred years ago seeing the potential for a mining town in an Indian village. That profound. This was the crux of my paper. See, Caleb comes in, sees this valley, not for what it can produce, but for what it does to people's souls." Jeremy pointed to his own heart, location presumably of his soul. "That's the future. And Caleb? He's the forerunner. I got an A, by the way, from this prof who never, I mean never, gives A's. What this town's gonna sell is nothing less than the intangible. Beauty. Think Taos. Small-town vibe, big-city amenities. People looking for self-actualization. Who appreciate this as the spiritual place it is. What Caleb saw in it. There's money in that. This bar? Enjoy the last of it. In five years it'll be one of those little places, those breweries, making their own delicious beers instead of selling us this piss."

The Poe line, memorized along with the first stanza in Mr. Bream's AP English class, flashed to her now: *Suddenly there came a tapping, as of someone gently rapping, rapping at my chamber door. "'Tis some visitor," I muttered, "tapping at my chamber door."* Thinking of her own chamber door—her vulva, as Georgia had insisted on calling what all Rebecca's friends dubbed "down there" or, worse, "privates," like some military officials keeping post—Rebecca smiled, an inward grin that Jeremy misread as outward admiration.

He rubbed his hands together in a washing-up motion. "See, this is great. I've actually been wanting to talk to you more. You're the kind of girl who might want to talk about things, pursue intellectual avenues. My only problem with Caleb, the only one, is that he's not intellectual per se, although he's weighty, but not, I mean, he's had my paper four weeks and still hasn't read it. He's not"—Jeremy prodded the table as if trepanning a brain to excavate the correct word—"*investigative.* Like me. Like *us.*"

Was this a come-on? Would this happen now? She'd been tap-tap-tapped near her chamber door, and now other men could see? Unwittingly she looked at Jeremy's crotch, the straining khaki fabric, the thick thighs, the blond commas of hair. Where was his penis sleeping? When she glanced up again at his face, she felt strangely unaware of how long she'd been staring downward. What if too long? She jumped up. "Just a . . ."

She stumbled over to Saskia and Nat, who were standing by the blinking jukebox.

"Rebecca you'll love this." Nat squeezed Rebecca's arm too tightly. "Like it's 1975. Every song. It's so cute."

She could hear Jeremy, adrift without an audience, calling to Mikala at the next table. "Wanna guess what this bar'll look like in, say, five years?"

Even alcohol didn't wash away Mikala's perpetually smug look. "Well, this is my eighth summer coming to the Motherlode, Jeremy, and I'd say that not even a lightbulb has changed in that time, so we know what it'll look like in eight more years. You're looking at it."

"Eight summers?" Rebecca whispered to Nat. "How old is she?"

"Old. Twenty-nine."

"She doesn't have a real job?"

"She became a teacher, so she can come back every summer. Scott, too. Maybe he's a sub."

Jeremy was saying, "Wrong-o. Yo, Scott. Your turn."

"Elvis will be here. Alive and living in the apartment upstairs. With Marilyn." Scott's jaws were busy with mastication, his normally sleepy eyes ablaze with candy bliss.

Jeremy voiced a buzzer blast and said in robot-voice, "That. Is. In. Correct." He threw a mini pack of Mike and Ikes at the next table, hitting the smooth, bare shoulder of Jamal, who was hunched toward Kai. "Jamal, one guess what this bar'll look like in five years."

Jamal twisted. "Dude, what?"

"Forget it. Let me lay it out. I fucking wrote my thesis on this." Jeremy further amplified his voice out of generosity toward everyone's ignorance. "Here's the Motherlode in five years. Over there, every kind of microbrew on tap. Maybe a little juice-bar kind of thing. Mountain bikers enjoying a brewski at the end of a long ride. Climbers coming in to fuel up. People who actually appreciate the nature here, who get it, not just freaking rape it. This town is headed for a big disruption. Big disruption."

"Um, Jeremy, not now," Mikala said. Because the bartender and both waitresses and the seventeen postshift coal miners on barstools and the family with the oatmeal-skinned children, all of them turned to see the source of that booming voice, the voice of intellectual investigation, ringing out louder than the song Saskia had picked ironically and forced the jukebox to play.

But Jeremy didn't hear or heed Mikala. He just swigged beer and continued. "Don, people like Don Talc. Sweet guy, but that's the past. Redneck culture is finished here. Caleb's showing us the future."

The song ended just as Jeremy paused to let his edification sink in, like rain on the arid mesas of their brains. A vehicle hit something outside, metal on metal. The swamp cooler whirred. "This is awkward," Kai said in her dulcet singsong.

◆ ◆ ◆

FEELING PROUD FOR SINGLE-HANDEDLY settling all the kids in bed, Caleb decided to reward himself with canned peaches in syrup. It didn't register that the kitchen lights were on until he opened the door. Three of the dinner ladies hadn't yet left, and they were gathered around the counter with Don and Denise. Nobody noticed him.

"Precious."

"Those lips? She'll be trouble."

"You gonna see her again soon?"

"Hard to get away in the summertime."

"Then they should bring her here."

"Aw, we'd love to see her. Little princess. And we'd all like to see Donnie, too—you know we would. It's been too long."

Caleb had sat with these ladies at the Motherlode alongside Don, asking about grandkids, bow hunting, Ski-Doos, rockhounding. He'd lived in this town for nearly a decade, had more than earned his entry to this conversation. But now he was nervous.

First, you shut down the oil shale plant. What a bizarre conspiracy Donnie had latched on to.

Then, you come and pretend you don't even know anything about Escadom. Did Don also believe that Caleb had somehow derailed the world's largest oil company in a scheme to devalue the Talcs' land? Caleb heard him cluck proudly. "She's a beauty alright. Takes after her mom, of course."

Caleb turned to sneak out. But too late. "You want your kitchen back?" Denise called. "All of us just gabbing." Everyone looked at him.

"No, not at all. Gab away!" He strode toward them and stood behind Charlene, the shortest kitchen lady, peering over her.

"Wow, is that Kiva?" Caleb reached for the photo, a bald infant with a concerned face. Donnie's baby. Someone had written in ballpoint: *Little Cowgirl.* Even as he said it, Kiva sounded wrong. He started to say Keira, but that seemed off, too, and he swallowed the second syllable, so that he just said Keer, and then repeated himself emphatically—"Keer!"— to make it sound intentional, cutified, a nickname. He held the photo beside Don's face. "She look like her grandpa? What do you think? Same eyes?"

Don took the photo from him. "Kayla. Name's Kayla."

"Right. Kayla. Sweet name." To make up for his blunder, Caleb filched the photo from Don's hand, went to the fridge, and clamped the baby under a horseshoe magnet, atop a yellowing Xerox copy of American Camping Association food regulations.

Don walked over and unfastened the magnet. The Xerox slipped down the length of the fridge and then skidded along the linoleum. "We'll want to put her up in the trailer."

◆ ◆ ◆

It turned out there were to be more firsts for Rebecca this night. Thanks to Mikala's largesse, Rebecca was drunk. To be precise, it was her third time inebriated, but the first time she was enjoying this state without associative anxiety, without worrying that she was letting down her parents, who themselves drank, but in an adult way, which meant unhappily.

Time folded up like a paper fan. One minute she was on the toilet in the stall beside Saskia; the next, she found herself standing at a table, wagging the newspaper she'd pulled from her backpack, claiming everyone's attention. "Actually, it's the most important paper of its kind. One of the only real correctives to both the mainstream and conservative media." The newspaper was, she continued—landing upon a new, brilliant analogy—a rope with twenty thousand ends, and at each one, another activist with a tin can pressed to his or her ear, listening to Ira's voice.

This was somewhat unnecessary. Over the past weeks, she'd told them as much. They knew about Angela Davis. They knew about Jane Fonda. But she hadn't shown them the physical paper and these twenty-five pages of four-color newsprint with the in-house cartoon would either expand or deflate their perception.

"Oh, *that*. Wow. Yeah, everyone knows that," said Mikala.

Scott and Jeremy concurred that the paper was "everywhere," and Kai added, "I read something from it in poli-sci last year. The prof was like, 'This is the shit.'"

Rebecca found this tenderly gratifying. Her parents. The shit.

She sat back down with the pleasurable feeling of receiving an award for which she'd worked hard. The notes that had been appearing in her mailbox—*Your mom says please call home. Your mom called, says to call her. Call your dad*—rose up in her mind, but she nudged them back into the murky subconscious. Looking woozily around the table, she realized she loved Mikala, who had her quite large head thrown back and was holding Scott's hand. And she loved Scott, who with his free hand was making the salt and pepper shakers talk, making Mikala laugh so hard she became young. And she loved Kai, who, despite being beautiful seemed to be genuinely interested in everything Rebecca said tonight and was now turning her open, receptive face toward Jeremy. And she even loved Jeremy, who clearly only wanted to be loved. All those theories so that someone would love him. And she loved Saskia and Jamal and Nat, but they were playing pool, and with her back turned to the pool table, she couldn't feel those particular rays of love, which, now that she thought about it, were probably all Caleb meant when he'd told them to hold their arms out at the Gathering and feel their vectors shooting away.

She loved David—of course she did. She always had.

When it was time to leave, she stumbled over a chair. Its occupant, a middle-aged miner with a walrus mustache, looked up at her in a way that she considered might be actually lecherous, because now she'd been tap-tap-tapped and also been happily drunk, and yet she remained Ira's daughter, remained so interesting.

Nobody else was on the streets as they made their way to Town Park, where Scott's bus waited to take them back to Llamalo. It was as if Jeremy's predictions had come true, and the town was just theirs, just kids from Berkeley and Reed and UC Santa Cruz out on a stroll for beauty.

Scott reached the bus first. He coaxed the engine, shoved a tape in the deck, and twisted the volume. Then he jumped out. *That's great, it starts with an earthquake.* Scott was first to start dancing, and the way Scott danced was like one of those wooden animals where you depress a button and the strings fall limp. *Eye of a hurricane, listen to yourself churn, world serves its own needs.* Saskia was next, and the way Saskia danced was more like pogoing, and the way Kai danced was hips and tits, like she was listening to an entirely different song, and the way Jeremy danced was to hop from foot to foot and huff out the words. *Team by team, reporters baffled, trumped, tethered, cropped, look at that low plane.* Lights went on in the houses across from the park. The way Mikala danced was to grab hands with Scott and to swing their arms from side to side. *You vitriolic, patriotic, slam, fight, bright light, feeling pretty psyched.* The way they all danced was to shout as one, *It's the end of the world as we know it.*

A truck drove slowly by. From a machine in its bed, it expelled a giant plume that rose into the blackness like a poltergeist, lit up red by the truck's rear lights, the candy smell of poison everywhere. It was awesome and horrible.

"What's that?" Rebecca asked, coughing. But all anyone said back to her was, *And I feel fine.* Jeremy grabbed her hand with his clammy one. *And I feel fine.*

They danced around a statue of a miner with a pickax slung on his shoulder. He looked into the middle distance, as if hoping to bring some solemnity to their folly. She saw that the names carved in stone beneath him were of Escadom's sons killed in its coal mine. Above him was the canopy of a large tree of a type Rebecca didn't know—maple? oak?—maybe even planted by the town founders, those dudes on horseback, with impeccable forethought about the need for shade in the future. The leaves unmoving in the still night.

THE REAGAN YEARS: EARLY OCTOBER 1982

CALEB TRAILED DONNIE INTO the kitchen, where Donnie leaned against the sink and said, "I already have the beginning of your article. It goes like this . . ."

Caleb, who couldn't see anything in the dimness after the undaunted sunshine of the outdoors, tried to make his body casual in a listening way, a strained hand-in-pocket, head-cocked journalistic pose. The lie was beginning to feel playful, like a costume or invisibility cloak, something he'd put on to allow himself to enter another world.

"Once upon a time," Donnie began, "there was this ranch called the Double L. It was homesteaded by a real pioneer, you know, who rode here and found this dried-out piece-of-shit land, all the prime riverside plots already taken, but he turned it into something. I mean, he dug out the ditch with horses and hard work, and *bam*—he grew crops and cows. You can say all that exactly. You got to make them understand it's a real American story. You'll want to say that it was three generations of men taking care of it, passing it down, father to son, you know? That's important. And one day, on this ranch, a baby was born, and they named him Donald, and that's me." Donnie snuck a little proud smile at the miracle of his own birth.

"And everything's really perfect. The mom's like this perfect mom, and the dad runs the ranch, just two-fifty cows. And the mom and the boy do the irrigating and shit, but also they play around a lot." Donnie paused. "*A lot.* And then we go to when the boy is nine—you'll have to figure out how to do that—and the mom dies, and nobody even told the kid that she was sick."

"Really? God, I'm sorry," Caleb said.

"Nah, nah, that's not the real point," Donnie said, with thin bravado. It took him half an hour to get to the real point, during which time Caleb's eyes adjusted and he could see the white wicker shoe holding plastic daisies on the windowsill and the smug crowned Jesus in a shiny frame, and he'd never been in a house like this.

He was wondering how to let on that he wasn't actually a journalist— or whether he should just leave without telling Donnie—but he followed this much of what Donnie said: In the years after his mom died, the Double L gradually sank into debt. Then, Exxon came to town, and the Talcs couldn't even find anyone to work for them, because you could get fifty dollars an hour constructing the oil shale plant. Donnie convinced his dad that the only thing to do was sell the herd, pay their debts, and take jobs in oil shale.

"I told him we'd be millionaires in five years—six, tops—and then we could buy more cows. And my dad said no, we work this land. That's our job. And I just started railing on him, telling him that this is our chance, until finally he agreed. And it was a good year . . ." Donnie raised his eyebrows. "A damned good year. I mean, it was like the center of the world here. A new bar opening every day. Whores coming in on a bus. Every night, my friends and I were partying down at the river. I mean, *hundreds* of people camped along the river. Some of the old people hated it. All these families just shitting in the river. Never seen anything like it in my life. Every morning at six, my dad and I would drive to Exxon's shuttle bus, and the street was lined up with new people looking for work." Donnie was grinning at the memory of it.

Lowering his voice to a whisper, he said, "I don't know if you can write this in your paper, but there were drugs everywhere. You go to the bar, no one's carding, and people just leaving lines of cocaine for tips." He shook his head. "Then just *one year* in, Exxon says it doesn't actually know how to make oil from shale. See you later, Exxon."

Now their land was useless again, he said, a dried-out piece of shit. Any day, the bank would pounce upon their ranch, send them into foreclosure. They were broke, but they were Talcs. This was their ranch. "The thing is, Exxon lied to us. They *lied*." Donnie pushed his hands into his pockets and gave Caleb a look that was both furious and imperious. "That's a story, right?"

Well, Caleb thought, staring at the floral wallpaper to avoid Donnie, it was a story, yes, but did Donnie honestly believe that his situation would improve if the world read about it over Pop-Tarts, over coffee, on the subway, on the toilet?

He glanced back at Donnie and was startled to see his mouth contorted in what looked like disgust. He realized that the boy was attempting to hide the childish signs of sorrow—pouting lip, swimming eyes. *"Fuck,"* Donnie muttered.

Sympathy swelled in Caleb. Here he was, at last, a guest of a real cowboy, and he was worrying about the cowboy's level of gullibility? He was thinking like his mom, like his stepdad, Aaron, their nightly outrage at everyone's stupidity. He'd inherited his mom's exasperation, the way she'd mutter, *Oh, come on, lady,* when someone ahead of her in line at the post office couldn't find her wallet. The whole point of being here was to become a different kind of a person, to act like his dad had acted in the world, slipping into different spaces, slipping away and fitting in, and so he looked at Donnie's anguished face as his dad would have. "It's a story alright. A doozy of a story."

Donnie stared for a moment, and then his face relaxed. "I knew you'd see that."

When Donnie's father returned home from the auction and learned a journalist was visiting, he invited Caleb to stay for dinner. It seemed innocuous enough for Caleb to ask to sleep out on the ranch—just for the night. He'd leave early, before they woke, and absolve himself of the lie by driving off.

"In the alfalfa field?" Don Sr. asked.

"Sure, if that's the best place."

The Talcs couldn't answer; they were laughing too hard. "He wants to sleep in the field!" Don was smaller than his son, sinewy instead of fleshy, and, with his homely, washed-out features, he seemed an unlikely progenitor of Donnie's dark handsomeness. But they laughed alike, hunched and shaking, silent except for an occasional breathy bleating. Then Don began coughing, unable to catch his breath. He rested a hand on Donnie's back, and Donnie reached over for the cigarettes, handed him one. Don put it in his mouth, still coughing. Donnie lit it for him as Don inhaled, his cough subsiding. It was this silent conversation between father and son that kept Caleb up at night in the field, tossing on the hard pea of envy while clouds rushed the moon and swallowed it whole.

He fell asleep near dawn and thus failed to make an early exit, waking to find Donnie over him, asking, "Are you ready? I'm gonna give you the grand tour." What could Caleb do?

As they walked alongside the irrigation ditch, Caleb wrote the names of the plants on a folded piece of paper he pressed against the palm of his left hand, as a reporter might—wild roses clinging to the bank of the trough; willows leaning over the water, oyster plants with yellow flowers, bindweed with white flowers, marsh marigold with orange flowers, spindly asparagus, while elsewhere grew only sage and grasses, the fecund so near the cracked, the lush opposite the prickly, water, no water—as they passed through all of this, Caleb thought, Holy shit. This is it. This is the place.

And so he stayed for eight days, during which the autumn colors emerged, the mountainside turning dandelion yellow, and the lie was like a toothache, a dull pain suggestive of rot. There were times he nearly believed it; he'd followed it so far. He found himself thinking about the article as if it existed, about Donnie as a character, how effortlessly sympathetic he'd be in the story, both furious and earnest. They got along surprisingly well—better, in fact, than Caleb did with most guys. Donnie was a gallant tour guide, a quick friend. He took Caleb to see the detritus of the bust, the abandoned "man camps" by the river, the school buses with blackened windows, where the hookers had worked, Escadom's half-built hotels and restaurants. U-Hauls passed by as they walked through town, and Donnie's hand raised in salute.

In the late afternoons, they walked along the ditch, and Donnie, never at a loss, told Caleb about a rancher who'd had a heart attack there, about the boy in his class who fell into the ditch. He said that since first grade, he'd walked the length of this ditch before school, looking for dead sheep or refrigerator doors wedged into a divider to divert water to another ranch. These diversions could choke a ditch and flood the road, and they'd all be trapped up here.

His favorite job, he said, was to burn the brush in the ditch, to clear it out in springtime before the water flowed again. He'd blast it with a blowtorch, all destruction behind him, like a movie. Once the brush burned, he'd run along stomping out sparks, pretending they were villages on fire, like fucking saving the day.

At dawn each day, Caleb would walk into the house, unhook a brown mug with a yellow sunflower from below the cabinet, and fill it with weak coffee. Don and Donnie would be waiting for him. Don would wipe a dishrag over the coffee Caleb dribbled onto the counter, and say, "Explain again why he won't sleep in the house if he comes in every morning to eat our food?"

"It's his wilderness experience, Dad. Just pretend you're not here. Or you're a mountain lion or something."

There was no purpose to the Talcs' early rising—no more ravenous cows, no more thirsty crops, no bus to take them to the shale plant while the stars still shone—and yet here they were, awake out of habit, their work boots tied. As they walked with their one-eyed eggs out to the porch, each grabbed a cowboy hat from the coatrack in the front hallway, as if setting off to work in the sun. Caleb followed in his sweatshirt.

On his fourth evening, they were again on the porch when Donnie bolted, just took off into the field, all those useless yellow and purple alfalfa flowers crowded out by weeds. He screamed, "Fuck, fuck, fuck, fuck, *fuck*," as he disappeared behind the barn.

Without taking his eyes from the darkening hump of the mountain, Don said, "You do understand what my son is expecting."

"I'm not sure what you mean."

"You're not?" Don's eyebrows were the yellow of a nicotine-stained mustache, and he raised them. "He's expecting you to write an article that will encourage people to feel sympathy for us, for what happened to us, when it was no different than what happened to everybody else. He thinks someone will read your article and ring our doorbell and offer us the money to keep our ranch, get it running again." He turned to Caleb. "You know why he thinks this?"

Donnie reappeared atop his teal ATV, zigzagging across the dimming field. Caleb shook his head.

"He's not stupid, you understand. But it was him who bugged me to leave ranching. There's the shame of that, along with our lost livelihood." Don half stood to untuck a pack of cigarettes from his back pocket, extracting matches from the cellophane. He lit his cigarette and crossed his thin legs, his manner tidy and feminine. "He's always promising that he's going to make the money himself, but ARCO's not hiring, nobody's hiring. For hundreds of miles, nobody's hiring, and the bank could give a shit."

Don stood and walked to his truck, his cigarette a red star. He climbed in and drove away.

Caleb sat alone. Don had barely spoken to him before this outpouring, and he felt humbled by his confidence. They'd welcomed him into their family, these people who didn't hold studious silence as their highest goal, who understood that the only important thing was to live here. There were no books in the house. They didn't read, which meant, according to Caleb's mom and stepdad, they didn't care about what it meant to be human. Oh well.

Soon the mountain was just an outline, a darker dark, and stars began to clog the sky. Donnie drove the ATV back to the barn and appeared on the porch. Don came back with two six-packs of Coors. Every time Don and Donnie drained a can, they chucked it into the darkness, and finally Caleb, who'd been lining up his empties beside his chair, walked to the edge of the porch and did the same. Like pitching himself into the blackness.

The next day, Donnie took him to Frank's Farm and Feed, on the mesa outside Hotchkiss, and pointed to the circular display of cowboy hats. "You should get one. Go back to work in *style*. Show them you've been to the Wild West."

Caleb took the hat Donnie was offering. "Definitely white," Donnie said. "No other color should be considered."

There was a feed smell, posters of men in Carhartts and Dickies, a linoleum floor punished by boot after boot. Caleb wanted the hat to make him look like he customarily shopped here. He appraised himself in the thin wall mirror with hope and then disappointment. "Doesn't it look like the hat's trying to eat my face?"

Donnie paunched out his lips, considering. "Nah. No, *no*." Clearly lying.

Caleb set down the white hat and reached for a brown one with a braided rope around the perimeter. It was the color of a chestnut mare. It was exactly the same hat Donnie wore.

In the mirror, he saw his hair sticking up, bushily, statically, as if its very DNA was ashamed and also titillated by the prospect of wearing a cowboy hat. He pressed the brown hat onto his head, and there he was, looking exactly how he'd always wanted to. John Muir and Ed Abbey and Caleb Silver.

"You'll look sharp going back to work in a Stetson," Donnie said. "'Holy wow,' they'll say."

"Holy wow? Is that even something people say?" he asked, trying to hide his pride.

Donnie grinned. "Yup. Holy wow."

They drove to the post office in Escadom. Donnie parked in front and went inside to check his mailbox, and Caleb walked down Founders Avenue, which already seemed more boarded-up than it had been when he'd arrived. Someone had written on the door of a flower shop: HAPPINESS IS ESCADOM IN YOUR REAR WINDOW. And on the hardware store, more to the point: FUCK EXXON.

The receiver dangled from the pay phone. Caleb depressed the tongue and found a dial tone. He asked the operator to make a collect call, pulling from his pocket *Our Side Now*'s masthead, torn from the paper and folded small. He read out the number.

When his uncle came on the line, Caleb described the ranchers he'd been living with, their generosity, their land—the perfect land. From the back of a parked pickup, a dog barked without ceasing.

"What's the problem?" Ira asked. "They can't afford it anymore but don't want to sell. And regardless of their preference, nobody else'll buy it. Within our current and deeply flawed system of supply and demand, you're a perfect match. So, what, are you calling me because of some class guilt? Sure! Feel guilty! Were they played by Exxon? Definitely. But I can't figure how you'd be challenging corporate-federal collusion if you walk away from this. This isn't exactly a boycottable situation. I mean, don't get me wrong—they're going to hate you. Don't expect them to thank you for moving them off their land, no matter how much cash you offer them. They'll fucking hate you. Class rage is real. But is that a problem you're going to fix?"

Caleb hung up and saw Donnie beneath the flag outside the post office, grinning and pointing. "Nice hat," Donnie bellowed down the street,
his hands cupped around his mouth. He was eighteen years old and large,
with shoulders the size of oar blades. Caleb had never had a friend like
this. Donnie waved his hat. Caleb wildly waved his back. Donnie shouted,
"Is that or is that not the most stylish journalist in the West?" Passersby
turned to stare just as Caleb achieved a somewhat effortless step-jump into
Donnie's truck. "Come on," Donnie said. "Let's get home."

THE FAREWELL DINNER BEGAN festively enough. Don, who'd removed
his Carhartt bib overalls for the occasion and was wearing a white button-
down, ordered a paternal round of beer. That morning, Donnie had said
they'd seen all there was to see but that Caleb should feel free to stay on
for as long as he needed for research. Caleb had asked to take them out to
dinner to thank them for their hospitality. "What hospitality?" Don said,
"You wouldn't even sleep in our house." But it was clear he was pleased by
the gesture.

The waitress brought a wooden bowl of tortilla chips and a saucer of
salsa, which sloshed onto the table when she set it down. Donnie, ever
the tour guide, gave a history of the building they were in, now inhabited
by The Casa, which had opened during the boom. "So before that, it was
empty awhile, but it used to be a bar—the Ute's Mirage—and before that,
this was where Frank's Farm and Feed was until they moved up on the
mesa. And before that . . ."

Caleb only half listened. It struck him that maybe Ira'd been wrong.
They might not hate him in the slightest. Why hadn't he thought of this
before? They were struggling, and he would help. They might, in fact, be
grateful. The word "savior" bounded through his head. Embarrassed, he
pushed it down, but it bobbed back up. The waitress returned with their
food—platters of beans and rice, and something yellow.

Before Caleb had a chance to reconsider, he blurted, "So, I had an idea
about your land."

They turned to each other with amused looks. Donnie said, "An idea?" Don said, "Oh no, he had an idea."

Caleb grinned along, but he could feel a nervous strain creep onto his face. He explained that he'd been planning for some time to start a summer camp and had been scoping out land. He paused to drink, heart pounding. "I know that you're in a bit of a bind"—he cringed at the euphemism, the alliterative British-sounding phrase—"with your land, and I thought, hey, if I keep you from foreclosure, this could be mutually beneficial."

Donnie's tongue covered his upper lip and then retreated. "Wait, I don't get it. Aren't you a journalist? Aren't you writing about us?"

Caleb didn't answer.

"We need to get this straight," Don said, carefully placing his utensils on the edge of his plate. "You're asking to buy the Double L?"

The Christmas lights on the window winked with desperate cheer. The ceiling fan wobbled on its orbit, hinting at decapitation. Oil pooled orange on their plates. Caleb offered a price per acre that he'd come up with by looking at the bank auction flyers around town.

"Are you or aren't you a journalist?" Donnie demanded.

Caleb couldn't bear to disappoint further. "I was. It's true—I was. But I'm ready to get out. Leave the rat race."

Donnie leaned forward. "And now you want our house? Where are we supposed to live?"

"Shut up, Donnie," Don said. "I don't think that's his consideration."

Of course, Ira had been right. The evening's joy had been trampled upon, neatly killed. Don turned his attention to his food, methodically cutting his quesadilla, taking small bites, and when he had eaten exactly half, he set his fork down and wiped his mustache. He kept his gaze down.

Donnie, however, couldn't stop staring at Caleb. Sauce dribbled from his fork. "You were lying?" he asked.

"Shut it," his father warned.

The waitress had abandoned them. She'd lose her job by the end of the week, judging from the other tables, all the empty chairs showing their bones. Caleb couldn't take it anymore. He set down a traveler's check worth four times the cost of the meal, and although he knew this display of profligacy would make everything worse, he walked away without waiting for change.

"Sorry," he said, although he didn't know exactly which crime he was apologizing for, and anyway his voice was drowned out by bells disguised as chili peppers that jingled as he opened the door.

NINE

Do You Love Me?

"SO, DO YOU *LOVE* me?" David asked little albino Caitlin, who was kneeling to tie her laces. He stabbed at her sneakers with her broom. "Do you love *me*? Do *you* love me?" It was the morning after Rumspringa, and David was rehearsing on the patio near the Gathering. Shauna, Tanaya, and Nicole, and their admirers huddled to watch. David continued. "If I have to ask, I don't want to know, right? Right?"

Rebecca, he thought, this is the mitzvah of not taking skits too seriously.

Rebecca, he thought, of course I remember the pier.

Caitlin rose, laces tied. "Do I what?" She sounded frightened. A rash had spread on her pink face. She was only eleven, a little young to be a shtetl bride.

"David, your line."

"Do you . . . ?" He raised the broom high, until its straw mouth kissed the willow roof, and he thought about adding a mitzvah of the willows to his list.

This mitzvah originated on a day that remained, in his calculation, as the greatest day of his life. It was the second summer of Llamalo, when Caleb had started to expand into the high desert across the irrigation ditch from the house; before that, they all slept in the alfalfa field. Caleb decided that campers needed some shade near the Gathering and asked only Suze and David to help quarry the sandstone for the floor of the patio. They spent hours slamming rock into the truck bed, but once they were done, the truck couldn't move. There'd been this hysterical camaraderie, David just swept up in Caleb and Suze's love for each other. She would tease them both, kiss Caleb, mess up David's hair. The sun had set by the time they'd unloaded half the rocks just to get out of Escalante Canyon. Drove back in the dark, all three of them in the front seat of Caleb's truck. The next day, they brought the rocks up to the Gathering in wheelbarrows and laid the floor as if they were solving an extremely heavy jigsaw puzzle. They dug postholes, secured the posts, placed supporting beams, and cut willows at the Upper Escadom Reservoir to rest across as a roof. At the start of every summer, Caleb and Suze and David—and then just Caleb and David—returned to the reservoir, slicing out a new covering with army knives.

"*Da*vid." Shauna fanned herself with the clipboard. Most kids couldn't handle the summer's deep heat like David could. "You can't space out like that."

David came to and handed the broom to his wife. "So, do you love me? Or have we just succumbed to the diminishing lust that plagues every marriage? Staying together out of habit, for the children, for society's sake. Society!" He raised a fist.

Matthew snorted. Nicole sighed, "The *actual* line."

A midsized girl ran breathless onto the patio, explaining that they needed more Dektol for the photography shack. Nat, who was supervising photography, didn't know where it was, and someone said David would know, and someone else said David was here, and so, did he?

David nodded, pleased. He knew everything about this place.

"Can you tell us?"

"I'll go get it." The bottle of Dektol was kept in Caleb's office, and David had few opportunities to visit that off-limits sanctum.

Shauna blew her bangs. "Now? Curtain rises *Friday night*."

"What curtain?" he said, heading off into the sagebrush. A few minutes later, he saw, in the distance, a shape that might be Rebecca. But all shapes looked like Rebecca now.

He remembered how after he ran into Rebecca at the Santa Monica Pier, it was awkward as shit between them. David would be guilted into going to the Silvers' with his mom for a potluck. Rebecca would talk to the adults loudly, flaunting her familiarity with the political terms of the conversation, in a sort of analog to the perfect spelling tests she used to leave out, and he'd try to disappear into the couch, attuning his vibrations to that split-pea smell.

The Rebecca shape resolved itself into Rebecca, her hair bouncing along.

It was strange to talk outside the barn, their faces in full color. In a manner that he hoped conveyed thoughtfulness, he put a hand on his chin to cover a small constellation of zits. "So, hey there."

"Oh, hi."

"Last night! Was it everything you hoped for?"

"Fun, actually. Really, really, really fun."

Two "reallys" would've been plenty. Even one got the point across. "Yeah, well, it's good I didn't come. Caleb really needed the help around here."

Really, really, really needed.

"So, I'm kind of in a hurry," she said. As if he didn't know the taste of her spit. She gestured to the woodworking shack, half of which she'd converted into her newspaper office by thumbtacking various quotes to the walls: NEVER DOUBT THAT A SMALL GROUP OF THOUGHTFUL, COM-MITTED, etc. Rebecca had started a camp paper here a few weeks earlier; of course she had.

"Bye then." He didn't move. Her spit tasted like Rebecca.

"Actually, I was just thinking about the, um"—she flung back a hank of her hair—"the barn." Just like that, the Rebecca of the barn, a bold and coy Rebecca, was out here in daylight.

"Yeah, I've heard of it. Cow-y in there."

"Bovine."

"It's always there. It's there right now. The barn is always in existence."

"Might be nice there in the morning."

"The morning, huh? Cooler then."

"I might be there in an hour or so. Before lunch. Just to look for some . . ."

"Tools" was the obvious word choice, but it appeared she couldn't make that pun. Or "wood." Plenty of wood in the barn.

"Rakes?" he suggested helpfully. "Spades? No newspaper office is complete without a full array of garden implements. Well, so, cool. Perhaps I'll see you there. Before lunch."

David continued on, smiling like a stoner at the dried grasses and the insects that loved them. Burrs huddled against his white socks. It was the Wednesday of the last week of camp, a week that usually trapped him in anxiety's mirrored hall. He would tell himself not to think about the ending of camp and rather to appreciate each moment as if it were occurring in a limitless expanse of days at Llamalo. But ignoring the ending was as impossible as ignoring an oncoming train when tied to the tracks, which meant he was always failing at appreciating the moments, and it seemed this failure was actually bringing about the camp's end and not the inevitable march of time itself.

David felt none of that today. He'd be back in a month. He knew where the Dektol was kept; everyone knew he knew. Rebecca would be waiting for him in the barn. The phrase "blow job" streaked across his phlegmatic mind.

Heading over the footbridge, he saw Caleb crouching to tinker with the pipe that led out of the shower house, and David realized he'd forgotten to include the mitzvah of taking a shower as a subset of the mitzvah of water, which he'd already divided into the mitzvah of potable water and the mitzvah of dishwater. Mitzvot, he was noticing as he tried to record them, branched out like dendrites. Every action, it seemed, could be broken up into even smaller actions, until what? The mitzvah of breathing? Of being fucking alive right now? Of being this happy?

In the office, he found the Dektol in a bucket against the wall, but he lingered. Sweat snaked down his forehead. The room was stifling, but fascinating for being forbidden, with the homey allure of a theater's backstage. He walked from window to door and back again, as if he weren't going to sit down at the desk.

Once in the chair, his hands grazed everything. He held a forefinger to the computer screen to feel the static. He pulled a few sheets of curled and strangely warm paper from the mouth of the fax machine. He wrapped his hand around the phone's receiver. "Hello. Llamalo," he said, practicing. Noticing an invoice with Caleb's handwriting on it, he pulled it closer. "Suze," it said, underlined twice, and a phone number.

So they talked. Standing, as if something were required of him, David held the invoice, put it down.

Of course they talked. There were all sorts of rumors about her. That she was married. That she'd died or joined a cult. Everyone else agreed that she and Caleb hadn't talked in years, but David never allowed himself to believe that. He knew they were meant to be together—king and queen, male and female, yin and yang—it was only a matter of time. Discovering that he'd been right seemed to demand action. Grabbing the fax as an excuse, he ran to the shower building.

"Caleb? Caleb?"

Caleb appeared in the doorway, his face brightening when he saw David. "Every week it's clogged with this foul mix of hair and soap. Why should hair smell so bad?" He jutted his chin toward the paper in David's hand. "What's up?"

David saw the flaw in his plan. The fax begged the question: What was he doing snooping? Still, he forged on. "Nothing. I was in the office and saw this. Thought you might need it."

Caleb laughed. He removed one leather glove and then the other, pinning the pair between his arm and side. "Look at you. You ran here? You need to know that as a rule, faxes are unimportant," he said with a teacherly tone that seemed to pleasingly reference their future together. "Usually invoices. Sometimes toner-depleting ads for new fax toner. Never an emergency." He reached for the paper. "But thanks. I appreciate your thoughtfulness."

David pivoted away and then back again to make it look like his true purpose was actually an afterthought. "Hey, I was wondering. Are you in touch with Suze?"

Caleb studied him. He wasn't smiling, but neither was he displeased. "I've spoken to her. Actually, quite recently. Why?"

"Does she ever think about coming back?"

"Suze?" Caleb asked as if there might be another "she." His expression was hopeful. "She didn't mention it. Although I suppose I didn't ask her outright."

"Would you ever?" David said, surprised at his brazenness, as if they were already equals.

Caleb smiled, clearly unbothered by David's forthrightness, another one of the ways he alluded to their time together without ever actually speaking of it. "I guess . . . well, I guess I've always been hoping Suze would get here somehow without me begging her to come. Why? What made you think of this?"

"I always think about Suze. I mean, we all do. I just didn't know whether she left on . . ." David struggled for the word. "Like, hypothetically, if she were to come, even just for a visit, would you like that?"

"Like it?" Caleb frowned. "I'd be thrilled."

David nodded, returning Caleb's frown.

Caleb added, "I wouldn't get your hopes up, though."

"Well, okay then," David said. "I won't." And he took off down the alfalfa field.

◆ ◆ ◆

CALEB REMOVED THE COVER page and uncurled the fax below, finding it handwritten. Not an invoice or an ad. Caleb let his gloves drop to the floor.

You can't deny this, asshole. <u>Proof</u>. You were in the Motherlode last night calling my dad a redneck. I heard from a reputible source who was there. He said how you're buying the Motherlode and planning to kick out all the rednecks just like you kicked us out. <u>Enviro Nazi</u>. Well guess again. I'll be there tomorrow. It's time for me to tell all those kids that your a liar. The truth about how you stole this land.

Here the handwriting became very small and hard to decipher. "And all their parents in their California" (the next word might have been "mansions") "are they going to want to hear that a liar is brainwashing their children?"

The entire last line was illegible, its bottom two-thirds cut off by the machine, leaving behind what looked like a child's drawing of grass.

◆ ◆ ◆

LIKE THE TWO PREVIOUS meetings of the camp's newspaper staff, this one was a disappointment. With only a few days left of summer, the kids remained unserious, only wanting to work on word searches, astrology, weather forecasts—fluff and filler.

Rebecca slid her hand over a tabletop welted with wax from batik and candle-dipping and tried to direct them toward the well-traveled path of reportorial curiosity. "If you think about it," she said, "the true purpose of a newspaper is to uncover and then speak truth to power."

No luck. A girl shrieked, "Wait, wait! What if I do interviews with animals?"

The others found this to be the height of newsworthiness. The girl laid out her plan: "We'll answer back in the animal's voice. Like, what's your favorite color, lizard?"

Rebecca's own muckraking was more literal. After the meeting, she scoped the barn to ensure emptiness and stationed herself in the back stall, kicking shriveled cow pies away. The barn turned out to offer little relief from the clamoring heat, and Rebecca had the good idea of removing her shirt. And then, with an unfamiliar gust of self-confidence, she unhooked her bra, peeled it from its mold, so that it became a shapeless piece of nylon falling to the ground. She looked down. Her nipples were courageous; her breasts, lopsided as ever, only the left acquiring the good shape of bra ads, the right listing shyly to the side. But she felt fine about it—sexy, even, for the first time. Topless, in cutoffs, she was finally Californian, which was a relief after spending her whole life in that beachy state without measuring up to its insouciant promise. The sneakers and socks detracted a bit from the image, but below was cow shit.

For a few ebullient minutes, she enjoyed the heat on her skin as well as her newfound audacity, but then problems appeared. Sweat under her breasts made her itch. Should she sit or stand? There seemed to be something desperate about any pose, but she was determined not to get dressed.

When David arrived, he found her leaning against the wall, arms crossed over her chest.

He stopped short a few feet away. "Whoa." A greedily astonished look on his face. Droplets of sweat on his forehead. She realized that she hadn't wanted him to make a big deal. She wanted her nudity to seem in character.

"Whoa what?"

Thankfully, he recalculated, eyes rising to her face. "So, tell me. How's *Our Side Now*? You read it yet?"

"The thing is, I've been kind of busy."

He was coming toward her. His hands were on her hips. "Really? Busy how?" His hands rising up her sides, thumbs on her breasts, mouth almost on hers. "Because I was hoping you'd tell me what it said, you know."

They kissed in the way he'd taught her the day before, until David pulled away, saying, "So, I was lying. Because I do remember that day. At the pier."

"You do?"

"Wasn't my doppelganger that time. Skee-Ball, right? You were standing in front of Skee-Ball with some girls."

"Mihui and Emily."

"I was flying. Stoned beyond all recognition."

"Stoned? You were thirteen." How much had he done that she never had?

"The age of manhood, according to the Jews. The age of mind-blowing, according to a tutor my parents hired. An intern at *OSN*, actually. John? Jim? Anyway, he brought me two pot brownies in a ziplock bag. Told me to wait until the weekend and then eat half of one and watch my mind expand. Being an idiot, and also thirteen, I ate both on the bus to the pier. My mind expanded so far I basically dissolved."

"That's why you wouldn't talk? You were weird. You touched the paddle of my yogurt."

"But let me tell you, it was the most beautiful paddle I'd ever seen."

She concentrated on his hands on her skin, on her nipples pressing against the cotton of his shirt. "I thought you hated me. Always after that, I thought so."

He shook his head. "How could I ever hate you, Rebecca? You're Rebecca. My friend Rebecca. I love you, Rebecca."

And now, as the past crashed up against the present, another good idea came to her: she wanted to feel his weight on her. But how to make that happen? She didn't quite understand how two people simultaneously descended from standing to lying, but surely couples did it all the time. She decided to collapse her knees while clinging to him.

"Yikes," he said, releasing her to catch himself and laughing in a way that made her regret her forcefulness. The straw bit her bare back.

They resumed kissing, but there were new discomforts. His teeth crashed against hers. His left elbow was pinning her right arm. His shins pressed against her sneakers, which seemed painful for him. But the weight of him was more than satisfying, precisely what she'd been waiting for.

Somehow his right hand appeared inside her shorts, but on top of her underwear. And in a gesture of solidarity, she did the same, pushing into his shorts, finding, in her hand at last, a dick, cock, penis, soft skin, pleasing. He rolled off her a bit, edged onto his side, and began rubbing, and she followed, a conversation of sorts, with their mouths fixed to each other's.

He was rubbing too hard, and she decided unhappily that there was no way to tell him without mortification, but then he pulled his mouth from hers to say, "Actually, it's too . . . um, can you do it gentler?"

"But you, too!" she said, expecting him to be humiliated as she was.

He simply laughed. "Like this?"

For a while, her brain continued its merry analytic work. Was this really, her brain wanted to know, so different than how it felt with her own hand? Sure, his fingers were colder and clearly external to her self, but was it really so phenomenal? Then her brain, skittering as if across ice, wanted to spend a moment remembering where she'd heard the word "epiphenomenon." And then her eyes were closing, and she was falling more slowly than she'd ever fallen. In fact, she wasn't even falling—*Oh god, oh god,* somebody said, maybe her—she wasn't falling; she was being carried by the only person to ever really see her, the real Rebecca, by which she now meant the wild one, the naked one, the one who was made of straw and air and tits and cunt, and she called out.

Opening her eyes, she found David looking at her with a sleepy, childish gaze, naïvely unembarrassed. She realized she'd dropped out of the conversation, her hand unmoving around him. He began thrashing against it. He closed his eyes. Grimaced. She held on as he flopped against her.

When he opened his eyes, she said, "You were so quiet. Was I loud?"

"Very audible."

"Fuck, let's get out of here." She stood, wiped her hand on the inside of her shorts, proud at her deftness with semen, dressed, and then bent down to his mouth to feel the lick of him again before leaving. The image that she had of herself was of a good fairy—beneficent, life-giving, flutteringly powerful. As she pulled away, she meant to say "Remember, the barn's always in existence" flirtatiously, but the existence of the word "existence" seemed suddenly questionable. Was that indeed what David had said? Subsistence? Existent? "Remember the barn!" she finally said. Which was not hard to do, because they were still in it.

◆ ◆ ◆

HAPPY BAR MITZVAH TO David. Mazel tov, David. Give the man a Swatch. A scotch. This hadn't been his first time, not at all, but he hadn't felt like this with Heather L., not with Aura, not with his own hand. He'd never told anyone that he loved them, because he'd never loved them. He waited the requisite five minutes and then walked out of the barn a man.

On the eating platform, he poured a mug of hot water from the thermos at the counselor's coffee-and-tea station. He spooned in Folgers, stirred. Ostensibly, campers weren't allowed to do this, but he'd found that nobody said anything when he did. It seemed like the appropriate action for a man, to bring a cup of coffee to the office and set it on the desk.

He was nervous when dialing, sure, but the doubts he harbored were overshadowed by the potential to please Caleb. A final gesture—and a grand one!—before camp ended and judgment was cast upon David.

Suze answered on the sixth ring, and he explained that he was David, from Llamalo. She might not remember him, he said, but he remembered her.

"Not remember you? David?"

"David Cohen," he clarified, just in case she was remembering a different David. He didn't recognize her voice.

"David Cohen then. Of *course* I remember. What a surprise. What a treat. Wait, are you okay? Is everything okay?"

"It's all fine. It's the last Wednesday of summer, though. You know how it goes. Final Friday is in two days. Then it's done. We leave. It's all over."

"So *sad*. The weeping and hugging. I'm sad just thinking about it."

The enthusiasm with which she spoke sounded like the Suze he remembered, but the voice over the line still hardly correlated with the woman he'd held in his mind all these years. He pressed on anyway. "So I wanted to officially invite you."

"To what?"

"Final Friday. Come here and cheer us up."

She laughed. "You sound different. How old are you now?"

"I'll be eighteen next month."

"A full-fledged adult. How are things at Llamalo? How's Caleb?"

"It's been a great summer. Maybe the best yet. Don't you want to see it?"

"You're so cute. Do you even know where I am?"

He blushed. "Actually, no."

"San Francisco. You're talking about a sixteen-hour drive."

"To the greatest place on earth? That doesn't seem like anything. I'd drive forty-eight hours to get here. Straight." He took a sip of his coffee. He hated it, but he was interested in liking it, so he persevered. "Here's what you do. Drive ten hours tomorrow. Camp by the side of the road. Do the last six on Friday. Get here by lunch."

"I can't even imagine seeing it again. What a trip that would be. We actually have friends in Crested Butte. I was telling Colin we should see them, and that way . . . God, it would be such a trip to come to Llamalo. Like, does it actually still exist? Sometimes I feel like it was all a figment of my . . . Friday? That's the last day?"

"This Friday."

"Honestly, I couldn't bring Colin. No way in hell. He hates roughing it *and* ex-boyfriends." She laughed and seemed to wait for him to laugh along, so he obliged. "But if I dropped him in the Butte and came for the day and then spent the weekend up in . . . Friday, right?"

Was she even listening? "Friday," he said for the third time. Had the last day ever not been a Friday?

"Okay, so I have a question for you, David Cohen. Did Caleb ask you to call me?"

"No! I just . . ." He paused. What to say? "I saw your number, and . . . well, I just missed you, I guess."

"You're so sweet. What a trip it would be to be there. I'm such a flake about keeping in touch with everyone that sometimes I feel like the past disappears. And then, here you are, calling me. Okay, I'm not promising, but I'll work on Colin. We'll talk it over."

Hanging up, he recognized that the pronoun she'd used was a problem. Perhaps a man would have asked her about it. Perhaps a man would demand, Who is this Colin of whom you speak? Perhaps a man might say, On second thought, if there's a Colin involved, don't bother coming. But he was just a junior man, a newborn man, and he decided that once she got here, once she stood on Aemon's Mesa, the most incredible place to stand, she'd become singular when she'd been plural. Colin? she'd think. Did I even know someone with that name?

The mitzvah of taking a shower, David wrote in his journal at rest time that day,

> *begins officially with the ditch water, which goes into the water storage tower on the alfalfa field and then gets piped into the shower house. The shower house, which I should describe, has a wood floor, a faucet on each of the walls, no roof. And a drain in the middle. On Mondays, we (the boys) stay at the river past dinner, eating sandwiches, and the girls go back to camp to shower and I have no idea what they do up there and I can't think about it too long, because here's what we boys do when we shower. We freak out. In a good way, a kind of* Lord of the Flies *way,*

but without the violence or conch shells. This is Tuesday, I forgot to say. We drop our swim trunks as soon as we cross the road and there's this ritual of spinning them and letting them fly. So we're waiting for our turns naked, except with our boots on, which we leave at the door of the shower, and we get back into them, the boots, as soon as we're done. And right at first we're freezing. The water heater is solar, that's cool but it never really gets the water warm. But nobody towels off, we just run around and because it's so hot, we're dry in a few minutes and still we keep freaking out and running and screaming until someone yells GIRLS COMING. And then we race bare-assed across the ditch to our platforms to get dressed.

David shook out his hand, cramped from writing. He closed his notebook, lay down on his sleeping bag, closed his eyes, and then sat up again to add one sentence:

Important: Of course if there's a thunderstorm, all showers are canceled.

TEN

Across Disney World

DONNIE SAT BY THE kitchen window the night after he sent the fax, waiting for the phone to ring. He could hear the Mexicans revving their lowriders. Someone set off Roman candles, and down the block the chained-up dogs howled in lust for fire that could fly. The wind was as warm as breath, and the phone didn't ring. He'd wait until midnight, and then, if Caleb didn't call, he'd start driving. Or maybe he'd wait until one. He didn't want to go. In his fax, Donnie had said, *Call me right away to discuss this.* He didn't want to go, but he wasn't being respected.

From the other side of the bedroom door, he could hear the bleating again, like the end of the world, like an accusation: What are you going to do about it?

Nothing. He was going to do nothing about it, because he was waiting for the phone. From the floor, one of Marci's magazines stared up at him, asking ARE YOU ON THE JOURNEY TO WEALTH? FIND OUT INSIDE! Also on the floor were Marci's underwear, a slump of towels, and two empty grocery bags with crumpled receipts. It all bothered him.

He picked up the magazine, flipped to the article: "Five Regular People Share Their Ordinary Journeys to Extraordinary Wealth."

Donnie's own journey to not-extraordinary wealth had started eight years ago, when he'd been one of six people living in two rooms in Montrose, picking corn while high. After a shitty winter cutting wood with the Mexicans near Olathe, Donnie had arrived in Telluride one March day, and, hallelujah, here was a town still alive, a town about money. He'd found a job fixing up Victorians, painting them lavender or teal or candy-cane stripes or camo green with yellow trim or maroon with gray—like team colors, all lined up on one block. He shared a rental on the wide mouth of the canyon with Ted and Shawn and Summer and Mark. It was a party condo, and he was a party guy, the one who placed the final can at the apex of the beer-can pyramid and then did a little Mexican hat dance. Da dá da dá da dá. His roommates adored their real rancher. All of them were from rainy places like Connecticut and Seattle, and they bought the pot and said, *Tell us about rodeos. Tell us about how bad the cows are treated.*

It was perfect until the October day he'd parked his truck outside the candy-cane house. The wind screamed of an approaching storm. Some hippies had just opened a shop that sold muffins, dense as boiled wool, and he'd bought one and was throwing bits of walnut and banana at the chipmunks. By the time his boss pulled up, the jays had become excited about the smorgasbord, and the sparrows, too, and Donnie was Francis of Assisi, feeding all the little animals.

But his boss had bad news. The Californian who'd thought he wanted to live in a revamped toolshed at nine thousand feet had decided he preferred the planed horizons of the desert. The project was over, and the building season, too, until April or May, depending on snowpack.

Donnie's roommates were all buying ski passes for the price of three months' rent, and they didn't understand why their rancher was riding off into the Western sunset. Or, actually, to Phoenix, where you could get construction work through the winter. There, he painted orange on stucco walls and laid terra-cotta on roofs like Legos, but in a few years, the rents climbed roof-high and his new roommates said, *No problem. Let's travel around in our van with the money we made*, and Donnie said, *You're crazy,* and moved to Questa, New Mexico, where everyone mined molybdenum at AmMiCo.

At the mine's cafeteria, he sat next to two brothers, who turned out to be members of a group called People for the West! (the exclamation point, he learned, was part of their name), and they taught him that everything was connected: the same enviros in Washington who had made it too expensive for the Talcs to grow beef were now making it too expensive for the mining companies to conduct their business. It was all connected, because the West wasn't owned by the people who lived in it or the state governments that understood it, but by the federal government thousands of miles away, bureaucrats with no clue how to take care of it.

Donnie joined the AmMiCo chapter of People for the West! and the mining company paid for his entrance fee and hotel room at the Wise Use Leadership Conference in Reno. The keynote speaker shared a stage with an overlarge ficus and talked about the "end result." Soon, there would be no way for honest people to make a living, and the entire West would be an amusement park, a sort of Disney World that people in Washington and Hollywood could visit to climb rocks or ski. The mines would move to South America, and our beef would come from Japan and our oil from Arabs, and the trees would be shipped from overseas as well. Our country would be the bitch of the rest of the world. The end result would be a land without its people, just tourists and animals frolicking around like Bambi.

He'd understood then what Caleb had done.

Donnie met Hobart R. Billings, Esq., at the conference, and he left with Billings's book, as well as pamphlets that asked ARE YOU IN CONTROL OF YOUR PROPERTY? and HOW CAN EXTRACTIVE INDUSTRY AND WORKING PEOPLE JOIN TOGETHER TO PROTECT JOBS? The evening he returned to Quartzite, he finally had the swagger to talk to Marci, who worked at the El Monte Carlo, a bar near the laundromat.

Donnie said, "Do you know the phrase 'custom and culture'?" She gave him a squinty, skeptical look.

She had obsidian-black hair, short as a boy's, and small winking earrings, like extra eyes. He was at the bar, and she was behind the bar, adjusting the radio. She looked too young to be there.

"Think of these words. Custom." He released his beer to raise his right hand. "Culture." He raised his left. "What do those words mean? Custom: How we live on the land. What we know about our animals and our crops and our minerals. Culture: The community we make out here. The morals we follow."

He repeated exactly what the keynote speaker had said, with the same rousing inflections.

She said, "Okay?"

Encouraged, he kept going, all the way to the amusement park. "*We'll* be the endangered species then."

He told her about his ranch, how he would be moving back there soon, taking control of his property. Maybe she'd want to visit sometime.

She said, "You're funny."

Marci stayed that night in his rented room, and for several nights afterward, until he felt certain they were dating. He told Marci how they were going to get married and work his ranch and have babies, by which he meant she should keep having sex with him and answering the phone when he called and resting her head right there on his arm. However Marci herself interpreted it, soon she was pregnant and then there was Kayla.

Kayla was tiny and terrifying. She was a spiderweb and a spider, all at once. She was a bouncy chair with a Winnie the Pooh pattern and a pink-roses diaper bag and a bottle sterilizer and a white crib and pink bibs and pink pajamas and little pink dishrags that were not to be used for dishes, and diapers and a camo-print stroller, and this took up all the space in their apartment and all his money.

For the first time since his mom died, he wasn't lonely, and he never wanted to be lonely again. He would think, Stop bothering me. Who are you? And then he would ache for them: What if they left! He wanted to tuck them under his coat, hide them under his wings. During the days after Kayla was born—those early days before Marci started crying all the time—Marci would say, "Can't we go now, live on your ranch, let Kayla ride a horse, our little cowgirl?"

He started writing the letters to Caleb when Marci started crying. He'd already been in correspondence with Hobart R. Billings, Esq., who believed that Donnie had a clear case. *Follow the money!* Hobart R. Billings, Esq., wrote, going on to say that Caleb was clearly funded by the enviro-Nazis; how else would a twenty-four-year-old kid be able to buy a ranch? He warned, however, that lawsuits took years and years. He said that there were quicker ways. Most recently he wrote, *We must band together and take back our land from the Jews and the Washington elites. We are all supporting you in your fight!*

It was with this encouragement in mind that Donnie sent the fax from the drugstore after talking to Craig, whose stepsister had been at the Motherlode last night. Donnie checked the messages when he came home from a half shift, but nothing. He had the next two days off, but Marci would be working at the laundry and Donnie was supposed to watch Kayla both days. He couldn't really leave to go to Escadom. When Caleb called, they could talk it through and he wouldn't need to go. If Caleb called by midnight. Or two. Or three.

He dropped the magazine. The telephone not ringing made Donnie want to crush things.

He waited until the bedroom was quiet, and then he went inside and shut off the TV. Marci had fallen asleep with her mouth open; she was so pretty. Kayla was just lying on the mattress, looking up at Donnie seriously: *What are you going to do about it?* He walked around to the far side of the mattress and sat down carefully. He held his breath to hear her breathe. She turned to him. Began kicking her legs. He picked her up, held her to him, smelled her scalp. Sometimes, to cheer up Marci, he flapped the baby's arms around and pretended she was speaking: "Hi, Mommy.

I wuv you." Now he took her little fisted hand and put it in his mouth, closed his lips around it.

He wasn't going to live in this apartment forever, waiting until AmMiCo moved to South Africa.

He would drive to Caleb right now if he knew where to put Kayla. Too near a pillow and she might suffocate and die. Too near the edge of the bed and she might fall. He poked Marci until her eyes shot open as if she'd never been asleep.

"Just *take* her, Donnie," Marci said, rolling over and away from him. "I need an hour. Just an hour—that's *all*." But he waved Kayla's arms around and said, "I need my Mommy. I wuv Mommy!" and pushed her toward Marci all the same.

Donnie slept on the couch so that he might hear the phone when Caleb called, but he woke at dawn, undisturbed.

♦ ♦ ♦

SOMETIMES THE SADDEST EVENTS are just a coincidence.

An enviro-Nazi is a fantasy, conjured up by corporate lobbyists.

A storm came and swept your life away, and I just happened to come by after.

Caleb was writing down things to tell Donnie. By storm, he meant global capitalism, the unstable price of oil.

It was two, then three, then five in the morning. Too hot to sleep, but that wasn't the problem. The problem was all he could imagine. For example, a gun. Small, the kind that fits a palm. He could hear the campers' screams. He'd been stupid not to call the cops, but "the cops" was actually just one cop, Glen Lebs. Glen had gone to school with Donnie. His father was on the board of the ditch company, in charge of Caleb's allocation of water. So maybe he hadn't been stupid not to call Officer Lebs, but he'd been stupid not to send the campers home. Instead, he'd decided to ship everyone to the river for the day so that he could receive Donnie alone and calm him down before the campers returned for dinner, a plan that now, considering his ignorance of both Donnie's arrival time and intentions once he got here, seemed half-assed at best.

But what more could he do? Caleb headed to the house before the wake-up bell to remind the breakfast ladies to set out supplies for bagged lunches. He'd left a note to this effect, but as he entered the kitchen amid the gassy fug of eggs, Charlene raised her eyebrows. "It's *far* too late to make changes like that." Despite her diminutive stature, she dominated the kitchen. In theory, the campers were responsible for cooking and cleaning, but this participation, minimal at best—baking the bread, setting the table, filling the condiments—was made possible by, and created extra work for, Charlene. She put her hands on her hips. "I set out the ground round to defrost last night. My menu says sloppy-joe lunch and burger dinner, and so that's thirty-five pounds of meat gone to waste if you cut out lunch. And besides, my lunch girls are already here. You weren't wanting me to send them home without pay, were you?"

Was Charlene in on it? Had Donnie called her and told her to keep the campers here? Caleb never argued with Charlene. "This is your kingdom," he usually joked when she wanted to make a change to the menu. But now he said, "It's just meat. Can we have some flexibility around here? You ladies want to take the day off and still get paid? Go for it. Live it up."

He'd gone too far. Clatter stilled. Hips shifted; heads turned. He patted the counter and attempted a smile. "Well, smells good in here. Smells delicious."

At announcements, his plan was met with wails of complaint. This was the last Thursday! Could the building crew stay back to finish work on one of the platforms? What about the cast of *Fiddler on the Roof*? Lines were unmemorized, sets unpainted.

He raised his hand to quiet them. "Hot, isn't it? At six this morning, I looked at the thermometer and it was nearly ninety. Six o'clock in the morning. I can't think of a better way to spend our last Thursday."

It seemed to take forever for the kids to gather swimsuits, water, lunches. The relief he felt once they disappeared from sight dissipated as soon as he found a note from Don thumbtacked to the porch in the usual spot. *Not feeling well—Home today.* In eight years, Caleb hadn't known Don to take a sick day. He'd been fine yesterday.

Caleb waited on the eating platform, which afforded him a view of the road. He tensed when he heard the drone of an airplane and when a kitchen lady slammed the basement door on the way to the walk-in freezer. Then the kitchen ladies and the laundry ladies drove away, leaving him alone. Silence like the day Aemon had arrived on horseback.

By 5 p.m., when kids and counselors had returned, Caleb realized he'd overreacted. Donnie was all bluster. Posturing, like a teenage boy in the hallway, stepping toward you, making you flinch. Caleb had been foolish to send them away, to give up a day with his camp. This had been the last Thursday until next year, and he'd given it up for fear.

◆ ◆ ◆

ALL DAY, WHILE MARCI worked, Donnie thought about escape. He thought about leaving Kayla with a stack of pink- and white-frosted animal cookies in her crib and driving alone with the window open. It was too hot, a cocksucker of a summer. Donnie and Kayla spent the whole day in the apartment, except for when he wheeled her to Walgreens for talcum powder, because she had a heat rash between her chin folds and under her diaper.

Near dinnertime, the phone rang. Kayla was on the floor with the cereal box and her yellow chicken, and the TV was on, muted. Donnie was lying on the couch in a mellow state, neither awake nor asleep. He was aware of Kayla's movements and chatter, and of the sweat on his back, and also of a staircase with gold balustrades that he knew didn't exist and yet was ascending nonetheless, with a real excitement about what he'd find at the top.

He was halfway across the room to answer the phone, pulling his damp shirt off his back, when he realized with grief that the staircase had disappeared, like a bubble pricked, and with it, whatever had been waiting for him. "What?" he said to Kayla, who was watching his travels into the kitchen area with delighted fascination.

"What?" he said into the phone. The man who answered wasn't Caleb. He wasn't Hobart R. Billings, Esq., although Donnie had called the Cheyenne number in the back of the book and had been waiting for a response.

"It's me." Don again. They'd talked this morning already.

Donnie leaned onto the kitchen counter and picked up the bag of frosted animal cookies, pink and white, with multicolored sprinkles that stained Kayla's lips when she gummed them, and he remembered his plan to put them in her crib, but what if she choked? He couldn't leave in the evening, after Marci came home, because Marci would say, "Don't go out, don't even go to the store, I just got here. I'm so tired, and the heat of the dryers, you wouldn't believe, it's destroying my skin, look at my hands, no, touch them."

"So you listened to me for once," Don said. "The kids'll be gone Sunday. You come any day next week and sit down and talk with him. Or just call him on the telephone."

Donnie reminded his dad about the lawyer's questions. How did Caleb buy the ranch? Who's funding him, and why? He reminded his dad what Caleb had said in the Motherlode. "You're not being respected," Donnie said, and he pushed Marci's Minnie Mouse collector cup into the sink. It was plastic and couldn't break, but still he heard Kayla, just a piece of fluff, crying like she understood sorrow.

"I have a job here," his dad said.

"A shit job."

"Caleb tries to be decent."

What could Donnie say to a man like that? A man who didn't stand up for himself, even with all the evidence Donnie had presented, who'd lived out his days since his wife died without even fucking another woman, living alone up there with Caleb so as to stay in the exact spot where he was raised up, like a dying tree.

Well, Donnie *could* say, "And you're his bitch." But wasn't Donnie becoming Caleb's bitch, too? Waiting all day for a polite phone call. Waiting for the kids to leave. What could Donnie do to Caleb once the kids left? Wasn't he falling inward, falling into the small shape of his father?

Early the next morning, he drove north toward the New Mexico border, toward Four Corners, where his mom once took a picture of him in a cowboy hat, sitting in four states at once, as all around him, at each point on a compass, Indians on blankets sold tin rings. He wasn't alone, but the windows were open, so he could barely hear Kayla cry, and when he did, he handed to the back seat a frosted cookie in the shape of a bloated mammal, a dead sheep in the ditch, and told her sweetly to shut up because he was bringing her home.

THE REAGAN YEARS: EARLY OCTOBER 1982

A SIGN AHEAD: ESCADOM. ELEVATION: 5,798. POPULATION: 702.

Caleb took the turnoff, driving across a river and into a wide valley like a salad bowl. He was twenty-four, with a stack of traveler's checks, thanks to Peter Finkel, and he'd been driving the small highways for three weeks, surveying the most remote towns of Wyoming, Utah, and the Front Range, but nothing he'd seen was right for his camp.

The road into Escadom hardly seemed to be heading into a town at all. Caleb passed arrow rows of arthritic fruit trees, two gray spotted horses in a field. A single-story school boasted a towering marquee that said ARCO COAL PROUDLY SUPPORTS THE ESCADOM HIGH CONQUISTADORS. It was a Friday afternoon in early fall, but there were no students milling. Beyond the school was another field and then a Mormon church and, finally, two blocks of narrow houses, but still no people, no toddlers in the small yards, no old men in lawn chairs.

As he crossed into a two-block downtown, he heard the screech of a megaphone and saw a rivulet of people heading the same direction along the sidewalk. The street was lined with pickups and horse trailers, improbably crowded after so much emptiness. Nowhere to park. He circled back to the residential block and stopped under a globe willow. From here, he could see all of the commercial strip—a row of short buildings on either side of the wide street, cut off by a cliff, from which a white cross loomed benevolently.

Caleb ran to catch up with everyone, feeling charged, expectant, like a child heading to a fair. He followed a couple who held hands but didn't speak to each other. The man wore a flannel shirt tight over his potbelly, and the woman sported a shellacked fountain of hair and magnificently long pink nails, and still Caleb couldn't help but see them—see everyone here—as sharing his passion for the wilderness. Despite the bumper stickers on their pickups saying PLEASE GIVE ME ANOTHER OIL SHALE BOOM AND I PROMISE NOT TO PISS IT AWAY THIS TIME! and I LOVE SPOTTED OWLS . . . FRIED and ON THE 8TH DAY GOD MADE RANCHERS TO CARE FOR HIS OTHER CREATIONS. Despite his knowledge, hard-gained in lectures and discussion sections, that ranchers and miners debased the land.

He walked behind the couple as they passed a stationer shop with a sign in its window—CLOSED INDEFINITELY. THANKS EXXON!—a post office, a restaurant optimistically called the Motherlode, a taxidermist. And then town ended, and he followed them across the train tracks, which the couple navigated in perfect synchronicity. Here, they came to a fenced-in area abutting the cliff. It had floodlights on poles at each corner, like a prison yard, although there was a sign insisting it was, instead, the Escadom Rodeo Grounds. The crowd funneled single file through chicken-wire gates, and Caleb trailed after.

He heard the yowl of a PA system and a voice, the words running forward: "*Wel*cometothefirstever*busted*r*usted*town*destroyed* auction, *every*thingforsale. Howitworksis *I*sayaprice, *you*holdupyourcard. *Sim*pleasthat."

Finally, Caleb understood. Over the past few weeks, he'd seen the breathless front-page headlines in the *Idaho Statesman* and the *Denver Post*: WE WOKE TO A NIGHTMARE and ROCKY MOUNTAIN HELL. The story, as he'd pieced it together, was that mighty Exxon had vowed to wring oil from the black shale beneath the western spread of the Rockies. And for two years, thousands came seeking jobs, creating commerce where there'd been nothing—hotels and bars and restaurants blooming like rare desert flowers, men camping in swarms along riverbanks, families living out of cars. Old people were kicked out of their trailer parks to make room for a shining new city to be built. Money, always so elusive, became comical in its near plenitude. Why not accrue a little debt and buy and buy and buy? And then, a few weeks ago, Exxon had changed its mind with, as one journalist put it, "the abruptness of a teenage driver making a screeching U-turn." Overnight, ten thousand became unemployed.

Caleb felt solemn to be so near these people, to brush up against their disaster, to examine the tables with their mammy cookie jars, Mixmasters, towers of plates, a congregation of teacups, buckets of wrenches, earrings, scissors, Bible figurines, piles of faded linens. Larger objects waited together on the ground: blank-faced TVs, basins with bloody rust stains, crayon-colored farm equipment, everything tagged with a black number on a yellow circle. The bleachers at the end of the lot were full, families settling down on pillows, lunches emerging from tinfoil. Only a handful of arms—arms, he figured, that lived in wealthier towns, in the ski towns and Front Range cities unaffected by the bust—raised to bid, and they bid on everything.

He found a place to stand beside the bleachers, with the eyelinered teenagers and the smell of cotton candy and beer. Next to him, a mother bounced a baby. A girl passed him a collection can covered in blue construction paper with Magic Markered writing. As he shoved twenty-seven dollars of Peter Finkel's money inside to HELP THE FAMILIES WITH BABIES WHO HAVE NOWHERE TO GO, he felt someone staring at him. He glanced over long enough to take in the angry stupor of three teenage boys against the fence, before returning his gaze to the auctioneer, a short man in a blue polo shirt tie-dyed with sweat.

A few minutes later, he twisted his head, and, of course, they were still on him. He turned away. He turned back. The boy on the right had long blond hair and a shirt with cutoff sleeves that said I'M OILFIELD TRASH AND GODDAMN PROUD OF IT. The boy on the left had sickly skin, a white tank top, and a dark mullet.

But the one in the middle, the one who stared most deliberately and most furiously at Caleb, was dressed in full cowboy—low hat, jeans, boots, and a fuck-the-heat blue denim shirt—an outfit that was all cliché; Caleb *knew* this. He was simply the person Caleb had wanted to be for his whole life.

Caleb turned away.

He took inventory of himself as they saw him: his North Face Rockhopper shorts and World Wildlife Federation panda T-shirt. He felt an idiotic desire to explain that, despite his looks and ancestry, he wasn't in the least bit Jewish.

Caleb glanced nonchalantly while stretching his arms to the sky. The cowboy's face was disgusted.

Caleb had survived high school; he knew the treachery of teenage boys. He forced himself not to look anymore, although he could hear whispering. He considered leaving but imagined them following him through the unpopulated streets. The auctioneer was relentless in his enthusiasm— "Sevensetsof*heir*loomqualitycandlesticks! *Per*fectforyourmantelpiece!" There was straw on the ground, an undersmell of manure.

Out of desperation, Caleb turned to face the teenagers. He gave a little wave and stepped toward them, saying, "Hey!" He told them his name, and then a lie just glided right out of him.

"I'm a journalist," he said, borrowing his uncle's trade, in which privileged people could eavesdrop and snoop without recrimination. He smiled nervously at his audacity.

The blond and the mulleted one began jabbing the cowboy, looking genuinely happy for him, as if he'd been chosen to step forward in a TV game show. "Told you." "That's what I said." "No, Craig, *I* said."

"Donnie here's been wanting to talk to a reporter."

"Who for?" asked the cowboy, jerking his chin with a practiced arrogance. Up close, he looked even more cinematically Western, with his heavily browed eyes, an angular, canine jaw, the squint of a telegenic young man looking out over the canyon. "*Trib? Post?*"

"*Our Side Now*," Caleb said, knowing they wouldn't have heard of it.

"Never heard of it." The cowboy frowned, as if this proved it didn't exist. And then he lit up. "You want a story? I got a story. Shit, I got a story that'll blow your mind."

"A story?" Caleb said, relieved. "Yeah, I want a story."

Sure, he worried where they were headed as Donnie maneuvered him out of the auction with a hand around Caleb's upper arm, but he was charged, too. He wanted to see whatever this boy would show him.

"Where's your ride?" Donnie said when they were standing on Founders Avenue, Escadom's main street. "You need to follow me."

Caleb followed Donnie's truck as it crawled out of town, winding along the river, the fading call of the auctioneer coming through the Honda's open window. They passed a few farms or ranches, fences, horses, rows of crops, waving arcs of irrigation sprinklers. Caleb followed Donnie as he zagged upward into what seemed like a canyon, the elephant toes of the mesa. Finally, they crested the cliff, and here was another world, hidden from the valley below. Brown earth like he'd never seen before, cracked and lunar, stubbled with grasses and sagebrush. Beyond this, the mountain.

They drove alongside a canal and underneath a wooden archway with a swinging sign—THE DOUBLE L—stopping beside a shy white house, its back to the road, its front door and porch facing the mountain. There was a barn, the wooden fence of a corral. Nothing else for miles. Caleb stepped out with a buoyant thrumming beneath his sternum. He walked toward Donnie, who was climbing the stairs to the house, and the tall, dried grasses stabbed his legs. It made him unable to swallow, how perfect it all was.

He trailed Donnie into the kitchen, where Donnie leaned against the sink and said, "I already have the beginning of your article. It goes like this . . ."

ELEVEN

Heat Wave

WHAT WAS THE MATHEMATICAL term to describe the shape of Escadom Mountain viewed at dawn from Rebecca's platform? Sine, cosine, one of those waves. Not tangent—she remembered that much. I remember it tangentially, she thought. It is tangential to my purpose here.

And what was her purpose here? Last night, after her girls had fallen asleep, she'd made herself come twice, urgently, with her eyes closed. This morning, as the first light manifested a difference between sky and mountain, her hand slipped back in her underwear before she was fully awake. She began rubbing lazily, eyes focusing on the deep-blue outline of the mountain.

Whatever the term, its shape was erotic, she thought, attempting use of a word that had always unnerved and embarrassed her, much like the word "occult." Against her wishes, she thought of the inscrutable exterior of Erotic Books. She'd been sure to look assiduously away whenever her parents drove her down Pico, so she never saw the clientele, although she'd imagined them. Even a girl without a TV knew what the clientele of Erotic Books was supposed to look like, the facial hair indicating furtive and unsatisfied desires.

Her parents visited bookstores that other parents didn't. Georgia periodically brought Rebecca with her to Sisterhood Bookstore, and Ira to

Midnight Special, and she would worry that someone from school might see her and assume these strange stores were a type of Erotic Books and her parents perverts, a worry that wasn't assuaged with the paintings of vulvas in the feminist store, although the Marxist bookstore was reassuringly sexless.

Returning her thoughts to the mountain, she considered that it was the shape of the swell she was currently chasing. *My purpose here: rise, apex, downward float.* Maybe this was why everyone liked mountains so much. They were the physical manifestations of fucking. "Fucking," as a verb, was another new word. Her parents used "fucking" exclusively as an adjective—the fucking president; the fucking idiots. Or, on further consideration, as a middle name—Jesus Fucking *Christ*!

There was sweat on her forehead, thighs, belly, hand. For two days, a hot wind had been whipping across the plateau as if blown from a hair dryer. She'd never felt anything like this in sunny California, where the ocean tempered all temperatures, so that the prevailing element was always water. Here, it felt like the brittle ground was about to burst into flames. All her girls had slept atop their sleeping bags; but she'd fallen asleep inside hers, so that her hand wouldn't be visible if anyone woke and looked over. Still, she couldn't stop the rhythmic *shh-shh-shh* of down-filled polyester.

She hadn't been able to meet David in the barn since Wednesday morning, when they'd had the experience she was currently reenacting with her own hand. Wednesday afternoon, he was on dinner duty. Yesterday, because of the heat, Caleb had sent everyone to the river all day. As they hiked back to camp, Tanaya approached Rebecca with surprising urgency and shyness. Her period had come suddenly, staining her bathing suit; she didn't want her friends to know. Rebecca snuck Tanaya inside the house, where they could wash her suit with forbidden running water in the upstairs bathroom. Leaving Tanaya hiding there, Rebecca rushed around to fetch a pad, clean clothes, Advil. It was pleasing to be needed in this way, especially by Tanaya, but it kept Rebecca busy until dinner. "I waited,"

David had whispered in her hair when he passed her table. "Tomorrow," she'd replied. Which would be today. Saturday, campers left early. Rebecca and the other counselors were expected to stick around for a week of cleanup, after which she'd take a bus from Grand Junction to Berkeley, where she'd sit behind a folding table in Sproul Plaza during orientation and invite the incoming class to join Students United for Justice.

Jenny L. sighed and rolled from her right shoulder to her left, her open mouth gaping inches from Rebecca. Rebecca stilled her hand until she was certain Jenny had fallen back asleep. Needing to hurry things along, Rebecca closed her eyes and set a scene in Samohi, a place where she'd always ignored David, and yet here they were in the windowless AV room in the basement of the English building. Broken overhead projectors like statuary. She was wearing a short red corduroy skirt that she didn't own. David's hand on her thigh, moving higher, pushing aside her underwear, David's mouth on hers, his finger rubbing, whispering, "Lie down, Zoomy." The floor was softened by hundreds of littered transparencies, their trig problems, World War II timelines, and diagrammed sentences never fully washing off. "Lie down," he ordered.

She finished just in time, opening her eyes as the sun broke over the mountain, lighting up the sage. Moments later, as if by force of sunlight, the wake-up bell rang.

Shauna sat right up, fully alert. "You guys, you *guys*. There's a mouse. I heard it."

The other girls squealed themselves awake. "Where? Where?"

"I couldn't sleep. I woke up so early and I heard it. This *noise*. Like it was in a sleeping bag." They all screamed, jumped off their mats, shook out their bags. Rebecca felt strangely unashamed, even as they gathered around her after determining the mouse wasn't in their beds. "Rebecca, shake yours out!" She obliged, and when nothing scurried away, she said, "Mice are nocturnal. It probably went off to sleep."

Later, as they walked through the sage toward the house, Tanaya again came up beside Rebecca and again grabbed her arm, making her stop until everyone passed.

"Aren't they attracted to blood?"

"Who?"

"Mice! What if they, because of my pad, what if they crawl on my . . . you know?"

As they walked together, Rebecca told Tanaya lies about rodents and their aversion to human blood. Reassured, Tanaya said she wanted to visit Rebecca in Berkeley, wanted to attend Berkeley herself when the time came, wanted Rebecca to promise she'd write, wanted Rebecca to come back and be her counselor next year. "Of course I will," Rebecca said. It was her last day, and she'd finally been adopted.

Tanaya insisted they sit together on the Meadow. When David showed up, Tanaya called out to him, patting the grass on the other side of her, not noticing the looks cast above her head as they all sang "On the Banks of the Ohio" and the hot wind blew and Rebecca felt herself nearly aflame with desire.

At breakfast, she crossed her legs and tightened her thigh muscles, putting pressure on her you-know. She rocked slightly back and forth on the bench and nearly lost it right there. She ran to the composting toilet stall outside the shower room, pulled the sheet closed, and finished in a minute, returning to the eating platform in a mood of blissful accomplishment, having climbed and descended Escadom Mountain before the others even finished their breakfast.

◆ ◆ ◆

IN PREPARATION FOR HIS son's arrival, Don left the ranch while the children were eating and drove to Ute's to buy Donnie's favorite cookies: Chips Ahoy. At least that had been true eight years ago. Who knew what he ate now? Marci knew, he hoped. He hoped Donnie had found that sort of comfort.

On his return, as Don pulled his car beside Denise's in front of their trailer, avoiding her potted mums, her statuettes of fairies, he saw her standing beside her car, reaching for him. The yellow sleeves of her blouse were rolled up, and her arms and hands were outstretched. Was this a truce? She hadn't spoken to him since yesterday, when he'd asked her to leave before Donnie arrived. But now she was holding out her arms to him as he stepped out of his car.

Denise had thought it stupid not to come clean. "Honey, we're fifty-five years old. Your son is twenty-six. Your wife's been dead for seventeen years." But he'd said no.

She wasn't reaching for him. There was a coil of rope on the grass, and the end of that rope was in her hand, which she was throwing onto the roof rack, trying to get it to hook. She didn't even look up at him. "Dini," he said, coming up beside her. "Dini, will you say something?"

"Pretty day." That's what she said, although it was hot as hellfire. "Great day for a drive."

The thing was, Don had been only thirty-eight when Pammy had died. Donnie had assumed that was elderly, that his dad's life was over. But it wasn't. He did fall in love again, and he could never tell Donnie. He was too volatile. What would he do? The boy grew up too much like Pammy, too impatient, always thinking the future held great mystery and potential. Don knew better.

The real thing was, Don had actually met Denise before Pammy died. Before Pammy even got sick. By "met," he meant he'd met her at the DMV in Delta, and then he met her for lunch, and then he met her at the Sleep Tite Motel.

After Pammy died, Don could be with Denise without committing sin. But it felt sickening. You shouldn't get what you want because your son has lost his mother. He kept Denise hidden from Donnie. The guilt ran through his life like a lode of coal in the mountain.

Denise and Don were practically the same person, and there was comfort in that, if a small amount of boredom. But they liked boredom fine. They liked mornings and evenings, and if that wasn't repetitive, wasn't boring, then Don didn't know what was. Donnie probably had never noticed a morning in his life.

He'd asked Donnie not to come. If Donnie managed to shut down the camp, as he believed he could, what job would Don get then? Where would he and Denise live? But when Donnie insisted, Don had told Denise to leave. Only for the duration of Donnie's visit, a day or two at most, but she'd packed everything. He'd told Charlene and the others not to mention Denise to Donnie.

"You'll call me when you get there?" he shouted now. She was going to her sister's in Casper. She opened the passenger door and climbed onto the car to thread the rope, humming. *She'll be coming 'round the mountain.* Why that?

"You'll call me?" he repeated.

She never said anything more. He went inside and came out with a glass of water as she filled the back seat with trash bags of her clothes and sheets, everything soft of hers. What a smart woman, he thought. If he were the one being kicked out, he wouldn't speak either. She drank the water, handing the glass to him and wiping her chin with the back of her hand as always, but she never said a word before driving away.

When he could no longer see her car and its cloud of dirt, Don brought the groceries inside and arranged the cookies on a plate. Donnie had said lunchtime, but who knew—maybe he'd come early. Maybe he'd grown into the type of man who came early. Don pressed his forehead against the diamond-shaped window on the front door. He stood there, sunlight washing over his face, and he waited.

◆ ◆ ◆

AT LUNCH, ERIKA SAID, "I carved a walking stick."

Micah said, "That's nothing. I can do five silkscreens."

Trina said, "Did you hear that Caitlin quit *Fiddler*?"

"Why's it so hot, Caleb?" asked Patrick.

Trina said, "The whole production's in jeopardy."

Micah pointed. "Who's that?"

A woman was walking from the parking lot. Caleb knew her immediately, although her bramble of hair had straightened. Her jeans were tight, then flaring. Her tunic, clean and white. She'd become someone else, as boring as soap.

"Who's that?" Micah repeated.

Caleb was suddenly mortified about all the years of willing her to reappear or disappear. Not to die, exactly, but never to have existed, for her body not to move about the world unknown to him. Yet now, he was sure that if he were to glance away, he wouldn't see her. If he held up his hand, she would vanish.

"That's just Suze," Caleb told Micah as she came to a stop at the edge of the cement platform.

By then, everyone in the camp had noticed, and a few people had left each table to run toward her. Suze threw her head back. "Do you know me? Do you know me?"

Teenagers who had been children, girls who had elongated into elks or pillowed out in oversized shirts, flocked to her.

"No way. You're not really Lindsay," Suze said. "You must be Lindsay's older sister."

It seemed crucial that the campers clear their tables the proper way. "Scrapers, passers, table cleaners, dishwashers," Caleb called out. "We need you guys. It's time." He was surprised by his own firm voice.

Slowly, they returned to the tables. Mikala had linked arms with Suze, but Suze broke away, pushing her sunglasses to her head, staring at Caleb. She came toward him, and he knew that this was still Suze. Suze of yellow. The letter *S*. He figured out how to free himself from the table. Once he had his hands on the small of her back, it was clear to him that it didn't matter if, from a distance, you could blot her out with your palm. She was familiar, the way autumn, when it comes again, looks familiar, and you can't remember what year it is, how old you are.

He wouldn't say, "I missed you." He'd been the one who stayed. "Suze," was all he said.

She pulled back. "I can't believe I'm here. I'm pinching myself. Is it real? Are you real?"

"What are you doing here, Suze?"

She twisted around, looking for someone. "No way. Is that him? That giant? That *man*?" She released Caleb to wave with both hands. Soon, David approached, slouching sheepishly but grinning. Caleb had to stand there as she threw her arms around his neck, saying, "I literally cannot believe it."

When they'd disentangled, she turned back to Caleb, grabbing his wrist. "*He* invited me. And it was the craziest thing I ever heard. But at the same time, *freakily* coincidental. All summer I've been thinking about"—she made a wide sweep with her palm—"*this*. Having these dreams where I can see it, in the distance, but I can't reach it, and when I wake up, I miss it like a phantom limb. And then there's David on the phone, and what could I say? I said yes!"

"You called her?"

David shrugged, still smiling. While this fact slightly diminished Suze's volition and evoked an unusual jealousy—they spoke? how often?—what did those concerns really matter? She'd come for Caleb. That was clear. Her lost limb.

Mikala began tapping on Suze's shoulder—"Come see Scott"—and Suze allowed herself to be pulled away from him. As the campers cleared dishes, Caleb walked from the eating platform. He didn't know where he was headed, but when he reached the far wall of the barn, he stopped and leaned against it. Here, nobody could see him, except for Don, who was spending another day in his trailer. Apparently, Don really was sick.

Caleb pressed his fingers to the wall behind him. He was shaking. His whole body was shaking; his feet were numb.

If some campers had passed by, they might have thought Caleb was doing nothing—how rare, how strange—but Caleb was as busy as a woman in labor. He was terrified. He was creating hope out of microscopic materials, tiny as ova, wriggling sperm. Hope born so premature it clung to his body, and he must not put it down.

Soon he heard the clamor of the campers on the Meadow. They would talk until he arrived. They would talk all day, until he walked toward them, and then they would look up at him and quiet.

◆ ◆ ◆

SIT HERE, SUZE. SIT here. No, next to me. We saved you a seat. From among the crowd, David watched Suze stand at the edge, considering. Who would she choose? To have her back among them was like a myth sprung to life, Aphrodite gliding in on sea foam, Persephone and her pomegranate seeds. She picked her way past the littlest kids, settled cross-legged beside him.

"Tell me things," she said, grabbing David's arm. "How are you? I mean, actually, *who* are you now?"

"Me?"

"Yeah, you," she laughed, pushing him.

He couldn't answer, because the sudden cessation of noise told him that Caleb had appeared. He turned to find Caleb looking downward, as if composing himself, as he usually did before speaking to the group. When Caleb looked up, however, he was uncomposed.

In this heat, they should drink more water than they could stand, he said, grinning as if hydration were the most wonderful thing. If they walked on the ditch road, they'd see the milkweed blooming! Would a counselor volunteer to fill the cistern? Those involved in this evening's production of *Fiddler* had asked to skip swimming, but come on, everyone, it was the last day at the river. They could rehearse before dinner. No, Tanaya, it wasn't up for discussion. And now he'd like to welcome a visitor. "Suze. Suze Guenther. Used to be a counselor here awhile ago. Stand up, Suze."

Giggling a little, as if enjoying the attention, she tiptoed around kids to join Caleb. He wrapped his right arm around her.

"How long has it been, Suze?" Caleb asked, cinching her toward him. "Five years ago since we last saw you? We're so glad you came back."

She tilted her head. Her hair fell against his chest, and Caleb beamed. David couldn't believe he'd pulled off this reunion. A fitting end to the summer.

He had, over the last few days, established a clear picture of how Caleb was going to talk to him this evening. It would be at the Gathering, after "Rocky Mountain High," when the campers hugged and wept and wrote phone numbers on hands, promising to write and visit and call. Caleb would find David, lead him aside to where no campers were standing. *You brought Suze here?* Caleb might say. *I already knew I wanted you to move here, but really, you brought Suze back? I can't thank you enough.* David realized he was imagining Caleb crouched on one knee, as if proposing. He made the Caleb in his mind stand up.

He didn't notice the man approaching until everyone on the Meadow had turned to look. He held a book in his hand, wore a baseball cap that said AMMICO. Jeans. Work boots. A white T-shirt with faded writing. Someone from the gas company, or maybe the husband of a laundry lady, bringing her lunch.

◆ ◆ ◆

CALEB WATCHED AN AIRPLANE move across the sky as laggardly as an ant along a blue plate. The world had slowed. A drop of sweat would take a day to fall from his forehead to the grass. At this rate, Donnie, who was walking toward Caleb and Suze, wouldn't reach them for a month. It would be cooler by then, and the kids would be gone.

He could hear Suze whispering. "Is that . . . ?"

In a way it wasn't strange at all to have them both back. "Here we all are," he wanted to shout. They were often here in his mind anyway, the two of them: his friend and lover, watching him as his camp grew.

"Should I do something?" she asked.

He kept his arm draped around her. Nothing would happen if he didn't say anything.

Or maybe it would. Donnie was a few feet from them. He carried a book in one hand.

Suze slipped out from under Caleb's arm and took Donnie's free hand in both of hers, saying loudly, "Donnie! Wow, *so* great to see you again. Here, let me show you around." She had this euphoric look about her, this gushing tone. She'd always risen to any occasion.

"You? You're still here?" Donnie smirked. "I didn't think you'd last."

She was undeterred. "It's amazing to see you again. You look fantastic. Let's catch up in the house. Jesus, it's hot out here." She spoke with the same enthusiasm with which she'd greeted Caleb.

Caleb glanced over at his camp. Those spaced-out faces in their post-prandial daze. The beauty of their open mouths, the sweat on their foreheads. Their hands brushing away mosquitoes. How could Donnie say anything that would take this from him? Caleb was part of no grand conspiracy. He'd built this. His every gesture had become a ritual.

Snapping out of his own daze, he said, "Hold up, Suze. Let go of him. You had something you wanted to say, Donnie? It's fine. We're here to listen." With a hand pressed against Suze's back, he led her toward the kids, relinquishing the limelight to Donnie.

"Are you sure about this?" Suze asked as they squeezed in with the front row of kids, facing Donnie. Caleb hid his own terror, but of course he felt it. He'd neatly tied the noose around his own neck. A car skidding off the road, and there was nothing for him to do.

"I've come here to tell you . . ." Donnie began so quietly he was barely audible. He shook his head abruptly to the right and then the left as if clearing it. "All this you see today . . ." Another head shake. "It's time everyone knows the truth, and not the lies . . ."

Come on, Caleb thought. Come on. Get to it already. He wanted to be back up there, contradicting whatever Donnie had to say.

"I've come here to tell you that all the lies you heard were lies, not truth," Donnie continued. "And this land, he's a thief. He's the one who stole this from me after he and the other . . . Okay, wait, I have to start earlier." Donnie looked around unhappily, as if being forced to give a class presentation.

Eight years had altered his face. Still chiseled and wolfish, but something had changed. Caleb couldn't put his finger on it.

Donnie twitched his head again. "I need to start . . . okay, back up to here. I need to start with Exxon and how we had this good thing going and everyone was making it, until they came and they shut it down. See, there's a custom and a culture . . ."

The real change, Caleb realized, was Donnie's demeanor. That arrogance had vanished. He stood with his head shoved forward, his gaze on the grass. The hand without the book fidgeted in the pocket of his jeans like a mouse in a bag. His voice was barely above a whisper. He had no idea how to do this, to address a crowd.

Caleb could feel an energetic hum start up behind him, and he knew that the campers' attention was spent, that they'd started poking each other; picking noses; twisting the stalks of what the boys had named "darthweed" into a loop that sent its seed pods flying; tugging on the arms of their counselors; saying they really needed to pee.

Someone tapped Caleb's back, and he turned around. "What's he even sa-ying?" Shauna's trademark whine. "I can't understa-and."

"Shh." Caleb turned back to see Donnie pull his hand from his pocket and hold it in front of himself, as if he wanted to keep an eye on it. It was trembling. The hand with the book kept hitting against his thigh.

"A custom and a culture. And the custom and culture of the West is the people who grow things here, who grow oil shale and cows and not treat it like Disney World for the rich tourists."

The throttle of the dishwashers started up inside the kitchen. Nat and Caitlin arrived from the infirmary teepee, waving at everyone. "What'd I miss?" Nat said loudly. "Is it the guy from the Forest Service for the fire safety talk?"

"I can't hear what he's saying," someone shouted.

"Me either."

"And then," Donnie continued, mumbling the crucial nouns, "when . . . took away our livelihood . . . That's when . . . shows up and pretends he's a journalist. So the very foundation, the bottom of . . . is built on a lie. He was in on it from the start."

Caleb stood. He could feel the campers turn to him.

Donnie ignored him. "But I learned from him." He held up the booklet, its cover a waving flag with TAKING BACK OUR LAND in gold foil. Caleb couldn't see the author's name, but certainly this was Hobart R. Billings, Esq. "That if you buy something under false pretenses, it's considered a fraud—fraudulent—by the United States of America, and you can get any lawyer—any lawyer—to back you up and get your land back."

Caleb stepped toward him. "Really nice of you to come by and talk to us. We need to let the kids go up now."

"Wait, I'm not . . ." Donnie drew himself up so that he was tall and focused, and he said, clearly and slowly, keeping his gaze on Caleb, "Motherfucker. Motherfucker. Mother*fucker*." The arm holding the book was raised in the air, and he punched his hand and the booklet forward with each "fucker."

"Okay, okay. We hear you," Caleb said, in a tone that implied they were all joking. "Let's rein in the language."

Now the kids were quiet and curious. Jeremy leapt up and then Jamal, the two of them standing among the kids like quivers in a bow, ready to be manly and protective.

"It's okay," Caleb said. "He's leaving. He's said his piece and he's leaving."

But Donnie didn't leave. "You don't get to steal this and get away with it." He spoke more audibly now that he was turned from the audience and addressing Caleb directly.

Caleb felt the pump of his own frightened heart. He wasn't sure how to intervene. And then, he didn't need to. A baby was crying.

The sound was as unusual on this high desert as the howl of a wolf. Don, walking toward them, held the source, a small thing in a pink sleeper. His hands were crossed around her belly, and she was trying to fly from his chest, to leap from his restraint. Her legs were pedaling, her arms were thrust forward, her face a red scream.

"She doesn't know me yet," Don said over the noise. "She was wanting you."

In a moment that seemed too fast for a bodily transfer, she was in Donnie's arms, his shirt in her fists, her forehead bumping over and over against his shoulder.

"I couldn't get her to nap," Don said. "She cried if I set her down. Worse if I picked her up."

Donnie frowned down at the baby, as if wanting to put her somewhere. Instead, he jostled a bit, and she quieted. Still heaving, she turned to look solemnly at Caleb. Sweat pressed her yellow hair against her scalp. Caleb was struck by the confidence of Donnie's hands on her, and also of the child's grip on her dad, the complete exclusionary embrace.

"Come," Don said. "You and Caleb can talk later."

"She's hungry," Donnie said accusingly to Caleb, as if *he* had been withholding her nourishment, and then Donnie walked the baby around the crowd, past the barn. Don followed a few paces behind.

Caleb watched them go. The baby had robbed something from him. The baby had thwarted Caleb's chance to put Donnie in his place, to restore reason and logic, to explain that there were no lies, just time moving on, cultures changing, legal transfers of land. Caleb clenched his hands, his adrenaline soaring with no outlet. He still felt like he was about to lose something.

He looked at Suze, who sat watching him expectantly, her arms around her legs like a young girl. She was still here. Caleb wouldn't think of Donnie anymore. Donnie was gone. He wouldn't think of Donnie for the rest of this day so that he could focus on Suze. With that decision made, he began to speak to his camp in his gentle way, thinking, as he often did when he made speeches, of Suze listening. And she really was.

He began by saying thank you to the campers. "Thanks for sitting quietly and listening to that man with me. Thank you." He decided not to refute anything Donnie had said or mention him by name. They could all wonder: That guy, the one with the trembling hands and the baby, what was he talking about?

"Sometimes, some people, they just need to be listened to," he said. "So many people in the world are never listened to. I'm sure you've had that feeling once in a while. You're trying to get your mom's attention, but there's your little brother, and she's only looking at him. Well, some people, these people, they feel like that all the time. They feel like nobody ever hears them. You know the people I'm talking about. You pass them on park benches on your way to the playground. You see them at bus stops. And mostly, we don't listen. We go about our day. We're in a hurry. But it's different at Llamalo, isn't it?" He paused. He was still shaking, his whole body like an aspen leaf, but he wouldn't let on. He was the incantor, the reciter, and he crouched down so that they couldn't see him shake.

"We're not hurrying here. We have time to let someone talk to us. Time to listen. Even if we don't really understand what he's saying." There was a scattering of laughter. "Even if it's the very middle of the hottest day of summer." More laughter. "And when we do that—when *you* do that—when you listen to someone who needs it so badly, it's a gift. A real gift. You should feel proud of yourselves today. Okay? Alright. Everyone's exhausted. It couldn't be hotter if it tried. Go on all of you. Get some rest. I'll see you at the river."

◆ ◆ ◆

THERE WAS A BURBLE of excitement among the counselors crowded around the pigeonholes on the side of the barn. *Weird. Who was he? Maybe Don and Denise's kid? Did you see how scared he looked? I'm sorry, I thought it was kinda . . . I know, me too . . . Funny? But that baby, she had lungs.* And then their attention drifted down to the mail they were shuffling through acquisitively. Kai held up an envelope sent by her boyfriend back in Santa Cruz so that everyone could see the gnar-gnar surfers he'd drawn. Jamal owed fines on six books at his college's sci-li. The encroachments of another life.

Rebecca had her own distraction. From the barn, there was no way to reach the footbridge without passing David. And David was talking to Caleb and Suze.

Suze was clearly a calamity, the type of woman whose very presence reminded everyone of the standard of desire. When she'd appeared at lunch, Rebecca had almost heard a collective sigh on the mesa: Oh, right, *right.* Beauty! Her symmetry exposed asymmetry around her. Beside her, Rebecca would be revealed as simply wrong. Why this oversized ANC shirt, and what dribble had formed its brown stain? What were these large flowered jean shorts with the pleats bagging out? Why were her hairy legs so hairy? Had she really thought anyone would find that seductive?

As if it might make her unnoticeable, she looked away from the threesome as she passed by, but this caused her to stumble on the threshold of the bridge, clutching on to her passel of mail and thumping heavily onto the wooden boards, which attracted their attention anyway. Caleb called, "Hey, Rebecca, come on over here! Have you met Suze?"

It was awful to have to stand so close to her and invite the inevitable comparisons, but Rebecca took the hand outstretched to her. Cool, small. She saw Suze's eyes twitch up and down her body, wondering, clearly, why Caleb had singled her out for introductions. The men gazed like idiots at Suze. Even Rebecca couldn't turn away from her.

"Rebecca's my cousin. First time here this summer."

A look of comprehension passed over Suze, and she released Rebecca's hand to hit her excitedly on the arm. "Serious?" She squinted. "I can't really see the resemblance. I mean, there's the Jewish thing."

There was that. She had all of Caleb's nose, none of his charm.

"She looks a lot like my dad, actually."

"So wait, that means, your dad's brother's kid," Suze said to Caleb, her eyes narrowing with recall. Turning to Rebecca, she said, "The radical newspaper, right? What was his name? Ivan?" She appraised Rebecca with a wrinkle between her eyes. Rebecca could feel the appeal of being the recipient of Suze's skittish enthusiasm; already, she wanted more.

"Can't believe you remember that," Caleb said with a proud smile, as if he'd been paid a compliment. Rebecca had never before seen him so obviously trying to please.

"Ira, actually," Rebecca said, but nobody looked at her.

"I'm an elephant. I can't forget anything. I still know the phone number of my best friend in seventh grade. Five two oh, one three one five. And her sister's birthday is April tenth. It's a morass of unimportant details up here." Suze affected one of those ugly expressions that, in pretty people, only serve to emphasize their inability to actually embody ugliness.

"The combination to my high school locker? Thirty-six, twenty-four, thirty-eight," she continued, further cheapening the significance of her ability to remember Caleb's family.

Mikala ran up to the group, her face blotchy with sun rash. "Who *was* that guy? He looked familiar."

Rebecca saw Caleb and Suze exchange a look. "God, absolutely nobody," Suze said. "Mikala! You're so gorgeous. Let me spend rest hour with you." Turning to David, she reached tenderly for his arm, a public ease with him that Rebecca wouldn't dare, and she felt the inner yelp of possession. "I want to know everything about you. Promise you'll tell me later?" Suze said, releasing David and grabbing Mikala's arm to run across the bridge in a girlish flaunt of best-friendhood.

"You should go up, too," Caleb said, turning to Rebecca and David with sudden impatience, as if they'd been dawdling, shirking.

Rebecca walked briskly ahead.

"Rebecca?" David said when they'd crossed the bridge.

"Can't talk here."

He came up beside her. "I'm pretty sure it's still legal for me to greet you."

"So, Suze. What's her deal anyway?"

"You'll love her. She's . . . uh, extraordinary, actually. As in not ordinary. I can't even explain."

The inexplicable was beauty, blondeness, an economy of flesh, a perkiness of breasts, a lack of "the Jewish thing." But she wouldn't teach David that. What she'd thought was sexy had been foolish. She walked faster. "Wow. High praise."

"Hey, are you mad at me or something?"

She wanted his weight on her again. No, that wasn't true. She wanted him pressed against the straw this time. *Lie down, David.* She wanted one leg on either side of him, to be atop him. "Mad at you? Who's mad?" She was surprised to find these words came out in precisely the same defensively embittered tone Georgia used with Ira. "I just need to be alone."

"Is it something I said?"

"No."

"Something I did?"

"I said it's nothing."

"Because if it's about that time, the barn, would you just tell me?"

They reached the Y in the path: girls' platforms to the right, boys' to the left. She stopped. "It's not about the barn."

"Well, that's a relief. Because I was kind of really wanting to go back there this afternoon." He reached out and dragged one finger down the length of her arm. "Maybe you could finally tell me all the news from *Our Side Now*. What *is* the cover story this week?"

"I'll see if I can catch you up." The word "catch" was suddenly suggestive.

Once she reached her platform, Rebecca distributed letters to the lucky girls, curled on mats like puppies. In a haze of happiness, she lay down on her own, reaching over the side to dredge the newspaper from her backpack, an act that seemed nearly sexual, continuing a joking foreplay with David. Since she'd carried it with her for weeks, the paper had acquired the softness of an already-read paper. It occurred to her that her parents had sent her only this one issue and then stopped, as if they'd known she wouldn't read it. As if they'd known she'd just lie here and think of David.

She opened to the Publisher's Note, which was, to be honest, the only part of the paper she consistently read. Scratched off in the hours before the paper went to press, it was chatty, a close approximation of her father actually talking to her.

Dear Friends,

How many of you have been with *Our Side Now* since 1971? Nineteen years ago, when we wrote the first issue, our daughter was a newborn; now, she's just finished her first year of college. *Our Side Now* is heading out of adolescence.

For the first decade or so as editor and publisher, I felt, and I may have been entitled to feel, vaguely self-congratulatory, attributing to the efforts of this newspaper a faint but palpable upswing in activism. Our readers wrote to thank us for alerting them to threats from privatization and unchecked capitalism. You asked for more articles about the gradual—and not so gradual—demolition of public education, health care, affordable transportation, public lands, immigrant rights, and decent wages for all. My assumption was simple: Devote enough column inches to the topic, and justice would come.

Today that strikes me as a particularly narcissistic delusion. Look around. Eight years of articles about Reagan led only to the election of Bush, who now threatens war against Iraq. The legacy of civil rights is starvation in South Central. We still pat ourselves on the back for ending the war in Vietnam, and yet we do nothing about the sickening accumulation of nuclear warheads, about an economy dependent on appalling gaps between rich and poor. We speak, but nothing happens.

My friends, we have done something wrong.

In an attempt to stop pretending that I'm having any impact on the horrors of our world, I'm shutting down *Our Side Now*. This will be the last issue you receive.

Ira

She was surprised at the stillness around her. All her childhood she'd known cataclysm was approaching—the blast of a nuclear bomb or at least the inevitable LA earthquake, her pink stucco house crumbling, the palm tree falling. It turned out, her world would end with the faint rustle of newspaper. She wanted more than anything to go back to the moment before she'd read the letter.

Tanaya draped her arm off her mattress and let *The Baby-Sitter's Club* #5,000 drop on the wooden floor. "I'm bored. Read to us, Rebecca."

"Read to us, read to us," Rebecca's girls began chanting. She'd been reading to them about Ishi, who was currently midway on his long trek from prehistory to modernity.

"No. I can't today."

"But you always read to us. We're bo-red. We're bo-red."

Their complaint was so naïve. Boredom? Rebecca closed her eyes and thought, Well, this is what it feels like to be old.

◆ ◆ ◆

CALEB STOOD IN THE doorway of his yurt, surveying. The floor was covered with carpet samples the size of prayer rugs. Pale pink with green roses, mottled beige, gray vines with leaves like mold. Two by two, he carried them outside, slapping them against the edge of the wooden platform. They exhaled dust, but that wasn't enough.

He squatted and dug his fingers into the fur and frantically began to pull up hair, which resisted, just like pulling hair from a head, having enjoyed its second life in the scalp of the carpet. He raked out sunflower seeds and toenail clippings, mud, oats. He pulled and pulled, but he was still trembling. The aftershocks of Donnie's visit.

A whole series of questions lined up in his mind, awaiting his attention. Had Don in fact been sick, or had he known Donnie was coming? Did Don bring the baby to stop Donnie, or was the baby in serious distress? Did Don believe that Caleb had been in the Motherlode calling Don a redneck, or did he remember that Caleb had been, at the time, in the kitchen making an ass of himself—*Kiva! Keer!* In short, was Don still his friend?

But no. He wouldn't think of the Talcs. He pulled the blanket from his mattress, exposing a sheet stained from nights with Kai. He flipped the sheet upside down, smoothed the blanket over. He saw hope, which had been a newborn two hours ago, toddling around the shorn floor, clapping its fat hands. He thought, She'll sleep here tonight.

The reason Suze left all those years ago was such a small one. She didn't "feel it" anymore. This had never made sense to him. You couldn't love Llamalo, as she clearly did, and then turn off this love, grow numb to the place. And yet, apparently this had happened to her the summer of 1985.

After the kids left, Suze took a weekend kayak trip down the Green with a counselor named Steve. She called Caleb from the Denny's in Moab. She told him that she'd counted seventeen bald eagles and four great blue herons. She told him that she might not be into dedicating her whole life to austerity. She actually couldn't stand another winter in Escadom. She wanted to see other humans. Caleb had reminded her that there were indeed humans in Escadom. "Humans like me," she'd countered. "Humans who want to eat decent Mexican food. Humans I can be friends with." She was, she said, moving to Crested Butte with Steve.

Now she missed him like a phantom limb. Caleb shoved his laundry in a bag, tossed a novel on his bed. A mixtape was already in the player. Hope entered the preteen years, years of substitutions: boys instead of ponies, girls instead of comics, TV for parents, the real Suze for the remembered one.

TWELVE

·

Down by the Riverside

REBECCA'S CAMPERS OBSERVED ALL their usual rituals on the thirty-minute hike to the river. They cut through the Sorgers' fields, jumping over black irrigation tubes, screaming, "Snake, snake." They ran down the trail that Caleb had built on the steep slope of the cliff; the rumor was that this was the path Aemon had originally taken. They avoided the rottweiler belonging to the man who squatted in an abandoned miner's shack. They jumped the train tracks with a scream, as if a coal train were bearing down on them. They sang as Rebecca had taught them: *Ain't gonna study war no more. I ain't gonna study war no more. I ain't gonna stu-dy war no more, no more, no . . .*

At last, she ushered them to the black-eyed Susans, where Jamal stood with a clipboard, checking everyone in. Nat made room for her on a towel under the shade tarp that Caleb constructed each summer. She and Saskia were dissecting Suze, her disappearance and reappearance, the waning or waxing of her beauty. Rebecca stared at the tarp's undulating blue shadow. "You're quiet," Saskia said. "It's the heat."

"I'm *fine*." How could she tell them that disillusionment was her true inheritance, the very opposite of the buoyant idealism she'd pretended was passed down like an heirloom? Before today, at least, the despair had been tempered by a golden aura of self-importance: nobody will come to the rally, but still we go; nobody will cover the rally, so we write about it; nobody will publish our point of view, so we'll start a newspaper, which nobody will read but us. With his letter, Ira had shoved off self-importance, leaving only despair.

She stood dizzily, black planets floating across the scrim of her vision, and walked to the shore, where David sat, lifting a dead dragonfly from the water's surface.

"I have to talk to you."

David glanced up and then pointed at a snorkel drifting out of the eddy and into the current. "Watch this."

"Can you hurry?"

He made her wait until the snorkel pushed out of the water attached to a nine-year-old boy, who released his mouthpiece, gasped, and said, "Dr. Livingston, I presume."

"Hilarious, right? He's been doing this since I got here."

"I need to talk now."

"Tilden," David called. "I gotta go. Do your Dr. Livingston bit where Scott or someone can see you."

The boy bowed. "Dr. Livingston, I presume." He sank underwater.

◆ ◆ ◆

WHEN CALEB ARRIVED AT the river, he angled himself on his rock so he could see both water and shore, which is how he usually kept an eye on all the campers.

Today, even with an angled posture, Caleb didn't see most of what went on. He saw that two little girls seesawed the inner tube, but he didn't see a big-bellied girl swim up, saying, "I can get on, too." He didn't see the two tubing girls say to each other, "Do you smell something gross?"

He saw Mikala swim across the river to Scott's lifeguard rock so Scott could rub sunscreen on her back, and he thought, Oh, they're sleeping together, and found it interesting that he hadn't noticed earlier. He saw that there were an unfortunate but predictable number of townies fishing upstream. But he didn't see the two men in jeans and ARCO caps, lying on their stomachs under the tamarisk, hands around warming beers.

He saw that some campers were gathered in a coven, and in the middle were the three witches: Nicole, Shauna, Tanaya. He didn't see that they were conducting interviews to compete for the role of David's wife and that the interviewees had to answer six questions, three of which were embarrassing, and then were either told to stay or leave.

He didn't see Rebecca and David walking together downstream.

He didn't see that one of the girls on the inner tube bounced on the valve and it pierced her skin. He didn't see the eleven-year-olds jabbing one another's arms with fingernails. He didn't see the boys slapping one another's thighs with sandy towels. He didn't see Kai watching Suze cross the sand toward Caleb. He didn't see two older girls tell Nat that the men under the tamarisk were looking at them and making a screwing gesture, with one finger poking into circled fingers. He could only see that Llamalo was at the river and Suze had returned. She was walking toward him. "About time," he called, raising his rescue tube. "Over here."

◆ ◆ ◆

"What should I do?" Rebecca paced back and forth under the calico shade of a cottonwood. She'd dragged David past the men in ARCO caps, into the seclusion of a copse of trees. "What am I supposed to *do*?" Snot from her nose, tears from eyes, calamity in her chest. "I've had this for *weeks*. I should be home with them. I should go right now."

She was sure this was somehow her fault. All that sex, petting, penis. She'd let this happen.

Nearby, two strutting crows called to the broken glass on the sand. David turned this way and that to follow her movement. "No, no, *no*. Here is exactly where you should be. Look, if you can just calm down . . . Rebecca, if you calm down, we can talk this through."

But she couldn't ever calm down. Surely, he could understand that. He'd always been there, pulled on the same raft at the YWCA, given a dollar to share and sent to browse the bountiful tables of political pins at rallies.

She wiped her face with the hem of her shirt. "The thing is, he's right. Ira's right. It makes me sick all the time. You go to a million rallies and make a million calls, and still your candidate isn't elected, or if he is, he takes money from Exxon and plays golf with the health insurance lobbyists. There's nothing we can actually do, right? Except buy a Christmas ornament made by a Nicaraguan women's collective or Palestinian scarves or South African bracelets woven out of flip-flops. We can shop. Or we can stop shopping. We can announce we'll never shop again, use the same paper bag for the rest of our lives and not give our kids birthday presents unless they're handmade out of that same bag, and it won't make a difference. Somewhere, right now, some guy is hauling away ten thousand plastic bags because they misspelled 'Safeway.' He's dumping them into the ocean. So hooray for you and your one bag."

"Oh wow."

"Don't laugh. Don't *laugh*."

"No, Zoom, I'm just laughing, because . . ." But he didn't stop. "See, that's what I always . . . Sorry. It's just . . ." He walked toward her with his hand raised, like a boy taking an oath, one palm held out. He took hold of her wrist and pressed her palm against his. It was warm and suffocating. "I used to ask my dad if once there's socialism and justice we'll be happy all the time. He would say, 'Don't worry about that—we'll never win.' And so I started to wonder, what's the—?"

"Did I ever tell you," she said, too full of her own thoughts to let him speak, "about the day I left for college? How Ira and Georgia drove me to the Greyhound? They stopped at that donut place on Bundy, and then just sat there, watching me eat, nobody talking. Finally, Georgia said they needed me to understand that there would be, like, different factions among the left at Berkeley. Some would advocate violence, and even though those people might be the most attractive, the most passionate, I should avoid them. It was like I was Kathy Boudin about to join the Weathermen."

"I can totally picture Georgia saying that." He was bending his fingers against hers, and she pressed hers back, one by one. That's all it was: a palm against a sweaty palm. And still it made it seem like there was nothing he wouldn't understand.

"They were so serious about it. When I boarded the bus, I felt like I was embarking on some clandestine mission, off to lay down swords and shields . . . that sort of thing." He snorted—of course he understood. "But there was nothing."

"So you started your own group, right? Because with Rebecca, there's never nothing. You come up with Unionionion and change everyone's life forever."

She blushed externally, glowed internally, said humbly, "I mean, I did start Students United for Justice, but there's only seven of us." She wanted to tell him everything, every meeting she'd gone to, every tall guy with glasses or dreads who'd lectured her about panopticons and the surveillance state; how she'd felt walking back to her dorm afterward as the eucalyptus leaves chattered and spores from the bottlebrush fell to the slate; and how she would lie in her bed full of the world's longing. She wanted him to know it all, every moment of her life. "My *point* is . . ."

"You have a point?"

As if on mutual agreement, they slid their fingers between each other's, like sliding legs between legs.

"Shut up."

His smile was the smile that said he knew her best.

"My point is that I still went to the meetings. That's the deal. We *know* futility—of course we do. We *know* it's useless, but we do it anyway."

His free hand found the waistband of her jean shorts, slid up along the satin of her one-piece.

His armpit hair was dewy and delicate. She wanted to grab it and bury her face in it. He had a zit on his shoulder, but what did she care about standards of desire and beauty? She'd rub her fingers over it. As soon as Scott blew the whistle, they'd leave the river separately and meet at the barn. She'd shove him into the straw.

"The marches, the meetings, the newspaper—we do it all, because without it, there's nothing. Without it, who am I? My dad runs this radical newspaper. That's who I am. That's me. That's *all* I am. What do I tell them now?"

He drew his head back slightly, gave a skeptical look. "Tell them? Who cares! Just tell the truth."

"And the truth is? What? None of it mattered? We tried and failed? I'm just like everyone else, except weirder?"

David removed his hand from hers, folded his arms. "Come on, stop. You're not weird. Just tell what you just said. How Ira's wrong. It doesn't even matter that he stopped the paper."

"But it *does* matter. That's not what I was saying at all."

"It doesn't. You *get* it—you just said it. What you couldn't see before." He was suddenly impassioned, impatient. "Listen, Rebecca, our parents are wrong. Their ideas are all wrong. For them, everything is anti, against. And this anger at everything, it means they're basically paralyzed. Like Ira . . . But Caleb . . . See, Caleb's figured out this *way*. About how to live here and not be stuck in unhappiness. It's like a system. Where everything we do actually matters. And if we follow that way . . ."

"A system?" She shook her head, roiling with frustration. "I'm not talking about Caleb. I'm not talking about *systems*. Jesus Fucking *Christ*, David, I'm talking about Ira. Ira's an important man, and he made a decision, which was, I think, brave. But it makes me sad. I'm sad. Do you see that?"

"But why? Fuck Ira. Your folks' paper was never the answer. *Never*. Fuck him. So it's over—who cares?" He looked triumphant. "You get it now. The answer is here. Now you see. We don't need our parents—we have this." He gestured wildly. "I mean, look at it."

She glanced in the direction he pointed. Through foliage, she could make out campers and counselors enjoying the meager delights of a sweltering rivershore in naïve oblivion. She looked back at him, and his face seemed newly ugly, his features dull and insufficient like his mind. "You never listen, David. You never have. You just drift away from everything that actually matters. And whenever I try to talk to you about anything real, you can't answer."

"Because it's stupid. It's stupid to waste your life trying to change something you'll never in a million years change. Even Ira realizes the futility. The stupidity."

"It's stupid to care about people who don't have enough food? Water? That's stupid? It's stupid to care about inequality and injustice?"

"Ira's been miserable. His whole life. I've never seen him unmiserable. But Caleb's happy. Don't you want to be happy?"

Of course not! she wanted to scream. But she wasn't done with her list. "It's stupid to care about the ongoing destruction of the Earth? Really, David? Or is it stupid to escape from it all and hide away in bourgeois delusion at a summer camp?"

"I thought you liked it here."

"I like it. It's great. But it's not life. It's a diversion. All of this." She gestured toward him. "It's been a great diversion."

David began kicking at the sand. "Don't be snide. It's my life. My entire life. I'm moving here. I've been wanting to tell you that. When I turn eighteen."

"Drop out of school?"

"Do you know what I'm leaving? I'm leaving nothing." His face changed, softened. He reached for her hand. "Come on, Zoom. I thought maybe you'd come here with me. Maybe on vacation. Or spend a semester.

Bring all your books, if you have to. Spend your days reading about how terrible the world is, but do it here. With me. Huh?"

She pulled her hand away. Her cataclysm had arrived. Her whole identity, her very self, blasted away. Nothing else could matter. Not him, not his plans. She wanted to hit him. Those shoulders, wrists, fleshless little bone bracelets, she wanted to break them. He was the only one who could grasp what was happening to her, and yet he didn't. He didn't understand her at all.

"Why would you think I'd ever do that?" Rebecca said, walking away.

♦♦♦

AT THE WATER'S EDGE, Caleb sat on his rock, enjoying the miracle of Suze standing beside him. They'd spent their first moments alone sharing incredulity. Donnie! Among them again! Who could believe the *insanity*? The *coincidence*. The very day Suze returned!

"But you did great," she said. "The way you took control. The way you managed him—respecting him, but without actually engaging in his rage. None of that typical male posturing. Which you could've done."

"Well." Caleb shrugged. He was trying to parse the compliment, which seemed to at once acknowledge and diminish his manliness. "It's part of what we do here. Part of what Llamalo's about. Respect, of course. Listening."

"Jesus, Caleb. You still talk like that? Like you're always giving a speech."

Was she already annoyed with him? And somehow this is what turned him on. All the girls since had been reverent, cowed, young. Suze had never conceded anything out of obligation. There'd been a friction between them that he'd loved. Only with her could he be completely honest. He leaned closer. "Alright then, I'll tell you. I was scared shitless, Suze. I thought he might have a gun. Donnie's always been unstable. The grudge he's held against me? The way he slept with you to get at me? Don't give that look—you know that's why he did it. Flooding the ditch? And he didn't exactly grow into a more reasonable adult. Those letters. You didn't even hear the worst of them. He believes that I'm an eco-Nazi, which is an industry term—"

"I know what an eco-Nazi is."

"An eco-Nazi is the way extractive industries slander environmentalists. He thinks I shut down Exxon's shale project in order to get his land."

"Okay, but you do see why he might want to come up with a narrative like that?"

"No, Suze, let me explain. You're missing the point. This isn't *Donnie's* idea. Not at all. It's all received knowledge. Total conspiracy theory fed to him by . . ." She was looking away, waving at someone under the shade tarp. He raised his voice. "The thing you don't understand is they'll say anything to get poor people riled up."

She turned back to him. "Okay, but—"

But he wasn't finished. "They encouraged him to come here and scare me. Unfortunately for him, I mean, as you saw, he's completely inarticulate, not an orator. And why should he be? That's not exactly what you learn as a miner. Different skill set."

"Well, apparently you *do* learn to soothe a baby. That was a surprise. Who's the mom?"

But he was done talking about Donnie, and he bugled his hands around his mouth in authoritative display. "Hey, Mikala, tell Josh to jump farther out next time." Back to Suze: "So you want to hear about the changes around here?"

"Well, sure, but . . ." She glanced around as if he might be speaking of the new sandbar cut by springtime snowmelt, the spread of tamarisk on the shore. "But in the grand scheme of things, it's the same."

And even though he agreed completely, in a theoretical way, there was so much he needed her to know. The lawn, of course. Suze's Meadow. How they'd tried seeding it with Kentucky bluegrass and, when that didn't take, switched to a hybrid bluegrass. Then, the platforms. When and where he'd built each of the new ones.

As he spoke, she nodded along, encouraging as always, murmuring "oh" and "uh-huh," her expressive face recognizing the amount of work he'd done, although she couldn't know how much of it was performed while imagining her as witness. He told her about moving the photography shack, building the blacksmith area, why he'd decided upon a new type of fence around the Gathering, the number of kids who did a solo up on Escadom this year, the number of returning campers this year versus last.

Each piece of news suggested something else he wanted her to know. Only when he began telling about the changes to the shower routine did she look bored, eyes darting from his.

"You'll find the yurt's the same, though," he said suggestively, daringly.

But she began turning her head slowly from beach to river and back again, shielding her eyes with her hand. "So who's the lucky girl this year?" Finally, she pointed at Kai standing in the water. "The beauty with the boobs. She's the one. Right?"

Before he could answer, Tanaya and Nicole approached the rock. They were both bikinied and covering their stomachs with an arm.

"We need to talk to Suze," Tanaya said.

"Over there," added Nicole, pointing. "It's about *Fiddler*."

Suze hit Caleb's thigh. "*Fiddler on the Roof*? At Final Friday? That's different. What's that about?"

He explained that the show was important to the girls fitting in here, shedding their former skin. Suze nodded, smiled, and then said to Nicole, "Sure, honey, let's talk."

As she slipped back into her sandals and walked away, his thigh burned where she'd touched it. She was jealous! He would need to reassure her that Kai was no competition. Hope passed through adolescence, the years of lockers and ticking classroom clocks, the years of masturbation, longing,

longing, longing. Hope reached young adulthood, twenty-four, the age Caleb had been when he'd met Suze, the age Ira had been when he'd registered voters in Mississippi, hope's earnest prime.

Scott blew the whistle. Only he could blow the whistle. It was time to leave the river.

THIRTEEN

First the Briny Silence, Then the Boom

THE BARN WAS ALWAYS in existence. Even when nobody was there, somebody was there. The mice were there beneath the straw. The bats, draped by their wings, in the high rafters. The *chit chit* of spider feet. Brown recluse, black widow. The barn swallows with their forked tails had left for the day. Had the barn grown to expect the people in their bathing suits? This was the time of day when they usually came. The sunlight strobed through the seams in the wooden walls. It had been nice to smell the muck of the river coming off the people. The alluvial smell, the smell of green algae and scum. The dampness. The barn was so dry and brittle. But the people didn't come. The mice woke from the quiet and fell back asleep.

◆ ◆ ◆

"THE WAY TO THINK about it," Rebecca said, "is that he's too radical to simply publish a newspaper. He'll do the one thing that can actually make a difference."

She stood in the girls' area with a group of counselors whom she'd waylaid on the way to their platforms. Still in their bathing suits and sneakers, they passed the torn-out editorial from hand to hand.

"It's noble," Saskia said. "He's calling us all out on our complacency."

"Nobody in my family would ever write something like this. They're basically illiterate racists," Nat said, looking over Saskia's shoulder. "He'd hate them all."

"What is it, then?" Saskia asked. "The one thing?"

"No, I'm not allowed to say. Not yet."

"You know, though, right?" Kai asked, pulling her hair out of its ponytail.

Saskia handed the page to Kai. "Is it going to be inside the system or outside?"

Kai said authoritatively, "It's got to be outside. Master's tools and all that."

◆ ◆ ◆

Suze patted the pages of handwritten lyrics that Shauna had given her and whispered to David, "They named some *grass* after me?"

"Technically, a meadow." David, his arms around knees, rocked forward, brushing up against Suze's white shirt. "Although, sure, on the small side."

"Petite," she said.

"It was Caleb who named it that."

"Caleb, Caleb, Caleb," she chanted, then turned from him to watch Nicole, still in her bathing suit, beg her matchmaker to make her a match, a request which, as a child, David had interpreted as a literal need for a stick that created fire. They were rehearsing on the Great Overlook before dinner. Flashlights were piled like kindling in preparation for darkness, but the sun and heat remained, as recalcitrant as a child who wouldn't go to bed. Suze had agreed to replace Caitlin as David's wife, a gesture of generosity and spontaneity completely in line with the way he remembered her.

Nicole had been told to snap in time, and she was not snapping in time. Shauna insisted they "take it from the top."

Suze glanced back at David. "He hasn't changed in all these years, has he?"

"Caleb? Should he?"

"Right, if you know you're the smartest person in the room, and by that I mean the proverbial room, because you never actually go inside a room, why would you change?" She laughed a little. "Can I talk to you?"

"Yeah! Of course. I mean, sure." David blushed with the understanding that he'd failed in his attempt not to seem too eager.

She looked at him intently. "The whole reason I'm here. Well, of course, there's you." She hit him on his upper arm with the back of her hand. "You called. Adorably. But the reason I came when you called is . . ." She started to sing: "I'm getting married in the morning . . ." Then she laughed. "Well, in September. In the sterile splendor of Colin's mom's home in Greenwich, Connecticut. You know it?"

"No, but I . . ." He considered offering to learn about it.

"Land of McMansions. Land of everything Caleb hates. Nature mani-cured for our comfort. Five Dominican gardeners working full time." She paused. Sucked in her cheeks. "So all summer, I felt Caleb's disapproval. Like literally"—she pointed to the dirt—"Caleb standing right here, be-side me in his cowboy shirt and . . . shall we say, pious demeanor, shak-ing his head when I paid eight dollars for a salad, rolling his eyes when I tried on a bazillion-dollar wedding dress, asking me how I ended up with someone like Colin."

Okay, okay. David calmed himself. "Marriage" was a frightening word, sure, but she was here because she didn't want it. She was heeding Caleb's disapproval.

"A frog in heating water, you know?"

He didn't.

"That's how it happened." She went on to say that in the first years after she left, she tried to keep up with most of the Llamaloian tenets. Lived in shitholes that gave her scabies, co-ops with stoned strangers always sleeping in the living room—roaches on the unwashed dishes, maggots in the bulk rice, blind mice babies born in her sleeping bag. She still bought nothing, not even a broom, before checking Dumpsters, borrowing from friends.

"But little by little . . ." She mimed stabbing her heart. "Kill me now—I succumbed to the delights of buying a new sweater. The wonder of Gore-Tex. I moved to San Francisco, where any experience of the great outdoors must be mediated by a truckload of expensive gear. And then I met Colin. He's great. He's a good person. He's not some idiot who hasn't considered the downside to consumption. His family gives a shit-ton of money away." She started accordion-folding a page of the lyrics in a way that seemed frenetic and sure to piss off Shauna. "Our mattress was handstitched by nuns! It's four layers of . . ." She looked away, then back at him. "Who gives a shit? I love my bed. I just thought, if I came here again . . . I wanted to be the person I was here. Do you even remember that person?"

"But you still are!" he said, although he didn't entirely believe it. "You're her."

A fake, tinny laugh. "I wish. Do you remember? I was like a queen here. Like the center of everything."

"But now you're here again," he said, a hopeful reminder.

She was staring at something beyond him. "Where else do you get some grass named after you?"

"Technically, a meadow," he repeated, but she didn't laugh this time.

"He didn't ask me a single question. He talked, for what? Forty-five minutes? Not 'How are *you*, Suze?' Not 'What's your life like?' Nothing. He won't change. I mean, I can see the attraction. That's easy. I can see why at twenty-two, twenty-five . . . All that intense focus—who wouldn't want to be the object of it? But then you remember what it's actually like."

A question? That's all she needed? But anyone could ask a question.

Surely, Caleb would soon ask her a question. And Suze would be satisfied. They'd live here together, with him and Rebecca, although he'd pissed off Rebecca without meaning to. An intestinal cavity to the left of his navel began throbbing with a sour pain. His anxiety was back. The usual last-week-of-camp anxiety: minutes ticking by.

"You're so sweet to listen to all this." Was she crying? She rubbed her eyes with the backs of her hands and then laughed in that horrible way again.

Now he was anxious about feeling anxious, because it seemed likely that anxiety was generative. The very act of worrying that something terrible would happen was creating that likelihood.

"Are you bored?" she said. "I'm bored. It's so fucking gorgeous here, and we're spending our time singing Catskills vaudeville? I've always hated this stupid musical." Turning to the singing girls, she said, "Hey, can I give a little suggestion?"

The girls ignored her.

He told himself not to think any further, and yet thought's filamental whisper floated by: You're anxious about being anxious about being anxious.

Louder, Suze called, "David and I need a different song."

Nicole stopped singing. Shauna said, "What?"

"Come on. This story, this . . . shtetl matchmaking stuff, what does it have to do with Llamalo? With the great and powerful Caleb? With Aemon's wondrous plateau? David and I want a song that makes us cry."

"We're cool doing it this way," Shauna said.

Suze jumped up and put a reassuring hand on Shauna's arm. "This'll be great. What'll we call it? *Fiddler on Aemon's Mesa*? No, see that's the problem—nobody fiddles here. I got it! *Guitarist on the Roof . . . On the Mesa*. Who plays guitar?"

Suze's emotions seemed to David a dangerous, unpredictable force, and he needed to do whatever he could to assuage them. Ask her questions. Sing a different song. Whatever would calm her down. "I do. I play guitar."

Suze gasped in either mock or real delight. "Everyone loves a guy who plays guitar. Don't we, girls?" She pushed him. "Well, go. *Go*. Get it."

To mitigate Suze's emotions, or so he told himself, David took Mikala's guitar from where she stored it in the living room closet, although nobody was allowed to touch it but her. On the porch, he tried to come up with the perfect song for them to sing, but he was distracted by the worry that Caleb wouldn't redeem himself by asking questions, and that even if Caleb did, the lack of questions was not actually all that bothered Suze. Because it couldn't be, could it?

"I got it," Suze said, thrilled, elated, the rising sun. "Do you know 'Blackbird'?" When she leaned forward, her necklace touched his arm. He tried and failed to not enjoy the silvery feeling of this.

"All your life," they sang, "you were only waiting for this moment to arise." They practiced three times, and each time it made the pain in his stomach burn louder, until the first campers and counselors appeared on the lawn to wait for dinner and Suze stood and adjusted her tank top and said, "You grew up. I'm amazed how you grew up."

He stood as well, holding the guitar by its neck. She was staring up at him. Was she expecting him to kiss her? He managed only monosyllables: "Uh. Yeah. Thanks. You. Too."

She laughed, and a group of campers called from the grass—*Suze, Suze, talk to us*—and she went to them.

◆ ◆ ◆

CALEB CHECKED THE TEMPERATURE on the thermometer on the wall of the eating platform. It was official. The hottest day of summer. The high peaks of the Rocky Mountains were blocking passage of the air that had settled on western Colorado like a headache. On the lawn, campers took bets as to whether it was 105 or 115 degrees "in the shade." At dinner, everyone was a lank of limp hair, was an untied shoelace stomped into dirt. It was 108 in the shade.

After announcements, which included Caleb's usual end-of-summer speech about how much everyone had changed and would be missed, he gave the cast of *Fiddler* half an hour to prepare for the show and sent the rest of the camp to sweep their platforms and clean the ground beneath. He leaned against the porch railing, hands clasped in front of him, watching the preparations below. Matthew arranged traffic cones, pilfered from the parking lot, to demarcate a stage on the side of the Overlook closest to the ditch. Suze walked by, swinging hands with an eight-year-old girl. It was the space above her breasts, the tautness of skin so near that heaviness. She waved to Caleb.

Scott rang the first bell, and now David arrived with a guitar strapped to his back. Soon he was on the dirt, strumming, Suze crouched beside him. It was the space above her hips, the small of her back.

His hope sauntered up, past thirty now, his own age, wearing a leather jacket from a thrift store, feeling particularly sexy, feeling juiced, pressuring him to do something, say something. He ran down the porch stairs and across the Overlook and crouched behind Suze, pushing his face near hers.

"Oh, it's you," she said, startled.

His mouth was dry. He licked his lips. The moon was just now intruding over the mountain.

His hope chanted: Come on, come on, come on. No problem, no problem at all. Piece of cake, slice of life, bowl of cherries. Meal time, swim time, no time like the present.

"Can I talk to you for a second?"

"Uh-oh," she said to David. "I'm in trouble." It was the space below her hips.

She followed him to the side of the house, saying, "Listen, I didn't mean to completely derail the performance. Honestly, I didn't think those girls would get so upset."

"Who?"

She hit his arm. "Hasn't the news spread? I gave some suggestions, and the girls got pretty offended."

She'd changed into a blue tank top. Her arms were tan, and she now shaved her underarms. When she lowered her arms, the exposed skin puckered, and he even liked that.

"Doesn't seem like a big deal," he said.

She leaned against the wall, and he stood in front of her, legs wide.

"They're not talking to us anymore. Total mutiny."

"Suze." This meant "Look at me," and she did. "I don't want you to worry about Kai."

"Kai?"

"She'll understand."

"Caleb." Her look and tone were indulgent, like someone half-assedly reprimanding a toddler.

"It's okay. It's you I want up there. In the yurt."

"Just stop a second and listen. I love being here—"

"I know you do. And you *can* be. That's what I'm saying. There's no impediment."

"This place. This place, if this is possible, is more beautiful even than I remember. The way I feel here, if I could somehow package that and bring it back with me. But—"

"No need. No need to package anything, Suze. Just be here."

"Can you stop interrupting? Jesus. The thing is. I don't know how to say this. You're the same. The same as always." A quick, hysterical laugh. "The same arrogant dick."

His heart was a water balloon slipping through cupped hands.

"Caleb, I'm sorry." She gestured vaguely toward the bushes. "I should check on the girls." She walked away.

She didn't mean it.

The sky was darkening. He stood in the middle of the flat ground.

Everyone was arriving. He closed his eyes, but he could hear their voices, yaps like coyotes circling. Somewhere, a girl cried. He was needed everywhere and nowhere.

When he opened his eyes, he saw that apparently all the girls had spent the last half hour trading skirts and dresses and butterfly barrettes and one tube of mascara. Caleb watched them scuttle in groups across the Overlook as if to prom, even the girls with chopped hair, who never wore skirts. They giggled to be seen.

Apparently, all the boys had spent the last half hour eating candy or snorting coke, because they ran circles around the perimeter of the Overlook, pumping their fists in victory, following Jeremy, who sang, "We are the champions."

"We are the champions," they echoed in bathrobes and scarves from the costume shack.

Caleb needed everyone to stop moving.

Nicole, Tanaya, and Shauna, dressed in leotards (pink, leopard-skin, teal) and miniskirts, appeared at Caleb's side. "We have to talk to you, Caleb. We have to *talk* to you."

Around and around the Overlook, the boys ran with Jeremy, now singing "Stayin' Alive." *Ah, ha, ha, ha.*

Caleb turned away from the girls and took off running after Jeremy, to tell him to stop running.

"Everyone. Sit down," David suddenly yelled.

Caleb stopped. David was standing on a milk carton on the makeshift stage. He wore a white T-shirt, on which he'd written in black Sharpie *Father, Husband, Jew,* and he clutched the neck of the guitar. "We have to start. Sit down!"

Caleb watched Tanaya, Shauna, and Nicole retreat to the sagebrush nearest the parking lot. He approached a group of younger girls and said, "Wanna sit here with me?" But they, too, wandered off. The wind screeched across the mesa, and he shivered, realizing the heat wave had broken.

Caleb had read that before a tsunami, the ocean recedes, exposing star-fish and anemones and urchins, and then it comes. It was like that the first cool night after a series of hot days at camp: first the briny silence, then the boom.

He needed them to shut up.

And still David shouted. "Be quiet. Sit down! Be quiet! *Sit down.*" But this only made it worse.

Caleb climbed between the few sitting kids to say to David, "Hold on. We need everyone to settle down before you start."

Suze appeared from dust and dusk. "Let me help." And Caleb, embarrassed, turned away to find Rebecca waiting.

"You have to talk to Shauna," she said.

"I'm already headed there," Caleb said with excessive pissiness.

In the center of the Overlook, Jeremy had started the boys doing jumping jacks.

"Hey, everyone," Suze said. "I think that David and I will just begin with our song, and when the rest of the cast is ready, they'll join. David, I'm going to start singing, and you start playing whenever you feel ready." It was the right thing to say, and Caleb, turning to watch her, hated the wind and the cool air and every living thing.

"What's he doing with my guitar?" Mikala said, coming up to Caleb. "Did you tell him he could use it?"

He didn't answer. David and Suze were singing some sappy Beatles song. And guess what? Suze sang like an angel, and David did, too. Together, they sang like they were meant to sing together, her voice high, his low.

It hushed everyone. Kids who were up sat down. Kids who were already sitting leaned against each other. Caleb stood there, mesmerized. He hadn't known David could play guitar and sing. Did David have a twang? Did David steal the twang Caleb had borrowed from Donnie? Did Suze dip and curve above his voice like a woman dancing, rubbing close?

All the while, Suze stared at David. David with his eyes half-closed.

After the song and applause, Suze said, "Let's play another. We'll give the residents of Anatevka a few more minutes." David, confident now, started strumming the saddest song of the camp's repertoire, and Suze began.

It was Caleb's Suze song: the song he imagined Suze hearing in a car in Santa Fe, Bozeman, wherever she was, and when it came on the radio, she would think of Caleb, the smell of Russian olive, the ceiling of stars. She would miss Caleb with the force of snowmelt. The guy next to her would ask a question, and she wouldn't answer. She would turn up the radio. *Our good times are all gone, I'm bound for moving on.* She would dump the man at a gas station and drive straight through the night until she arrived at Llamalo. But she was already here, singing their song with David.

♦ ♦ ♦

KAYLA, THE SNEAK, WAS asleep, but every time Donnie lifted his hand from her belly, her eyes opened. When he set his hand back down, they closed. He was stuck in his dad's bedroom forever, his hand riding the breath of her belly, the fan twisting its head from one side to the other, saying no, no, no.

Donnie dozed off, and when he woke, it was dusk outside. He sat up from the bed, rolled up towels, and placed them around Kayla so she wouldn't fall out. He walked into the trailer's other room, which was somehow cramped even though there was hardly any furniture in it, nothing on the walls. His dad lived with nothing after all these years, lived like a shadow. His towels were old and crusty, his TV was old with a bent antenna, and his toaster was so old it made old burned toast. All this in grief for a woman Donnie could hardly remember. His own mom and he couldn't remember.

"She sleeping?" his dad asked. He sat at the table, tapping his cigarette into an old ashtray. The dishes were washed beside the sink.

"If she wakes, put your hand on her belly and pretend you're me," Donnie said, stepping into his boots. They'd been fighting all afternoon. His dad wouldn't even admit that Caleb had trashed the place. All those ugly half-assed buildings with no system, no order. It was a disgrace. A teepee? Even if the Talcs did get their land back, it would take a long while to clean it up.

"Where you going?"

"Taking a walk."

"Stick to the road then, and don't bother Caleb. We're not allowed up there in the evening."

Donnie opened the door, and the wind poured in. He walked against it to the house where he grew up, the house that Aemon built, now with an ugly cement patio stuck to the back of it. Picnic tables and painted signs. He opened the kitchen door. It was dark inside, but his hand reached up in exactly the right spot to find the string light pull that still hung in the center of the room.

When the light switched on, he saw that the rest of the kitchen was new, tricked out with a restaurant-sized dishwasher and stoves and fridges. And still his dad insisted that a twenty-four-year-old had just happened to have cash for all this. "He was a journalist," his dad had said earlier today. "He earned his money." Well, who did his dad think owned the newspapers? The same people who shut down mines. It was all related, but his dad wouldn't listen.

Donnie walked into the living room, his living room, the living room where his mom sat in his memory, because of course he remembered her. His mom on the floor in her green dress, playing rummy, screaming and laughing. *That's my card. Give me that card. Donnie, I'll pay you for it.* Taking out a dollar from her purse and throwing it at Donnie. Like the entire world was a joke between the two of them, while Don just looked on from his chair.

He walked through the front door to the porch, and goddamn but the moon was rising full over the mountain. This was his. He used to sit on this porch with his Grandpa Conway, who would talk to him. And Donnie should've listened, but he never did, because he had too much to think about. He wished he could remember anything, either what Grandpa Conway had said or what he used to think about as a kid.

Donnie could hear the kumbaya song as he walked down the steps. Nobody even turned to look at him. They were all crowded around on the dirt watching Suze, who was singing with a boy. All this lawn and they chose to sit on the dirt. Only Caleb stood, arms folded at his chest, like he was too important to sit. The boy strummed his guitar like all the boys in Telluride had strummed their guitars, like he was in a porno, like everyone would want to see the expression on his face when he was fucking.

This afternoon, Donnie had called Marci when she got home from the laundry. "So, did it happen like you said it would?" she'd asked. "Should I pack? Are we moving to Colorado?" She'd laughed like she never believed he would pull it off. Then she started crying. He said, "I'll see you tomorrow, baby. We'll be home tomorrow." She said, "Put Kayla on. I want to hear Kayla." He held the phone next to Kayla's ear and could hear Marci say, "Did Daddy get you a ranch like he promised?"

The kumbaya song finished, and he saw Suze throwing her arms around the boy's neck, pecking him on his cheek. Poor, poor Caleb, watching his girl love on someone else. And then a hippie lady ran up to the boy and said, "Are you using my guitar? I really hope not. I'm pretty sure I didn't give you permission to use it."

"Fine, take it," the boy said, swinging the guitar cockily. All pumped up with a kiss from Suzy-Q. "You weren't even using it."

◆ ◆ ◆

CALEB FELT AN OCEAN rise within him. "Come with me, David. Now." He turned and began walking.

"What is it?" David asked from behind. "Everything okay?"

Caleb wove between tables on the eating platform. He held the kitchen door for David to enter. After which, Caleb shut the door hard and leaned against it. The kitchen ladies had left the light on, and it bothered his eyes.

"Look, I'm sorry about Mikala's guitar," David said, moving to the center of the kitchen before noticing that Caleb was still standing at the door. "I didn't think she'd mind."

"You're sorry? *I'm* sorry. And not about Mikala's guitar. I don't give a shit about Mikala's guitar. Mikala's guitar is the least of your concerns. Let me ask you a question: Are you the social director of this place now? You're making phone calls? You're inviting people to come see you here?"

"What?"

"I'm talking about Suze, David. I'm talking about Suze."

David began biting his lower lip. "I thought you would like it."

"Me? I would like it? Me or you, David? Who were you really thinking about? Me or you? Because I'm trying to get this straight. You went up to my office, somewhere you're not allowed. You looked through my papers and found her number. You picked up the phone and decided to make a call, also not allowed. So tell me, David, was this a case of poor judgment or utter idiocy?" After a day of restraint, it felt amazing to scream. He couldn't stop himself and wouldn't even if he could. He was coasting on his anger, riding the downhill of it.

David said nothing. The pull string of the overhead bulb was swaying from the wind that snuck through the windows, hitting his forehead rhythmically, but he didn't move away.

"Right. You can't even answer. Can you answer? Do you even understand the first thing about this place?"

"But it was Suze. She's about this place. Everyone wants to see Suze."

"Not me, David! I didn't want to! But you didn't think about that, did you? Completely oblivious. Just thinking about yourself and what you want. A fucking unmitigated disaster."

I thought . . . I mean I didn't think . . . I really am sorry." His voice was growing high-pitched, prepubescent. "Is this a problem?"

"Is it a problem? That's what you want to know? Is it a fucking problem? Yes, it's a problem. It's a goddamn problem." He crashed his fist onto the counter and opened the door, leaving David below the swinging cord. "Wait."

Caleb turned to see the boy's face scrunched, his arms wrapped around himself. "I mean, is it a problem with our plan?" he said, nearly inaudibly.

"Plan?"

"For me to move here. Like we talked about?"

"Move here? Move here, David? Honestly, I can't see you coming back here in any capacity. I don't imagine you'll have anything to do with Llamalo after tonight." And with that, Caleb was spent. The ocean settled, just gentle lolling waves now. He walked out into the night.

On the Overlook, he saw three girls shimmying their little hips, lamenting their singledom. *Matchmaker, matchmaker.* The beams of flashlights crossed, hit the bushes, illuminated the traffic cones. The moon had risen and shrunk, pursued now by a satellite. The cool air pushed the lingering heat up over the Rockies and into the Great Plains.

He saw the white eyes of a car backing up. *Make me a match.* Later, on the way to the campfire, Caitlin stood small in front of him. "Um, Suze said to say bye to you. She had to go. She couldn't find you. She said to tell you bye."

♦♦♦

AFTER THE PERFORMANCE, REBECCA sat on the porch steps in the dark, hoping, and admonishing herself for hoping, that David would seek her out. Her mind kept showing a short movie with David's response to the shattering of her life (*Fuck him. So it's over—who cares?*), followed by him singing with Suze in that blissed-out way, tra-la-la, like nothing had happened. It would be best to never see him again, but she listened for him among the shapes passing below, and she imagined him apologizing, redeeming himself by asking to see the letter, which, as it happened, she had at the ready in the pocket of her shorts, as well as a flashlight by her side to shine on it. Together they would read her father's despairing words and contemplate the bleakness of her future and the meaninglessness of all action.

Then, footsteps on the stairs.

"Rebecca? I couldn't find you anywhere."

"Well, I was just here." She forced relief from her voice.

"I have to talk to you." He sat, his bare arm touching hers. She wanted to fall on him, to push him down, but first he'd have to acknowledge her suffering and his role in it.

As campers and counselors streamed by, David told her he needed help. He'd messed up; he didn't explain how, only that Caleb was angry and he needed Rebecca to intervene. He spoke in rapid bursts, none of it apology. "If you could tell Caleb . . ." David paused. He licked at the crease between his lips. "If you could just convince him . . . If you could *assure* him that I actually did this for him. Because I thought he'd like it. That was the only reason."

"Oh my *god*," a passing camper squealed. And then the Overlook was empty as everyone headed up to the Gathering for a final fire.

"Caleb's just an asshole sometimes," Rebecca said. "I wouldn't worry about it."

"Not *him*," David snapped. "He didn't do anything wrong. *I* did."

David's ardor for Caleb seemed to be a delicate glass bauble forged in a decade-long fire, held out before Rebecca in his trembling hand.

"I'm sorry, but you shouldn't idealize Caleb." She was lifting the bauble from him, palming it, feeling the cool smoothness of the glass. "He's just as fucked up as everyone else. He's so pious about his rules, and then he breaks them all. He drinks every night. He sleeps with a different counselor every summer. He arranges the seating charts based on what girl he wants to sit near."

"Don't mess with me right now."

"Well, it's true." And whether or not it was—the alleged bottle of whiskey in his yurt, the way his hand seemed to linger on the backs of certain counselors—whether or not it was the truth did not matter right now. Or so Rebecca told herself as she dropped the bauble and stepped on it, feeling the crunch of broken glass underfoot.

"It's true," she went on. "He has no special knowledge. No special rules or, I don't know, system of how to live. Believe me, he's as lost as anyone. So what do you care if he hates you? Plenty of people hate you, right? And you don't care. So fuck him." She stood. "Who gives a flying fuck."

David was shaking his head. "Seriously? Can't you just help me?"

But why should she help him when he hadn't helped her? Rage filled the space carved inside her by desire. It fit perfectly and felt more familiar. She longed to hurt him, to pound upon the chest she wanted to lie on. But instead, she jumped down from the steps, headed toward the faint chirr of campers singing. "Have to go add my voice to the choir now, David, that sort of a thing, but maybe I'll catch you later, okay?"

◆ ◆ ◆

THE WIND THRASHED THE tarps like a woman beating rugs. It swung the branches, creaked the wooden platforms, ululated to the owls. The camp had gone to bed, which meant David had gone to bed, but he wouldn't sleep.

In eight years, David had never walked away from his platform in the night. Now, as he descended the steps, he was disappointed to learn that it was as simple as leaving school. It was simple to walk downhill. He left his duffel but wore his backpack, which he'd stuffed with his sleeping bag, flashlight, and sweatshirt. It was simple to barge into the ranch house and turn on all the lights. Nobody came, and nobody noticed.

Nobody noticed that David knew everything about this place. He knew that the small room off the kitchen was full of silver trash cans with bungee cords fastening down their lids, a whole room of these cans, like some giant science experiment, breeding pods for aliens.

David lifted lids and let them crash down like cymbals. Still, nobody came, nobody noticed. He pulled out a sticky plastic bag of dehy chili and another of powdery green flakes—SPLT P SP—and tossed these aside, dove for the MC N CHS. From a cabinet marked POISON—KEEP OUT, he slipped forbidden chocolate bars and a waxy envelope of graham crackers.

He scavenged packets of oatmeal, peanut butter in a salsa jar, saltines, a red bowl scratched and softened with use, a fork, a dented saucepan, a knife that he sheathed in cardboard torn from the cache of boxes under the table.

He descended to the basement, which housed the coal furnace, legions of spiders, and craft materials dusted with a shadow of coal. The walk-in freezers hummed. From a box labeled ORANGES, David retrieved a water pump, an insect-legged stove, a fuel canister, and a book of matches.

The lawn was pewter in the moonlight. David packed as Caleb had taught him, lining everything up on the grass like tin soldiers before marching them into his bag.

It was simple to leave Llamalo, to walk up the road past Don's darkened trailer, to follow the familiar route. It was simple to be gone.

Nobody noticed that David was made from this place, his skin from the cracked clay ground, his legs from the branches of a Russian olive, his teeth from a king snake's skull, his fingertips from the soft lobes of sage. The strange thing was, when he reached the edge of the cliff, he stepped onto the trail to the river, and the trail wasn't there. He stepped into air.

THE REAGAN YEARS: JULY 1982

TO REACH PETER FINKEL in the overgrown Berkeley Hills, Caleb hiked past houses of dark wood, where purple wisteria drooped over potted succulents and Frank Lloyd Wright stained-glass windows. Finkel's house was set back from the sidewalk, behind a koi pond. A woman in a black smock, with a bowl cut of gray hair, answered the door and told Caleb to wait, eyeing the whole length of him before vanishing. The foyer was mirrored on three sides, and a black stone vase with white calla lilies like swan necks rested on a low table. Caleb could see at least fifteen clean-shaven Calebs in suits, and they looked like dorks, like eager little boys. He straightened his spine, and the crowd of Calebs transformed into young-but-visionary leaders.

Ira had said, "The guy I'm setting you up with is a former radical, deep underground kind of guy, who went soft, made a fortune on computers and is choking on guilt, looking for ways to spend his cash. His nom de guerre was Peter Pan. You'll call him Peter Finkel, which is close but not identical to the name he was given at birth." Caleb had heard "computers" and went to Sal's Army, where he bought a suit the color of a Girl Scout uniform. Now, staring at his selves greenly multiplied, he was sure it was a mistake.

"We remove our shoes before we enter the house," Peter Finkel said when he appeared at last: a short, thick man, bowing at Caleb. Unshod, Caleb followed him into a large room with tatami mats on the floor and two blue ovoid meditation cushions, like the eggs of some passing dinosaur. There was no furniture other than a small shrine on a shelf in the corner with a stone Buddha who had a lei of dried marigolds at his feet. Peter Finkel folded his body onto a cushion, like a gazelle kneeling, and Caleb perched on the other, his knees in front of him, pants hitched up to reveal unfortunate white tube socks.

"So here we are." Peter Finkel smiled stingily. Caleb waited for him to continue. A wall of this room was mirrored, too, but Caleb avoided it, unsure of which self he'd find there. "The nephew of the great Ira Silver."

Caleb offered Peter Finkel the folder containing his mission statement and budget, but Peter Finkel waved it away. "Just speak. Bring your idea to life for me."

Caleb said he wanted to start a summer camp that was like no other summer camp. He used hollow nouns: nature, harmony, self-discovery. He felt his earnestness ooze from him like molasses.

Peter Finkel played with a toy on the mat, five silver balls hung from five silver wires. He pulled one back and let it go. *Click-click. Click-click.*

Caleb talked about utopia, that glorious word. *Click-click.* He talked about homesickness, about being at home in the outdoors. *Click-click.* He talked about Drop City in Colorado and the Hog Farm and New Buffalo and the other communes—the topic of his senior thesis—and how he believed that even though they'd failed, the promise of a new society wasn't over, but it was children—who'd been ignored in the 1960s communes, left to wander around naked and dosed—who needed it most, *click-click,* who needed to be released from nuclear families, who need to be *click*-transformed-*click* before they grew up.

Usually, Caleb felt an onrush of love for these hypothetical children when he spoke about them, love for the actual thirteen-year-old boy he'd been the day he learned his father had killed himself, but now he felt only ridiculous and far too warm in his suit. Peter Finkel was wearing a purple T-shirt and running shorts. Caleb mentioned the feeling of trees and rocks talking back to him, albeit in a pre- or post-verbal way, and beneath his poly-blend shirt, molasses dripped down his back.

Caleb could see the rest of his day stretch ahead. When he finished fucking up this interview, he'd eat dinner burritos with his roommates at El Farolito, followed by pub trivia at Flanahan's. Half-drunk and not at all revived by the trivial victory, he'd retreat to a bedroom that used to be a fire escape, the walls gummed with Ansel Adams prints and that Thoreau quote: IN WILDNESS IS THE PRESERVATION OF THE WORLD. He would read from the stack by his bed: *The Call of the Wild*, Gary Snyder's *The Back Country*, *Desert Solitaire*, the books his dad had given him the last time Caleb saw him, all of which he'd already studied devoutly, highlighting and scribbling *This is it!* in the margins. He'd jack off. He'd sleep.

Panicked by the dour unspooling of his day, he found himself shouting, "I can save people, sir. I know it."

Peter Finkel glanced up as if he'd just noticed that a visionary—or an idiot—was sitting across from him.

"What are you, twenty years younger than me?"

Caleb nodded. At least twenty.

"And you're saying exactly what I said twenty years ago."

"Seems unlikely."

"Do you have any idea how depressing that is?"

"It can't be exactly the same."

"You can *save* people. Really?" Peter Finkel paused to slide his jaw back and forth in a way that made him look both enraged and uncomfortable. "Because *I* have no idea how to save anyone, least of all myself. And I kind of want to smash your head for the hubris you have." Peter Finkel raised his fist toward Caleb's head, and Caleb flinched.

Peter Finkel shook his own head slightly, eyes cast to the floor, as if to apologize to his peaceable self. "And then to think that in twenty years, you're going to be like me, disappointed with everything you did, wishing more than anything you could get that feeling back, that confidence, that ballsiness, but knowing you never did save anyone. *God*, that's depressing."

Caleb knew that he would never be like Peter Finkel. Peter Finkel had scaly white islands on his bald tan head and small hairs protruding from his earlobes. Caleb's body could climb mountains, could bike across the Golden Gate Bridge in the rain.

"When Ira called and told me about you, I thought, Okay, sure, my job now will be to nurture the young blood, to mentor, to help out, to pass the baton, so to speak. But then you come here with your suit, and Jesus Christ, you look just like I did, with your hair cut short and your ears sticking out. But that doesn't matter, because everyone's always told you that you're smart, so you think you can save people."

He bugged his eyes at Caleb. "And so I'm thinking, sure, I'll teach you. Do you want to learn about disillusionment? You want to learn about a pervasive feeling of failure?"

Caleb tugged at his socks. "I understand your reluctance, sir, but isn't it somewhat of an exaggeration to insist that failure and disappointment are inevitable? I mean, of course I'm not working at this scale, but consider—"

"Hold on. You're *not* about to say Gandhi. You're *not* going to say MLK."

So Caleb, who had been about to say Gandhi and MLK, said, "Ira."

"*Ira?*"

Caleb regarded Peter Finkel, the scorn scowling his face, his bare knees shining and broad as skulls, his fingers twitching at his toys. The person he used to be was dead. His days were spent mourning Peter Pan, mourning optimism. Caleb felt a sudden sharp love for him, for how old he was and all he'd lost. He stood up, relieved to be released from his blue egg, and began gliding around the room, the straw mats springy and smooth under his socks. "Think about it: Ira's still doing what he set out to do. His paper arrives in my mailbox every Wednesday. *He* hasn't lost his ideals. He hasn't succumbed to disillusionment. You don't have that, right?

But what if that's Llamalo in twenty, thirty, *forty* years? Forty years of kids being transformed. Going back into the world as these transformed people and then changing *it*. What if *you* made all that happen?"

"You're a cocky motherfucker."

Caleb stopped abruptly a foot away from Peter Finkel, forcing the man to look up. He put his hands in his pants pockets, hitching up the pants. "How about you give me the money, and then in forty years you come visit Llamalo and see what it's become?"

Peter Finkel squinted at him. "And if Llamalo—which is a crazy name, by the way, you might want to think about changing the name—doesn't exist anymore?"

"You can gloat. You can say you were right. But that's not going to happen."

Peter Finkel stared ahead. "That's fantastic, but in forty years I'll be dead."

"In forty years, Ira will still be writing his outraged editorials—"

"Hunched and arthritic," Peter Finkel said.

"And I'll be waiting for you at Llamalo." Caleb opened his palms.

"You want me to give you money so that I won't be outdone by Ira in my dotage?"

Caleb didn't answer, and Peter Finkel didn't say anything for a while, just tilted his head back, considering the ceiling. Then he stood. "Fine. You're on. I'll back you for one year—start-up costs not to exceed fifty thousand dollars. Because if I live, I want to be able to say, 'I told you so.'" He was much shorter than Caleb, and he looked up as he spoke. "I'll pay fifty grand for the privilege of saying it to you."

Caleb reached to shake his hand. "You won't be able to, sir."

Peter Finkel bowed with his palms together, offering his eczematous baldness to Caleb. When he returned to vertical, he stared into Caleb's eyes. "You don't get it. I *was* you. I was a motherfucker like you. It doesn't last. I wish it did. God, I wish it did."

FOURTEEN

Miss Clavel

CALEB CLANGED THE COWBELL on the porch. The hem of his jeans was wet from crossing the dewy meadow. Wind flattened his shirt against him. It was five thirty on Saturday morning, and there was darkness all around, stars above. He sounded the bell again and again, until everyone on the plateau would know: this was the last morning.

A baby cried. Donnie was still here.

Caleb entered the house, passed through the living room, and set a pot of water to boil. The kitchen held the fermented smell of a crate of apples rotting under the table. Today, the kitchen ladies wouldn't come until dinner, when they would feed the counselors one last time. After that, he'd see them only in the bank and Ute's Market and the Motherlode until next summer. Soon he'd be cooking for himself again, taking one plate from a shelf of ninety, or heading to the trailer to see what Denise had made. That is, if his friendship with Don hadn't been soured by Donnie's paranoia. And if it had been, then what? Entirely alone up here?

But first, he reminded himself, with a firm enjoinder to calm the fuck down, there would be Counselor Week, six days when the counselors helped Caleb clean and store supplies, remove tarps, and repair the structures. With skills honed in college, they'd prepare meals of overspiced slop, legumes softening in the cloying embrace of curry powder.

Our Week of Infantile Foods. That's what Suze had dubbed Counselor Week. Remembering this, Caleb felt doused with a fire hose of embarrassment, and he turned away from the window, as if to avoid being seen thinking of her. Would he always feel this humiliation at memories of Suze? He could not bear it.

Knowledge, it turned out, was not preferable to ignorance. Send Caleb back to the garden, to his innocence and longing, to his belief, however false, in her inevitable return, anything but this finality. Better to never have seen her again.

Caleb poured the boiling water into two mugs, added Folgers to both, sugar and creamer to one, and was ready by the side of the road just as the headlights came toward him. When the bus heaved to a stop and Don stepped down, Caleb held out the sweetened coffee.

"You planning on taking time off next week? Just let me know—it's no problem," Caleb said nervously, as this was his oblique way of asking about Donnie's visit.

Don sipped his coffee. "Might head to Junction. Let me know what you want me to pick up. Been having these headaches. Denise wants me to see some Chinese healer she's heard about. She says they know a lot, the Chinese. She says they have ancient wisdom." Don laughed in his wheezy way that was indistinguishable from gasping for breath, then he added, "Donnie'll leave today, I'm pretty sure. Or tomorrow. I apologize for any interruptions."

I told you so, Caleb thought, being both subject and object of that sentence. Of course Don harbored no ill feelings toward him. Of course they were friends. For eight years now, they'd stood in the dark, drinking coffee.

"Ancient wisdom, huh?" Caleb said. "I'll tell you what has ancient wisdom. Tylenol. You tried that? You tried a little something I learned from the native peoples called Advil?"

"How about you go round up your kids."

"We'll be fine," Caleb said, grinning over his coffee. Don believed flight times were merely suggestions. Every year, he'd worry that the planes would get spooked like horses and fly away before he could get the campers to the airport.

"There's the coal train to think about."

"It's going to be fine."

"I know you'll insist on a breakfast stop. You want to ring that bell of yours again?"

Caleb let Don fret for a while as the sky lightened around them and objects took their usual shapes, and then he relented. "I'll move them along."

Walking toward the ditch, he could see campers laden with sleeping bags and backpacks; soon they called to him: *Caleb! Help! You woke us up in the middle of the night. My bag is way heavy.*

For the next half hour, Caleb and Jeremy and Jamal hefted suitcases from the platforms to Don, who loaded them in the bus's storage. When they were finished, Caleb boarded the bus, standing with one hand on the driver's seat. "Shit, they're loud for six thirty in the a.m.," he said to Don.

The lucky campers with window seats rested their cheeks on the glass. Nat and Saskia stood in the aisles to count kids. Kai, whom Caleb had turned away from his yurt the night before, climbed the stairs, slipping past Caleb without looking at him. Rebecca headed up the aisle to where Caleb stood. "Where's David?"

Caleb shrugged, gestured his thumb out the door. "Ask Scott."

He turned sideways to allow Rebecca to pass down the stairs. From the doorway, she called to Scott, who was approaching from the eating platform, bent over a mug. "Where's David?"

"What?"

"Where. Is. David?"

Once aboard the bus, Scott looked down the aisle. "He's not here," Rebecca said, coming up behind him.

"Gotta be. He came down early this morning. Was gone when we woke up. Duffel bag by his bed, everything packed. Figured he had something to do with Caleb."

"Me? Why would he?"

"He's not here," Rebecca repeated.

"We can't wait around," Don said.

Caleb calmed everyone down. "I'll bring David myself. He must've decided to take a walk. Pretty irresponsible of him." He gave Scott cash to buy the traditional breakfast donuts in Delta and patted Don on the shoulder, still relieved at the reassurance of their friendship. "See you at the airport." He hopped off the bus, but Rebecca followed.

"I'm waiting with you," she said, with a fierceness he didn't have time to address.

Don honked the horn.

"Okay, okay," Caleb said to Rebecca. To Don, he said, "Get out of here!"

The doors closed; the bus exhaled and left.

Caleb told Rebecca that he'd check David's platform again. "You hang around here and give him hell when he returns." He grabbed a box of O's from the pantry, eating from it as he walked, impatiently awaiting the return of prodigal—and hopefully penitent—David.

The sky brightened. Nothing moved but the shaking heads of sage. Nor was David on his platform, where Caleb saw only Scott's sleeping bag and eight stripped and stained mattresses. On the shelves, the usual left-behind debris. An uncapped bottle of Off. A pink bandana. One sock. A composition book, its black cardboard cover with a constellation of white spots.

He picked up the notebook, and it opened to the middle, where the pages were sewn together. On the lined paper, indented with ballpoint pen, he found a sort of family tree or genealogy chart. "Water" branching off to "shower" and "drinking" and "plant," which was crossed off and "garden" written above it. "Singing" branched to "Meadow/informal" and "campfires." "Walking," its own category with three subcategories. And so on. The writing became minuscule toward the bottom and edges of the page. Dropped onto the edge of a cot, he turned the page and began reading. *The mitzvah of the generator, which is similar to the mitzvah of sundown . . .*

He flipped forward a few pages: *The mitzvah of looking at the ~~silloehtte~~ sil-lohette of the Dobies when you wake.*

He read awhile; he couldn't say how long—he was simply gone, fallen into this curious encyclopedia of sorts. The mitzvah of John Denver. The mitzvah of standing at the Gathering and feeling your vectors go shoot-ing out. The mitzvah of guitar before eating. The grammar was juvenile, "your" and "you're" methodically transposed. The handwriting was ter-rible, the "vah" of "mitzvah" barely legible, like the silhouette of the Dobies when you wake.

He turned back to the front page to look for a name or explanation and found a ripped-out sheet of paper, folded once, stuck between the front cover and first page.

> Hey Caleb. I think you should have this. I was keeping a sort of record of Llamalo—how it actually works. I don't know if you know the word mitzvah. Actions to bring you close to god. Jewish people—actual Jewish people not like me—say you don't need to believe in god, just do the actions and you get there. What-ever god is, right? Act this way and belief will follow! Anyway I was going to explain this all to you, the whole point of the book. But since we both know that my time here is over—that I <u>won't have anything more to do with Llamalo</u>. Well, I guess I won't get the chance. You could keep this if you want. Love, David

Book in hand, Caleb descended the platform steps and headed to the house. After a few minutes, he picked up his pace, just slightly. Was David running away? Caleb didn't want to give in to panic. It was early still. The kid was surely nearby, could return. Caleb began walking faster. A discon-certing image from *Madeline*, which he'd read hundreds of times to his half sister, appeared. He had a sense of himself as the feminine and ineffectual teacher—or was she a nun?—speed-walking toward disaster at an impos-sible angle to the ground.

Ignoring Rebecca on the porch—"What's wrong? What is it?"—he headed to the parking lot, tossed the composition book onto the floor of his truck, drove all the way to the Sorgers' before he thought better of it. He skidded around and returned to Llamalo, parking beside the house. Ignoring Rebecca again, he ran up to his office and found the number in the phone book for Escadom Search and Rescue.

Chase from the Forest Service answered. "Caleb! Bright and early. Been meaning to ask you about your truck. Glen Lebs said you might be selling it. You called on the Search and Rescue line, not my home line, just FYI."

"I'm missing a boy."

"Seriously?"

"Seventeen-year-old kid. He left this morning, couldn't have gone far. Maybe five eleven. Blondish hair. Can you start looking?"

"Hold up." Chase began asking useless questions. Date of birth. Parents' names and numbers.

"He could be at the river. Actually, I think probably that's where he went. You know, I'll hang up now, go down there myself and check."

"Hold *on*. Wherever he is, he'll probably come back on his own. That's by far the most likely scenario. And now that you've initiated a search, I'll need you by your phone. You'll need to stick around to call us, so we're not scrambling up your cliff all day when he's back there eating marshmallows."

"You know my trail to the river? I can show you," Caleb said while searching for David's file in the box of such.

"All your kids hoofing it every day when I'm trying to count birds? I think I'm familiar with it. Stick by the phone."

Caleb found David's registration and shoved the paper and cordless at Rebecca, who had appeared in the doorway. "Answer his questions. And stay in the house. The phone has a tiny range. Only goes as far as the barn."

He pushed past her to descend the stairs and didn't stop running until he reached the river, a shock of green willows by the blue water.

"David! David!"

A kingfisher flew by, three great blue herons. A bald eagle circled. Tamarisks swayed their lacy fronds. Had he drowned himself?

They would have to dredge the river. He would insist on it. Caleb ran back uphill to find Rebecca on the porch, to ask if Chase had called. But Chase hadn't.

Caleb ran through camp, past the Gathering, climbing into the foothills, so that he could see farther. But he could see nothing. He saw the mountain rising to the east. He saw the Dobies to the south. He saw the green cut of the valley to the west and the mesa beyond, stretching nearly to Utah. He saw nothing. There was no emergency. If there were an emergency, wouldn't he see it? Our eyes are useless tools. Our eyes could see a boy and mistake him for a Russian olive.

Returning to the house, he grew fatigued and unable to run. He jogged and then walked, bent over, a sharp pain between his ribs. He was passing the photography shack when he noticed a small figure moving near the ditch. "David?" he screamed in a high voice. "David?" He felt the wings of endorphins, and he ran effortlessly.

But it was only Rebecca, waiting on the bridge. "Chase called. He's pretty banged up—that's all he said. Banged up. They're bringing him to a hospital in Delta."

"Where was he? Where'd they find him?" Caleb grabbed the phone, as if it held the answers.

"I didn't ask."

"Did you talk to him?"

"To David?"

"Of course David."

"I didn't even ask to. Why didn't I ask?" Rebecca began to cry, and Caleb led her to the truck and slammed her door, his muscles overactive with relief. David hadn't drowned. Nobody was dredging the river. He'd taken a walk, gotten a little scraped up. Caleb found he was still holding the phone, and he set it in his lap as he drove.

After Escadom, the road to Delta dipped into a canyon, crumbling reds and ochre on either side, leprous earth, and then they were stopped for eleven minutes while the coal train rushed by, a passing storm. Once the barrier rose, Caleb drove twice the speed limit. He knew this road.

He'd driven this way so many times, for so many reasons, and all of them were what he wished he were doing; all of the days that came before this one were perfect, he knew now. This was the way to the courthouse for his DUI. This was the way to the bulk-food run. This was the way to the airport twice a summer. This was the way to the Kmart, the way to the hog farm, the way to discount windows, the way to the public swimming pool in Montrose.

This was the way to Delta County Memorial Hospital, a facility only slightly larger than the Kmart. He parked, followed signs to the emergency room, the doors opening for him.

"I need to see David Cohen. Where is he?" he asked at reception. A woman typed slowly, stared at her computer screen. "No, nobody's been admitted by the name of David Cone."

"Cohen," Rebecca said. Caleb turned to her, surprised. He'd been only barely aware of her presence beside him.

"Cone?"

"Cohen," Caleb said louder. "C-O-H-E-N."

"Oh, Co-*hen*."

But no, she couldn't find any patient by the name of Co-hen either and sent them to wait on the molded plastic seats, underneath the muted TV. A toddler was smashing his hand against the buttons on the vending machine. A radio on the reception desk played the country hits of the summer. The boy's mother picked up a newspaper from the floor and began fanning herself with it. She caught Caleb's eyes, rolled hers. "They can't even turn on the swamp cooler for us?"

Caleb sat for a few minutes and then returned to the desk, where the receptionist had begun a word search. "Look, I'm legally responsible for David Cohen. I'll need you to find him now."

"I assure you we're doing all we can."

Finally, a young man in scrubs came out of the triage room with a clipboard in one hand. He walked over to Caleb. "You're the one looking for David Co-hen?"

Caleb nodded.

"We helied him to Denver Trauma about half an hour ago."

Caleb stood up, stepping close to the man. "Didn't you want to tell me? Didn't I need to authorize? Weren't you planning on telling me this?"

The man looked at his clipboard. "Looks like his dad was contacted. Dad's on his way to Denver. Mom was called as well." He had the lilt of a native Spanish speaker. "Mr. Co-hen will be getting the best care possible. You can try to calm down now. You can rest assured."

FIFTEEN

Rocky Mountain High

FACTORING IN THE HOUR they'd spent in Grand Junction to rent a car, because Caleb said his truck might "explode into flaming shrapnel" at the speeds required on the highway, the drive from Delta to Denver took seven hours, during which time they followed the unspoken code of emergency: you don't talk, you don't speculate, you grimly move forward. Caleb switched lanes often, passing eighteen-wheelers, tailgating tourists. Although Rebecca had never spent a day quite like this, had never, for example, driven the breadth of the Rocky Mountains, much of childhood had felt similarly under the sway of crises beyond her control, and she felt like a child again in the passenger seat, hoping Caleb would stop for a bathroom, for food, not wanting to ask. Far worse than her bodily needs was the pain of culpability. She'd wanted to hurt David last night, and this morning he'd fallen and hurt himself. She'd asked for this. But her pain at least could be relieved. She'd apologize for how snide and unhelpful she'd been, and David would forgive. *What does it matter?* he'd ask. She'd come all this way to see him.

Childlike, she'd brought nothing—no wallet, not even a sweatshirt—and when they reached the hospital, it was Caleb, with his ID and authority, who stood in line for the receptionist, sending Rebecca to the waiting area. There were men moaning in their wheelchairs. A protestation of lap babies. An elderly woman lay across three chairs with newspaper over her body. People sat staring at nothing, ignoring the magazines, arms crossed in front of their chests. There was a line for the pay phone, two lines for the receptionists behind plexiglass, but no sense of movement, just the purgatory of waiting in the bracing wind of air-conditioning.

When Caleb returned, it was with good news. He shook her shoulder giddily. "It's going to be fine. He fell, broke something. They wouldn't say what—let's assume arm, maybe leg. Ouch. He's in surgery now. His folks are with him."

"Joe and Judy are here?"

"Waiting in a hallway by post-op. Non–family members aren't allowed, but a nurse suggested we go to the cafeteria, away from this madness. She'll tell them to find us as soon as we can see him. It's going to be fine."

Released from the strictures of emergency, Rebecca couldn't stop babbling as they made their way through brightly lit hallways, up an elevator, down another hallway, explaining that Joe and Judy were like family, second parents. She described Judy's thwarted career with the New York City Ballet, Joe's physical resemblance to Gandhi, which had led to, or perhaps derived from—the causality, now that she thought about it, unclear—an obsession with the great man. For Christmas, Georgia and Ira always gave Joe a Gandhi biography or photo or figurine. Caleb would love David's parents. And they, him.

Outside the cafeteria, Caleb stopped at a row of pay phones and placed a collect call to the counselors. After a failed attempt, he hung up, laughing. "Of course they won't answer. I have the fucking phone. It's in my truck. I drove off with it." It felt like a tremendous joke: how naïve and scared they'd been just a few hours ago.

It wasn't just their good humor that made people turn to stare at them as they pulled open the doors of the cafeteria and entered into the humid smell of disinfectant and spaghetti. It was, she realized, watching Caleb set a plastic tray on a metal counter, that they came from a land of dirt.

Their boots shed mud with every step they took; their shirts held several generations of stains; their hair was greasy, the texture of straw from swimming in the river, with curls matted together. The denim of her shorts, like that of his jeans, had turned brown with dust. As Caleb walked ahead of her around the circuitous lines of food, the smell of him rose above the institutional stench. And she surely smelled the same or worse, she realized proudly.

When she'd met Caleb at the start of summer, she'd been surprised by his appearance. A tree of a guy with lines like bark on his face, he wore odd, ill-fitting jeans, a snap shirt, a cowboy hat. She'd wondered whether it was all a calculated performance. Now, she knew that he simply lived outside the world of commerce, outside of culture and aesthetics, preference and reference. And after eight weeks at Llamalo, she was becoming like him. Everything here seemed antiseptic, unnecessary, funny. What was this greasy meat? These glossy red apples? This case of colored drinks? What were these walls? This TV? This roof? Why be inside at all?

Even electric light, flickering from rectangles in the dropped ceiling, seemed an unnecessary and profligate hindrance to sight.

As they ate, she told him about Ira's letter in *OSN*, reciting much of it from memory. Caleb leaned forward to nab a package of salt from her tray. "This must be devastating for you."

It was, she admitted. Encouraged by his response, she told him at length how she'd begun to question her very identity and purpose. Would she still study media and its role in the uprisings in the third world or run her student activist organizations? And if not, who would she be? If progress toward justice was hopeless, as Ira insisted, then what?

Caleb listened attentively, although he admitted he had no answers. He'd lived too long without even reading a newspaper, except the *Grand Junction Tribune* for the funnies and classifieds. "Although for me," he said, "the way I do live is its own political act."

"That's not systemic," she said quickly, feeling slightly bad about putting him in his place, but it seemed necessary to his understanding of all she'd lost. "Not fighting to change the distribution of power."

"Power, huh?" He shrugged, apparently uninjured. "Maybe not. I guess I've always been interested in something really basic. How it changes you just to live out there, on the plateau. I don't think these individual changes happen in a vacuum. I think they do ripple out into the world. Anyway, I heard you talk about Ira a bunch this summer. I can understand how this would shake you."

It was a momentary disappointment when his focus turned from her to the door behind her. "That's gotta be . . ." he said, rising out of his chair. She turned.

Standing by the stacks of trays, peering around for her, were Joe and Judy—she, with short curls and impeccable posture, he, bald and tan with frameless glasses.

Rebecca and Caleb headed toward the couple. As they passed the cashiers, Caleb stopped her with a hand on her arm. "Just so you know, David might be a little pissed at me at first. We had a bit of a thing last night."

Then his face turned affable, his arm stretched out. "I've wanted to meet both of you for so long," she heard him say, while she hugged Judy, and more briefly, Joe.

"How is he? How is he?" Rebecca asked.

"Let's find a table," Joe said, releasing her.

"We already ate, but the two of you should definitely," Caleb said. "Why don't we go keep him company?"

"Let's find a table," Joe repeated, and there was nothing to do but follow him through the grid of chairs to the far, unpopulated reaches of the room. He came to a stop by a window that looked out on a cement courtyard of smokers and wheelchairs and gestured to Caleb. "Sit."

Rebecca moved to sit as well, but Judy reached for her hand, intertwining her fingers with Rebecca's, keeping her standing beside her.

"So, how's he holding up? We can't wait to see him," Caleb said as Joe pulled out the chair opposite him.

Joe cleared his throat, crossed one leg over the other, sat back in his chair, folding his arms in front of his chest. Finally, he said, "I don't know how much you know about tort law."

"Not much, I admit. Why? Is there something we should be thinking about?"

Rebecca saw a discomfiting differential in their facial expressions. Caleb was open and curious, Joe, tight and controlled, as if working hard to maintain neutrality.

"At seventeen, David's my dependent. I'm responsible for his medical expenses, which means I can, and I will, sue you for the following. The cost of surgery. The emergency room visit. The helicopter." Joe's eyes were focused on a spot in front of him. "There will be rehab, I'm told. Perhaps weeks, but more likely months, of physical therapy."

Caleb jumped in. "Sure, that makes sense. And thanks for the heads-up. You shouldn't have to pay for any of this." He gestured around the cafeteria as if Joe were asking him to underwrite the bowls of Jell-O, the Lipton tea. "I mean, you know that David wasn't on my property when he slipped. Left on his own accord. Just took off. But sure, this shouldn't be on you."

"As I was saying, I can claim medical expenses against you. David has no lost earnings, so you won't be liable for that."

Rebecca was remembering that Joe, unlike Ira, became placid in inverse to his anger. When happy or bored, he might appear jokingly mad, but when truly outraged, he became as calm as salt. It was clear from the way Caleb chuckled amiably that he didn't understand this. "Yeah, right. They still don't pay you to go to high school, do they?"

"Still, I can sue for David's pain and suffering of all sorts," Joe continued, as if Caleb hadn't spoken. "Not just physical, but emotional. Any fears about the future, any psychological trauma caused by the night."

"Night?" Caleb smiled and shook his head. "He left this morning."

Joe turned to his ex-wife. "Did you hear that, Judy?"

Judy nodded. Her rings were digging into the bones in Rebecca's fingers.

Joe resumed his cool regard of Caleb. "We've been wondering the extent of your negligence. In his few moments of lucidity this evening, although of course he was on a high dose of medicine to ameliorate the extreme pain, David described the ordeal of last night. The terror and pain magnified by darkness and isolation. Thankfully, he must have lost consciousness for some of it. When the EMTs found him, he'd begun to enter shock from blood loss. Judy and I have been trying to imagine a night like that. A broken pelvis. Unable to move. Nobody answering his screams. Nobody, apparently, even aware he was missing. As a father, it's not easy to imagine my son like this. You could argue, and many have, that you can't or shouldn't place a financial figure on pain and suffering, and yet that's exactly what our legal system does."

A train had begun to hurtle through the cafeteria, a train with broken brakes, unable to stop, and Rebecca was both passenger and onlooker. Judy's grip, while painful, was keeping her upright.

"It was his pelvis?" Caleb was agitated now. "Look, nobody's given us any information. We've been asking."

"What I'd like you to understand today is that none of this will shut down your camp."

Caleb threw up his hands. "Great. Thanks, I guess. Thank you for not shutting me down. Now can I see him?" He pushed his chair backward, but stopped short of standing when he noticed that Joe hadn't moved.

"No, the lawsuits won't shut you down. Depending on the length of the docket in Colorado, it could be years before you pay a penny. And insurance, which I'm assuming you have, will cover some, although not all, of it. Eventually, you'll see a drastic, perhaps untenable, increase in your premiums. It's likely that, at some later point, you won't be able to find a company willing to insure your land. But, ultimately, you will not be enjoined to cease operations as a result of my tort suit, which means—"

"Enjoin? You lost me there."

"As I was saying, I can't get a judge to issue an *injunction* against you. And so, you should understand, I will need to shut you down through other means, and this will be immediate and irrevocable."

"I'm sorry, but are you threatening . . . ? David *ran away*. This wasn't something I could control."

With one hand, Joe began sweeping the table's crumbs into a pile. "My son spent a night holding on to the side of a cliff, bleeding and unable to move. And you? You didn't even know he was gone." He paused to gently nudge the collected crumbs over the table's edge and into his upturned palm. "So think of this as a promise. I will personally call every parent—every mother, every father—who has ever sent a child to your camp. I will convince them—it shouldn't be hard—not to send their children to you. And if you find *new* children, I will track down *their* parents. I will visit each family individually if need be. I will inform newspapers not to sell you ad space. I will come to any meet and greet you hold. I will make sure that, starting right now, you will never care for children again."

Rebecca watched Caleb's lips open in surprise, but her thoughts were with her own immediate future: what she would say when she saw David, how she might apologize for her terrible stinginess. *Can't you just help me?* he'd asked her last night.

"Look," Caleb said, leaning forward. "I understand you're upset. *I'm* upset. But shutting me down isn't what David wants. Not in the slightest."

"Don't you dare tell me what it is that my son wants." Joe stood, wiping his hands together, releasing the crumbs to the linoleum. "Come on, Judy. I want to get back to him."

Only Caleb was sitting now, elbows on the table, forehead dropped into his hands. "Can you wait here for me?" Rebecca said to him. "I'll be back."

"Oh, hon." Judy released Rebecca's hand, glanced over at Joe. "The thing is, David doesn't really . . . He won't see you right now."

"So, I should wait here?"

"No, hon, look. He was adamant about this. David says he won't see you at all." Judy's tone was soothing but laced with a deep maternal reproof, the likes of which Rebecca had never heard before; she'd always been so good.

"But you said he's groggy. He's medicated. So I'll wait. I can wait. I'll wait." It seemed important not to stop this pathetic pronouncement of her ability to wait, and so she repeated it until Joe said, "Rebecca, just go home. Ira and Georgia would love to have you. Get on a plane and go home. We're not here to disturb David."

As they walked away, Rebecca, guilt clinging to her like an unwashed smell, was struck with the cool scientific knowledge, as if this were happening to someone else, that she would never feel happy again. *Can't you just help me?* he'd asked.

No. She couldn't. She'd wanted him hurt.

"OF COURSE HE'S UPSET. He's a father," Caleb said after nearly an hour of silence. It was 9:22 according to the clock on the dashboard of the rental. They were back on I-70, crossing the Rockies westward, but in the darkness the mountains had disappeared, and they could see only the white lights of cars in the oncoming lanes, the red taillights ahead of them. "But calling the parents? No. He'll realize that's overboard. He'll cool off before that."

Did he really believe this? "Joe? Cool off?" Rebecca said. "He only goes in one direction."

"The thing he needs to understand is, David *loves* Llamalo. He doesn't want this. A broken pelvis is terrible, sure, but . . . it heals. At least David'll be able to explain everything."

"You don't get it. This has nothing to do with what David wants. There's not going to be some consensus meeting. Joe's decided to ruin you, so he will. It'll become his extracurricular, his hobby."

She described how Joe had fought farmers for years to get them to stop forcing laborers to use the short-handled hoe, "El Cortito." She described how he could team up with his friend Ralph Nader to bring national attention to safety at summer camps, using Llamalo as a case study, how friends at *Mother Jones* would write the article, how Ira, perhaps the best investigative reporter alive, outside of, say, Sy Hersh, could find the names of any camp parents, current or prospective. When she finished speaking, the only noise was the whoosh of cars passing in the fast lane.

CALEB DIDN'T SPEAK AGAIN for half an hour, at which time he hit the steering wheel with both hands. "I'm fucked! I'm fucked!"

Caleb was indeed fucked. But what about her? The only boy she'd ever loved didn't want to see her again. The only place this boy cared about was gone. Which was on her. All her fault. And the center had fallen from her life. Nothing mattered. El pueblo unido would be defeated. The schools would never have all the money they needed; the military would not be holding a bake sale; it would never be a great day. Wasn't she fucked, too?

CALEB EXITED THE HIGHWAY at a town called Frisco. He parked in the empty lot of an office complex, all the windows dark, although spotlights on the façade illuminated white letters that spelled GROCHEMCO: GROWING A CHEMICAL COLORADO.

"So, I'll rejigger," he said, still looking straight ahead, hands on the steering wheel at ten and two, as if maneuvering traffic. "No kids. I'll invite adults to live up on the land with me. A year-round thing. Better than a two-month camp. We don't need campers. We don't need tuition. Everyone participates for their keep, maybe pays some room and board. We could break even." A moment later, he breathed out heavily. "But fuck. The lawsuits and the fucking insurance. How do I pay for that?"

"Can't you grow something on the land? Wasn't it a ranch?"

"Costs way more to ranch the land than to let it sit there." He slammed his hands against the steering wheel. "Fuck!"

He drove back to the highway on-ramp, and Rebecca imagined coming back here in two years and finding that GroChemCo had taken over the entire town. And in five years, the company would own the state of Colorado. And in ten years, GroChemCo would be her entire country, and nothing she or anyone did would stop it.

AT 12:17, CALEB AGAIN exited the highway, this time parking at a Taco Bell in Glenwood Springs. "I figured it out."

"What out?"

"Are you hungry? I'm hungry. Let me buy you dinner."

In an otherwise-empty restaurant, over seven-layer burritos and Sprite, he described a plan so fully formed that it seemed he'd spent months devising it, taking notes, weighing philosophical and practical concerns. He would sell the ranch, set aside a portion of the money for lawsuits, and with the rest, he'd buy cheaper land—perhaps in Colorado, but he'd consider Wyoming, Utah, Idaho, anywhere with a similar relation to mountains and the horizontal axis. He'd invite counselors and, when they turned eighteen, former campers. David, of course. Word would spread, and soon he'd be attracting other young people as well. College students on a semester off or in their aimless years after graduating, when life's purpose glowed brightly but held no shape. Before they hardened. Before they were distracted by babies and debt, before they'd relinquished their plans of living a life of wonder.

It had been a mere four hours since he'd learned that Joe would destroy his camp. Already rising from the ashes? He was taut with confidence and optimism, radiant in the ugly fluorescent light.

He asked her if she knew the word "mitzvah."

"Is that a Hebrew word? I'm not really Jewish, not in any synagogue-entering way. Is your mom?" She already knew of the atheism coupled with disdain for all religion—especially their own—on their shared paternal side, the way Ira could not even sit through a revised feminist Seder, where all mentions of Pharaoh were replaced with Reagan, and the hope for next year was never to be in Jerusalem.

"No. But it's a useful word. I've been thinking about it. So, Christians have to believe in God, right? That's what gets them saved—*I take Jesus into my heart*, that sort of thing. But Jews, those skeptical people, don't expect anyone would simply believe in the intangible. So they set up certain actions—or mitzvahs—and by doing them, again and again, you might start to believe. One way to think about Llamalo is that it's not a place, but a series of actions we do."

"I don't get it. You never mentioned God before."

"No, Rebecca. Not the biblical God, but a feeling, a holy feeling. You know it. The feeling of standing on Aemon's Mesa. That's what I've wanted to share with kids. That's what can change them forever. But they can't access that feeling simply by showing up and standing there. I mean, take yourself. Did you feel anything when you first came to Llamalo?"

She shrugged, rightly accused.

"See, it's the actions we do, the rituals, the *mitzvahs*—repetitive, mundane collective acts—that grant us that feeling. We can take these actions anywhere. *They're* Llamalo. And the first mitzvah we'll do, the very first, will be to walk to this new Llamalo all together."

As he spoke, not in the casual way he'd talked all day, but as a camp counselor, as if there were hundreds listening, she thought him brilliant. What an agile, fascinating way to consider Llamalo. And didn't it have echoes of what David had said to her? Was it just yesterday? *Caleb has this way, this system.*

Then his tone switched. "I have five fucking days to figure this out."

"Why five?"

"What do you think?" He spoke sharply, as if annoyed by the slowness of her mind. "Then they leave. The counselors leave. I can't walk *alone*. I can't do rituals *alone*. It doesn't work that way." He pulled the straw from his drink, twisted it tightly around one finger. "Some of them have to come with me. Jeremy? Mikala? They might. Saskia, sure. Maybe Kai. Scott? But I need to convince them. Now. Before school starts and they get distracted and then I'm alone."

He released the straw, and it sprang onto the table. "What about you, Rebecca?" Now his voice was intimate and cautious.

"Me?"

He reached over their trays of food to touch the tips of two of her fingers. "Want to help me save Llamalo? I've seen you here this summer. I've seen how much you changed."

It was true, she realized with a thrill. She wasn't at all the same person. That sexless girl? That prude? Here, she was turned on by the very earth. "Yeah," she would say to her friends back at Berkeley. "I took a semester off to help my cousin start a community. A commune-type . . . A way of living." She'd have to work on the precise vocabulary. "I'll be headed back there in May when classes are out. My boyfriend lives there. David. You should come sometime."

"I think you have an understanding I need," Caleb continued.

She saw herself visiting David tomorrow in the hospital she was currently driving away from. Don't worry, I'm saving Llamalo for you. As the rest of Colorado became subsumed by GroChemCo, only Llamalo remained, a light of resistance. Not systemic? Well, what was? *My friends, we have done something wrong.*

"So what do you think?"

Dive in, she heard him say. Dive in and ride this wave with me. She turned to the window, which, in the darkness, had become a mirror. She saw them both leaning forward, looking so much alike, and who could tell whether it was familial resemblance or the Jewish thing or the determination of a diver. "I could take a semester off. Maybe longer."

SIXTEEN

Metamorphoses

A SMALL GLITCH: DONNIE'S car was still parked at the trailer.

Caleb had seen it in his headlights when he and Rebecca returned to camp at two thirty in the morning, and now he was lying in his yurt wondering what to do. His only goal over the next few days was to convince the counselors to leave with him for the new Llamalo. But who would do this if Donnie, inarticulate as he might be, found a way to share his rumors and rageful fantasies? Donnie wanted nothing more than to sow chaos. His only goal was to fuck things up for Caleb.

He imagined calling Donnie in the morning from the ranch house.

"Hello, Donnie. It's Caleb. Please leave my property immediately."

"Hello, Donnie. Guess what? You're not allowed to visit your dad anymore."

"Hello, Donnie. It's Caleb. You can stay, but I forbid you to talk to the counselors."

When had Donnie ever done what Caleb wanted him to do?

Well, once he had.

At this thought, Caleb threw off his blanket and walked out of his yurt, its canvas walls too confining for his excitement. Barefoot on the wooden platform, he tilted back his head to breathe in the stars. All that mattered, he reminded himself, was the invitation.

Over the years, Caleb had learned that if you invited them the right way, people generally acted how you wanted them to act. If you made sure to invite them into something grand and purposeful. If you told a compelling and urgent story into which they could enter. If you gave them a role, a small but crucial part.

WHEN HE WOKE, HE was startled by a strange light. He'd never been in his yurt midmorning in the summer, and it was like being trapped within a glowing white orb, what a caterpillar might see midway to becoming a butterfly.

At the house, he found the counselors doing nothing, directionless, under the halcyon illusion that everything hadn't just changed. They were squeezed around one table on the eating platform. Four played hearts; two, cribbage. On the table were boxes of cereal, bowls crusty with oatmeal. Caleb stood behind Kai, placing his hands on her shoulders, pressing his thumbs along the knobs of her spine to the velvety nape, and in that way, he apologized for his distance of the past few days. As he rubbed, he told everyone that David had been in a good mood, despite some injuries he'd sustained when he'd fallen while on an ill-conceived farewell walk yesterday morning. (Caleb had told Rebecca, and she'd agreed, that this was a simpler story to present.) Caleb then gave instructions for the work that the counselors needed to do that day, but he made sure to praise them, too, to tell them he trusted them to set whatever pace they needed, to take trips to the river, to have a good time.

"Wouldn't it be so fun to bring the baby to the river?" Nat said. "She's such a squish!"

"She's like the cutest thing," Kai said, leaning into Caleb's hands. "Don was walking the ditch with her, and we all got to hold her."

Caleb tried to keep his tone casual. "Was anyone else with them?"

They said no, they didn't think so.

Caleb sat with them until he saw Don drive away. He told the counselors, in a demanding tone that negated his previous laissez-faire sentiment, that it was time for them to head over the ditch. Once alone, he walked across the alfalfa field to the trailer.

"My dad's not around," Donnie said, filling the doorway so Caleb couldn't see inside, although he could hear a baby's emphatic babbling.

"No, that's fine. The thing is, Donnie, I was looking for you." Standing at the threshold, Caleb was a step down from Donnie, a bothersome deficiency in height he wasn't used to.

"Not exactly in the mood for a chat." The door began to close.

"Wait up," Caleb yelled. And since all that mattered was the invitation, he said into the diminishing space between door and jamb that Donnie had made some really great points when talking to the campers.

The door stopped moving a few centimeters from shut. "Really smart thinking. I listened to you, and I thought about it. This is your land, Donnie. When Exxon left, it was a terrible time for everyone here. I didn't mean to take advantage after what Exxon did."

The door opened. "Wasn't Exxon."

Caleb nodded several times, trying to agree with this irrationality without convicting himself. "After the . . . unfortunate circumstances. Look, Donnie, you belong on this land. You're right about that. And I wish, man, I *wish* I could give it to you outright. I really do. Unfortunately, I've got debts, as you might imagine. But how about this? I'll give it to you as cheap as I can." Caleb named a price. It was slightly less than he'd paid eight years earlier but still significant, although, as he'd been telling himself all night, surely mining jobs paid quite well and Donnie's expenses were minimal. Besides, wouldn't Escadom Savings loan the Talcs whatever they needed? "How's that sound? You think you could come up with that?"

Donnie turned away, retreating into the trailer. Caleb leaned in and saw Donnie, responding to a noise, crouched and tugging something from the baby's mouth. "Drop it, Kay-Kay. I said drop it." When he returned, he was holding the girl. She had a red shirt, diaper, yellow flyaway hair, a grave expression like her dad. Her starfished palm was hitting his chest.

"I mean, if you can't get the money, I do understand," Caleb said nonchalantly, his heart pounding as if a palm were slapping his own chest.

"You think I couldn't? You really are an asshole."

"Sorry, I didn't want to assume. Well, I was hoping to get this going as soon as possible. How much time will it take to get it together?

"Like I said, no problem. Whenever you're ready."

Caleb shoved his hands into his pockets. "There are a couple additional things I'll need you to do, though."

"Things?"

"Just two." Caleb paused. With an anxious little smile, he said, "Number one is, I need you not to speak to the counselors. You don't tell them anything. I just want to be clear, and I wish I didn't have to ask this, but if I find out you even come near them, I'll have no choice but to sell to someone else."

Donnie stared at Caleb. It was a wolfish stare, both vulnerable and accusatory. "And two?"

Caleb laid out the second condition. He told him what time to come to the Overlook on Friday, what to wear, what to say. He said that if this went as planned—and he had every reason to believe it would—on Saturday morning the two of them would meet at Escadom Savings and begin the land transfer.

"You're bribing me?"

"No, no. *No.* Not a bribe, Donnie. This is mutually beneficial. Come on—you can see that."

There was a noise—a thunk and then a scratch, like a branch scraping glass—and a shuffle of blue-and-white feathers in Caleb's peripheral vision. A bird flying across the alfalfa field had hit one of the trailer's windows and dropped to the ground. They moved together from the doorway to see. A magpie lay still.

For a few seconds, nothing. Just Kayla pointing. Then it shook, and without discernible effort, it was aloft, showing off the oily black underside of its wings, their crisp white bands.

"Thank god," Caleb said.

"Stupid bird," Donnie said.

But the way they stood there and the sound of their voices made it seem, to Caleb at least, like they'd finally said the same thing.

AT LUNCHTIME, CALEB FOUND the counselors on the porch. He crouched to get their full attention. On Friday, he said, after all their tasks were done, they were going to do something they'd never done before. They would have a kind of ceremony, during which he would give them news that, quite frankly, would change their lives forever.

"What?" Kai asked.

"Rebecca knows, but she's not telling, are you Rebecca?" He caught his cousin's eye, shared a smile.

Nat said, "This is so freaking mysterious."

Scott said, "Whoa."

Caleb grinned. "Good. Get excited. You should be."

◆ ◆ ◆

THERE WERE INDIANS EVERYWHERE on Charlene and Hein's coffee table that evening. Seated warriors with ribboned headdresses. Barechested bucks on horseback. Men smoking the peace pipe inside a teepee. A whole clique of kneeling maidens, breasts just pouring out of leather dresses, one of whom Donnie had picked up and was examining. "Your mom loved Indians, just like me," Charlene said, coming up beside him. "You remember that about her? How she used to say she must be part-Indian because she loved the Indians so much?" Charlene was child-sized, had been old even when Donnie was a kid, and she had to reach onto her toes to pinch his upper arm when she said, "It's good to see you back, Donnie."

It was Sunday night, and she'd filled her house for him. Charlene and Hein's daughters and their families, and Press and Amy-Lynne Sorger, and Glen Lebs, who'd been just a skinny, nervous fucker and was now the cop, and his parents, Eugene and Sue Lebs of Lebs's Orchard. Also Craig and *his* parents and brothers and their families, and the Kinneys, who owned Frank's Farm and Feed, and a whole flock of teenage girls in Escadom High shorts and ponytails, one of whom brought him a banana split in a red plastic bowl, blushing cutely. And whenever he was thirsty, some woman would say to some kid, "Go get Donnie a beer," because he was the guest of honor, the king, the one they'd all come to see, after his years in banishment, and they didn't even know it was over yet.

The teenage girls had set Kayla on the rug and brushed makeup on her cheeks, and last he saw, she was back in the kitchen, where some women were feeding her succotash from their fingers. Donnie discreetly felt up the Indian maiden. He'd never been an honored guest before, never even had a birthday party after his mom died, and here he was, basking in love coming at him from all directions.

He could kiss Charlene in gratitude, pick her up and spin her around. If Charlene hadn't planned this party for him, he would've left yesterday. Instead, he'd called in sick and was around this morning for Caleb to tell him he could have his land back. He hadn't thought he'd convinced Caleb, but apparently he had. He waited until there was a unified lull in the conversations, and then he set the maiden down, saying to no one in particular, "Well, it looks like I'll be moving back here."

The heads nearest turned to him.

Donnie nodded, as if in response to a question. "Yup. Caleb's ashamed of how he acted. Moving on. Says it's Talc land."

Charlene sucked in air between her teeth. "Don't joke, Donnie. That's my job you're talking about."

"Not a joke. Apparently, he grew tired of being a liar and a thief." If Donnie's mom was part-Indian, this made him part-part-Indian, and he war-cried and whooped until everyone in the room was looking at him. "Sayonara, asshole."

"What's he saying?" Sue Lebs asked from a chair in the corner.

"Caleb. Up on Aemon's place," Gene Lebs called. "Giving it to Donnie."

"He didn't mention this to me," Press said, turning to Don, who sat beside him on the couch. "He tell you?"

Don was staring at Donnie. They hadn't had time to confer. His dad had been gone all day, driving kids from church camp in Naturita. "He's *giving* it you?" Don said. "When did this happen?"

"Selling it."

Don set his plate on the coffee table and walked out of the room, just as some Sorger girl entered from the kitchen, saying, "Did I hear right? My *job's* gone?"

"*You* gonna hire us now, Donnie?" asked one of Charlene's daughters.

Gene Lebs said, "Well, good for you, Donnie. Good for you." Finally, the mood turned the way it should. Everyone started saying how glad they'd be to have Donnie back, and when would they meet the famous Marci, and wasn't it great he'd earned enough money to buy his ranch back, wasn't he responsible, and the Sorger girl, who was worried about her laundry job, told her daughter to get Donnie a beer.

After which, Donnie went to the bathroom, saying hello to his mom, whom he found in a photo in the hallway, a bridesmaid at one of Charlene's daughters' weddings, in a lavender floor-length dress with ruffles and high collar, her hair in two wings. She was captured midsentence, but what was she saying?

On his way back to the living room, he saw that the door to Charlene and Hein's bedroom was flung open. He looked inside, and there was his daughter. Don had removed his boots and was on the bed with his legs stretched out; little Kayla, part-part-part-Indian, a papoose on his chest, her dreams, whatever they were, caught by the circles of webbed string and beads above the bed.

"Where you getting the money?" Don whispered, patting Kayla's back.

"I'll get it. Everyone has money. Money's not the problem."

Later, sticking around after everyone else had left, even Don and Kayla,

Donnie asked Charlene if she could give him a loan. She was at the sink, hands gloved in bubbles, and she turned to him.

"Oh, Donnie. I loved your mom, and I love you. But I got nothing." Donnie looked through the living room to where Hein was watching an enormous TV. Charlene was lying. "I got two of my daughters working the kitchen with me. That's our income. What we make in the summer from Caleb takes us through the year. I'm happy for you, Donnie, but I don't know what we'll do."

THE NEXT DAY, DONNIE found Logan Sorger in his upper corral and asked him. Logan took off his hat, wiped his forehead with his sleeve. He was two years older than Donnie; they used to get drunk and push each other into the ditch. "Don't you get it? There isn't a single person we don't owe money to."

He went to talk to Glen Lebs and heard the same shit. The Lebses were drowning, their orchard insolvent. He drove over to Frank's Farm and Feed, and Kevin Kinney told him that they were going through a temporary hard patch. He even asked Craig, who worked at the coal mine and whose dad worked at the coal mine, and both of them made less than Donnie made at AmMiCo.

That was Tuesday. On Wednesday, he called human resources at AmMiCo and said he was quitting. Then he called Marci and told her to come to Colorado. She said, "With what car? You took it." When he asked if her dad could give them a loan, she said, "I knew it! I knew it!" And then she grew hysterical and screamed that he needed to bring Kayla back right away. Still, it didn't seem like it should be hard to get the money. There was money all around.

The woman who led him into her cubicle at the bank was plump and pretty and smelled of floral shampoo, but soon it became clear she pitied him. His credit rating wouldn't allow her to approve a mortgage of that size. No, not even a mortgage half that size. But she did know a real estate agent who specialized in starter homes and trailers he could talk to.

All week, he could hear the counselors shouting to each other, playing their music. From the trailer, he couldn't see their ratty ways, except when two of them lay on the top of the picnic tables like they were lawn chairs. He didn't walk by the house, didn't speak to them. Not once, not even when the Jewess with the sharp face and the tufts of hair in her underarms came right up to him when he was sitting with Kayla outside the trailer.

"So what's your baby's name? She's so cute. Are you Don's son?" She was polite and serious, and it would be fun to flirt, to make her blush. It would be fun to tell her the truth about Caleb and watch her react.

"I'm not allowed to talk to you," Donnie said finally. He did what he was told. Walked inside the trailer, where it was so hot Kayla's skin pimpled.

◆◆◆

"Sorry, sorry," Rebecca said, backing up, apologizing instinctually, even though she hadn't done anything wrong. She'd only tried to be nice. The man was always alone, sitting outside his dad's trailer in his USA shirt with his baby on a towel beside him. He was the man who'd tried to talk to them on the last day of camp and who'd been too shy and flustered to get his words out. She hadn't wanted to bother him. She'd only wanted to tear down hierarchies! Wasn't that a noble impulse? It wasn't right, the way the counselors hung out day and night, like at a movable party, and he sat alone, a single dad, hardly older than she was.

She'd simply wanted to extend friendship across class lines. It seemed bizarre that he wouldn't let her. He wasn't allowed? By what religion, what law?

In the grip of embarrassment, she marched toward the house and entered the little upstairs office with the darling wallpaper. She hated this room now. She came here every day, ignoring messages littered across the desk—*Rebecca, your mom called; Rebecca, call your mom*—instead, calling David at the hospital. "Oh, Rebecca, hon," Judy had said on Monday, Tuesday, and Wednesday. "He's busy now. I'll tell him you called."

Today was Thursday. The counselors were at the river, but she'd stayed back to use the phone, to finally tell Georgia that she'd be leaving school to help Caleb.

"After what he did to David?" Georgia said. "Judy said that Caleb acted unconscionably, that he was *dangerously* negligent. I only reached her once, the day after it happened. Joe won't speak to us at all. Like everyone else, they're furious about *OSN*. You don't know this, because you won't return my calls, but all our friends are absolutely enraged at Dad. I get blamed, too, you know."

Rebecca patiently explained that Caleb didn't *do* anything. David had done it himself, run away, attempted to descend a cliff in the dark, all because—here she became a little flustered, since she still didn't know why he'd left that night. Was it because she'd bad-mouthed Caleb? Was it because David and Caleb had fought? When she'd asked Caleb what they'd fought about, he'd brushed it off, saying, *Just a little thing.*

"All because he loves it here!" she said finally, in an adamant tone that made up for the gaps in logic. He loved this place Joe was destroying, this place Rebecca would now save. Or, if not the place, exactly, then the spirit of it, the ethos, the *way*.

"Well, Joe'll never forgive Caleb," her mom said. "You know that. But what I'm hearing is that you're reacting to what's happening here. You're having a reaction, which is understandable."

"It's not about *there*. I love it *here*. I love Caleb's vision," she said, realizing too late that this was not the way people in her family spoke. They didn't care about "visions." They just did their work. Until they didn't.

"We need to talk about what Dad did," Georgia said. "I need to know how you're feeling. How *is* this for you?"

"I'm fine."

"You've had the paper for a month without calling us. We gave you space, but you have to talk to me now. It's a big change. I can admit, as I'm sure you've guessed, that it wasn't my plan. It was all Dad. I hope you don't mind me telling you that I'm furious, too. Like you, I'm completely enraged."

The feelings Georgia apparently wanted to talk about were her own. "Everyone asks me why Ira thinks he was the only one who could do it. His voice is all that matters? Someone could've taken over as publisher. What about all the work everyone else did? What about the subscriber base? Everyone's asking if *I* wanted the job, but you know he couldn't have watched me, just sit by like that and watched."

"So, I'll call Berkeley and take a leave of absence."

"Don't be ridiculous—you can't stay there. You'll be so relieved to go back to school. I only wish I had that kind of distraction."

Ira must have walked into the room, because Georgia began screaming. "Don't put it there. Ira, *Ira*. Ira, stop. I'll do it. Here, you talk to Rebecca. She says she's leaving school. Because of what you did. She's upset, like I told you."

"Pumpkin. I appreciate you calling finally." Her father's voice shocked her. That he still existed! That he had not, with the letter, somehow offed himself. "I know how mad you must be at me."

"I'm not mad."

"It's natural for you to be furious. It's not how you would want things to go. But school is exactly what you need. The sadness you're feeling, the sadness we're all feeling, will be mitigated by school. You'll have your clubs. Your classes. Your friends."

"Are you listening to me? I'm not sad."

And she wasn't. She'd spent the past few days floating on an eddy of happiness. Or if not happiness, then a wondrous type of energy. She enjoyed watching and talking to Caleb, who had several times taken her aside to seek her insight about the counselors and their possible commitments. Caleb was brilliant and decisive. He didn't quit or fail. He cared so deeply about giving everyone the feeling of standing with so much space all around. David had been right about him, after all. And David, whom

Llamalo had transformed so thoroughly, who was so entirely different here than at home, David would be thrilled when he finally learned what she was doing.

Often, when Rebecca walked about camp, she felt outside of herself, as if she were watching a movie about a woman who had come to save a dying town. And the woman in this movie was beautiful and sexy and also somehow her. Because she had transformed as well. How had she ever thought she could go back to Berkeley, to the loneliness of that neutered existence? Here, Scott smiled at her, Jamal gave her a back rub, Jeremy put his hand on her thigh and asked if she wanted to go look at the stars with him. They were on the Meadow at the time, the stars abundant above them, so she said no, she had a boyfriend, didn't he know?

She listened as Ira screamed at Georgia. "Put the phones in the closet. No, not in there. I told you to give them away. I told you." To her, he said, "It's a mess here, pumpkin. We have to clear out the office before the first of the month. So tell me, is this an emergency? Are you actually serious about leaving school? Because I'll drive there. I'll come, and we can talk this through. Is that what you need? You need me to come there?"

"No. I don't."

He went through his schedule aloud anyway. He had a lunch interview that afternoon and a radio appearance the next day. He told her he was always giving interviews now. The *Nation*, NPR, the *San Francisco Bay Guardian*. They all wanted to know why he stopped the paper and what his thoughts were about the invasion. "You know about that, right? Iraq invaded Kuwait—done deal, now it's really happening. I'm sure you've been reading all about it. I can leave Saturday. We'll talk it through. Actually, Saturday's tough. I'm sorry, pumpkin," he said regretfully, as if unable to accept an invitation she'd extended.

"Don't worry about it."

"Just get yourself back to Berkeley and we'll come see you there. I'll come next week. We'll go out to lunch and talk about everything."

She could hear Georgia's voice in the background.

"George, I get it," Ira said. "So, Mom says to remember, it's okay to be angry. It's okay to be sad."

"I'm happy," Rebecca screamed, hitting her hand on the desk. "I am very, very happy."

THE CARTER YEARS: OCTOBER 1977

IN THE BEGINNING, OF course, there was no myth, just a younger Caleb, a skinny, nervous Caleb, standing beside his car's open trunk at the end of a dirt road.

He knew how the story should go: A young man walks into the wilderness, unheeded and alone, and he finds purpose, strength, surety. Caleb knew the words "Rocky" and "Mountain." Put together, they erupted into snowy peaks passable only by mountain goats, wolves, bear, and himself.

Perched on the ground beside him was a backpack with a metal frame like a railing for the disabled. Into the pack, he pitched a silver can opener still clinging to its cardboard backing, a can of refried beans, a fork. He looked for the mountain but could see only foothills furry with low brush. He hoped the mountain wasn't too high. He shoved batteries into a flashlight's plastic canister and dropped that into the backpack as well. On the other hand, if the mountain were too short, would it really count?

He'd left DC nearly two weeks earlier with a simple, glorious plan, which was to climb the mountains of the West and learn the secrets of people who did such things. People such as his father, dead now six years. Caleb was taking a semester off from college; there was no better time to uncover these secrets. "It was gnarly," he would say when he returned to his job at Kinko's. "It was *insane*," he'd say.

But he'd driven to the Bitterroot Mountains and the Wind River Range and the Uintas and the La Sals, and he hadn't climbed anything. Instead he ate at Denny's and slept in hostels, including the hostel in Moab with a live alligator in the bathtub and the one in Lander with three girls lying shirtless on the roof. The other young men wore sunglasses on little leashes and read topo maps before setting out for the wilderness without inviting Caleb. They looked at him as if they knew he'd never slept outside except for that one night on the lawn between Temple Emanuel and the Dunkin' Donuts to raise money for the cross-country team.

Caleb crouched to tie the laces of work boots as large as teakettles. He was due at Kinko's in three days and should really be driving through Nebraska right now, but last night he found himself on a small highway somewhere past Montrose, Colorado. There were no billboards. No stores. No suburbs, no subdivisions, no woods, no apartment complexes, no intersections, no overpasses, no cemeteries. Nothing he was used to. When he saw a sign for Gunnison Mountain Road, he took it. Although he couldn't actually see a mountain, he decided that this was the Rockies, and Gunnison would be the mountain he would climb before returning home. He slept in his car and woke at dawn, figuring he should be able to ascend and return by nightfall.

There was no marked trail, so Caleb headed off between huddled juniper trees. After fifteen minutes, he turned to look at his Honda, which was actually his stepdad's Honda, orange and bereft, like a homebound pet. He waved, just a small lift of his hand, because he was embarrassed to be waving to a car, although no one could see him, not even the Honda.

Soon Caleb grew pleased with the sluggishness of his leg muscles and the blisters ballooning on his heels and toes. This pain meant that he wasn't the same Caleb as he'd been in DC, when his body had felt nothing. Here, red crevices had been cut into the earth. Maybe he, too, was cut away, all that was distasteful about him, all he'd inherited from his mother—his worry, arrogance, pessimism, all eroded.

As he walked, he found himself keeping pace to the iambic first line of a Thoreau quote. *The-West of-which I-speak. The-West of-which I-speak.* And, unbidden, it came back to him: The first time his dad took him hiking, how he'd strained to keep up. He'd been nine, naïve, sycophantic. Even now, a decade later, he cringed with embarrassment, remembering how, at the dizzy peak, with patchwork Vermont spread below them, he'd tried to impress Robbie by saying solemnly, "Now I understand wilderness."

Robbie had laughed like a delighted baby. "This? This is sweet, but shit, it's not wilderness. It's not really even a mountain. What is it? Second-growth forest on a hill? A mound? A trumped-up anthill? You want real wilderness, you should come to Utah. Or Wyoming. Colorado—*that's* wild."

Robbie had then explained that the reason he didn't visit Caleb more often—and he would like to, really he would—was that when he hung around humans after a stretch in his cabin in Utah, the anxiety that came off them was so heavy he could smell it. "Like burning rubber. I can *literally* see the fear of death on them. I just kind of sit back and watch them buzz around, rush and stress and freak out. Just so they can gorge themselves and buy crap and watch television and make lists. *You* see this, right? They're trying to distract themselves. And the funny thing is, they don't even have to feel that way!"

Later that day, Robbie had dropped him back at his mom's, where, a week later, a letter arrived with no message, just the quote in his dad's handwriting, the words crawling across the paper. "*The West of which I speak is but another name for the Wild; and what I have been preparing to say is, that in Wildness is the preservation of the World. —Henry David*"

The quote, he later learned, after checking out every book by Thoreau from his jr. high library, came from an essay titled simply, "Walking." And here he was at last, walking in the West, the Wild. "Colorado," he said, and he liked the round sound of the word.

It was not yet noon when he finished his beans and realized his life's purpose. He was meant to be a wilderness pioneer, a leader through the unknown, an interpreter of the desolate high-altitude expanses. His laces were stippled with burrs, like a feasting of aphids on stems, and although he didn't know the name of the burrs, he wanted to teach the name to a group of people who walked behind him.

He wanted to say "butte," "mesa," "abutment," and he wanted the people walking behind him to ask "Which is which, Caleb?"

He wanted to show them how to find a stream to drink from, but there were no streams— only the moldy green of sagebrush. His water bottle was either half-full or half-empty, depending, and he began to suspect he was walking in a wide circle.

A few hours later, still walking, he thought about a chicken club with bacon. He heard behind him a rustle that could be mountain lion or rattlesnake. He thought about a hamburger and cheese fries. He would like it with grilled onions. He would like there to be a pink glistening pool of grease veined with ketchup when he finished. He would lean to the plate and put his mouth to this pool, like a hungry bear dipping his head into a pool of snowmelt.

It was the muddy middle of October; all around him hungry bears were looking for one last meal.

Just before dark, he came upon a butte or mesa or abutment rising from the flatness. He could barely make out a grove of trees on its ledge; perhaps, finally, this was the base of the mountain. He walked toward it, steadily, without rushing, without running, chanting to himself as he stepped: Look at me, Ma. I am walk-ing, Ca-leb walk-ing, walk-ing Ca-leb.

And then he began running, fitting between the shrubs, snagging and freeing his coat. Look at me, Ma. I am run-ning, run-ning, run-ning.

And then he was climbing, and very worried indeed, because Caleb was still Caleb, and the earth slipped out from under him with every step, and the plants he grabbed hold of had tiny thorns.

At the top, he could see neither the mountain nor his stepdad's Honda, and the grove of trees was actually just two trees without leaves, so leafless in fact it seemed they were dead and not simply wintering. It seemed they hadn't had leaves in years, had grown from a seed leafless, had been saplings without leaves, like hairless deer.

He was surprised to feel, more than terror or exhaustion, the warm flush of envy. All he wanted was to be the kind of man who belonged here, who would know where the hell he was and what to do next. "Just *tell* me," Caleb called out. "What am I supposed to *do*?" But his father, still dead, did not answer.

SEVENTEEN

The Invitation

"YOU'RE JUST PLANNING TO let the crud fall on the floor?" Don said during Kayla's Friday morning nap.

Donnie was standing barefoot on the back of the couch with a screwdriver to remove the lighting fixture, making his dad feel short and unagile, linoleum-bound—and thus, unable, despite his promises to himself, to let his son be.

"Look at the mess it already made."

Donnie jerked his head, and his body undulated to regain balance. "And what would you recommend doing? Just let it sit up here filthy, like . . . ?"

Like everything else in this place. The rest of the sentence didn't need to be uttered. When Donnie had arrived home and set Kayla on the floor, he'd said, "This is how you live?" Denise had taken everything of hers, her herbs and rose soap, the mosaic coffee table, the still life of amber beads and peaches she'd painted. And all the old stuff, all of Pammy's stuff, had been given to Caleb years ago. "Just a double-wide on the Double L," Don had joked, but Donnie had turned away, and who could blame him?

Now, Don coughed and wiped his eyes to make a show of the dust. It was pretty, actually, in its slow fall. Donnie had done nothing wrong, not really. All he'd done was ask every single person in town for a loan, and each one had made a point of telling Don about it. *Sorry, Don. You understand.* How did Donnie think this would make Don feel? If anyone should help buy back the Talc land, it should be Don. He was fifty-five years old and had nothing to give his son. The shame gripped at him.

So when Donnie let a screw drop behind the couch cushions, Don didn't stop himself from yelling, "Great. Now what?" Donnie thudded onto the floor.

Don chuckled while Donnie stripped the couch, diving for the screw, retrieving pennies sticky with crumbs. He realized with a shock that Denise's hair would be there, long and black, and suddenly, desperately, he wanted Donnie to find one, to hold it up and ask, "What life have you been living, Dad?"

But all Donnie said was, "You're blocking the light." He couldn't find the screw and had to climb back on the couch to remove the swinging fixture before it fell.

"Here, Dad, catch." Donnie held out a half sphere of clouded glass, the bowl filled with dead bugs, like letters fallen off a page. It was this cockiness that broke something in Don, who these days had to hold on to the sink when he brushed his teeth.

He didn't know what happened next. Did he even reach for it?

Perhaps his fingers didn't close. The glass dropped onto the orange linoleum and shattered.

"I'll sweep." Donnie jumped off, and Don flinched to see those bare feet and the crystalline winks of glass. But he didn't say, "Don't" or "Watch out."

Instead, he lit into his son: Didn't Donnie know that he had no hope of buying back the ranch? Did he think he'd find the money floating in the irrigation ditch? No, he had to embarrass Don by asking all his friends. This was childish behavior. Donnie was still a child. Not like Caleb. Maybe now, Caleb would stay. Caleb was steady. Caleb was dependable. Caleb was a Jew; he understood the value of money. On and on, until Donnie stepped over the splinters on the floor and walked out the door barefoot, holding his new brown cowboy boots by their pull straps, saying he was going into town for the afternoon, telling Don to feed Kayla the prune juice mixed with punch and to use the powder on her rash, leaving Don to think, But I am a father, too.

◆ ◆ ◆

Donnie parked in Caleb's lot, where his dad couldn't see his car, and walked toward the house. He hadn't been back up here all week, and it was more a mess than ever. Nobody here, but sweatshirts sprawled on the grass. Mugs on the stairs. On the porch, the military drone of wasps over an open jar of jelly.

He heard them before he saw them, squawking like migrating geese. When he caught sight of them on the road, he hid in the barn like he'd done as a kid, standing flat against the doorway to watch the outside world from the dimness inside.

They came like characters in a storybook. Little hairy elfin boy. Bald giant boy, bare-chested except for the straps of a backpack. Sexy black-haired lady in a bikini top. Caleb wasn't there, just the others.

They weren't all Jews. The sexy one looked like she could be from Hawaii. The girl with huge tits was pale as sugar. One of the boys was African or maybe dark Mexican.

The boys carried tamarisk branches, which was dumb, since if you so much as lay one of those branches down, six plants would grow immediately in that spot. Two girls had their faces hidden behind huge passels of sunflowers. Another gripped a tired bunch of Queen Anne's and columbine. Finally, he saw the little Jewess, wearing the same shirt as when she'd tried to talk to him. She called to the others, "I'll get marigolds!" His lucky break.

She unlatched the garden fence, closed it behind her. Donnie watched her crouch over a fishing tackle box, retrieve clippers, then squat again by a bed of flowers. When the others were across the ditch, out of earshot, he walked up to the fence, pulling down the brown hat he'd bought at Frank's three days earlier. That's when he'd bought the snap shirt he was wearing. He was all dressed up like a cowboy again, just like Caleb had asked him to be.

He grasped the fence with both hands, poked the pointy toe of his new cowboy boot into a diamond of fencing, feeling like an ape up against its cage, although it was technically the girl who was inside the enclosure.

He didn't say anything, just let her notice him, those thick eyebrows registering surprise. Was there something he wanted?

"You grow all that yourself?"

She earnestly explained that everyone here worked collaboratively, taking the time to define the word in case he was an idiot: "Like, worked together."

"I figured someone as pretty as you could make the flowers grow all by yourself."

She was quickly flustered, splotches blooming on her cheeks until she was gloriously pink. "Well, no . . . I mean, thanks . . . I mean . . ."

"Right here." He pointed at the bed of yellow and orange flowers. "Right here exactly is where Caleb used to sleep."

"He slept in the garden?"

"Weren't a garden then, just a field. He made a point of sleeping in the field back when he was a journalist."

She shook her head, leaving some strands of black hair caught on her mouth. "Caleb? I don't think so."

"Sure, he was a journalist. Didn't he tell you about that? He wanted to write an article about me for his paper. He took notes on me for a week, wrote down everything I said."

Funny he'd ever believed this story, even at eighteen; it was so obviously false. The girl clearly thought so, too. A whole week writing an article about *him*? That's what her face said.

"Article never appeared, though. I called them once. Strange little newspaper that he worked for. Name was *Our Side Now*. I got their number and called them maybe a year later and asked them to send me the article about me, but they couldn't find nothing with my name in it. Funny thing is, at the end of the week interviewing me, he had a change of heart. Left his career as a journalist and bought up my land."

"Yeah, no. I think you misheard. He didn't work there."

"Really?" Donnie acted shocked, pushing away from the fence. "Is that so?" As if he'd never figured this out on his own. Still, it was good to have corroboration that Caleb hadn't bought the land with money he'd made. Why should Donnie pay for it when Caleb hadn't? When he'd been given money by any number of groups, maybe even by the feds. He'd read about situations like this in the brochures from People for the West! Called an illegal taking. As illegal as it got.

"Funny thing is, he told me I wasn't allowed to talk to any of you. I wonder if this is why. Or if maybe there are other things he don't want me to say. I just keep wondering about that."

Then he walked back to his car, even as he could hear her ask, "He told you not to *what*? Wait. Wait, could you just . . . ?"

◆ ◆ ◆

BRIGHT ORANGE, REBECCA TOLD herself. Overlapping petals. She smelled one: Wet dog. "Really feel it. Smell it. Roll it between your fingers," her math teacher at Samohi had said after coming back from a retreat in Ojai and placing a single raisin on a napkin on each desk. "Have you ever truly tasted a raisin? Use all your senses to live in this moment, this wondrous moment."

Although Rebecca had been bored by the raisin then, she tried it now with the marigolds in her hand. The petals against her lips were as soft as . . . petals.

Caleb was good and brilliant, deserving of her help. This was her very last certainty. She might doubt everything else, but not this. He'd never forbid this man to talk to them. But hadn't he asked Rebecca to lie about David? Think about the marigold and nothing else.

The marigold was boring. Pain slipped into the wings of her ribs as she carried the flowers to the Gathering, singing with cheer even she understood as false, *You are my sunshine, my only sunshine.*

◆ ◆ ◆

When Donnie didn't return by midafternoon, Don dropped Kayla and her snacks at Charlene's and drove to where his bus waited in the Escadom High lot. The girls' basketball team shoved on, headed for a preseason game in Montrose. The coaches were driving separately, so it was up to Don to maintain order. Good luck to him. Even the kids he'd driven to school every day for years didn't say, "Hi, Mr. Talc" after not seeing him for a summer. They were too busy chewing gum, fiddling with the radios on their heads, yelling, *That's my seat. Get out of my seat.*

The Mexicans boarded last, eyelids down, not talking. Probably didn't even understand English. Don had wondered why there were so many more of them these past few years, and Donnie had explained it. Since the enviro-Nazis had shrunk the mines, the only work was shit work, housecleaning and bussing tables, work that was not in our custom or our culture. Work for Mexicans. But to think of Donnie made Don feel ashamed again, and, as he turned onto the highway, he turned his thoughts away from his son.

All the way to Delta, a Kmart semi was tailgating. His head was hurting a little. He wanted the kids to stop shouting, but he'd learned that if the bus driver screams, "Quiet down," kids just laugh, even girls.

Outside Delta, where the mesas opened wide until there were no mesas and just desert, Don saw a flash of nighttime. He pulled to the shoulder and shut off the motor. He watched the Kmart semi pass by. Then he let himself fall against the steering wheel, the way Kayla fell asleep on his shoulder.

◆ ◆ ◆

The Gathering was decorated with flowers woven through tamarisk. There was wood in the fire pit, a bucket of water beside it. The counselors were waiting on the Meadow for Caleb, who stood watching them at the living room window. He was pleased that they'd dressed for the occasion—at least the girls had, wearing skirts or dresses, colorful earrings. He could nearly see the anticipation coming off them. He checked his watch again.

At 4 p.m., he ran down the steps to join them. "Hello! Hello!" With one hand, he squeezed Saskia's shoulder; with the other, Jeremy's. "I'm so excited for this. We'll start by taking a walk. After that, the news. Then, we'll head over to the Gathering for fire and celebration." He told them that they couldn't talk, but they could sing, which they did, the entire camp repertoire as he led them south into the Dobies, along the remains of the trail the campers had made.

This was the mitzvah of walking nowhere. Not to be confused with the mitzvah of walking somewhere.

Now that he'd been reading David's notebook, he thought of everything as a mitzvah: the mitzvah of looking at listings for tracts of land in the Re/Max office, the mitzvah of talking to the woman at the bank. He often found himself explaining these to David in his head, or asking David about his. *The river gives us only what we don't need, and that's its mitzvah*, David had written, like a koan. Caleb was still trying to figure that one out.

After an hour, he circled around and brought the counselors back to the Overlook, because in 1985 a girl forgot her sleeping bag, and so he always told the 1982 Night story here. The late afternoon sun hovered over the far mesa, making everyone here more beautiful and, concurrently, connected by their beauty, unified, as if it meant something to be the recipients of this light.

He stood on the bank of the ditch. The counselors formed a semicircle around him. He checked his watch. He looked toward the barn, the parking lot, the road, any direction from which Donnie might be coming, but Donnie wasn't coming from any of them.

Soon, the evening would lose its magic. The endorphin buzz from walking would wear off. The sun would set. The counselors would remember about dinner and last fucks and bus schedules. Tomorrow, they'd leave. He had no choice but to start without Donnie.

He explained the mitzvah, what can be accomplished when a group does these mundane, repetitive actions together. He talked about the homesickness that comes from having a home and a nuclear family. He spoke on and on, words coming to him like white blossoms falling. He ran through a hurricane of them, until Donnie's car finally pulled up beside the house. Donnie stepped out and made his slow way to them, wearing a cowboy hat, hands in his jeans pockets, his face glowing in the setting sun, just like theirs.

"What's this plateau called?" Caleb said theatrically as Donnie approached.

The counselors looked around. Were they allowed to talk?

"Shout it out. What's this plateau called?"

"Aemon's Mesa," Jeremy bellowed, one fist pumping into the air.

"That's right. And this here is Aemon's great-grandson. Come here, Donnie." Caleb gestured for Donnie to stand beside him. "This is my friend Donnie. You might remember him from the 1982 story." He quoted himself telling the story: "And then Donnie said to me, 'Caleb, all my dad and I want is for our land to be saved.'" He draped his arm around Donnie's shoulder. "Remember how Donnie said, 'I'd be thrilled if you could help us out. I'd be thrilled if you took care of this land next, but it's a lot of work.' Remember that?"

They nodded.

He could feel Donnie's shoulder muscles beneath his arm. He looked over and saw his eyes darting back and forth like trapped fish. "Well, something wonderful happened. Donnie recently let me know that he's ready to protect this land himself. Did I get that right, Donnie? You're ready?"

Donnie nodded and said, "Ready," just as Caleb had asked him to.

Caleb raised his free hand. "I can see what you're thinking. Why is this *good* news? Well, it means we've accomplished exactly what we set out to do. Look all the way to the mountain. Nobody built anything. Nobody paved it. Nobody dug up the earth for the minerals below, the oil shale below. We've kept it wild. And something happened to us in the meantime, something incredible. While we were guarding this land for Donnie, we changed. We became guardians, protectors. That's what we are. That's what we've become. All of us together."

He looked at their expectant faces, felt Donnie's breathing beside him. All his nervousness, the adrenalized emergency of the past days, had dissipated, and he felt nearly calm as he slowly quoted Thoreau, drawing out the *W*'s and *S*'s in the sentence that had become like a nursery rhyme to him. "The West of which I speak is but another name for the Wild; and what I have been preparing to say is, that in Wildness is the preservation of the World."

He repeated the final phrase. "In wildness is the preservation of the world." Then he repeated it again, enunciating each noun with wonderment. "In *wildness*. Is the *preservation*! Of the *world*! Each of you should feel proud. Think of what we did, protecting Llamalo all these years! But now it's time to ask ourselves, what is Llamalo? Is Llamalo this dirt beneath our feet? Is it the view of that mountain? No. It's the way we live together, how we live without the distractions of modern life, the rituals we perform, the mitzvahs. Llamalo is a verb, not a place."

He looked at each person in turn. He loved them; he felt the love in his body. This was the invitation: his love. He said their names. Jamal. Saskia. Kai. Rebecca. Jeremy. Nat. Scott. Mikala.

He told them that he'd chosen them, this particular group, to be the ones to make a new Llamalo, to *do* a new Llamalo. "The preservation of the *world*," he said once more. "See, the world needs our help now. We can't wait until next summer."

He explained that, by finishing their work on Aemon's Mesa, they'd moved beyond a summer camp. Llamalo was meant to be performed year-round. The next place they moved to would not just be protected, it would be a *training ground* for protectors. He would be leaving for this new place, walking to it as soon as Donnie was all settled in. He said, "So answer me this. Why's it called Llamalo?"

"Llama*lo*!" Jeremy again.

Caleb lowered his voice in counterpoint to Jeremy's bellow, making them lean in to hear him. "I want to hear from everyone. Why's it called Llamalo?"

"Llama*lo*!"

"So will you come with me? Will you create the new Llamalo?"

The answer was by now inevitable. Hands in the air. "Llama*lo*!"

Then, a rumble, an earth rustle, a vibration.

Noise travels on the mesa strangely, the wind bringing distant sounds you shouldn't be able to hear, so he kept talking. He told them that Donnie had asked for a chance to thank them for the years they'd spent protecting this land, but the noise was growing—a motorized whirr, a chain saw, a helicopter. He couldn't deny the noise, and nobody was listening to him; they were all turned toward the glare of the setting sun, shielding their eyes with their hands in order to see the two guys on ATVs coming across Aemon's Mesa, coming across Llamalo.

♦ ♦ ♦

ONLY TWO? Donnie shoved off Caleb's arm, squinted down the road for the others. All he could see were Craig and Travis. Of course. It wasn't hard to figure out. Glen? Kevin? Logan? They never meant it when they said they'd come. They were placating him like a baby. They were Caleb's pussies, just like Don.

♦ ♦ ♦

THE MEN CUT THEIR motors a few yards behind the counselors. There was quiet again, or near quiet: Rebecca could hear Caleb's voice. "What's going on?"

She turned back to look at him and found Donnie's face animated, unlike the stoical mask he'd worn while Caleb had been talking about him. "Simple," he said, walking backward, away from Caleb. "You got my ranch for free. Now I get it back the same way. It's moving day. Me and Craig and Travis are moving into the house. Other friends are coming, too. We'll stay all night. Shit, we'll stay all month. As long as it takes."

Caleb's arms flung out. "You brought them here to scare us?" He took a step forward, a step back. "No. This is *not* what we agreed on." Rebecca had never heard him so unhinged.

Donnie smiled, clearly enjoying himself. "You're scared? Wow. Sorry." He squinted in Rebecca's direction. "Tell *them* what you told *me*." Unsure if he was addressing her, she twisted around to his friends. "No, you. Yeah, you, princess. Tell them how Caleb wasn't a journalist. How he lied from the very start. How every word he said today was a lie."

"Don't be ridiculous, Donnie," Caleb said impatiently. "We are not dragging this up again." He turned to the counselors. "Alright then, let's head to the Gathering. Give them some time to clear out."

He began walking toward the bridge. The counselors followed like ducklings.

"No!" The noise came without premeditation—or even permission—

as if the scream had, on its own volition, forced its way from Rebecca's throat.

Caleb whipped around.

Everyone was looking at her. Mikala and Scott, holding hands. Jeremy, with fingers pressed against each temple. Kai, in a muddy dress. Donnie. Behind her, the men on their ATVs were probably looking, too.

For once, she couldn't think of what to say. She was Rebecca, but no longer Ira's daughter; that meant nothing anymore. She'd lost her inheritance of outraged certainty. When at last she spoke, her voice sounded high and unfamiliar. "I think you should let him talk."

She saw Caleb close his eyes, heard him breathe out heavily. Then he opened his eyes, gave a little pained smile. "There's nothing more he needs to say. He's ready to take the land back, like he said. That's the entire story." Caleb added, in the reassuring tone with which he might speak to a young camper, "It's all fine, Rebecca. Come on now."

She would have liked to follow, to forget that Caleb had indeed lied about his reasons for leaving Llamalo, with no mention of David's fall or Joe's retaliation. Because so much of what he'd said had been beautiful. The preservation of the world? What could be more beautiful? What more did she want than to be a protector? She, too, felt the homesickness of home. She wanted to do the mitzvahs. Who wouldn't want to wash dishes a certain way and have it mean something glorious? She wanted it all to be true.

But it wasn't.

"How do *I* know that?" she said.

"How do you know what?" Caleb said sharply, his hands held out like he was balancing a platter.

"That it's the entire story. If you never let him talk. If you tell him he's not allowed to talk to me."

He began shaking his hands, the platter tipping, falling. "Fucking hell, Donnie! We had an agreement."

"Fucking hell, Donnie. We had an agreement," Donnie mimicked in falsetto, and his friends laughed loudly.

She hated all of them—not just Caleb, but Donnie, too, and both his friends—hated them all, but still, she wanted to understand. "You told him you were a journalist?"

"I can't *believe* we're talking about this right now. I can't fucking believe it."

"Then explain why he's so mad at you. Just tell me." She realized she was standing just like Georgia did when she fought with Ira, arms crossed in front of her chest, head pushed forward.

"Really, Rebecca? You want to do some muckraking at this moment? This is how you help me?" He began pacing in the center of the large triangle made by Donnie in front of the ditch, by Rebecca and the friends on ATVs on the Overlook, and by the counselors on the edge of the Meadow.

"Okay, fine. I'm a journalist. You're a journalist." He pointed wildly. "Saskia, Kai, Jamal—they're journalists. Who isn't a journalist? You don't need a degree. It's not like being a doctor. Years and years ago, when I first arrived in this town, Donnie threatened me. I can barely remember the situation. I know I was scared. I needed to give a reason for someone like me being here. Yes. Technically, it was a lie. But the sort of white lie we all say all the time. What could it *possibly* matter now, a decade later? How is it at *all* relevant?"

"But I don't get it. Did Donnie say the stuff you said he did? How he wanted you to protect the land? How thrilled he was? Is that true?"

She heard one of Donnie's friends erupt with a high-pitched, sarcastic "Yeah rii-iight," but she didn't take her eyes off Caleb.

"Or did you make all of it up? And why? To make them love you?"

"That's what people do, Rebecca! That's how we get things done. What's the alternative? You want the whole truth? Fine." He took a few steps toward Donnie, pointing. "Donnie here is delusional. He believes there's a conspiracy of evil liberals." He pivoted and stepped toward her, his finger still jutted out, prodding the air to punctuate every sentence. "You want to know more? He believes the newspapers are in on it. The whole federal government. *You're* in on it. All the Jews are in on it! We all joined together to shut down Exxon, the wealthiest company in the fucking world. And why? To screw him. To strip people like Donnie of their deserved fortune. It's pure propaganda by mining and oil companies to fool idiots like him. My god, Rebecca, do you get it now? How else am I supposed to deal with this idiocy? You're defending someone without a firm grasp on reality. A dupe!" He was screaming. "Are you a dupe, too?"

"Hey now," Jeremy said.

Silence. The sun slipped away, taking with it its golden light. In response, the night birds appeared, streaking above them toward the river, one after another.

Caleb turned his gaze behind Rebecca. "Craig? Travis? How's your mom? She still cooking at the Motherlode, making the eggplant parm I love? You're really planning to sleep in my house? Because I think I get it now. He can't afford it, can he? Donnie invited you here, because he doesn't have the money."

Rebecca saw Donnie stretch his arms above his head, perform an exaggerated yawn. "I think it's time to settle in, boys. Hope these kikes left us some beer. Hope the girls cleaned the place nice and neat for us. Logan'll be here soon. And Glen Lebs. And Kevin Kinney. Hope there's beds for all of us rednecks. Don't want to sleep in a Jew bed, though."

"Do you hear him?" Caleb shouted. "Now do you understand? This is the man you want to defend? How stupid are you?"

Rebecca couldn't think of the right response. Quite stupid? Not at all stupid? On a scale of one to ten, moderately stupid? She found herself, in a strangely calm voice, a voice of authority and decisiveness, addressing the counselors. She told them that she was leaving, that something was really wrong here and they should come with her. It was time to go. "I'll give you ten minutes to pack your stuff. Meet me in the parking lot in ten minutes."

Nobody moved. If they didn't come, how would she leave? She had no car. After an endless second, she added in a rush, "David's in the hospital with a broken pelvis. He fell from the cliff, stayed there all night. It's his dad who's shutting Llamalo down. Donnie has nothing to do with it. Now will you come?"

"Wait . . ." Mikala said, crossing her arms.

Rebecca shook her head. "There's no time. Just get your stuff."

Jeremy took off, crossing the bridge and heading toward his platform. Mikala said, "I have to find my guitar, don't leave." Jamal said he'd be right there and followed Jeremy. Saskia, Nat, Kai—they all asked Rebecca to wait for them.

Without glancing at Caleb, Rebecca ran to the parking lot. She climbed into Scott's bus, closing the door behind as if someone were chasing her. She was wearing her Rumspringa skirt. She'd leave everything else here. The stained shirts, the shorts with denim turned the gray of Aemon's Mesa, the sleeping bag Ira bought for her summer in nature camp. She had no money, no credit cards. She'd leave her backpack with the hair ties and WILL YOU BE READY WHEN THE MILITARY DRAFT RETURNS? and *Things Fall Apart* and the final issue of *Our Side Now*.

From the open window, she could hear Caleb screaming, "You're fucked, Donnie. You fucked yourself."

"Really, Caleb? I did? *I'm* fucked?"

A door slammed. From inside the car, she watched the moon rise above Escadom Mountain like a balloon released from a toddler's hand.

◆ ◆ ◆

DON TALC KNEW THAT he was in a bed, but he was not sure where. A man with a stethoscope necklace sat down beside him. "Can you tell us your name?" The doctor held open Don's eyelid and drowned the iris with light. Don thought it wise to keep quiet.

"Who's your next of kin?" The doctor pulled open the lid of the other eye. "Who do we call?"

Don tried to say "Denise," but nothing came out. The doctor sighed as if Don were intentionally failing to cooperate, and told the nurse to look for some identification.

Don's brown wallet was outstretched in the nurse's hand, but Don couldn't reach for it.

EIGHTEEN

Arise, Ye Wretched of the Earth

WELL, THIS WASN'T WHAT the Pizza Hut delivery guy had expected. With an order of four large pies on a Friday night—or, actually, Saturday morning, 1 a.m.—at the Antler Lodge, the lowest budget skank motel in Glenwood Springs, he'd expected a party, a glimpse of hookers, or at the very least, kids from Glenwood High with something for him to smoke.

But instead, these dour hippies were on the floor looking up at him. Faces like roadkill and muddy tracks everywhere from their boots. They paid with smoothed-out singles and coins they piled into his palm. No lights on, like they were having a séance. And when he asked to turn one on to check the cash, a little hobbit-like dude with beaded necklaces said no, please, they didn't use lights.

The energy was really fucked up in there.

◆◆◆

DONNIE WAS STILL WEARING the cowboy outfit when he stood at the nurses' station at Delta County Memorial, asking for more blankets. He'd slept the night in a chair in Don's room after Craig's dad had found him drunk in the kitchen of the ranch house. "Where's Kayla?" is what Donnie'd said when he heard. Kayla was with Charlene; she was fine. Donnie drove alone to the hospital.

"Blankets for Mr. Talc?" the nurse asked while typing with the tips of her curved nails. "Unfortunately, he won't be needing any." She explained that she'd spoken with the representative at Blue Cross, who'd said Donald Talc hadn't been a client since 1982. "Your dad," she said, "will be discharged in a few hours."

"But how? He can't feed himself. He can't take a crap by himself."

"As the doctor said, it's highly likely he'll regain many of his functions." She tore the cover off her Cup-a-Soup. Steam rose between them. "I'll give you a printout of numbers for home-care nurses, but most of them insist on insurance." She handed him the expired insurance card, scratching his palm with her talons.

He already owned sippy cups. He bought Ensure at Ute's on the way home, leaving Don in the car. He called Charlene from the pay phone outside the post office. "Don't you worry about Kayla. Get your dad situated, and I'll bring the baby by later. I'm telling you, it's a godsend that you're visiting now, what with Denise away to god-knows-where."

"Who's Denise?" The phone crackled. Charlene said she had to go.

It was nearly impossible to get his dad into the trailer. The wheelchair he'd rented wouldn't unfold. Sweating in his snap shirt, he smashed his foot down on it like he did on Kayla's stroller. Once inside, he fell asleep on his dad's bed, but then Don made a noise he'd never heard before from a human being. It was the sound of a cow in distress. He rushed into the other room, but Don had fallen silent, and his face held no sign of pain or effort.

When Donnie turned away, the noise returned. He wondered if it wasn't his father at all, but some injured wild thing that was trapped inside the trailer. He crouched by his dad. "What is it?" Donnie fanned out the hospital's cards on the coffee table. "Point to what's wrong." Don didn't even twitch.

♦ ♦ ♦

"Aren't you coming?" Mikala asked Rebecca, the only one not tying boots or standing up.

It was seven in the morning, and they were getting ready to leave the room they'd been sequestered in for ten hours, fighting like a jury. At stake was a contest over who was losing the most. Each person defended only himself or herself, using details of psychological pain from twenty years of life. *You don't understand. See, my mom . . . The thing you need to know is, Llamalo was the only place where . . . Caleb was the only person who ever treated me like . . . If it turns out he's a liar, then who can I . . . ?*

Rebecca found the others particularly unconvinced by her case. She'd only been there this one summer. "So, you're sad about your dad? Is that what you're saying?" She was sad about David, too, she tried to explain. But they insisted they were all devastated, all of them implicated in his leaving. And to think Caleb hadn't even told them about David's broken pelvis. Can brilliance justify deceit? Yes. No. Yes. No. Rebecca's few minutes of testimony ended as the rest of them returned to Caleb, chasing after a car that was driving away from them.

No verdict had been reached. Only this: As Scott opened the door to let in the Colorado sunlight, they all suddenly agreed, although nobody said as much, that they'd wasted their last hours together. They were about to swim alone again in the ocean of oblivious humanity. Nobody else would understand what they meant. *Llamalo? Yama Low? Weird name. I hated summer camp, those creepy cabins. Yours didn't even* have *cabins? Huh.* For the rest of their lives, they would dream about trying, and failing, to get back to a wide plateau and a tall mountain with the white shape of an animal on its side, where Caleb was waiting for them, and they would wake up in their city or suburb and spend their days in longing, nothing and nobody measuring up.

The very last group of counselors was saying goodbye. Saskia, driving east, would drop Jamal and Jeremy at the Port Authority in New York. Scott and Mikala, headed northwest, would take Nat and Kai to the Greyhound station here in town.

"We'd be psyched to drive you there, too," Mikala said, brow furrowed with concern. But Rebecca, whose parents had never had time to drive her anywhere, who had always taken buses—to the orthodontist, to orchestra rehearsal, to Llamalo at the start of the summer—Rebecca had another idea, and she'd asked Mikala to loan her the money for a second night at the motel.

◆ ◆ ◆

"YOU HAD A GIRLFRIEND? All this time?"

Don shook his head. No, no, no, no. Then he started crying again, tears leaking from the unfrozen eye. The doctor had explained that this was physiological, not emotional, a common response in stroke patients, but Donnie hated it.

"You can't deny it. I got proof." He pulled a tissue from the box on the kitchen table and dabbed at the sagged face. Stretched his legs, crossed them at the ankles, all the dexterous things he could do. "I'll lay it out for you. First to spill the beans was Charlene, but she was cagey. Then . . . hold on."

He sprang up and opened the fridge, casting light upon the foiled casseroles cooked by the ladies of the town. Macaroni splendor, cream-of-mushroom mystery. A banana pudding made especially for Kayla, although she'd left for New Mexico yesterday evening, clinging to Donnie's arm and shrieking while he buckled her into Marci's mom's car.

Donnie reached for a can of Coors. It was Sunday morning. Already today, he'd lifted his dad onto the toilet and wiped him and laid him on the bathroom floor to put on his diaper and shoved him into his wheel-chair and held up two cartons and said, "Chocolate or vanilla?"

Donnie sat back down and cracked his beer. "And then Amy-Lynne, when she came by yesterday, told me that before the party Charlene told everyone not to say anything, but she had to tell me now. This Denise person lived up here with you. Said she never saw one of you without the other in an evening. Said that in the wintertime, when Kebler Pass is all icy, you'd drive her over to Snowmass and wait in the car all day while she cleaned condos. Am I getting this right?"

Don looked back at him, his right eye melting, left eye blinking.

"Said the two of you kept mostly to yourselves, but she'd see both of you with Caleb at the Motherlode on Fridays. Said that you were great friends with him all along. You and Denise and Caleb sitting at your own little table. All of you lying to me."

But he couldn't mess with his dad, not like this. "You want to know what I think about that? Hot damn, Dad." He slapped the table. "Hot damn."

He imagined a woman with them in the trailer doing the womanly jobs. A woman Cloroxing and changing Don's diaper, but not just that. A woman kissing on Don, lying next to him, loving him. Denise—whoever she was.

It was the best fucking news Donnie had ever heard.

With the bunched-up tissue, he wiped at the cheek again. "But the thing is, nobody knows how to reach her. I even walked up to Caleb's this morning, woke him up in his tent to ask him. He said Denise is at her sister's in Casper, but he didn't have the number. Nobody does. So now you and I'll sit here until we find a way for you to give it to me."

He held the beer can to his dad's lips, brown liquid dribbling down his chin and onto his shirt. Then he picked up a pen and wrapped his dad's left fist around it. "You can try to write with your good hand. And if that doesn't work, we'll come up with some secret code, some number of blinks. Somehow, you're gonna give me this lady's phone number and I'm gonna call your girl. I'm gonna call your lady."

◆ ◆ ◆

ALL THE WAY TO Glenwood Springs, Ira felt proud of the extravagance and selflessness of this gesture. Rebecca wanted a ride from one state to another? Was there no bus? But she'd sounded like hell on the phone, claiming emergency. He'd set off directly, drove twelve hours with a rolled towel shoved behind him, spent $39.99 on a motel, woke at five to drive the rest of the way, all with an expectation of gratitude he only realized when, at the rendezvous—noon, Sunday, Antler Lodge parking lot—she wasn't grateful. She was sullen, greeting him with a perfunctory hug and then getting in the car and untying her boots, pressing her bare feet against the glove compartment and staring out the window, as if she were bored by her father and could not get enough of the landscape of Colorado, where she'd spent all summer.

"Well, my drive was long and tedious, I won't lie, but the best part," he said, as he joined the meager traffic toward the highway, "was stopping in this town Fruita. Typical American diner—waitress had no idea how to make iced coffee, even when I said, give me a cup of ice and pour coffee on it. All this small-town hoopla, all adorable, almost makes you nostalgic for somewhere you've never been—why can't life be this simple, et cetera— until I realize why I know the name Fruita. It's where the uranium was mined. *Above thy fruita planes. America, America,* et cetera. And then on the way out of town, I see a billboard paid for by the John Birch Society: 'Get the US out of the UN.' Jesus, the ignorance. Anyway, how are you?"

It was an affable invitation for conversation that she declined. In the silence that followed, he felt superfluous, his sciatica electric. There was no reason she couldn't sit in similar silence on a bus, leaning against her backpack to sleep, like he'd done so many times. And then he realized she didn't have a backpack. No bags in the trunk. Where was her stuff?

She turned to face him. "I forgot it at Caleb's camp."

"Forgot it? Are we supposed to buy you new stuff?"

"It's fine. I hardly had anything." She bit her lip until the skin blanched. She was so lovely. "Stop it," he wanted to say. "Not that lip. Don't bite that lip."

Unhappy with the gas prices in Colorado, he held out for cheaper offerings in Utah, where it turned out there weren't any gas stations at all. His gauge hovered on empty, and the alchemy of dusk made the desert around them look more water than rock. He turned off the highway onto a ranch road and cut the engine. To the south, snowy peaks rose from the flat expanse, looming judges. "So, we'll sleep in the car," he said, careful not to admit any misstep. "An adventure!"

They ate the peanut-butter sandwiches he'd packed, and darkness colored in the windows, and then there wasn't anything else to do but recline their seats. He unfurled the Mylar earthquake blankets from the trunk and handed one to her.

But before he allowed her to hide behind the isolating scrim of sleep, he said, "Want to tell me what the emergency is? Why you're not on Greyhound as planned?"

"I really don't."

"Actually, I think you owe me an explanation. You made me drive this far."

"I just want to know why." She was flicking the flashlight he kept in the glove compartment off and on, irritating his eyes. "I wanted to hear it in person."

"Why what?"

"Why'd you shut down the paper, Dad? And don't tell me everything I already know."

Ira hadn't expected this. "The paper? Call it a heart attack. Doctors tried all they could, but Western medicine is its own musty gamble, controlled as it is by the pharmaceutical industry."

"Really, no bullshit. Please."

"No bullshit?" He turned to her but could only see her outline. "Jesus, Rebecca. It was me. You know that. Mom wanted to keep going, same thing every week, but for years I was bitter. A constant state of rage because the world hadn't gone the way I told it to, over and over, week after week, editorial after god*damn* editorial!" He shouted this to the air around them, to the cows sleeping standing up, to the lizards scurrying, to the fossils wedged in the shale beneath the car. "The superiority I would feel every time I saw one of the inane bumper stickers. 'May Peace Prevail on Earth.' 'War is not the Answer.' And for what? What was I doing differently?"

"But all those years you could do it, and then suddenly you can't?"

"Obviously, I've given this plenty of thought. And you know"—he sighed—"I'm just not sure. But I have thought this. I've thought that maybe everybody has one decade, call it an optimistic decade, when the world feels malleable and the self strong. And then it's over. It doesn't come back."

"A decade? Like ten years exactly?"

"Well, a metaphoric decade."

"Oh, one of those." He loved making her laugh.

"Maybe mine lasted longer than ten years, but not much. I was going through the motions." It was a strange way to talk, side by side in a dark parked car, and he felt the tremendous intimacy of a long airplane flight; night and the tectonic plates below, and nobody mattered but the two of them.

"You know, there was this guy living up at Caleb's." She paused for a long time, and he worried she wouldn't continue. "Donnie. A miner—as in gold, coal, et cetera. Not underage. Anyway, he wore this USA shirt. Flying eagle, red, white, and blue sleeves. And it always made me think of that song." She began to sing: "Arise, ye prisoners of starvation! Arise, ye wretched of the earth!"

He smiled at the surprise of it—this song he knew so well. "Okay, okay. I know the words, hon."

But she didn't stop singing, and there was nothing to do but join her, belt it out for all cows to hear. "For justice thunders condemnation: A better world's in birth! No more tradition's chains shall bind us; arise, ye slaves, no more in thrall."

He trailed off in order to listen to his daughter. "Something, something *some*thing something thing thing thing . . . The international working class shall free the human race!" How had she known to call him for a ride? Had she guessed how badly he needed this time with her?

"But, okay," she said, "will the international working class arise? No.

Will it ever do anything but collude with industry? And will the result of this collusion be anything but the increase in every conceivable measure of suffering?"

"Well, sure. That's the other option. Maybe optimism as a whole has ended. But honestly, Rebecca, I've thought about this, and I don't know. Is it there's no true intervention possible, or have I stopped being able to see how to intervene?"

"And?"

"And what did I conclude?"

"Yeah."

It was so kind of her to care about what had happened to him, the great rift in his life. He wanted to give her something more than his confusion, but what could it be? He reached for her hand across the stick shift, and it comforted him. "Let's get some sleep," he said, squeezing her fingers. Maybe in the morning, he'd know. Maybe when they woke hungry and sore and had not even the most American of substances to take them home, maybe then he'd have her answer.

NINETEEN

Winter

FOUR WEEKS BEFORE THE Persian Gulf War, six out of the seven members of Students United for Justice committed a misdemeanor by unfurling a banner from an overpass on I-80. Rebecca, who had, back in May, conceived of this Action—everything done by SUJ was called an "Action"—was not among them. At the time, Rebecca was eating dinner with Michelle, the roommate assigned to her in late August, when Rebecca had told the dean of students that she could no longer move into the Peace and Justice Cooperative because each of the three nouns in the name of the Peace and Justice Cooperative held a promise that could never be fulfilled. Similarly, Rebecca had changed her major from Third World Revolt and Media Studies to English and had been surprised to find that her new classmates cared deeply about made-up people and their made-up problems.

The dinner Rebecca and Michelle were eating during the Action was dinner only in the temporal sense. It was dinnertime. Michelle, who was premed, had taught Rebecca many things, including the practice of bringing plastic Baggies to the dining hall at breakfast, filling them with cereal, and eating this cereal dry for all other meals. They were sitting on the floor of their room, half a dozen Baggies between them, as Michelle talked about Christmas. Only six days away and she hadn't bought anything for her aunties or her two nephews. Michelle's side of the room, usually neatly stacked with organic chem textbooks and color-coordinated flash cards, had lately been overtaken by gifts and wrapping paper. Michelle had, on several occasions, announced that she loved Christmas so much. The lights! The love! The presents! Michelle was a woman of surprisingly intense passions. She loved U2 so much! She loved Peanuts so much! She loved her little figurines of Peanuts characters wearing Santa hats! She loved the Gap so much, although she believed the Gap in Berkeley was a pale imitation of the Gap in San Jose, which was the best Gap in the world.

Rebecca had tested this theory herself when she went home with Michelle for Thanksgiving to avoid seeing David, who, along with Judy, had been invited to Ira and Georgia's. What could Rebecca possibly say if she saw him? I tried to save Llamalo for you, and instead I ruined it? Sorry the guy you idolize is a liar? Sorry I caused your fall by wanting you to be in pain? She'd left him dozens of messages—first with Judy and then, when he moved out, at the number Judy gave her—but he'd never called back. He didn't care about their time together, those minutes in the barn. Swimsuits and the light coming through. So instead she went to San Jose and bought, at Michelle's urging, khakis and a red V-neck at the best Gap in the world. When she wore this outfit, she felt as if she were in disguise, although, as Luke had explained to her, all clothes were costumes, everyone was posturing, there was no true, immutable self beneath these consumer choices. "We are each only the sum of our signifiers," Luke liked to say. Luke was a senior she'd met in a seminar on postmodernism. After he'd eviscerated a paper she'd written—"Who Is the Dreaming Animal Really?: Representations of the Other in Kingsolver"—he'd asked her out to coffee, where he explained that all politics was aesthetics. Protest was an aesthetic choice. Capitalism had subsumed rebellion, making it just one more thing to purchase. Now, they were dating, which meant that every week she'd sit on Luke's floor, his Panasonic cassette player between them, and he would lecture her. It was important to him that she learn which was the best Sonic Youth album, exactly when Nirvana was "dialing it in." At some point in the evening, he would put on Galaxie 500 and they'd have quick sex on the floor, a jabbing in the general direction of her clitoris, a frantic humping. The main erotic actions, as far as she was concerned, had to do with the condoms. Luke standing with a foolish and gorgeous erection, searching for condoms in his dresser drawer. Luke sitting on his bed with a serious expression, tongue peeking through his lips, as he unfurled the rubber slowly down the length of his dick. Luke on top of her, the smell of condom on his fingers. Luke dexterously tying the knot in the spent, baggy condom, tossing it overhead into the trash basket, after which Luke would take a short nap and then the music tutorials could resume.

Sometimes, she would say that she liked a song and Luke would say no, that song was derivative and once she knew more, she wouldn't like it. It was somewhat funny what you needed to go through to see the erection. The first time he visited her room, Luke had complimented her minimalist vibe, calling it "a bold move." She hadn't taped any photos to her walls, although Mikala had sent thirteen from the summer, through which she'd looked hopefully for David and found only a blur of blond hair and red headband in one shot. Nor had she hung any of her posters, not NUCLEAR POWER? NO, THANKS! or ATOMKRAFT? NEIN DANKE! or АТОМНАЯ ЭНЕРГИЯ? НЕТ, СПАСИБО! or 原子力?さようなら! She did still have her five albums autographed by Pete Seeger, hidden from Luke's derision under her bed, but she understood now that any emotion she felt while listening to them was just familial sentimentality, not a response to Pete's call to action. If she'd been born to different parents, she would no doubt feel an equal upsurge listening to these parents' apolitical favorites—"What a Wonderful World" maybe. Or "Scenes from an Italian Restaurant." Or the Bobs—Dylan or Marley.

Still, some evenings, despite her determination to be a sophomore with sophomoric concerns, she'd tell Michelle she was too tired to study with her in the library, and she'd lie in bed and listen to Pete. Not the records; she didn't own a record player. But she'd slip a cassette into her Walkman, pull on her headphones, and listen as he said, "And the most important verse was the one they wrote down in Montgomery, Alabama. They said, 'We are not afraid.' And the young people taught everybody else a lesson. All the older people who have learned how to compromise and learned how to take it easy and be polite and get along and leave things as they were, the young people taught us all a lesson."

Then everyone would sing, *We are not afra-aid, we are not afra-aid, we are not afraid,* today! *Deep in my heart, I do believe, we shall overcome some day.*

"I just can't decide," Michelle was saying now. "I mean, I pretty much figured out that I'll get Jake a Nerf basketball and Troy one of those cars that you control. You know, with a remote?" But for the aunties, she was torn between scented candles or gloves, a conundrum that must have been presented as a question, because she looked accusatorily at Rebecca. "Are you even listening?"

Rebecca wasn't, not really. She'd noticed that it had started raining, hard patter hitting sideways against the glass panes of this fourth-floor window. She was thinking of the other six members of Students United for Justice. There was nowhere in the world she'd rather be than on that I-80 overpass with them in the rain and wind.

They would tie a sheet to the chain-link. NO BLOOD FOR OIL, it would say, "blood" in red, "oil" in black. They'd all wear black sweatshirts to feel like renegades, and they'd tie kerchiefs over their mouths to look like revolutionaries. The wet white sheet would cling to itself, and the writing would begin to bleed, washing the cars below with pink raindrops. Three weeks later, it would still be there, twisted, faded, because nobody cared, because all the drivers underneath were still driving, because even if they did care, none of them could prevent the war, and the cops had more important things to do than pull down torn sheets. Nothing would happen.

Michelle was waving her hands. "Earth to Rebecca! Earth to Rebecca!"

Deep in her heart, Rebecca was afraid. "Well, the candles would be beautiful," she said, reaching for a bag of Chex. "Buy them candles."

♦ ♦ ♦

FOUR DAYS BEFORE THE war was supposed to start, American flags flew from all the commercial buildings in Escadom, except for the Motherlode, which flew a GRAND OPENING flag and was no longer called the Motherlode. In Escadom's Town Park, each leafless cottonwood and maple had been banded with yellow ribbons in support of the waiting troops.

Up on Aemon's Mesa, the ranch manager of Coyote Junction Ranch was walking from his trailer across a field sheeted with snow. Already, the barn had been demolished; the garden fencing was down. Soon, it would all disappear, even the house. And then, come spring, Caleb had been told, construction would begin on the spec houses, the gate around the gated community. The DeWitts had hired an architect from Aspen who specialized in modular modernism with a Western flair. They'd hired a building manager from Snowmass who really understood their vision. "What's my job then?" Caleb had asked. "Energy and enthusiasm," Anders said. "Keep things on track." It was a made-up job, an act of generosity, as was allowing Caleb to stay in the trailer, to live up here on the plateau, where he needed to be.

On the porch, skis and kayak paddles leaned like poplars. Lacey answered the door wrapped in a towel, her hair in another. "Caleb! You're early. That's great," she said in a tone that implied it wasn't. "Anders! Caleb's here."

A voice shouted, "I'm on the *phone*, baby."

Lacey stepped back to allow Caleb to enter. "Wait in the kitchen? I guess you know where it is." She laughed abruptly, as if to say *Sorry for the change in fortunes!* and then disappeared upstairs.

The living room looked undressed without the Talcs' plaid curtains, without their couch, their secretary, their commemorative plates, but Caleb had to admit that the kitchen had improved without the camp's oversized appliances. What remained of the Talcs' wallpaper was mostly obscured by photos of Lacey and Anders in Costa Rica, in Patagonia, in winter, in summer, always outdoors. A framed Ansel Adams photo of a pueblo in moonlight, a poster of the taxonomy of chilies, actual dried chilies tied to cupboards painted Ed Abbey peach.

When Anders DeWitt had heard from Suze, who'd heard from Mikala, that Llamalo was for sale, he drove there right away from Aspen. Caleb barely recognized him from the camp's first summer. He still wore wire glasses on his unruffled face, river sandals on his skeletal feet, but he'd gained an air of astounding confidence, a smug joviality. The secret to happiness, he told Caleb, was simply prioritizing happiness. He was only twenty-nine, but he had an MBA from Wharton, a trust fund from his maternal grandfather, and a commitment, he said, to conscious investing. "That one summer I spent up here"—he waved one arm around the thorny, seductive grounds of Llamalo—"changed my entire outlook. Reset my life course."

He'd bought Llamalo for four times what Caleb had offered it to Donnie for, and then doubled its size when he bought the Sorger ranch as well. And then he approached the owners of the Motherlode.

For months, the town's single restaurant was dark, a note scotch-taped to the window. THANK YOU TO ALL OUR PATRONS. AND ESPECIALLY THE COAL MINORS WE ARE SO PROUD OF. WE ARE SAD THAT WE MUST SAY GOODBYE. But it opened under the name Coyote Junction Restaurant and Microbrew just in time for Christmas Eve.

"Caleb!" Anders boomed into the room. "Don't tell me Lace left you empty-handed." He wore a T-shirt with a cartoon drawing of a triangle for a mountain traversed by a man on stick skis—a cuneiform of joy—with three words, IT'S ALL GOOD. He fetched two unmarked brown bottles from the fridge, and they sat.

Anders jiggled his knee beneath the circular table, tapped his turquoise ring upon it. "Are you cold? Lace says she's freezing. I can't get the fucking coal furnace to work right."

"I'll take a look at it."

"Well"—Anders smiled, either embarrassed or relieved; it was hard to tell—"thanks. That'd be great." He looked uncertainly around as if for a clue as to how to continue the conversation and then brightened. "So, there's awesome news about some prospective buyers."

A New Year's article in the *Grand Junction Tribune* had gloated, *Welcome to 1991. Nearly a decade after the collapse of oil shale, could Escadom be headed for financial recovery?* It quoted real estate maverick and restaurateur Anders DeWitt: *"I think we can safely say that the cycles of boom and bust are over. Unlike the extractive industries, real estate and tourism, if managed thoughtfully, are economically stable."*

Anders smudged one finger across a wet circle on the table as he described a couple from the Front Range who, because of something called telecommuting, could work in Boulder but live in Coyote Junction Ranch, during which monologue Caleb listed for himself the plants that would sprout along the ditch when the snow melted. Twistflower. Tumble mustard.

Lacey entered, wearing jeans and a red sweater, followed by the dog, Arapahoe.

Prince's plume. Asparagus. Devil's beggartick. Caleb remembered a time, so recently, when he'd pointed out Gardner's saltbush to a crowd of kids walking behind him.

Anders said he was super-excited about the entrepreneurial synergy between the new residents.

Shad scale, hedgehog cactus, spindle bluebell. There was the mitzvah of knowing the names of the plants.

Lacey, opening the fridge, asked Anders why he'd bought mild salsa when she'd told him to get picante.

In a few months, before the snow melted and the high mountain streams poured into the reservoir, Caleb would walk the length of the ditch, setting fire to it, part of his job now.

Turning to Caleb, Lacey said that she totally got why Anders wanted to move here—"He's an idealist, you know"—but the skiing sucked, and it was such a haul to get to Crested Butte or Snowmass.

Was the feeling of standing on Aemon's Mesa a holy feeling if Caleb was standing there with synergistic entrepreneurs? Was there a mitzvah of modular modernism with a Western flair?

And what if, after the snowmelt poured into the ditch, the ranch manager of Coyote Junction Ranch (which—someone should tell Anders—was no longer a ranch and had never seen a coyote) wedged a fridge door in a divider and flooded the road? Nobody could leave. All of them stuck here, staring at their computers. Would they even notice?

Caleb set down his beer and stood. "I have to go."

"Whoa, man. What happened?" Anders jumped up. "You came for dinner. Lace makes a mean enchilada."

Caleb reached out his hand to shake Anders's, but Anders was placing something in it. "Just try this bottle—hints of pumpkin! Come on, man, don't go. You know, it's strange to admit it, but I get kind of lonely out here. We should hang out, man. We should *do* stuff."

Lacey said, "Anders, if he needs to leave . . ."

There was the mitzvah of needing to leave. Caleb set the pumpkin beer on the table. "You have snowshoes? To walk in the snow. You have a pair I could take home?"

◆ ◆ ◆

ONE DAY BEFORE THE war began, Rebecca woke when the bare bulb switched on in the garage. "Hon?" The muffled maternal call came through stacks of paper. "Can I come in?" Georgia asked after the fact. Through the open door, the oceanic smell of fog hurried in.

Rebecca reached out from her bedroll to turn on the battery radio, expecting Daniel Schorr and the coming war, but finding herself deep into local food programming. Apparently, she'd slept through the day's promising beginning. The room was dark; bamboo had grown over the garage's windows. All night, she'd heard the leaves rustle like newspaper against the glass.

She'd arrived home by Greyhound two weeks earlier, in time for the annual *Our Side Now* after-Christmas potluck not to happen for the first time in her life. Nobody found the shoe boxes of political buttons in the linen closet. Nobody brought the potted pine in from the front yard. Nobody pinned the political buttons to its boughs and then draped on silver tinsel. Nobody stood on a chair to affix, at the very apex of the tree, in lieu of a star, Georgia's prized possession: a green button with yellow writing that said WEARING BUTTONS IS NOT ENOUGH.

The production assistant wasn't drunk in the bathroom. The paralegals from Joe's office weren't huddled by the oleander talking shop. People who, due to political rifts, hadn't spoken to each other in twenty years, weren't not speaking to each other. The UCLA professors and the renters' rights organizers and the good city councilors and school board members and Rose from Bread and Roses in Venice weren't refilling their cups with cheap wine in the garage. David wasn't sitting on the couch with his headphones on. There was no discussion of whether it was Joe or Judy's year to come. (It was Joe's.) There was no debate over when the contingent of United Farm Workers folks would arrive or whether Chavez or Dolores would be among them. There wasn't a single member of the Chicago Eight, not even Tom Hayden. The movie star Ramón Estevez and his friends, the former nun and priest with whom he got arrested each Wednesday morning at the Federal Building to protest nukes, hadn't brought their black bean dip.

Only Jerry came—Jerry, who sold bumper stickers on the Venice board-walk in his Speedo—but Georgia sent him away.

Since Rebecca's bedroom was being used to store file cabinets and IBMs from the newspaper office, she was sleeping in the garage for the dura-tion of her visit. Back when Rebecca was thirteen, the *OSN* office had moved from their garage to a storefront on Pico, and the garage had turned into the newspaper's morgue, shelves stacked with papers in chronologi-cal order.

Now Georgia maneuvered around these shelves with her worried look and a plate of buttered toast. She sat on the edge of Rebecca's mattress. "Can I sit?"

"Did anyone call?" Rebecca asked, reaching for the toast.

"You keep asking us this. Who're you hoping for?"

"Nobody, Mom. It's nothing."

"Is it Luke? Is everything okay with Luke? He was very sweet when I spoke to him yesterday. Were you hoping he'd call again? It hasn't been twenty-four hours. You really like him, huh?"

"It's not Luke."

"Is it someone from Samohi? Is it Mihui? Didn't you go to the pier with Mihui a couple days ago?"

"It's not Mihui. It's nobody. Forget I asked." She willed her mom to guess, to say, "Is it David? As a matter of fact, David did ask about you. David did call." At the very least to say his name. David.

Instead, Georgia sighed. "Fine. I have to go to work. How about you get dressed and come with me this time? Aren't you tired of moping around here with Dad? We could always use another canvasser."

"CalPIRG? Door to door in Pacific Palisades?"

"I know, I know. What am I selling?" Georgia smoothed Rebecca's hair from her forehead. "Let's see. I'm selling a way for some housewives to stop feeling guilty. They don't pay their maids a living wage, but they gave twenty dollars to save the sea lions! There. I beat you to it. Did I miss anything?"

"No, that's basically it."

This was her parents' life, postnewspaper. Ira had his book deal. Georgia, unable to find other work, ended up with an organization she and Ira had always mocked for its Band-Aid solutions.

Rebecca switched off the radio. "The war's about to start, you know."

Georgia gave the automatic responses. "Terrifying, disgusting . . . That man."

"Apparently, there've been protests at the Federal Building. There's an encampment."

"Are you going?"

Rebecca took a bite of toast, chewing as she said, "Me? To stop the war? Nineteen-year-old white girl sleeps in North Face tent on the well-watered lawn of the LA Federal Building. Bush reconsiders bombing Iraq. War in Middle East thwarted forever!"

Georgia picked up the plate and stood. When she reached the door, she turned around. "It wasn't very nice of us, was it?"

"What wasn't?"

"We made sure that from the earliest age you were outraged by injustice. And then we told you that there wasn't anything you or anyone could do about it."

Rebecca shrugged. "It's not like you had a choice, right? The end of the optimistic decade and all."

Georgia frowned, her hand on the light switch. It was automatic, muscle memory; when you leave the morgue, you shut the lights. "What's that?"

Rebecca explained it the way Ira had. How everyone got just one, and hers was over.

Georgia tossed her head back. "That's such bullshit! Such typical Ira bullshit, creating a universal theory out of his own personal malaise. One optimistic decade! Just because his ego wasn't being rewarded sufficiently, despair's on all of us now?"

Georgia flicked the light off—"Sorry"—and then on again. "Hon? You know why I was so furious when Dad stopped the newspaper? It wasn't because I disagreed with him about its efficacy. I can't argue—and I didn't argue—that we were creating substantive change. No, I was mad because I loved it. God, Rebecca, I really did love it. I loved the weekly deadlines, all that anxiety. I loved the sense of being in it with everyone else, of being in the trenches, if I can, on this day, use a war cliché. Ira worried for *years*—'Are we still relevant?' And I would reply, 'It feels good.'"

"You wanted to keep it going because it felt good?"

"It made me happy to do the work. Or, I guess more accurately, it made me happy to decide that the work mattered. Because it is a decision. You should know that, hon. So many things in life that you think are definitive are really just decisions. Does the work matter?" Georgia frowned and folded her arms, leaning against the doorway. "I made a decision, despite evidence to the contrary, to believe in . . . what? In the collective power of all of our seemingly insignificant steps? I guess that's it. Your dad always likes to say 'Maybe the arc of the moral universe doesn't bend toward justice after all,' and sure. It doesn't. Not unless we pound on it. But that's my decision, to believe in the pounding. That's what makes me happy. This afternoon, I'm giving a presentation to the other canvassers about mollusks, our latest campaign. Mollusks! Did you know your mother cared about bivalves?"

"No, Mother. I didn't." Rebecca knew she sounded snide, and she felt bad about it. But deeper down, she felt the smallest rustle of hope, a palm frond moving in the windless sky.

◆ ◆ ◆

"Do-nnie," Denise called, later that morning in Colorado.

"Do-nnie," Marci called.

Donnie tensed his leg muscles and then released them again to the soft embrace of the couch cushion. Don was sitting in his chair beside the couch. Kayla, her hair in two pigtails, busily crawling in and out, dropping plastic pop beads like prizes on Don's lap, on Donnie's belly. The TV panted, "Desert Storm!" There were yellow ribbons wrapped around the front doorknob and pinned in cheerful florets on Denise's sweater. In September, Craig had flown for free to Kuwait, via Texas, after signing up with a recruiter at the Grand Junction mall.

"Donnie, we know you can hear us."

"Get in here."

Donnie groaned to rise, beads tumbling to the carpet. He didn't work until 4 p.m. No need for verticality before then. In the kitchen, the two women seated at the table had the same disapproving expression on their dissimilar faces.

"Didn't we ask you twice to check in on Caleb?"

"Twice." Marci played the important role of echo.

"We need you to do it this morning."

"This morning."

Donnie stood above them. He was the man of the house now, but not the hero. Caleb was the hero, after all, the good son. He'd bought Don this two-bedroom in town, across from the park, where they could all live together. No vista, no mountain, but out the kitchen window, they could see the statue of the miner, snow landing on his helmet and streaking across the names of the dead.

"It's been, what, three days?" Donnie said, still hopeful he could get out of this. "Probably on a trip. Skiing or whatever he does." Until this hiatus, Caleb had been coming every afternoon to sit with Don for a stretch. He'd drag a kitchen chair into the living room, hold Don's left hand, talk to him about god-knows-what.

"Well, we should know that," Denise said.

"We *asked* you," Marci said.

Getting out of the tasks the two women required of him was Donnie's current fight against society, but he could tell he wouldn't make headway today. In the silence of their insistent gaze, he heard Kayla in the other room talking like Don, to Don: *Caw caw, da da.* They were learning together.

He drove up onto the plateau before work, and there was Caleb's truck in front of the trailer, snowbound. He'd let the women know they were worrying for nothing. Caleb had simply stopped his visits. Even good sons go bad sometimes.

But as Donnie turned onto the field, he spied some yellow paper nailed to the front door, fluttering slightly.

Dear you,

I'm sitting on what I used to call the Great Overlook, nothing to the south but the grays and whites and browns of winter. Escadom Mountain in its winter pelt keeps guard to the northeast. This is the view that I've seen every day for nearly a decade, and I love it.

If you found this note, you've seen it. You know how perfectly mind-stopping it is. You know how every morning it can shock you anew. I've spent these past years trying to understand why we crave so much open space and mountains. I can only figure that there's something reassuring about grandeur. That it helps us believe that there could be eternity, there could be forever. There could, at the very least, be a very, very long time, long enough for us to finally tire of this world.

When I sold Llamalo, I was determined not to lose this, too. The feeling of standing on Aemon's Mesa. But I was holding on to something I didn't need. This view is actually nothing special. There are lots of grand places, plenty of mind-stopping views. For a few days, I understood this. I thought I would make a new Llamalo. I thought we'd walk there together, find a new piece of land. But I see now, I got the order messed up. I'm the one who's supposed to start Llamalo, to do Llamalo, to be Llamalo. Nobody will follow until I start. Well, here I go.

There's nothing holy about this plateau. This is NOT Llamalo. I'm headed out to find it. You're welcome to join along.

"Jesus, Caleb," Donnie said out loud, slipping the note into his back pocket. "It's the fucking middle of winter."

At Coyote Junction Restaurant, where Donnie was a busboy and Marci a lordly waitress, he was distracted from the skilled labor of carrying water glasses, because Marci was flirting with Glen Lebs, who'd asked to be seated in her section. While they worked, Denise watched over Kayla and Don and the demon boy from across the street and Charlene's grandbaby. "My daycare," she called it. Honey Nut Cheerios for all.

Donnie stayed late to mop, returned home beat, eyeballs throbbing, spine twisted. And still, because he was the man of the house, he went into the basement to remove clinkers from the coal furnace before he dropped into bed between Kayla and Marci. Fell asleep on his back with a hand on each of them.

When he woke at noon, twelve hours before the war started, he passed the note on to Denise, who called Chase at Search and Rescue.

TWENTY

Llamalo

"YEAH, I KNEW ALL that," David said with surprising matter-of-factness. "All of it?"

Rebecca had just told him everything. She'd taken the bus to the address Judy had given her, knocked on his door, and said, from the hallway, "I know you don't want to see me, but there's some stuff you should know." She didn't omit anything: Joe's threat; Caleb's idea to remake Llamalo according to some Jewish idea—she couldn't remember the word; Donnie. She told him that Llamalo had been sold to a former counselor, and Caleb was living in Don's trailer.

David's hand gripped the door as if he might slam it in her face. "Pretty much verbatim. Mikala and Scott just showed up one day after I refused to talk to them on the phone. Parked their van in the lot here. It was maybe early October, and I was still high on Percocet half the time. At first, I was so embarrassed I must've apologized a hundred times for being such a fuckup. Go on a little walk and fall down a cliff. Really swift, huh? Really shows how I was king of the place. Can't even find the trail. What a joke. But finally, Mikala and Scott—they're so rad—they insist they're not angry, and we hung out for a week, went bowling and shit. We hashed it all out. After that, I must've talked to everyone at least twice. Kai, Jamal, everyone. All my friends. Once Tanaya learned, she told everyone." He took a few steps backward, waved one hand into the apartment. "Are you coming in or what?"

She stepped inside, quickly took in the room. A blow-up mattress against the wall to her right, his sleeping bag unzipped, a headlamp beside it. Against the wall to her left, toward where David now headed, was a cupboard and counter with a hot plate, toaster oven, no sink. An open box of Pop-Tarts, a can of Pringles.

"Where do you wash dishes?"

"Bathroom's in the hall. Same as the pay phone. Gets quite congenial out there. Nine apartments on this floor and about nine hundred cats. I'm sure you smelled the piss as you walked through. But the view—you need to see the view."

She crossed the center of the room—boom box on a crate, beanbag chair leaking Styrofoam pebbles, wetsuit like a shadow shed on the floor—to the window. Expecting the ocean, she looked down seven stories to a Dumpster with its mouth open, displaying black bags like rotted teeth. She turned back around, leaned against the sill.

Her mission to tell David all he'd missed, a mission which had seemed so important and serious when she'd called Judy and waited for the bus, now was rendered useless. All morning, she'd thought only about obligation. She hadn't thought about his bed, his height, the slant plank of his chest, his himness. She hadn't thought his body would still be so interesting. She could feel the air molecules between them, feel the air shift as he moved.

But perhaps, she thought, watching his hands, those unvirginal hands, those copulating hands, she was wrong about her mission. She hadn't wanted to disseminate information; she'd wanted to gather it. What did David think of Rebecca? Or did he?

"So that's why you never returned my calls? Because you heard I defended Donnie? Who, as it turns out, wasn't worth defending? You're mad."

"Nah. You were a rabble-rouser, a truth seeker. You were just being Rebecca."

"So what then? Because I didn't help you? That night?"

"Like I said, only one person tripped and fell down a cliff. And it wasn't you."

"So you talked to everyone. *All* your friends. And you never answered a single one of my calls. I was shocked you even opened the door for me."

He shrugged. "I thought it was Yuji or Toast. They usually come by around this time. During Spanish. Listen." He held up one finger.

There'd been a constant low-level chatter that she'd been tuning out, but now, tilting her head, she tuned it in. A woman, deeply upset, screaming in Spanish.

"Señora Martinez, next door. It's her telenovela. Just as good as Mr. Thacker's tapes. Remember those?"

She wouldn't answer his question, since he hadn't answered hers. She crossed her arms over her chest. "I can go then. I don't want to disturb your language session."

"Rebecca, come on." He sucked his lips into his mouth, released them with a pop. "Look around. *This.* This is why I didn't call you." He jutted his chin at his room. "It's lame. There you are in Berkeley, all your clubs and shit, and I'm a high school dropout living in an SRO. Cool!"

"But," she began, not sure how to contradict him.

"No, it's true." He was looking down, rubbing his thumb at something on the counter. "I'm not the same here as I am in Llamalo. As I *was* in Llamalo. I'm a different person there. That's the David you liked." As if to change the subject, he looked up at her with a Howdy Doody expression, eyebrows raised, phony enthusiastic grin. "But, hey, it's not just any SRO. It's an SRO on the motherfucking beach. You got some time? You want to vamos a la playa with me?"

She watched him find his sweatshirt, keys, put the Pop-Tarts in the mini fridge. He wasn't wearing the red bandana, and his hair was lionlike around his head. There was a haltingness to his movements, not the languid way he moved across the plateau. Whether this was from embarrassment or physical pain or physiological damage from the fall, she didn't know. But he wasn't the boy she'd seen at Samohi either. He wasn't furtive, wasn't sullen or awkward. Still, he scared her. What would he do with his life? What would he care about now?

Outside, the dazzling world mocked the gloom she'd felt in his room. Right in front of his fetid aquamarine building, grandly named the Sea Castle, were a multitude of delights: the bike path, a playground on the sand with swings and seesaw, circus sounds coming from the pier, the slow turn of the Ferris wheel at its end. "Behold!" he said. "The sparkling ocean!"

They slipped off their shoes and walked past a homeless encampment and the lifeguard tower to the water's edge, her feet numbing in the cold sand. Surfers paddled toward the dying afternoon swell. An oil tanker on the horizon, the white triangles of three sailboats, contrails of airplanes spelling out messages from above: CORONA GOLD FOR YOUR THIRST. TAN DON'T BURN. HOT HOT GIRLS DANCE PARTY.

He kept his gaze seaward, not on her. Clearly he wasn't as aware of her body as she was of his. Dejected, she realized that only she could feel the distance, the molecules, now salt-watered, between them. Even as he talked to her, she felt forgotten.

Their conversation was perfunctory. How was her mom? How was his? He asked when she was headed back to Berkeley. A few days, she said, adding that she was an English major now.

"A fine language," he said, not seeming to understand the significance, what she'd given up.

Or maybe he did understand, because he turned to her. "I still miss being there, you know. I miss it all the time. I miss Caleb. Look, I'm not naïve. I've thought a lot about how flawed he is. He yelled at me the night I left. And apparently, he yelled at you, too—that's what I heard. He lied.

All that shit. He's a deeply flawed human, but who the fuck isn't? The thing is, Rebecca, I'd go live there, I'd go in a heartbeat if I could, even knowing what I know."

An elderly woman—seventy? eighty?—passed right in front of them, slowly jogging through the surf in a metallic bikini, her skin a deep tan, her short hair canary yellow, bangles jingling on her wrists.

"The thing about the mitzvot, though," David continued, nodding hello at the woman, who fluttered her fingers back at him. "This idea of his. I know where Caleb got that from."

"Where?"

He smiled his usual smile, crushed tin. "Zacky. Remember my friend Zacky Reznick? Caleb got it from Zacky Reznick's rabbi."

"How's that even possible?"

He shook his head; he'd tell her some other time, he said. Right now, he had six dogs to walk before dinner. One of his less strenuous jobs. In the mornings, he delivered the *LA Times*. Four thirty a.m., if she could believe it.

She said she'd walk him back to the Sea Castle. He stopped short, though, just past the bike path, everyone rolling by them, a wheeled parade. He looked at her.

"Rebecca."

She was nervous. She didn't know when she'd see him again or how to say goodbye. She started telling him about the classes she'd taken this semester and how politics was aesthetics, and everything was aesthetics, really, if you thought about it. A man in a turban and white tunic glided by on roller skates. A woman in a wheelchair held the leashes of two dogs that pulled her along the path, American flags waving from the back of her chair. There were bikinied women swaying back and forth on Rollerblades. Teenagers on lowriders eating cones of soft-serve while biking. Men biking while holding boom boxes. A girl like a statue on a skateboard, carrying a Coke can which held a single bird-of-paradise stalk. Rebecca explained at length why the supposed literary canon wasn't actually canonical. The world might end if she stopped talking, she would talk on and on for the preservation of the world, as all the world's peoples rolled by, oblivious to their salvation, just hours before the war started.

"Hey, Zoom."

"What?"

"Can you just shut up for a second?" He brushed her hair from her face, curled it around her ear, leaned to her. She opened her mouth like she'd learned, and they returned to the dark woodland at last.

THAT NIGHT, JUDY CAME over after dinner to listen with Georgia to NPR's live countdown to the war. Ira sequestered himself behind the closed door of his bedroom. He said he needed to work on his book. Why should he stop to hear the news? He knew the news.

Rebecca sat at the kitchen table. Judy, looking like an aged child in white billowiness, stood at the counter, fiddling with the radio dial to try to avoid the unavoidable static. Georgia was removing everything from the fridge in order to sponge the shelves, lining up comestibles on the counter. Mustard, horseradish, a flotilla of butter pats on a plate, an opened can of cream of mushroom.

"When did I even use that? Six months ago?"

Judy pressed her thumb into the spider plants on the windowsill to check for dry soil. "They're David's age. Exactly his age. The boys there."

"Here, a stub of cheddar from the eighties!" said Georgia. "From the Reagan administration. Eat it!"

Instead, the three of them ate the entirety of the Entenmann's pound cake that Judy had brought, right from the box. They drank a bottle of red wine. And although the radio commentators kept talking of bombers poised to set trails across the sky, Judy and Georgia began to distract themselves with the analgesic details of gossip.

They did nothing, because there was nothing to do.

As Judy mocked each of Joe's girlfriends, Rebecca remembered a time when she'd been driving with Ira—on their way to San Diego, where she would color her Chinese village while he interviewed a human coyote—and he was trying to explain a dialectic. Consider, he'd said, the speed of this Volvo heading south on the 405 and the delicacy of *The Pirates of Penzance* playing on the tape deck. The two were in opposition: Gilbert and Sullivan's meanderings, variations upon variations, chirrup, chirreep (*For he is a pirate king. Yes, yes, he is a pirate king*), and driving's simple forward thrust.

Why was she remembering this now? But of course. The synthesis. "Marx's true delight," Ira had said, hitting his thumb against the steering wheel in time to the music.

She wanted to call David and explain. Whoever he'd been on Aemon's Mesa—that boy, that beautiful and confident boy, was with him still. Just as Caleb was both visionary and deceitful. There was no line, fine or otherwise. One carried the other. And Rebecca was just one person, prudish and desirous, optimistic and hopeless. Just one Rebecca. For it was, it *was* a glorious thing to be a pirate king.

Standing, she told Georgia and Judy that she'd be right back, and she tugged open the sliding glass door. In the newspaper's morgue, she dressed quickly, shoved her driver's license and twenty dollars into the pocket of her jeans, leaving the rest of her wallet behind.

When she returned to the house, all humor had slipped out the open door. The mothers were seated at the table, listening.

"Jesus fuck," Georgia was saying. "Jesus *fuck*."

Judy patted a chair.

"Sit with us, Rebecca."

"Actually, can I use the car?"

"What for?" Judy asked.

Georgia stared at Rebecca for a moment, then turned and shouted, "Ira! Rebecca wants the car keys!"

He emerged from the bedroom, removed his glasses with his right hand, pressed the fingers of his left onto his closed eyes. "It's late. It's too late to go anywhere."

But Georgia said, "Let her, Ira. One of us should be there."

IT WAS NEARLY MIDNIGHT when Rebecca parked in Westwood, in front of a closed taqueria. After she locked the car, she knelt to thread its key with the lace of her left boot, tucking the key behind the tongue and retying her laces. The traffic signals flashed yellow, caution.

She walked past the sleeping homeless, the gated apartment buildings. Already she could hear it, like being inside someone's body: the stethoscope boom of the heart, the high-pitched gale of blood flowing.

Two cop cars drove slowly in the direction she was walking, pausing to look at her. Then, in sync, they turned on their lights but not their sirens and raced ahead, as if responding to silent screams in the night.

She saw the weary or worried leaving, walking toward her. A young man hoisted a sleeping toddler. There was a white-haired couple with handwritten signs, the man saying, "It really felt like it could get violent. I never appreciate being pushed." A middle-aged woman, her quilted coat pinned like a general's with buttons: WAR IS NOT HEALTHY . . . GIVE PEACE A . . . VISUALIZE WORLD . . . ANOTHER MOTHER FOR . . . IMAGINE ALL THE . . . Rebecca's bile rose.

But what if Caleb were right? Not about everything, of course. But what if, in the visionary hemisphere of his being, he'd landed on something. Or Zacky Reznick's rabbi had. Maybe all you had to do was act as if it mattered.

Turning a corner, she could see the blocky Federal Building, its two white columns lit up in the night, and the crowd—two thousand people? ten thousand?—gathered on the lawn in front of it, some on a makeshift stage. Placards bobbed like coral polyps from a reef. Banners swam eel-like in the current. She could hear whale calls from those giving speeches into bullhorns. At the edge of the crowd, sprinklers were rhythmically dousing a village of tents.

Why join two or ten thousand people when just now in Kuwait teenagers in dun-colored fatigues that never can mimic the blandness of sand played gin rummy as they waited?

Llamalo? Belief will follow.

She heard a voice shout into a bullhorn and the crowd roar in response. "What did she say?" asked a man coming toward Rebecca. "They started the bombing," his friend responded. "It started."

She took off toward the noise, running slowly, then faster. And then, overtaking her, charging down the middle of the street, was someone camouflaged to asphalt, a guy in black pants, black sweatshirt, black ski hat. She watched him tear by like a panther. But then he faltered, glanced over his shoulder at her. She caught his eye; he circled back.

"Hey. Haven't I seen you camping here?"

"No, not me."

"I could've sworn." He leapt from foot to foot, his breath rapid. "Did you hear? They started the bombing."

"Yeah, no, I heard."

"We're going in, taking over the building. A group of us. We're going inside." He cocked his cocky head. "Are you up for it?"

A black mittened hand outstretched to her.

Llamalo.

ACKNOWLEDGMENTS

FIRST, AN ENDLESS MESA of thanks for that most wonderful thing—friends who are stellar writers and generous readers: Jessica Bacal, Lila Cecil, Emily Chenoweth, Rachel Graham Cody, Jenny Gotwals, Lisa Jones, Lisa Olstein, Jon Raymond, Claire Reardon, Scott Rosenberg, Gabe Roth, Mary Strunk, Tali Woodward, and Leni Zumas. For the weekends writing with dogs and the occasional baby, the constant joy: Matthew Brookshire, Alison Hart, Luis Jaramillo, and Abigail Thomas. For an optimistic decade of belief in this book: Dale Peck. For invaluable support of all sorts, thanks to Ingrid Binswanger, Carmen Hernandez, Andrew Kidd, Wylie O'Sullivan, Lisa Papademetriou, and Maud Macrory Powell.

Thank you to the women who cared for my daughters while I wrote, including the teachers at Fort Hill, and especially to Mary and Kathleen Bordewieck. And to the places where I wrote: the Writers' Mill, the Brooklyn Writers Space, and the office provided by the Five Colleges Women's Studies Research Fellowship.

Ira's "Dear Friends" letter was borrowed in part from the far superior letter my grandmother, Miriam Borgenicht Klein, wrote to the Barnard College class of 1936. Escadom is an entirely fictional place, with its fictional landscape and woes. My knowledge of actual western Colorado was augmented by *Boomtown Blues* by Andrew Gulliford and *Naomi & Dev's*

Plant Book by Naomi Sikora and Dev Carey, as well as by time spent living there, for which I thank Ed and Betsy Marston, Jackson Perrin, and Lisa Jones.

I'm so grateful for Doug Stewart. There would be no book without his unfailing enthusiasm, kindness, and advocacy. And huge thanks to everyone at Algonquin, especially to Kathy Pories for her wisdom and discernment and for saving David's life.

Erin White read over every word and then read them again, all except for this sentence, and now I find my gratitude for our friendship is beyond words. To think someone with such intelligence, insight, and love of the high desert could appear in a cold New England office and bring me the sun!

Thank you, family. To Emily and Rick Abel for belief in me, in books, and in this troubled world. Thanks to my sisters, Laura and Sarah Abel, and to the families you created. Thanks to the Zuckers for bringing me into your family.

Lastly, gratitude to my loves, Susannah and Rose, for each day of you. And most of all, to the brilliant and patient Adam Zucker, who has made not only this book but also my entire life smarter, funnier, and more grammatical. You are my favorite place.

THE OPTIMISTIC DECADE

Something Wrong: An Essay by Heather Abel

Optimism and the Colorado High Desert:
A Conversation with Heather Abel

Questions for Discussion

SOMETHING WRONG

An Essay by Heather Abel

"CLASS OF '36, I guess we did something wrong."

I was in college when I first read that sentence, and its author—my grandmother—had just died. She'd been charismatic and uncompromising, equally critical of capitalism and sentimentality. In her life as a Westchester housewife/radical leftist, she'd planned protests, played tennis, and published mystery novels. When her children were grown, she moved to Manhattan, waking every morning at five to walk briskly around Central Park (mugged only a few times), spending the rest of the day writing and tending the ivy she'd planted to beautify the trees along her block. Every Saturday she organized against US atrocities in Central America.

Days before she died in 1992, she dictated the final paragraph of her eighteenth book to my mother while attached to an IV, a blood transfusion, and oxygen. The book was, she explained, the first in a new series she planned to write. At her memorial, a week later, held in a classroom at Barnard College, her five children yelled and laughed and interrupted one another. She'd taught them to rebel against society's mawkish ceremonies, like memorial services, as well as its unjust institutions. Her children all inherited her radical politics, and they raised us, her twelve grandchildren, in the same mode. You can be anything, they joked, as long as it's a public defender. Interpreting this broadly, we complied.

A month after the memorial, I received in the mail a thick, spiral-bound book of my grandmother's unpublished writing, compiled by my aunt. I'm looking at it now. While most of the pages are filled with witty poems that my grandmother composed for celebrations, there is also a photocopy from her Barnard College fiftieth-reunion book, one of those alumni books to which you're invited to send in a list of your degrees and progeny along with a brief life update. My grandmother's entry is preceded by a Barbara Graham Junge, who has "arrived at a point in which the whole world has opened up for me" and followed by a Marion Wright Knapp, who doesn't "have much to say for or about myself other than that I'm enjoying life enormously and have given up that nonsense about being of any great value in my world."

Between Barbara and Marion sits Miriam Borgenicht Klein, offering not an update, but a condemnation in five sentences. "Anyone our age has to stand abashed at the state of the world," she begins. "For thirty or so years after we graduated, we felt, we may have been entitled to feel, vaguely self-congratulatory: if we preoccupied ourselves with such matters at all, we could assign to our efforts a small but perceptible effect; things were getting better. That comfortable illusion no longer seems to me possible. Put a finger anyplace on the globe today, and there is warfare, harassment, piles of dreadful weapons, appalling gaps between rich and poor." She finishes with her biting summation, the first-person plural opening its arms to include every alumna: "Class of '36, I guess we did something wrong."

How did I feel when I first read this? Well, proud. Mine wasn't your average grandma. And like her, I wanted to rail against the apathy of my college classmates. Dutifully rebellious, I'd started a chapter of the Children's Campaign for Nuclear Disarmament when I was ten. At seventeen I'd brought busloads of other students to the Nevada desert to protest the nuclear test site.

But I was also frightened. That despair in her words? I knew it well. As a family of atheist Jews, our only god was cynicism. I'd been told my whole life: Work hard to change the world, but guess what? Despite your efforts, the world will grow increasingly fucked.

Her words reminded me, more than anything, of a picture book I'd read as a child about an old, witchy woman who tried to rid the world of nighttime. Since I associated night with dread—of kidnappers and loneliness and nuclear war—I fully supported her attempt. With her broom, she swept frantically at the sky all night, resting victoriously when morning broke, only to be devastated when darkness fell again. I was horrified by the book's metaphoric implications. It was my earliest introduction to futility.

After college, I tried peripatetically and desultorily to do something right, first by teaching gardening in housing projects in San Francisco, then by writing for an environmental newspaper in Colorado, while all around me night continued to fall; things were getting worse. Finally, conceding that I wouldn't be doing anything right for the world, because I wanted to write a novel, I moved to Manhattan, not far from my grandmother's block, where the ivy no longer grew.

My book began, as so many first novels must, out of a sort of rage. I wanted to write about being my grandmother's granddaughter, about inheriting an idealism laced with disillusionment. I wanted to explain how it felt to grow up with a feverish love for Woody Guthrie's anti-fascism and Cesar Chavez's hunger strikes and for linking arms at a protest, for singing "We Shall Overcome," and for that love to be tarnished, as if under dark clouds that spelled out the words DOOM and NOT GOING TO HELP.

The book began out of rage and, I'll admit, hubris—a youthful idealism. I remember a professor telling me that no novel could be written in less than two years. I nodded and inwardly disagreed, confident that I'd finish in a year, eighteen months tops, after which I'd finally go to school to become, in the narrowest sense, a public defender.

In fact, it took me fifteen years to finish this book. I wrote other things during that decade and a half. I taught classes, raised babies. But still, intermittently for fifteen years I worked on draft after draft, each one somehow *wrong*.

A strange thing happened to me during this time of failure. I'd begun the book furious about the end of idealism, but as the years passed, I began to understand that when idealism ends, well, that's when things get interesting. After all, you don't need to simply desist when disillusioned. No, you can show up for work anyway, not with earnestness or sentimentality (my grandmother would shudder at that), but with a buoyant sense of the absurd. It's absurd to write another draft of a book that isn't working. But there's beauty in this absurdity and plenty of humor, too.

How did I finally learn this? From my characters. I saw how each of them, while really trying to do something right, kept doing something wrong. Their egos got in their way, as did their lust and pride and greed, yet I was full of love for them anyway. I could forgive them more easily than I could forgive the rest of us, the wide first-person plural. I forgave Caleb, who wanted to create a back-to-nature utopia for kids, but who lied out of fear and bravado. I forgave Donnie, who, in his desire to reclaim the ranch he sold to Caleb, regurgitated the xenophobic propaganda of the mining industry. I forgave Ira, a radical journalist who shut down an entire newspaper when he stopped believing that his work was influential. And I forgave Rebecca, Ira's daughter, who wanted so badly to rebel in a dutiful way but couldn't figure out how to do it without being told.

You'll have to read to find out which one of these characters gets to say my grandmother's reproof to the class of '36. It's somewhere in the book, albeit in an altered form.

But her five sentences no longer frighten me as they once did. Back then, I was angry at myself and everyone else for not figuring out a way to do something unequivocally *right*. Now I'm beginning to understand what it means to live with an idealism conjoined with despair, with cynicism (and I have a feeling I couldn't finish my novel until I figured this out). It means you work *despite* futility. You go to a protest, shout alongside strangers, and come home to read the terrible news. You plot out your new series of mystery novels while dying in a hospital bed. It's easy, I see now, to write five lines of condemnation. We do it on Twitter every day. It's harder to live absurdly, as my grandmother did, to drag the folding table down to Greenwich Village to collect signatures on petitions that will most certainly not remove US death squads from El Salvador, to water the ivy even though one day it, too, will die. We fail and fail. We stand abashed. We are doing something wrong, but look how beautiful we are as we keep sweeping the darkness back each night to allow one more day to arrive.

OPTIMISM AND THE COLORADO HIGH DESERT
A Conversation with Heather Abel

This interview was originally conducted by Corey Farrenkopf for *The Coil Magazine*.

Set in the high desert of Colorado, Heather Abel's debut novel, *The Optimistic Decade*, dissects the issues dividing Left from Right, positioned against the backdrop of a back-to-the-land commune-esque summer camp called Llamalo. It sounds like a comical setup, but Abel's characters are never satirical or lampoonish. Abel doesn't ridicule one side or the other, allowing the sad realities of individuals' lives to speak for themselves, eliciting sympathy from readers where they'd be surprised to find any. Beyond the timeliness of her novel, Abel explores the various forms of love, the awkwardness of teenage years, and everyone's eternal search to belong. The plot follows teenagers Rebecca and David as they navigate a tense summer at Llamalo, both trying to figure out where they fit into a divided world. The novel's true humor arises from their socially awkward relations and angst-ridden missteps. Alongside her fully realized characters, Abel's depiction of the high desert is exacting. Her mesas and scrublands, ranches and depression-wracked towns are painted with vibrant clarity. I was lucky enough to speak to Heather after she did a reading at Sturgis Library. The following encompasses some of the highlights of that conversation.

Corey Farrenkopf: In a particularly politically charged time, your book navigates both sides of the political spectrum, while never overly condemning or lampooning either. Caleb and Donnie are perfect representatives of the polar extremes of Left and Right. Could you speak to the challenges of writing sympathetic characters, even when their worldview doesn't align with your own?

Heather Abel: When I worked for a newspaper in Colorado, I would spend time with men like Donnie, miners and ranchers who had lost their jobs, whose lives were not turning out as they'd believed they would. I'm always interested in dashed dreams. As a reporter, you're out to get a quote, but I wanted to do more, to follow these men home (in a non-creepy way), to see how their anger and sadness expressed itself in dailiness. How did they spend their days? What did they eat for lunch? How did they treat their children? I actually loved writing of Donnie's humanity, even as I didn't shy away from some of his abhorrent politics. I wrote a bunch of his scenes just after the 2016 election. I was aware that Donnie would have voted for Trump. I was aware that I believed that I hated everyone who voted for Trump. And I was aware that I loved Donnie. More of a challenge for me were Ira and Caleb, the men on the left. My politics are as left as you can get, but I am painfully aware of the faults of many of us who hang out on this end of the political spectrum—our self-righteousness, our narcissism, our ego, our provincialism. I wanted to write these men with all their contradictions laid bare, but I didn't want to lampoon them. This was delicate, and I'm so glad you found it successful.

CF: Some critics have compared the main struggle in your novel, the ranchers versus the campers, to the Israeli/Palestinian conflict. Was that intentional on your part? If so, could you speak to how you threaded such narrative through the book and how it influenced your decisions? If not, what are your thoughts on such a reading?

HA: First off, I was honored to get such a thoughtful review in the *New York Times*, which came with the online headline "In the Colorado Desert, a Debut Novelist Finds a Metaphor for Israel and Palestine." Books operate on many levels, of course, and on the main level—the level of plot and character—I meant this as a book about the American West. Donnie and Caleb are influenced by and reacting to a very particular Western mythology and masculinity. And the camp, Llamalo, has a very American history. It belonged to the Ute Indians until they were forced off. Under the Homestead Act, the government gave it to Donnie's great-grandfather, a white pioneer. Exxon's disastrous oil shale project bankrupted Donnie, forcing him to sell the land to Caleb. This is such an American story of power, conquest, resources, and succession. Llamalo's story is not the story of Israel and Palestine.

At the same time, books always swim in the ocean of metaphor, and I was consciously working with the metaphor of the Promised Land. I was thinking explicitly about how we ask particular swaths of land to create community and to transform us. In service of this, we create borders; we keep people out. I was also thinking about the Jewish idea of mitzvot, actions we do to get close to God. Early on in my writing of this book, I read *Sabbath* by Abraham Joshua Heschel, in which Heschel explains that the holiest place for Jews is not a place at all, not even a synagogue. It's a day, a period of time—the Sabbath, a mitzvah. I was so interested in the idea that actions are holy instead of places, especially since I was writing about the myth of place. Of course, I did think about Israel when I read that. I decided that I wanted the spiritual development of my book to reflect this understanding. All that is to say, yes, the metaphor was there, but it was super low level. How cool, then, that the reviewer picked it out.

CF: Auto-fiction has been big in recent works of realist fiction. How much of *The Optimistic Decade* is pulled from real life versus your imagination? Where does Rebecca fit into all of it?

HA: So much of writing is sitting in a chair reaching for objects that we can't see, all the tangible stuff our characters touch as they go through their lives. When I wrote Rebecca, these objects were easy for me to find. She grew up in Santa Monica, like I did. Her parents were journalists, and I'd worked as a journalist. Like me, she spent her childhood going to protests and meetings and potlucks with other LA leftists. It was fun for me to reach for her objects: the spiral-bound reporter's notebook, the beer poured into apple juice bottles for a picnic, the sand in the bottom of the beach bag, the pin on the Christmas tree that says Wearing Buttons Is Not Enough. (In this way, David's objects were easy, as well.) Auto-fiction implies, I think, a cohesion between the author and the character's internal states as well as fluency with the external objects. There's definitely some distance between Rebecca and me emotionally, and often I feel closer toward Suze or Caleb or Georgia. But I was trying to say something in this book about masculinity, which I navigated through Rebecca and her growing understanding of men and their power and privilege. I still feel really emotionally close to that part of the story, and I hope it's speaking to young women. (And men!)

CF: Llamalo is a kind-of-commune, back-to-the-land summer camp utopia. Where did you get the idea for that setting? Why the high desert of Colorado? Any interesting firsthand accounts of commune life or the search for a supposed utopia?

HA: When I was nine or ten, I was home from school with the flu, and I found a book about the kibbutz in my dad's office. I was enthralled. People didn't always live in nuclear families? How fantastic! I studied intentional communities and communes in college, and I read pretty much everything I could about them. My own personal experience is not with a commune but with a back-to-the-land summer camp in northern California. I worked there for six years. It's not as rugged or ramshackle as Llamalo, but it definitely taught me that camps can be myths come to life.

CF: I know you said it took several years and many rounds of edits to create *The Optimistic Decade* as it is now. I get hung on the time it takes me to finish my own works of fiction. Could you fill us in on the publishing process that went into bringing your novel into being? What would you say to other writers who struggle with the fear of writing too slowly?

HA: *The Optimistic Decade* had a comically long gestation process. I started it in graduate school, but when an agent asked to represent me based on some short stories a professor had sent her, I stopped writing. (Oh, naïve youth, what I wouldn't do to get those years back!) I was thrilled, but clearly overwhelmed. I put the novel aside for some years to make money, and when I finished a draft, my agent said it wasn't quite right. I was nine months pregnant at the time. After my baby started daycare, I scrapped that version of the book and wrote it anew. When I had another draft, I sent it to a friend's agent who offered me representation. He spent over a year doing a very belabored line edit, and then he gave up agenting. By that time, I felt distant from that version of the novel, so I wrote much of it new again. I sent this to the fantastic Doug Stewart at Sterling Lord, because I loved a book he represented—*Bobcat* by Rebecca Lee (read it!). Two weeks later—and about a decade after I started the book—Doug sold it to Kathy Pories at Algonquin. I had a wonderful experience with Kathy, who is such an astute and kind editor, and the plot of the book changed drastically once again.

There is so much about publishing that is out of our control. Agents leave. Editors might work slowly. The market slogs along. Capitalism is not our friend. The only thing we control is how truthfully we write our stories. Sometimes it takes a long time for this truth to come out. We get sick, have babies and jobs and crises.

That said, I now see the purpose of pushing myself to write quicker. One of my teachers told me I should finish the book before my first baby was born, because the experience of motherhood would change me, and I wouldn't be able to keep writing the same book. I didn't listen to her, but she was right. I had to rewrite my book. When my second baby was born, I was changed once again; so once again I changed the book.

For this next novel, I'm trying to challenge myself to write quicker, to get a draft done before I change or the world changes. The world is morphing so quickly now that I wonder if our stories—even if they're set in the past or the future—won't seem as relevant to us if we take a decade to write them like I did. But I can do this (or at least try to) because my kids are older, my chronic illness is under control, and I'm in an entirely different place financially. I want to give everyone permission to love their slowness. I know that I love reading the books written by authors who took years and years. I appreciate the complexity and richness that comes from a snail's pace.

CF: Rebecca and David are very authentic teenagers. The fluctuation of their emotions is spot-on, along with their social anxieties and desires. How did you get in the headspace to write from their perspectives? Any advice to writers struggling to nail down that authentic, angst-ridden teenage voice?

HA: Do we ever really leave our teenage selves behind? I found it perhaps too easy to write from the teenage perspective. It's such a hyper-aware time, a time when we fluctuate so quickly from self-aggrandizement to self-flagellation. Two things did help me, though. First, I played music from my teenage years, because music is a failsafe vehicle for time travel; put on "I Melt with You" and I'm gone, back to the Lincoln Junior High gym, watching Nick dance with Wonnie and wondering if I might conflagrate from jealousy. Second, I became friends with my embarrassment. Adolescence is constant humiliation, and we find ways to contort ourselves in adulthood to avoid some of these feelings. When I shoved myself back into teenage-size to write David and Rebecca, the constant embarrassment returned. Rather than push it away, I grew fond of it. How vulnerable we all are! How odd and soft and searching.

CF: In a lot of ways, *The Optimistic Decade* can be read as multiple variations on the traditional love story. There's the standard narrative of romantic love, but then you complicate that with the love of ideas and the love of a place. Can you talk about balancing all three throughout the narrative? Did you find one more challenging than the others?

HA: Oh, I'm thrilled that you call it "multiple variations on the traditional love story." That's exactly what I was hoping someone would take from the book. I actually found the love of place hardest by far. My love for the West is so primal and deep; it too easily relies on the language of cliché. The wide-open spaces! The grandeur! Romantic love is societally sanctioned—it keeps society chugging along—and love of ideas is honored in my family, but not everyone goes through life strung out on a place. I can feel myself becoming a little defensive of this love, a little too insistent. Many of the novel's false starts were because I didn't know how to express this love. Finally, I just gave it to a cadre of characters—Donnie, Don, Caleb, David, Suze, Rebecca—and let them all enact it in their idiosyncratic ways.

CF: I really enjoyed what you said in your audience discussion about setting, how you anchored your fiction in places from your past that you missed. Could you speak to the idea of visiting old stomping grounds through fiction?

HA: I fell in love with Colorado's stories and landscape when I moved there at 23. Five years later, I left Colorado for New York to get an MFA in fiction. At one of the first parties I attended, I told a guy that I'd be moving back as soon as I finished my degree. This guy became my boyfriend, then my husband, and his job took us to Massachusetts, where the mountains look like anthills and all my neighbors vote just like me. I began *The Optimistic Decade* in mourning for Colorado but soon realized that by writing it, I could live in Colorado again. Every day I would travel to the high desert, walk between sage and rabbitbrush, climb up into the pinyon-juniper forest, visit with the ranchers and miners and hippies who had been my neighbors.

CF: What are you working on now? Any work coming out in the near future you'd like to talk about?

HA: I can barely speak about my current project for fear that it will evaporate. But I can say that my new work is set in Northampton, where I live. As I alluded to above, for many years I hated living here. I couldn't see it as a place of story. I felt uninspired, turned off by the landscape and the lives of the people I met. Finally, I realized that to fully exist here, to open myself to the place, I needed to write about it, to learn its history and think about its future. It's worked! This is the first autumn that I've been fascinated by New England, especially by the way seasons rule over people here. Now I find Northampton to be both a much more haunted place and a much more real place. It's no longer the site of my dislike but the site of my curiosity.

CF: Any final *Optimistic* advice to readers and writers living in our not-so-optimistic decade?

HA: Ever since I decided to leave journalism to write fiction, I've been doubting myself. Through the Bush years and the Obama years, I would fret: What is the point? How is this helping anyone? Should I do something else with my life? Part of this is because I was raised in an activist, academic family. I remember my mom giving me a bumper sticker that said Art Saves Lives. She said, *I thought you would like it, but I'm not sure it's true.* Sure, I agreed. How did art actually save lives? Can art perform surgery? Can art give everyone health insurance? Can art reunite a child with her parents?

Oddly, it's been the disaster of Trump that has quieted my doubts. They seem like indulgences from a more naïve time. We need immigration lawyers, definitely. We need journalists. We need social workers and teachers and domestic abuse counselors, and we need people to run for Congress. But we need art, too. We need storytellers. We need our world reflected, analyzed, altered. I think we feel this need every twisted day, every day spent on the internet watching horror, watching a man try to become a dictator. So my advice to other writers is really just gratitude. Thank you, all of you, for the stories you're telling, for doing this hard work, for moving at a snail's pace in this fast world, for saving my life.

QUESTIONS FOR DISCUSSION

1. Ira and Caleb offer two very different ways to respond to a messed-up world. Ira has spent his life engaging with societal problems, writing about them and protesting them. Caleb has decided to retreat, to form his own utopian community where he introduces kids to a different way of living: "with kindness and love, without buying shit, without watching shit." Do you identify with either of these approaches?

2. Did you have an optimistic decade—those years (not necessarily ten) when, as Ira says, "the world feels malleable and the self strong?" When was yours? Do you think you need to be young to have one?

3. Many of these characters have a passion for the landscape of the West. Is there a landscape that speaks to you, where you feel you belong?

4. Caleb believes that kids need to be separated from their nuclear families in order to fully flourish. He considers the nuclear family a place of sadness ("There's been pain . . . There's been love withheld"). Why might he think this?

5. What is Suze's role in the book? Why do you think the author had her come back to Llamalo on the hottest day of the summer?

6. Like many teenagers, Rebecca responds very differently to her mother and father. How does her relationship with Georgia change throughout the book? What events or realizations brought about these changes?

7. David uses the Jewish idea of mitzvot to think about the camp's rules and rituals. What are the mitzvot of Rebecca's family? In what ways is the mitzvah of protest similar to a religious mitzvah? Can you think of any mitzvot of your life?

8. *The Optimistic Decade* is crowded with fathers. How have Ira, Robbie, Joe, and Don Sr. tried to shape their children in their image? Which of their children rebelled and which went along with their fathers? Donnie is the newest dad in the book. What did you think about his relationship with Kayla?

9. When Caleb first arrives in Escadom in 1982, he is excited to become friends with Donnie, a friendship he ultimately ruins. Do you have friends who are different from you in terms of class and culture and politics?

10. In the book's opening scene we watch Rebecca convince herself that she wants what her father wants for her. When does she start thinking for herself? What precipitates her independence? How does it prepare her to stand up against Caleb near the end of the book?

11. Caleb and Ira are morally ambiguous characters. They do good work in the world, but they can treat those around them poorly. What was it like for you to read sections from the perspective of someone you might have disagreed with? How do you feel when you don't like a character in a book?

12. When Rebecca is disillusioned with Ira and Caleb, she gives up on politics altogether. At their last meeting, David tells her that even knowing what he knows about Caleb's flaws, he would go back to Llamalo if he could. Do you react more like Rebecca or David when leaders disappoint you?

13. Don and Donnie were raised to embody a certain stereotypical masculinity associated with the American West. In what ways does Caleb imitate them? What about David?

14. Why does Caleb lie to Donnie at the auction? How might their friendship have evolved if he hadn't lied? Why does he lie about David's accident? What would have been different if he had told the truth to the counselors? At one point Caleb says, "Sure he hadn't told the truth this morning, but the myth stood in for the truth, which was all anyone wanted anyway." Do you agree with him that the camp needed this myth?

15. Historically, people have come to the American West, seen its beauty, and wanted to control and alter the landscape. *The Optimistic Decade* tells this story through the ownership of a particular swath of high desert. Who does the land really belong to? What would you like to have happen to this land?

16. Don Sr. is one of the few characters who doesn't seem to have a strong ideological position. What do you make of the relationship between him and Caleb at the end of the book?

17. Early in the book, Rebecca's parents worry about how she'll react when she hears that the newspaper will close. What does the newspaper represent to her? How does she change after learning of its closing?

18. The tension between Llamalo and Escadom is one that occurs all over this country when impoverished neighborhoods or cities begin to be gentrified. Does Caleb help Escadom? Will the real estate boom that Anders is a part of help the town?

19. If you were to start your own utopian community, what would it look like? Who would you want to join you? What would be some of the rules, rituals, or mitzvot?